Always a Wedding Planner

4-in-1 Romance Collection

RL Ashly, Leeann Betts,
Toni Shiloh, Davalynn Spencer

BARBOUR
PUBLISHING

Finally a Sweetheart

by Toni Shiloh

Dedication

To the Author and Finisher of my faith

And now abide faith, hope, love, these three;
but the greatest of these is love.
1 Corinthians 13:13 NKJV

Chapter One

The musical strands of Mozart's Piano Concerto No. 21 filled the air as Felicity Edwards carefully piped intricate scrolls on the future Schwartzes' wedding cake. The light coral swiss buttercream frosting popped wonderfully against the khaki-colored fondant. The bride had been adamant about her colors for the beach-themed wedding. Although Loveland, Colorado, was far from any ocean, Lake Loveland remained a frequent destination where couples from around the world pledged their love and undying devotion.

She rubbed a palm over her heart. *Always the baker, huh, Felicity?* She sighed.

She'd made scores of beautiful cakes, but she'd never had the opportunity to hold that shiny ceremonial knife with the man of her dreams and cut into spongy layers of confection perfection. When would she finally be a bride? When would Mr. Right sweep her off her feet and present her with a diamond that would shock her friends and family?

Her lips twisted, tongue poked out as she turned the cake to continue forming the scrolls. Since starting Weddings by Design with her best friends, she'd been to more than her fair share of weddings. She'd had no choice—not that she actually minded.

Being a wedding cake baker was the best job ever. Filling her Instagram feed and all the other social media outlets the company used with her creations brought her joy. Nothing made her heart melt more than to see the bride cry happy tears and the groom high-five his best man when his own cake was revealed.

Plus, she simply enjoyed taking photos of her creations. Not just for her portfolio, which was expertly displayed in her office for consultations, but for her personal collection as well. She added them to the scrapbook started by her mother—photos taken with a Polaroid camera, labeling the images with the date and occasion for the cake. Since her mother had passed, Felicity used an Instax to take the pictures. The Schwartzes' wedding cake would be her next entry.

Stepping back, she looked it over. "Perfect." She smiled and noted the music had come to an end.

"Felicity?"

She glanced up to see her business partner Cassie entering the kitchen.

"Hey, what's up?" Felicity pulled off her latex gloves and tossed them into the trash.

"Your one o'clock appointment has arrived."

The clock showed five till. "Thanks."

"I had them wait in your office. Hope that was okay."

"Sounds great."

Cassie smiled and left the kitchen. Felicity turned to her assistant, Jill. "Let the cake sit awhile and then store it for me, please?"

"Sure thing."

Felicity paused at the industrial sink to scrub her hands. She didn't like the coating the disposable gloves left behind. A quick peep in the mirror revealed that her mascara had persevered through the intensity of piping icing. She stepped into the closet within the kitchen, removed her chef's coat, slid on a turquoise silk blouse over her tank top, then removed her hair clip to tousle her curls. "Ready or not," she murmured.

Thankfully her office was right in front of the kitchen. She hated keeping a potential client waiting. *Lord, please help this meeting go well. Help me envision their desires and design a cake that will bless them.*

Felicity took a deep breath before opening the door. The couple turned at the sound of her entrance. She froze, heat filling her cheeks as she spied the groom-to-be.

"Felicity?" He stood, his mouth dropping open.

"Hi, Will." She forced a smile as she hurried around her white-lacquered tabletop desk.

Being single in her thirties was bad enough, but did she really have to create her high school crush's wedding cake?

"Wow. You look great!"

How could he say that in front of his fiancée? Felicity pressed her lips together and turned away to focus on the bride. "Hi, I'm Felicity—the wedding cake designer and baker." She forced a chuckle she didn't feel as she held out her hand.

She'd never been this nervous meeting a couple before. *Because Will Davenport wasn't sitting across from you the hundred other times.*

"Nice to meet you," the bride said.

She had the same stunning blue eyes as Will shining out from her caramel skin.

Same blue eyes?

Felicity looked down at her desk calendar. *Olivia Davenport.*

They were related?

"You're Olivia, right?" She swallowed, looking at the woman and then over to Will.

Could one of them put her out of her misery and say how they knew one another? Were they not the bride and groom?

"I am." She beamed. "My fiancé is deployed overseas right now, so my big brother stepped in to help." Olivia squeezed Will's hand.

Felicity sank into her gray office chair. They were brother and sister. How hadn't she known Will had a little sister?

"Olivia was five years behind us in school. I graduated before she was even a freshman," Will offered as he sat.

It was like he could read her mind. A little uncanny but welcomed. "Oh, that makes sense." This time a genuine smile found her face. "Do you know what the groom wants in a cake?"

"I hope so." Will stretched his legs out in front of him. "He's a good friend of mine."

"Oh, then if anything goes wrong, it's your fault?" She winked and then froze in horror, her head swiveling in Olivia's direction. "Not that anything will go wrong."

Olivia chuckled. "I knew what you meant."

Thank goodness. She hadn't been this flustered in. . .in. . .a really long time. It was time to get down to business and stop her heart from mooning over Will Davenport. But wow, he looked even better than in his high school days.

Felicity pulled out her consult journal. "Well, Olivia, tell me what you're thinking for the cake. Do you have your colors picked out? A theme for the wedding?"

"Elliot, my fiancé"—a dreamy smile covered her face—"he's a

pilot in the air force and will most likely wear his uniform. I was thinking the theme could revolve around his career. Our colors will be navy blue and steel gray."

"Wonderful. Please thank him for his service." Felicity jotted down the colors then grabbed her iPad to open the cake design software.

"Will do." Olivia tucked a strand of her dark brown hair behind her ear.

"Do you know what shape you want for the cake?"

"I was thinking the traditional round shape with tiers."

"I like to use a design software instead of sketching." Felicity focused on pulling up the app. "I'll be asking questions while I'm working on my iPad, but I promise you, I'm not ignoring you."

"No, I understand."

"How many guests are you planning for?"

"A hundred."

That would require at least three tiers. "Do you know what kind of flowers you want?"

"Sunflowers."

Hmm. The flowers would look stunning on a cake but may detract from an air force theme. Felicity bit her lip as she dragged the rounded tiers with her fingers. She saved the first option and then opened a copy to try a few tweaks.

"Do you like fondant?"

"Yes."

"Do you have a cake topper in mind?" She looked up to gauge Olivia's reaction.

Although it was important not to waste time, Felicity slowed down to remind herself to include Olivia in the process. Plus, she needed to peek at her info sheet to see what the bride had listed for the cake budget.

"I found a penguin topper that has the groom wearing Air Force blues and the bride a wedding dress."

"I love it." The laugh lines that fanned Felicity's eyes had probably popped out, emphasizing the time that had passed since she last laid eyes on Will Davenport. She cleared her throat and studied him. "Do you think Olivia's fiancé will like the air force theme?"

"Definitely. I think if you could incorporate some airplanes somewhere, it would be a great touch as well, since he's a pilot."

Hmm. That's a thought. She bit her lip as she pored over her iPad again. "What does he fly?"

"Fighters."

She grinned and pressed SAVE on the third option. "Okay, I have a few options."

Olivia nodded.

"First, let me say, if you don't like them, it's fine. Anything can be changed in the preplanning stages. Once the cake is made. . .that's a whole different story."

"Completely," Olivia stated. "I'm not a bridezilla type of girl."

How many times had Felicity heard that? Instead of contradicting the bride, she smiled. "Here's option one." She turned the iPad around. "We'll go strictly traditional. Three tiers with a broad navy ribbon and a thin steel gray one above it. I'd then add a sunflower on each tier."

"That's gorgeous," Olivia whispered as she clasped her hands together. "It's classic."

Felicity allowed a slip of a smile. She didn't want to appear too eager. Swiping the screen, she brought up the second option.

"Keeping the same shape and number of tiers, I've removed the ribbon and the sunflowers on each level. Instead, I placed the sunflowers at the top and added a jet and its stream scrolling across each tier."

"Wow." Will leaned forward. "You could really do that?"

"I can. It would be even better if I could make it look like the exact plane he flies."

"I really like that." Olivia exhaled. "I'm so glad I chose Weddings by Design to plan my big day."

"We aim to please." And they really did. Each of her partners had a specialty intent on making their clients' dreams come true.

Felicity scrolled to the last option. It left off the sunflowers and incorporated the ribbon and the airplane together. "What do you think?" She peered at Olivia.

The younger woman bit her lip as she examined the 3D image. "I don't know," she said. "I didn't expect it to be so hard. I love every option for one reason or another."

"Okay. Why do you like the first one?"

"It's classic. I feel like it would match the tone very well. He'll be dressed up, I'll be wearing white, and the bridesmaids will be in gray. Our wedding will have that classy feel, you know?"

Felicity nodded to let Olivia know she was still with her. "And the second one?"

"Elliot would love it." She bit her lip. "I should probably pick it for that reason." She turned toward her brother. "Don't you think so, Will?"

⌒

Will couldn't believe he sat in front of Felicity Edwards. When she'd first walked in, those old feelings of inadequacy from high school rushed back. His palms became clammy and his words stumbled over themselves. Now he sat in complete awe, looking at the cake designs she'd drawn up in a matter of minutes.

"Will?"

He peered down at his little sister and cleared his throat. "Elliot would want you to love the cake."

"And I want him to love it."

Felicity piped in. "There's always the option of a groom's cake."

"What's that?" Will shook his head, trying to straighten his thoughts.

"It's a fun cake purely to please the groom while the bride gets the more traditional one."

Will leaned forward. "What would that look like?"

Felicity intertwined her fingers and rested them on her desk. "Well, we could do one in the shape of a plane. Or have a sheet cake decorated to match his uniform. Is he wearing his dress blues or mess dress?" She had dated a military man once and always preferred his mess dress.

"I don't think he's decided," Olivia said.

"He has." Will interjected. "Just wants it to be a surprise."

"Well, either way, the color is navy blue." Olivia's lips quirked.

He chuckled, thankful for his sister's easy personality. Another woman might not be so accommodating when it came to the details of her wedding.

"You can certainly let me in on the surprise if we decide on a groom's cake." Felicity met Will's gaze.

He swallowed, heart suddenly thumping in his ears. "I could."

"Great."

She shuffled papers around, and Olivia looked at him, raising her eyebrows in question. He shook his head. There was so much to say and not say. His admiration of Felicity had always been from afar and would likely remain so.

But you're not in high school anymore.

Still, she ran a wedding planning business, and he was a barber.

No, you own your own business as well.

He had to keep reminding himself of that instead of listening to the past jabs of his ex-fiancée. Will slid his palm across his pant leg to refocus.

"I don't think I want a groom's cake," Olivia announced. She glanced at him then Felicity.

Felicity leaned forward. "Okay, share your thoughts."

"Well, we're supposed to become one on our wedding day. If we're one, then we should have one cake."

Will squeezed his sister's hand. He couldn't believe how mature she'd become since dating Elliot. "Be sure to share that sentiment with him." Elliot would turn into more putty than his sister already made him.

"Since I want it to be one cake, I'll go with option two."

"Perfect. Let's discuss flavors."

"It has to be red velvet. We shared a piece on our first date."

Which happened to be on Will's birthday. Guess now he couldn't have red velvet cake whenever he had his own wedding, since Olivia was commandeering it first. *If* he ever married.

Jackie had crushed that dream.

"It's a great choice." Felicity leaned on her elbows. "How about we make it blue instead? I can replicate the exact shade to match your colors."

Color me impressed.

"That sounds perfect." Olivia clapped her hands.

Felicity amazed him. Will looked at her, cataloging all the changes time had wrought. She was still pretty, but in a more classical sense now. She'd lost the chubby cheeks and baby fat that made her adorable in high school. Now her svelte figure brought attention to her frame and slender neck underneath the gorgeous mane of curls. Her bronze skin glowed in the sunlight streaming through the windows.

"I can schedule you for a taste testing. That way we can discuss different icing options."

"I thought you would use fondant?" Will hadn't meant to jump into the conversation. But what was the point of a taste test if Olivia knew what flavor she wanted?

"I can. They have different flavors. I can also manipulate regular icing to look smooth and still have the same look if that is preferred. Of course, we can also do fondant with icing underneath."

"Okay." Olivia looked at him. "Could you open your schedule for that? Come with me as a second opinion?"

"Of course."

Felicity tilted her head. "What do you do, Will?" Her pink, glossy lips parted with the question.

He averted his eyes, wondering why it was so hot in the room all of a sudden. "Um. . .I'm a barber."

"He owns his own shop," Olivia interjected.

He prayed his face maintained its normal color instead of turning red. All the while a river of molten lava ran up his neck.

"That's amazing. Here in town?"

Will met Felicity's gaze. "Yes. Davenport Clips."

"That's you?"

He nodded, surprised at the lack of condemnation. Where was the sneer over the fact he "played with hair" for a living? "Awesome." Her lips curved into the most beautiful smile he had ever seen. "I never even put the two together."

"Loveland's not small enough for you to have."

Her smile widened, and his heart dove for his feet. *Uh-oh.* This was high school crush 2.0. And he wasn't sure he could handle another rejection.

Chapter Two

"Will Davenport." Felicity stared at the closed office door in bemusement.

The bride's brother. That was so much better than him being the groom. How awful would that have been? Chill bumps pebbled her arms.

All through high school, she'd mooned over Will in every class they'd shared. Well, there had only been two, but it had been enough for her to daydream what her name would sound like attached to his. Felicity Davenport had sounded great to her teenage mind.

She grinned, remembering the many hearts and signatures she'd drawn her junior and senior years. Will had never seemed to notice how interested she'd been. Not even when they were lab partners. Still, he'd always been nice to her.

Felicity grabbed her cream cardigan off the back of her chair and left her office. Hopefully one of her business partners slash best friends would be free. She needed girl talk, stat.

She, Cassie, Ronnie, and Kiki had remodeled a house near downtown Loveland to be the headquarters for their business. The bedrooms had been renovated into workspaces for each of them. A quick stop at each woman's office proved they were all busy. Felicity went to her kitchen, tapping her toes.

Jill had just started working for Felicity a couple of months ago, and they were nowhere near the sharing-secrets-of-the-heart stage. Perhaps she'd run by her dad's place and talk to him. *Ugh.* Discussing guys and her interest in them with her dad would be too awkward. Which left her stepmom, Heather.

Felicity's nose wrinkled. Heather wasn't bad or anything. She loved Felicity's dad—as well as the two kids they had together—fiercely. But even after fifteen years, Heather and Felicity's relationship continued to be lukewarm at best.

Felicity had tried to bridge the gap. There just hadn't been a lot of opportunities for her to get to know Heather. Her father had tied the knot with her a month before Felicity graduated from high school. A couple of months later, Felicity had left for culinary school. Then she'd spent a couple of years overseas before coming back home and settling into her own routine. If it weren't for the weekly meals at her dad's house, she'd barely know he had a wife.

Despite the awkwardness in her family relationships, her friendships had bloomed. She'd joined the singles group at Loveland Community Church and had met her best friends there. They had all come together as the other members of the singles group married off. Then she, Cassie, Kiki, and Ronnie had decided to form their own group. When they discovered they all shared a love for weddings, they opened Weddings by Design.

Life was great—lonely at times, but great nonetheless.

If you keep saying it, maybe you'll finally believe it. She rolled her eyes and headed for her office to grab her purse and car keys. She didn't have to talk to Heather, but maybe being at her dad's house would center her. She couldn't believe how much seeing Will had sent her mind into a tailspin.

She was reminded of her past boyfriends and how short lived those relationships had been. At her age, the guys she dated were looking to settle down and start a family. Only she couldn't have kids. The removal of her ovaries—thanks to a cancer scare—had clinched that.

They'd leave her with an "it's me, not you" farewell and never look back. A snort escaped her. One didn't have to be an expert to read between those lines. Then there were the guys looking only for one thing—well, she was a no in that arena.

She shook her head. Why was she feeling so strange? Just because Will Davenport waltzed into her office and set off feelings long forgotten didn't mean she had to be maudlin. Besides, he probably had a girlfriend. She froze, standing in front of her car. Of course Will had a girlfriend. The man owned his own business. Dropped everything to be with his sister. What woman wouldn't snatch him up?

Her shoulders sagged. She'd gotten her hopes up for no reason. No need to bare her heart to Heather or anyone else. Felicity turned back to the house, watching as the sunlight bathed the gray siding. Maybe she'd bake a cake and take it to her dad's for dinner later. Satisfied she had a plan to occupy her time, Felicity headed back inside to get to work.

A few hours later, she stood on her father's doorstep, dessert in hand. She'd baked a strawberry cake with lemon buttercream frosting for dessert. A candied lemon zest garnish perked up the presentation and tantalized the senses. The door unlatched, and Dad's face split into a grin.

"Felicity Love! How's my baby doing?"

Her lips curved with affection. "Hey, Dad." She kissed his cheek. "I'm good. You?"

"A lot better than you, it seems." He chucked her under the chin then took the cake from her hands.

"Why do you say that?" She hung her cardigan on the entry-way coatrack.

"You made cake. And a nicely decorated one at that."

Okay, so she liked to self-soothe with baked goods. What woman didn't? "Had some extra time on my hands, Dad."

"Sure you did. How many cakes did you make?"

"The girls all took one home." Her voice rose with each word, her face heating under his scrutiny.

"Hmm. Boy troubles?"

"Dad, at thirty-three I'd hardly call them *boy* troubles."

"Well, I'm sixty-three, so boy troubles it is." He stroked his graying beard and motioned for her to follow him into the kitchen. "Where's Heather?"

"She went to pick up Tabitha from theater class."

Felicity's half sister wanted to be an actress when she turned eighteen. Luckily, the town had a local theater that always had an open cast for kids.

"Where's Junior?"

"Upstairs playing video games."

"Of course." She leaned against the counter as her dad checked the pot on the stove. "Something smells good."

"Making your mom's stew."

She sighed. "My favorite."

"Heather suggested it when you said you'd be coming over."

Felicity was thankful that Heather had never tried to take the place of her mother. How could she? Her stepmom was only fifteen years older than Felicity. Whenever Heather was around, Felicity tried to be nice, but it was just weird that another woman was in her childhood home, raising two children with her father. It was like her dad had a whole different life that didn't include her.

Of course he does. Life moves on.

Coming home was supposed to pull her out of the funk, not make it worse. Seeing her dad live a life apart from hers—with a wife and two younger children—made her life-goal clock tick louder than ever.

Lord God, I don't want to be alone. Please send the perfect man for me. One who loves You and would cherish me. She bit her lip as Will came to mind. Why hadn't she asked if he was married? Glanced at his ring finger or something?

Stop dreaming.

"Felicity?"

Her dad's voice broke through her reverie. "Hmm?"

"You going to tell me what's going on?"

"I'm okay, Dad."

"If you don't want to talk to me, consider talking to Heather."

She scrunched her nose.

Her dad sighed. "I know she's not your mother, but she is a woman and might have some advice."

"I appreciate the encouragement."

"All I can do is try."

Wasn't that the truth. Her dad was always encouraging her to seek Heather's wisdom. Trying to bridge the gap and forge some kind of relationship between the two of them. She loved him and his efforts. Maybe if she stopped thinking of Heather as a mother figure and thought of her just as a fellow woman, things between them would go more smoothly.

"You've given me something to think about."

"That's what dads are for."

Felicity gave him a hug, and the tension slowly seeped from her shoulders. She just had to be patient and wait on the Lord's perfect timing.

The bell over the shop door rang as Will's little sister strolled in. The men waiting all averted their eyes to magazines or cell phones. Will glanced around, nodding with pleasure. The sign along the back wall worked.

Keep Your Eyes off My Sister.

He'd put up the warning after Olivia had made a couple of visits when he first opened the barbershop. The men had followed her every move until she left the building. Thankfully none of them made any rude comments, but their actions were enough for Will to tack up a sign and breathe easier when they took heed.

"Hey, Willie." Olivia smiled at the use of his childhood nickname.

"Hey, Livie. What's up?"

"I need to know your schedule so we can make the cake tasting appointment."

"Oh, right." He used clippers to edge the back of his client's neck. "Give me a moment. I'm almost done."

"Sorry," she said, peeking around his shoulder to apologize to the customer.

George chuckled. "No worries."

Will brushed the hairs off George's neck and unclipped the barber cape. "All set, my man."

"Thanks, Will." George stood and shook Will's hand, leaving the tip in Will's palm.

He slid his hand into his pocket and gave a two-finger salute goodbye with the other. Olivia plopped down into the empty chair and crossed her legs. "I have tomorrow off."

"I don't."

She pouted. "Friday?"

"I can do Friday afternoon." Though he'd have to move some stuff around first.

"Perfect." She marked her calendar then slid her cell into her purse. "Now let's talk about the lovely Felicity Edwards." She batted her eyelashes.

"Nothing to talk about." He grabbed a broom, hoping she'd get the message and scat. Little sisters could be such a pain.

"Right. You didn't talk then, and you won't talk now." She glared at him, folding her arms across her chest. "Spill, Will."

"Listen." He sighed as he leaned against the broom. "Felicity was in a couple of my classes in high school. We got along. We graduated. We had a miniature reunion in her office the other day. End of story." He resumed his cleaning duties.

"You blushed when she smiled at you."

Great. Of all the things for Olivia to notice. "Must have been the lighting. Don't you know men don't blush?"

"Whatever." She rolled her eyes. "I saw you flirting about Elliot's wedding garb."

"Because I told her I'd let her know what he chose?"

"It was *how* you said it." She arched an eyebrow as if to ask, *Am I wrong?*

"She's cute?"

Olivia shook her head. "She's not a little girl, Will."

And did he know it. Felicity had blossomed into a beautiful woman, not that he'd admit that to his younger sister. "Then what would you call her?" he goaded.

"A woman, Will. One you're attracted to."

He shrugged. If he said yes, Olivia would make his life miserable. If he hedged, she might let him take things at his own pace. And from the moment he left Felicity's office, he'd been planning and praying about what to do next. This chance meeting seemed like another shot, blessed by God. One he wasn't going to let pass him by.

"Are you ignoring me?"

"Trying to." He chuckled at Olivia's expression.

Her eyes squinted in a glare as she tapped her hand against the seat rail. "Let this be a warning to you, big brother." She pointed her finger at him. "If you don't do something by Friday, I will." She winked, hopped off the chair, and strolled right out of the barbershop.

Sisters. He shook his head.

"Couldn't help but overhear your dilemma," Isaac chimed in while cutting Deacon's hair in the next chair over.

"I'm sure." Will put the broom back. Why was everyone intent on offering him advice?

"So, you going to ask the lady out?"

"I have a plan."

"Maybe it needs another set of eyes." Isaac cupped his ear. "Or ears."

"I'm good, man."

"Man, you never share any good news."

"Hey, just because we run a barbershop doesn't mean we need to be gossips."

"That's exactly what it means, Will. People come in. Sit down. And spill their guts while we shape them up."

Deacon nodded, listening intently.

And sadly, Will couldn't argue. Barbers, beauticians, and bartenders probably heard everyone's problems, whether they wanted to or not. Most of the time, Will didn't mind, but it was different when he was on the other side of things. "You forget, Isaac, I'm not sitting in anyone's chair."

Isaac turned his attention to Will and then circled him, squinting at his hair. "I could edge you up, and you can tell Dr. Carter what's up."

He chuckled, shoving Isaac away. "Go finish Deacon's hair."

Isaac did so and thanked the man as he left. "All right. It's quiet now. No one else to hear."

Will peered in the mirror in front of his chair. His hair had grown at least an inch since his last cut and the edges were a little jagged. "Fine, but no advice."

"Do I at least get to listen?"

He stared at his friend. "Fine." He sat down, waiting as Isaac jacked up the chair. "I knew Felicity in high school."

"What does she look like?"

Will sighed. "Curly hair. Brown eyes. Light brown skin." And an undeniable beauty he'd always been attracted to.

"Would I know her?"

"Her dad is Roy Edwards."

"He's the tall mailman, right?"

"That's him."

"Oh, *her*. The older one. She works at that wedding planning shop, doesn't she?"

"That's her." Did everyone know that but him? "How did you know that?"

"Clarissa's dream is to have a wedding done by them. She gave me the 411 on all of those ladies. There are four of them, and each has their own specialty."

"Felicity does the cakes."

"Be careful. You may gain some extra weight messing with a woman who can cook."

"Like you did?" He pointed at Isaac's stomach. Ever since he'd started dating Clarissa, the man had packed on weight around his middle.

"Clarissa likes to feed me."

Will snorted. "She's trying to find a way to your heart. Haven't you ever heard that ol' wives' tale?"

"Well, I told her I loved her last week, so it must be working."

Will laughed, careful to keep his head still as Isaac held the clippers to his neck. The buzz wasn't loud enough to interrupt conversation.

"So, are you going to ask this Felicity woman out?"

"I want to, but—"

"No buts, man. Don't let your ex mess up a future with someone who could be a better person than she'll ever be. Felicity sounds like she has it all together. You guys can bond over entrepreneurship."

"Maybe."

"No *maybes* about it. Ask her out. Let her feed you, and life will be good."

Will wished it could be that simple. As Isaac finished his hair, he turned his thoughts toward the Lord.

Lord, I'm in my thirties. Asking a woman out seems like it should be a lot easier by now. It probably would have been easier to ask Felicity on a date in high school. Now Jackie's words ring in my head. Telling me I'm not worthy and that I have nothing to offer. Is Isaac right? Does owning my own business sound attractive, or will all women turn up their noses when they find out it's a barbershop?

The image of Felicity's smile when he'd told her came to mind. She hadn't turned away in disgust, but he also hadn't divulged his feelings for her.

Give me strength so I don't chicken out and give Livie an opportunity to take matters into her own hands.

Will shuddered. He should have just led his prayers with that. Suddenly, talking to Felicity didn't seem that daunting.

Chapter Three

Felicity set the white rectangular serving plate down in front of Olivia and Will. She took her seat across from them at the round dining table. "I've made some different options for you today." She pointed to the pieces in front of them. If all went well, she wouldn't have to retrieve the backup flavors in the kitchen.

"I love the color." Olivia's infectious smile broadened. "It'll match perfectly."

"Fantastic." Felicity breathed a sigh of relief. She had stayed up late working to match the color palette Olivia had left with her, experimenting with the dyes until the batter was the perfect shade of navy blue.

Now to see how she likes the flavor combinations. Felicity pointed to the first piece of cake. "This has a vanilla bean fondant over the red velvet—well, blue velvet in your case—with a light dusting of powdered sugar between the fondant and cake." Felicity bit her lip as Olivia and Will took bites.

"Good," Will said after he swallowed.

Olivia's face flushed red. "Not my favorite," she murmured.

"No worries." Felicity scratched the flavor off her notepad. "Why don't you try this one?" She motioned to the next piece. "This is white chocolate fondant with cream cheese frosting underneath. I thought you might want the traditional white coloring."

"Mmm." Olivia took another bite. "This one is good."

Felicity made a check mark. "The next one has been paired with buttercream instead of fondant."

After tasting, Olivia set down her fork. "It's okay."

Will nodded in agreement.

"All right." Felicity inhaled, pushing the nerves back. At least Olivia really liked one choice, but Felicity would rather the bride have multiple flavors she enjoyed to choose from instead of defaulting to the only option she thought was tasty. "This last one is the traditional cream cheese frosting. It'll be prepared so I can decorate it as we discussed before."

Olivia considered. "I like that one, but so far the chocolate fondant is my favorite." She intertwined her fingers, tilting her head to the side. "I don't suppose there are any other flavors to try?"

"I have four more in the back. Let me go get them."

Felicity retrieved the next set from the kitchen and went back to the living room that had been transformed to a sitting area for tastings. She placed the final offerings before the Davenports. "If you don't like any of these choices, Olivia, we can always schedule another tasting." She perched on the edge of her seat.

"I appreciate that, but I'm sure I'll have a favorite after I try these." Olivia offered a reassuring smile.

Lord, I hope so. Felicity exhaled slowly. "The first one is an almond buttercream fondant with a powdered sugar dusting underneath."

Olivia took a bite and covered her mouth with pleasure. "Oh, that's wonderful."

The tightness in Felicity's shoulders eased as the bride-to-be took another taste.

"Do I get a bite, Livie?" Will smirked.

"Sorry." She set down her fork.

Will forked some of the cake into his mouth then grinned. "I can see why you took more than one bite."

Felicity placed a star next to the flavor on her notepad. "The next one is a simple vanilla frosting. A classic." After two shakes of Olivia's head, Felicity pressed on. "The third option is a mascarpone cream frosting."

Olivia took a delicate bite then shook her head, nose scrunching with disgust. "What's the last flavor?"

"Swiss meringue buttercream."

Will slid his fork into the slice, studying her before he took a bite. "Tasty."

Felicity tried to smile, but heat rushed to her cheeks under his gaze, freezing her lips in place. Her imagination wanted to run away with a picture of her cooking for him alone, even spooning some of her creations to his lips. *Get it together.*

Olivia looked at Felicity. "It's between the almond one and the white chocolate."

"Would you like to try both of those a second time?"

"I would, if that's okay."

"Certainly. Let me get you some cold water first. Clear your palate."

"Thank you." Olivia's blue eyes twinkled.

Felicity grabbed the water and another slice of each of the two contenders. She loved red velvet cake, but paired with chocolate fondant would be too sweet for her. Then again, if she were to get married, she'd probably go for light and airy flavors. Maybe lemon layer cake with fresh berries?

You're not getting married.

She frowned. Her singleness was a reality she lived with every day. When had she last been on a date? *Oh yeah.* Mrs. Spencer had set Felicity up with her grandson. It was one of the curses—or blessings—of being single at a big church. Every woman over fifty wanted to parade her eligible bachelor relatives before Felicity. Unfortunately, none of the relationships lasted past the first date.

She shook her head from her musings as she crossed the sitting area and stood in front of the Davenports. "Here you go." Felicity bit back a sigh and sat back down. Half the job had her on her feet, so she treasured the moments of rest.

Peeking through her lashes, she examined Will. She could happily get lost in his incredible eyes. They complemented the warm tone of his brown skin. His teeth gleamed behind pale pink lips and were accented by his close-cropped mustache and beard. She couldn't help but note the way his chin curved. *Who looked at people's chins?*

Will sampled the first piece of cake, and she jolted. *You're doing a cake tasting. Stay focused, Felicity.* She took in Olivia's expression. "What do you think? Is there a clear winner?"

"Definitely." Olivia sighed. "The almond buttercream is delightful. I may have to lose a few pounds to enjoy a bigger slice." She turned to Will. "Do you think Elliot will like it?"

"Of course." He squeezed her shoulder. "You picked a winner, kid."

"So, what happens next?" Olivia tucked her hair behind her ear. "Do I have to do anything else?"

"No, ma'am. You've picked your design and your flavors, so all I need to do is make your cake. It'll be ready for your big day and eating pleasure."

"Fantastic." Olivia clapped her hands together. "Oh wait." She frowned. "Does that mean I won't see you until the wedding?"

Odd. She didn't interact with her clients beyond the cake tasting. Felicity proceeded cautiously. "Well, you'll see me around here whenever you come in for wedding plans with the other ladies. Although I do most of my work in the kitchen, I come out every now and again to talk to my partners."

"But your part in the planning is over?"

"Yes."

Olivia turned to Will. "Then I guess you need to ask her out now before you lose your chance."

Felicity's mouth dropped open, and her gaze found Will's.

His face flushed and he rubbed his jaw. "I think you need to scram, Livie."

"Oh, I will." She slid her purse strap over her shoulder. "My job here is done. It's all you, big brother." She slapped his back and waltzed out of the room.

Felicity held her breath, afraid to look at Will. Would he feel obligated to ask her out now that Olivia had thrown down the proverbial gauntlet? She wanted to slide under her desk and hide. As it was, her face felt like she'd just opened a preheated oven. *Lord, a little help here would be nice.*

Will cleared his throat. "Little sisters."

"Ha." She bit her lip. That was the sorriest excuse for a chuckle, but her nerves were stretched too tight for a genuine laugh to escape.

He rubbed the back of his neck. "Olivia claimed I'd take my

sweet time asking you out if she didn't intervene. Unfortunately, I thought she was bluffing."

"Then you do want to ask me out?"

His baby blues locked onto her. "Most definitely."

A tingle of awareness went up her spine. *Oh boy.* "Would you have asked if she hadn't forced your hand?"

"I planned on getting your number before I left." He shrugged. "Didn't want to do it with her watching."

Felicity felt the beginnings of a smile. "Then I guess you have something to ask me, huh, Mr. Davenport?"

Will's gorgeous mouth curved, and her stomach dipped under the force of his full grin. The urge to fan her face overwhelmed her. Was she having hot flashes? No, she took hormone therapy to prevent that.

"Felicity Edwards, would you do me the pleasure of going out with me this Saturday?"

A quick peek at her desk calendar showed that day was absent of wedding business. "I'd love to."

"Great. Could I get your number?" He unlocked his cell and passed it to her.

She typed her name then her number before saving herself as a new contact, all the while biting the inside of her cheek to prevent her own smile from spilling out and erupting into squeals of delight. She handed him back his phone, waiting to see what else he'd say. Instead, her cell buzzed against the desktop as a notification flashed across her screen.

"Now you have mine."

"Thank you."

"My pleasure." Will stood. "See you Saturday?"

I can't wait. "Yes, Saturday."

"I cannot *believe* you just did that." Will held the passenger car door open for his sister.

Olivia grinned impishly at him, her eyes twinkling with mirth. "You weren't going to do anything."

"I was."

"R–i–ight. How many times did you have the whole *ask her out* or *don't ask her out* conversation in your head, big brother?"

Will growled. "Get in the car." He shut the door and came around to the driver's side to get in. "God and I just had to have a little conversation before I moved forward."

"Which you probably had the first day you saw her."

True, but Olivia didn't have to know that.

"And I'm sure you had one the next day and the next," Olivia continued as he pulled out of the driveway of Weddings by Design and headed to her apartment. "You study a problem from all sides before making a move, *if* you even do."

"Livie, that wasn't for you to decide."

"Doesn't it bother you that I'm getting married before you?"

"That's a girl thing."

She snorted. "Please. You want a family. I see your eyes get all squirrely looking when you see a family pass by. You were built to provide and take care of others. It's why you're helping me."

"I'm helping you because you're my sister and Elliot's my best friend."

"You're helping me because that's how God *designed* you. I bet every time you take a spiritual gift test you get helping in some capacity."

Will stared forward. When Olivia was passionate about a subject, she became almost predatory in nature. Like a vulture waiting to tear into roadkill. And as irritated as he was, Will couldn't help but be thankful Felicity had said yes. Olivia's meddling could have very well made things between him and Felicity awkward past the point of no return.

"Livie, you know I love you, right?"

She huffed. "Yes."

"And you know I appreciate you, right?"

"Yes. But you don't want me in your business? That's what you're going to say."

He glanced at her. "Not that I don't value your concern, but my love life is that. Mine."

"But, Willie." She wrinkled her nose. "You'll end up alone if I don't step in."

"Like you did with Jackie?"

"Ugh."

He looked at her to see she had folded her arms across her chest.

"I should apologize, huh?"

Will held back his laughter at her petulant tone of voice. He resisted the urge to look at her again. He'd lose all composure if her bottom lip poked out like it always had as a child. "Only if you mean it."

"I don't want you upset with me. And I know I can get a little carried away at times."

"Just like Mom."

She chuckled. "Maybe."

"Shift that over to a yes."

"Fine. I'm sorry for interfering in something that wasn't my business. And for embarrassing you, because I'm sure that's your biggest problem."

He shook his head. *Sisters.* "Thanks, Livie. And since you're being so magnanimous, I'll put you out of your misery and tell you we have a date Saturday."

"Yes!" She squealed, clapping her hands. "Where are you going to take her?"

"Uh." He scrunched his brow. "I'm not sure."

"It has to be somewhere spectacular."

"I was thinking a picnic."

"No! It's still a little chilly for April."

He pulled into Olivia's apartment parking lot and stopped the car. "I'll figure it out."

"Chophouse?" Her eyes gleamed.

"That's expensive."

"But you want to make a good impression, don't you?" She peered up at him, eyes wide and round, looking the very definition of pleading.

He rubbed his chin. "Look, Livie, I don't want to travel the same path I did with Jackie. Felicity has to know up front that I can't splurge for expensive dinners and champagne-and-caviar taste."

"Fine." Her lips twisted. "That makes sense." She stared off, tapping her chin. "Oh, I know. Candlelight Dinner Playhouse? You get dinner *and* a show, which is a lot better than dinner and a movie."

"But we can't get to know one another and catch up if we're watching something."

"You and your ill logic."

He raised an eyebrow. "You mean perfect logic."

"Anyway, big brother." Olivia opened the car door, got out, and turned to him. "Whatever you pick, I hope she enjoys it."

"Thanks, Livie."

"See you later." She shut the door and gave a wave.

He waited until she walked up to her first-floor apartment and opened the door before driving off. As he made his way home, Will brainstormed all that Loveland had to offer. Sure, it was a little chilly, but maybe Saturday would find them in the low sixties. If that ended up being the case, then a picnic could work. Or a walk through Benson Sculpture Garden. Of course, they could go hiking through Devil's Backbone.

As much as Olivia's interference had annoyed him—talk about beyond awkward—still, coming away with a date with Felicity Edwards was definitely a win. All he had to do now was plan the perfect date.

Chapter Four

DRESS COMFORTABLY. WEAR TENNIS SHOES.

Felicity stared at the text from Will. They'd chatted a couple of times by phone since he'd asked her out. They'd even shared a few texts, but this one had her mind whirring and wondering what today's date would include.

She looked toward her closet. *What do I wear?*

Today was a rare day when she had nothing scheduled. No weddings. No cake prep. No new client meetings. Her calendar had a big fat nothing except for her date with Will. So, like every normal woman would, she'd washed and styled her hair, then painted her nails a nice spring coral shade. Now she just had to pick a comfortable outfit.

A *cute* one at that.

A glimpse of aqua caught her eye. Felicity grinned at the eyelet top. It would go perfectly with her skinny crops. Luckily, she had a pair of matching Converse to go with her outfit. By the time she dressed and added a day makeup look, Felicity's nerves had peaked, bringing a slight jitter to her hands. Which of course had her jabbing her earlobe trying to find the right place to insert her dangling earrings. Thank goodness she'd done her mascara first; otherwise she'd probably be crying with a poked eye. After donning a white cardigan, she headed toward the front of her apartment.

Her cell buzzed. APARTMENT NUMBER?

Her fingers typed out a reply.

Felicity blew out a breath. *Okay, Lord. It's almost time. I have no idea what to expect or what we'll be doing, but I pray we have a good time together. I hope I can relax instead of feeling like I'm going to vomit from nerves.* She squeezed her eyes shut, placing a hand to her stomach. Slowly she inhaled and then exhaled.

She jumped at the sound of a knock. *He's here.* She stared at her front door then willed her feet to move. First the right, then the left. Finally, she peeked through the peephole. It *was* Will.

With a smile, she opened the door. "Hey there," she breathed out. She gulped, trying to contain her emotions. He looked amazing in a baby blue polo that brightened his eyes and made his skin glow like decadent caramel sauce.

"You look. . . That color on you. . . Wow." He spread his hands out as his mouth quirked into a half smile.

Her heart picked up speed. How had the high school boy turned into such a stunning man? "Am I dressed okay?"

"More than."

She could feel her cheeks bunching. "Thank you." Turning, she grabbed her over-the-shoulder purse.

After she locked the door, Felicity turned back to Will. "Ready."

"Great." He cupped her elbow as they descended the stairs from her second-floor apartment.

Warmth coursed through her elbow down her arm. She could feel her body heating from his touch. Felicity asked a question to distract herself from her thoughts. "Where are we going?"

"Do you really want to know, or would you rather be surprised?"

She bit her lip. "I don't know." She breathed out a chuckle. "I love surprises, but sometimes I think anticipation will make my heart stop or something."

"That's the fun, right?" He winked.

The urge to place something cool against her face welled within her. But she couldn't. Her red cheeks were enough indication of her feelings already. Maybe he'd just consider the pink hue makeup. "It is. So, I guess I'll be surprised."

"Great." He stopped in front of a gray sedan, his hand dropping from her arm. "This is me."

"Really?"

An uneasy look crossed his face. "Yes. Why?"

"I have the same car." She pointed across the lot, a couple rows back. "That's me."

"Oh." His lips curved as he made his way to the passenger side and held the door open for her.

Felicity got in the car, inhaling Will's crisp cologne that lingered in the interior. Her heart thudded in her ears as she waited for him to round the front. She blew out a shaky breath.

You can do this. Just be yourself. But what exactly did that look like? She knew how to act in front of clients and her best friends, but with Will—well, her insides were all mixed up like a pack of multicolored sprinkles.

Will started the engine and backed out of the parking space. "Do you want to listen to some music?"

"I don't mind it as background noise." But she didn't want the volume so high they couldn't talk.

"My thoughts exactly."

She gave a mental hand clap. Still, she remained flustered. Why couldn't she think of anything to kick off a conversation? What could she say? *Be honest with maybe a little sugar coating.* "How do you like owning your own business?" Maybe not the most intimate of topics, but if she could make it past the small talk, then points for her.

"I love it. I get to make my own hours. Have the days off I want."

"Really?" She turned, staring at his profile. "When are your days off?"

"Sunday and Monday. What about you?" He glanced at her, a hint of surprise widening his eyes at her stare.

Her face heated and she faced the windshield. Hopefully he wouldn't catch the blush she assumed was in full bloom now. "We have Sundays off as well. Usually we're doing some kind of work the rest of the week."

"At least you get one day of rest."

"Well, I get two this week. I had nothing scheduled today, so I relaxed at home." And primped for this date. She picked imaginary lint from her jeans.

"You had all day to think about our date?"

Her head whipped in Will's direction.

He slid a finger along the collar of his shirt. "I didn't mean to say that out loud."

A laugh rose unbidden. "I'm so glad to know I'm not the only one feeling awkward."

"Right?" He shook his head as he stopped at a red light. "We're in our thirties. What's wrong with us?"

"I don't know. But you'd think it would be easier."

"Maybe it isn't when it really matters." His eyes caught hers.

Held hers in their depths. Her breath suspended, heart thumping away in her ears. Maybe God knew something she didn't.

A car honked, breaking the moment. Will blinked and cleared his throat, facing forward once more as he moved ahead. Had he felt the impact of that moment as much as she had? It probably only lasted a split second but seemed like an eternity.

Thank goodness they'd been at a stoplight. No need to get in a car crash gazing into each other's eyes. Her lips twisted in a wry grin. Tension had fled, but something new lingered in its place. Hope? Anticipation? Whatever it was, Felicity wanted to explore it and get to know the man who caused the wide array of emotions.

"Do you have any other siblings besides Olivia?"

"Isn't she enough?" He laughed, taking the sting out of his words. "No. It's just us two. You?"

"I have two half siblings. A sister and brother. Thirteen and eleven."

"Wow. How's that?"

"A little strange. I'm old enough to be their mom, but I'm not. I'm their sister." She shrugged. "I try and spend time with them like you would a sibling close to your age."

"Really? Do you take them out?"

"Sure. We go to the movies. Hang around the house for game days."

"Sounds like you're a great big sister."

Funny how the compliment warmed her. "I try to be. Tabitha's into theater, so we're always dissecting what makes a movie or play worthwhile. Or we'll go horseback riding, since she likes that as well. Junior is into coding and video games."

"Do you play with him?"

She nodded then spoke, remembering his eyes were on the road. "Yes. He loves Minecraft and Lego video games. They bore me a little, but it's the one thing that makes him talk a lot. I find out all about his friends and school when we play."

"And do you ever hang out with them at the same time?"

"Sure, if we do something like watch a movie or have family game nights. Plus, my dad and stepmom invite me over for a family dinner once a week." What would it be like if Will joined her? Would he get along with her family?

"My parents were really big on family dinners growing up."

"Are they retired?"

"No. My dad actually got a promotion last year. They ended up moving to Florida. My mom loves it there but misses us."

"I bet. Is she flying back for the wedding?"

He snorted. "Are you kidding? You couldn't keep her away. She flew out a week after Olivia got engaged so they could go dress shopping. I know they video chat a lot to talk about the little details that make Elliot's and my eyes glaze over."

Felicity chuckled at the image. "You've been a good sport. Agreeing to come with her for the cake tasting."

"I had incentive." He turned and winked at her.

Heat filled her cheeks as her heart set into a gallop. Would she blush all evening from his flirting?

"In all seriousness, they were good. I could have stayed all day tasting your food."

"That could be arranged."

They settled into a comfortable flow of conversation until Felicity noticed the time. Will had been driving for a while. "Where *are* we going?"

"Don't worry. I promise you'll have fun."

She pointed to the road sign indicating they were entering a new town. When did she miss the sign saying they'd left Loveland city limits? "There wasn't any place fun in Loveland?"

"We'll have plenty of time to go on dates in Loveland." His face colored with embarrassment.

"I'm glad I'm not the only one whose face gets red."

"I just realized how presumptuous it sounded."

"Oh no, it was more like hopeful."

After a few twists and turns, Will parked in front of a miniature golf center. Felicity bit her lip as her mind raced. Her palms became clammy, and she wiped them on her jeans.

Will turned to face her, a spark of happiness in his eyes. "Ready?"

"Uh, Will?"

"Yes?"

"I'm not very good at golf."

"It's just mini golf. No one is ever good. That's why it's so much fun."

He wouldn't be thinking that much longer. She and sports did *not* mix.

⌣

Will placed a palm in the middle of Felicity's back as he guided her toward the first hole. Since they'd walked in and paid, Felicity had looked everywhere but at him. At first he thought she was just taking in the amusement center. But when he began to ask her questions and her replies came out in one-word-monotone responses, concern had snaked its way through him.

He couldn't help but notice how she kept wiping her hands on her jeans. Just how bad was she at golfing? "You know how this works, right?"

"In theory." She grimaced. "I hit the ball, hoping it goes into the hole."

"Right." He pointed to the number at the front of the first hole. "That tells you how many tries you want to aim for. If you get it in there under that, it helps your score."

Her eyes widened, the whites shining back at him. "Score?"

Will bit back a chuckle. "Yeah. It's friendly competition only. I promise."

"Right." She visibly swallowed. "What happens if it takes more tries?"

"It hurts your score."

She glanced behind him and leaned forward. "I mean, how many times do I try before I give up and we move ahead. I don't want anyone who's waiting their turn to get angry."

He raised an eyebrow. "I don't think that'll be an issue."

She muttered under her breath. Almost sounded like "That's what you think," but he couldn't be so sure.

"Do you want me to go first?" He offered a smile to reassure her.

Will wanted her to have fun, not regret saying yes to him. Maybe he should have forked over more money as Olivia suggested. *Don't give up yet. Just put Felicity's mind at ease.*

He stepped forward. "Here. I'll show you how easy it is."

"Sure." Her lips thinned.

If that was a smile, it was a poor excuse for one. Will lined up his putter and aimed for the hole. His ball went past and stopped a couple of feet away.

"Nothing to it. Your turn." He moved out of the way, gesturing for her to take her place.

Felicity's shoulders rose then lowered as she exhaled. "O–okay. I can do this."

"Remember, it's just for fun."

Her eyes squinted as she concentrated on her shot. Her grip opened and closed repeatedly over her putter. She licked her lips then clamped down on her bottom lip. Will averted his eyes, looking at her hands on the putter. She raised the club into a swing and. . .

Oh Lord, help!

He grabbed Felicity around the waist and moved her to the side as her putter bounced off the windmill and ricocheted straight for the spot where she'd been standing. He turned, thankful the putter merely swooshed by them. Only his thankfulness quickly turned to dismay as the putter hit a man on the arm.

"Kill me now," Felicity murmured.

Will squeezed her shoulders. "It'll be fine."

But right now, he needed to make sure the stranger was okay. He walked over. "I'm so sorry, sir. My date swung a little too. . .enthusiastically." He picked up the club. "Are you okay?"

"No worries." The man gestured to the two teens next to him. "My wife is the same way. Hence the reason she's out getting a manicure while I have the kids."

His son nodded vigorously. "We learned better than to bring my mom here. It's dangerous to all involved."

Will glanced over his shoulder. Felicity's head hung low, her arms wrapped around her waist. He turned back to the family. "Surely it won't be that bad. I can give her pointers."

"Good luck. Before you do that, mind if we go first and get out of your way?"

Will gaped, then closed his mouth abruptly. "Sure. Again, sorry about that."

"No worries. But next time you might want to take her to dinner and a movie." The man winked and continued forward, his kids following him.

Will walked over to Felicity. "I told them they could go first."

"Great idea." She sighed. "I can't believe I hit somebody."

"It's okay. He was cool about it. Next time, just hold on to the putter."

"Right."

After the family left, Will handed her club back. "Do you want some pointers?"

"Sure."

He gave her some, emphasizing the need to hold on to the handle. "You ready to give it another try?"

She nodded, tucking a curl behind her ear. "I can do this."

"Of course you can." *Lord, let it be so.* If she hit another person, he'd lose his cool and finally let the laughter out.

"Okay, I'm going for it." She swung her arms with less height than before and hit the ball.

He ducked as a draft of air wafted over his head. Felicity covered her mouth, eyes wide with horror. He winced with every clang and let out a low groan at the sound of glass breaking.

"Oh my word." Felicity's face balled up.

"Don't cry." He wrapped his arms around her. "*Please* don't cry." *Lord, please don't let that window cost a lot to repair.* This date was supposed to allow them to get to know each other better. He pulled back, missing the warmth being close had provided. "How about we go somewhere to eat?"

"That sounds like a better plan."

"Maybe one day we'll laugh about this?"

"Don't hold your breath," she muttered.

A laugh escaped. "Okay, I'll laugh about this one day."

She shook her head, a hint of a smile curving her lips.

After speaking to management regarding the broken window, and paying for repairs—after he assured Felicity he didn't mind paying—they headed toward the car.

Will cleared his throat, his hands resting in his pockets. "So, is it just golf you have trouble with, or all sports?"

"*All.* Not to mention anything that takes me off my own two feet. God made me to be planted firmly on terra firma."

"Good to know." He wiped his mouth, trying to keep from laughing.

Felicity peered up at him. "Are you regretting asking me out?"

"Not at all. But I do think we'll need a do-over." Hitting a random stranger and forking over money for a broken window hadn't been in his plan. He needed to prove to Felicity that a date with him would lead to a good time.

"I think that sounds doable." She grinned at him, and relief settled into his chest.

All wasn't lost.

Yet.

Chapter Five

Felicity knocked on the door to Cassie's office.

"Come in," Cassie called out softly.

Felicity pushed the door open and sank into the chaise located in the corner of the room.

"Uh-oh. Bad day? Client? Something else?" Cassie propped her chin on her hand, tapping her pen against her desktop.

Felicity fidgeted in her seat, trying to gather her thoughts. She peered at her friend. Cassie was a couple of years older than Felicity, but the gap didn't matter when it came to their friendship. They just clicked. "Bad date."

"Oh, your date with Will already happened?"

Felicity nodded as she stared up at the ceiling. Gone were the popcorn ceilings. Instead, an ivory coat filled her vision. "He took me miniature golfing."

Cassie slapped the desk, her guffaws filling the room. Felicity tried to keep a stoic face, but her lips twitched at the memory of the shocked look on Will's face when she hit the stranger with her putter.

"Oh Cass, it was awful!" She gave in to the laughter as tears streamed down her face. "I shouldn't be laughing considering I hit a bystander with a flying golf club."

"Say you didn't." Cassie tipped her head back and fell into more laughter.

"What is all this noise?" Ronnie stood in the doorway, her hazel eyes wide, darting from Cassie to Felicity.

Through hiccups, Felicity repeated the tale of the failed night of miniature golf. Soon Ronnie's face about matched the red highlights in her hair, she was laughing so hard.

"Did you really break a window?"

"Well, the golf ball did. But I guess I did by proxy."

Cassie wiped tears from her face. "That's hilarious. Did it scare Will off?"

Felicity smiled, remembering Will asking for a do-over.

"Oh, judging by that look on your face, I'd say no. Right?" Ronnie asked.

"He felt bad I did so awful, as if he was personally responsible for my horrible athletic skills."

"Points for him," Cassie said. "Do you want to go out with him again?"

"Yes." She smiled, thinking of how easy talking to him had been. "The only problem I had with the date was the location. He could have picked anything else—"

"Not sports related," Ronnie chimed in.

"And I would have been over the moon."

"Have you heard from him since?" Cassie asked.

"Sunday. He texted to thank me for the good time and to let me know he'd like to go out again once he got a look at his work calendar."

"What does he do?" Ronnie took a seat in front of Cassie's desk.

"He owns his own barbershop. Davenport Clips."

"The one near Lake Loveland?" Ronnie pointed over her shoulder as if she could see the spot.

"The very one."

"Then you guys already have something in common." Cassie smiled.

"Yeah, his sister mentioned how we're both business owners. I think it's amazing he can run a business like that in today's climate. I feel like I'm always hearing about someone closing their doors."

"Maybe you should drive by his shop. Take a peek around," Ronnie suggested.

"But I don't need a barber. It'd be so obvious why I was there."

"Agreed," Cassie stated. "Save that for when you're falling in love and want to surprise him with lunch or something."

Felicity laughed, but inside her thoughts whirred faster than the paddles on her Kitchen Aid. Would she end up falling in love with Will, or would he find out her situation and say, *Thanks but no thanks,* like the others before him had?

She gulped. How would she know the right time to let him know she couldn't have kids? Obviously, it wasn't the first date, because that would be beyond awkward. But were you supposed to say something on the third date when it seemed like you wanted to keep seeing each other? Or after you agreed to be exclusive?

Not that she'd ever made it far enough to be exclusive. Dating in a person's thirties almost guaranteed the guys wanted a family. In her twenties, most of the men she'd dated didn't care to delve deeper into a relationship, so she'd been the one to end things.

"What does that look mean?" Ronnie pointed at her face.

"I was just wondering when to tell him, you know?"

Ronnie's brow furrowed, and she bit her lip. "You have a secret?"

"You know. How I can't have kids?"

Recognition dawned.

"When do you usually tell a guy?" Cassie asked softly.

"Too early?" Maybe that was just a good reason to excuse all the guys who had never called her after telling them. She'd tried a bunch of different times in a relationship, and they never seemed to work out.

"Or maybe you just haven't told the right guy?" Ronnie suggested.

"We'll see. I'm not telling Will on the second date."

"Just pray God leads you," Cassie suggested. "Don't put a number on it."

"You're right." Felicity slid her hands along her pants. "Wait." She tilted her head and looked at Ronnie. "I thought you were working from home today."

Ronnie only came into the shop when she had a tasting or consultation. She preferred to cook in her industrial-grade chef's kitchen at home. Which actually worked out perfectly, because then Felicity could use the kitchen at Weddings by Design and not worry about stepping on Ronnie's toes.

"I have a consultation coming in about thirty minutes, and I forgot something in the office."

Back in her own office, Felicity pulled up her appointment calendar and began making notes for the upcoming brides. She had a wedding this weekend, but thankfully it would be performed at dawn. The couple wanted to look at the sunrise as newlyweds.

Which meant by noon, she'd have the rest of the day to herself.

Her phone buzzed with an incoming text. *Will.*

Hey Felicity, are you available Friday night?

She bit her lip. I'd love to say yes, but it depends on how late you want to get together. I have an early wedding Saturday.

Okay. Would lunch on Friday be possible?

Felicity peeked at her Friday calendar. She could do lunch. Yes. That would work.

Great. Pick you up at your shop at 12?

I'll be ready.

And she would be. She'd take Cassie's suggestion and pray that God would lead her in when to reveal her fertility issues to Will. Until then, she would anticipate seeing him again.

⌣

"I've got the goods, brother dear." Olivia preened as she set a picnic basket on Will's desk.

He stood, inhaling the tantalizing scents of deli sandwiches. "Thanks, Livie. You got the Kid?" The Kid was the name of his favorite club sandwich.

"I did and took a guess on Felicity's choice. You did say she has no allergies, right?"

"Yeah." He'd texted her last minute, realizing he didn't want her to go into anaphylactic shock just because he wanted to surprise her with a picnic lunch.

"I do hope this will go better than that flying golf club fiasco." Livie placed her hands on her hips. "I told you to take her to a restaurant." She tilted her head. "And what if she hates bugs? Sometimes picnics aren't romantic."

Will groaned. "You're killing me. First you told me to ask her out before you butted in and ended up outing me anyway. Then you say I can handle everything but keep insisting I listen to your date ideas."

"Which, if you had, you would've avoided mayhem by golf club."

"But I would've never known she's such a terrible sportsman."

Livie's lips parted in shock. "So, wait, you didn't think the date was a disaster?"

How could he when he got to spend time with the woman who had occupied most of his teenage thoughts? Lack of athletic skill wouldn't damper his thankfulness at a second chance. But he wouldn't tell Olivia that.

He cleared his throat. "Not at all. We got to know each other better, and I saw how she handled a little adversity. She was actually. . .adorable." His lips twitched at the memory of the chagrined look when her golf ball almost hit him upside the head.

"Oh my goodness."

"What?" He blinked to focus and found Livie gaping at him.

"You like her," she whispered.

"Hence the reason I asked her on a date. What's wrong with you?"

"No, sir. I mean *like* her, like her." She placed her hands on the edge of his desk, leaning forward. "Why else would you call her adorable? Guys don't talk like that unless they're headed for the chapel."

"We've been on one date. Slow your roll. The only wedding I'll be going to this year is yours."

Olivia rolled her eyes. "No one is saying you're getting married tomorrow." She straightened and folded her arms across her chest. "But you've got the bug, and I can't wait to watch you fall, brother dear."

"All right. Get out. I'm going on my date without your proclamations ringing in my ears."

She giggled and waggled her fingers at him. "Be sure to sing 'Going to the Chapel' on your way to see her. Give her my *love*." Livie smiled mischievously and left the room.

Sisters.

Will grabbed the picnic basket and headed out the back door of the shop. Soon he was pulling up to Weddings by Design.

He couldn't recall how many times he'd passed this place and never gave it a second look. If he'd known Felicity Edwards worked here, he would have made up some lame excuse to stop in. He walked up the sidewalk to the cute gray-sided home and stopped short as the front door opened and Felicity stepped onto the front porch.

His breath caught as she grinned at him, her full lips curving, making her cheekbones stand out and the joy in her eyes sparkle. Was that for him? Was she really as happy to see him as he was to see her? He took a few steps, meeting her halfway.

"Hi."

"Hey there."

A tantalizing hint of sugar tickled his nose. "Did you bake a cake today?"

"I did. Do I smell like flour or something?"

"Sugar." He grinned down at her.

"Phew. Better that than something worse."

They walked to Will's car, and he blew out a breath, trying to slow his rapid heartbeat. This date *had* to be better than the previous disaster. As cute as Felicity had been in her inexperience—*more like worst golfer ever*—Will wanted to show her a good time. And to prove to himself that he didn't need a ton of cash for a woman to like him. He just wanted to be liked for himself. Was that too much to ask for? He opened her car door.

"Thank you."

As he drove to the park, Will glanced at Felicity. "How's your day going?"

"It's been pretty good actually. We got business from two new couples, and I spent the morning making a cake for tomorrow's wedding."

"Oh yeah. You said you had an early start."

She laughed dryly. "If you consider a sunrise wedding early."

"Really? Who would wake up that early?"

"Apparently a couple that wants to greet the day as Mr. and Mrs."

"That's actually a nice sentiment."

"Agreed, but I'd be dead on my feet. I'm still trying to figure out how much makeup the bride will need to cover up those circles from lack of sleep. Not to mention how long it'll take to get her hair ready."

Will glanced at her to see her shudder. "So, no sunrise wedding for you?"

"Oh no. Any time after noon sounds good to me."

"What about a midnight wedding?"

"I don't know. I could see doing that for like a New Year's Eve wedding, but personal preference, I'd rather be done with my wedding day by then. What about you?"

"No sunrise or midnight weddings for me. I'm a middle-of-the-day person."

Felicity laughed, and Will puffed his chest like he'd just won a prize, even though he wasn't exactly sure why his comment inspired that reaction in her.

"Yes! That's me." Although maybe he shouldn't have admitted that.

"I'm not an early bird, and just thinking about night owls makes me want to reach for a blanket."

"Well," he said, putting the car in park, "if you need a power nap before going back to work, I did bring picnic blankets."

"You thought of everything, huh?"

He smiled at her, hoping his nerves didn't show. Truth was, dating Felicity made him realize how long he'd been out of the dating game.

After finding a spot in an open grassy area, Will knelt on the blanket's edge and pulled items from the basket.

"You ordered from my favorite deli."

"Really?" The sun illuminating her flawless complexion fascinated Will.

"I always get the turkey sandwich."

"Thank goodness." He passed her the sub. "That's what Livie ordered for you."

"She got the food? Tell her I said thanks."

"I will. She grabbed everything for me so I could finish up with my clients and not take all of your lunch time."

"That was sweet of her."

"Nah, that's her evil genius at work."

Felicity snorted. "What do you mean?"

"Olivia is nosy. She can't help but stick her nose where no one asks her to."

"But isn't that the beauty of siblings? Having them know your secrets?"

He cupped his ear. "Did you say siblings were trouble? Yes, yes, I agree." He delighted in the sound of her laughter and took another bite of his sandwich. He swallowed. "In all honesty, Olivia's a great little sister. Annoying at times, but I love her."

"It's so awesome you two have such a close relationship. Do you go to the same church?"

"We do. We've been going to Good News Baptist forever. What about you?"

"I go to Loveland Community Church. It's actually how I met my friends. Where we dreamed up owning our own business."

"Tell me more." Will ate his food quietly as Felicity shared about her business partners.

Well, actually, they sounded more like friends who happened to be co-owners. He was glad she had friends who could share her passion.

"What about you? Do you own your barbershop on your own or have a business partner?"

"I'm the sole owner."

"Wow, Will. That's amazing."

He nodded, his thoughts a mess as her words seeped into his soul. Jackie had made him feel like being a barber was nothing to be proud of. Could he trust that Felicity really admired him? Or would the proverbial shoe drop when he let down his guard?

Chapter Six

Today was perfect. The Colorado sky glimmered a bright blue, letting the sun's rays shine down on her and Will. Felicity tipped her face up, loving the warmth of the sun as the boat Will had rented bobbed steadily over the lake.

"What are you thinking?" Will's voice sent shivers through her, and goose bumps popped on her arms in response.

"Just what a beautiful day it is," she said.

"How can you tell with your eyes closed?"

"They were open before I shut them."

Will chuckled, and Felicity couldn't help herself. She righted her head and opened her eyes to gaze into his blue irises.

His lips curved into a smile. "You're beautiful."

"Thank you." Heat filled her cheeks. "You're not so bad looking yourself."

His laughter filled the air. "High praise coming from the woman going around proclaiming a day's beautiful with her eyes closed. Then again, maybe I should be worried. Are you really calling me ugly?"

"Oh you." She gave him a light shove. "You know you're not ugly."

"I don't know. Have you really looked at me to make sure?"

Felicity turned in her seat and studied Will. She leaned forward, keeping her face devoid of emotion as she scanned his features. Noted the faint lines in his forehead that would probably be more prominent in a couple of decades. The way his nose seemed perfectly symmetrical and centered, not to mention his full lips that held a touch of pink. And his skin reminded Felicity of the brown sugar buttercream frosting she'd whipped up yesterday.

"No. Ugly you are not, Mr. Davenport."

Will closed the gap between them and slid his hand up her back. "I think I might have to kiss you now."

"Please do."

He brushed his lips softly over hers. Once. Twice. A third time. He pulled back. "I've been wanting to do that forever."

"Who said you had to stop?" Any other time Felicity would have hushed herself from being too forward, but those bare brushes of the lips weren't going to cut it. She'd been wanting to know what Will's lips felt like since their first date.

"Forgive me." Will leaned forward, pressing his lips against hers.

Felicity sagged in his arms as his kiss ignited a fire within. Being in his arms, feeling the rightness of the moment, the excitement, enhanced the depth of his kisses. Maybe, just maybe, things would work out in a forever kind of way.

When Will pulled back once more, he settled his forehead against hers. "Wow."

"Mm-hmm." She kissed his cheek, then scooted back. She needed to put some space between them and cool down. "Thank you for bringing me out on the lake. I've really enjoyed myself."

"Because it's such a beautiful day?" He winked.

"Maybe the company had something to do with it," she teased.

Will chuckled. Every time she pulled a laugh from him, giddiness filled her, making her head swim with delight.

"Good. I still feel like we're recovering from the miniature golf fiasco."

Felicity dropped her head into her hands, muffling the groan that tore through her. "I still can't believe that." She peeked through her fingers. "And you know I'm not better at any other sport, right?"

"Don't even want to try? Maybe we could go bowling next?"

"Lord help us if we do."

"Okay, no bowling."

"No *sports*." Felicity splayed her hands, hoping he'd get the point. "You know what? How about I plan our next date?"

"Yeah?" He kissed her cheek. "I'd love that."

"Then it's a date." She squeezed his hands.

"What about church?"

"Hmm? What about it?" She tore her gaze from the beautiful scenery.

"I know you go to a different church than I do. Would you ever want to visit mine? Or maybe I could visit yours?"

She paused, thinking about what he was asking. Were they ready to start visiting each other's church? Was their relationship that far along? They hadn't had a conversation about exclusivity or anything like that, but Felicity didn't necessarily need it, did she? She didn't get the vibe from Will that he would romance her today and another woman tomorrow. And obviously, if he was asking to visit her church, he had longevity in mind.

She hoped.

"Okay. That sounds good."

"Great." He beamed. "Then how about Sunday I join you? See where you and the ladies first met and thought of your wedding shop brainchild."

She added how he made the effort to know everything about her to the mental list of his positive traits. He was serious boyfriend material. "Sounds like a great plan."

Right now, Felicity would focus wholeheartedly on living in this moment and not worrying about the future and what it could bring. She just wanted to enjoy Will and getting to know him. He wasn't flashy with their dates. Didn't talk solely of himself. She felt seen and heard, and those were two very important things for her.

No more overthinking. She would continue floating on the lake and enjoying the day that the Lord had made.

Sunday arrived too soon. Will groaned and tugged at his tie to loosen it. How many times had he tied and untied it? He couldn't get the top centered. The material kept knotting to the right and looked foolish. In the back of his mind, Will knew the tie wasn't what had him twisted on the inside. The real culprit of the sudden onslaught of tension was church. The one thing that brought him joy no matter what now had him ensuring his suit and tie looked right.

Lord, please help me make a good impression with Felicity's family and church family. He actually had no idea if Felicity's dad and family went to her church. He'd assumed, then texted her to verify. A quick yes from her had sent his stomach rumbling as if a group of motorcycle riders had flooded the streets.

He was going to meet her father, stepmother, and half brother and half sister. It was definitely too early in their relationship for that. Wasn't it?

His phone chimed, and he stared at the incoming text.

Willie, Elliot just surprised me. Want to ride with us to church?

So he could see them make eyes at each other? No thanks. His thumbs flew across the screen.

I'm actually going to church with Felicity.

Olivia sent a GIF of a person doing a slow blink.

Are you serious? When were you going to tell me?

How about never?

Brothers.

Three dots danced across the screen as Will waited for Olivia to type more. Most likely a dissertation on how he was wrong to keep that from her and she wanted to get together so she could pry the details from him.

Will Davenport, you are coming over for dinner tonight at Elliot's place. AND you should bring Felicity, because if I have to rely on you for any type of information, I'll have two feet in the grave.

He chuckled. She was so predictable.

Yes, Livie.

Don't yes, Livie, me.

I'll be sure to text Elliot the magic words as well.

She sent a GIF of a kid doing an exaggerated eye roll. He chuckled and slid his wallet and phone into his suit pocket. He'd given up on the tie. He couldn't be late or he'd make a worse impression than the slight tilt of the Windsor.

By the time Will pulled into the parking lot at Loveland

Community Church, the anxiety that had been drumming through him like a live wire had settled down to a quiet hum. He walked up the sidewalk with the other congregants, scanning the premises for Felicity. She said she would be keeping an eye out for him. He didn't know if that meant she'd be waiting in the lobby or in the sanctuary.

As he nodded in greeting to the man holding the lobby door open, he heard someone call out to him. He turned his head, searching for Felicity, pretty sure that was her voice.

"Over here, silly." A light touch on his arm stayed him.

"Hey." He smiled down at Felicity and trailed his fingers lightly across the back of her arm in greeting. "Fancy meeting you here."

"Do you come here often?" she asked, a bright smile on her face.

"Can you believe I never have?"

"Then I can't wait to see what you think." She motioned him to follow her with a tilt of her head. "My family's already seated. They're saving the two end seats for us," she said as he fell into step with her.

In the sanctuary, people quietly chatted, shook hands, or exchanged hugs while the worship team softly played instrumental music. Will leaned down toward Felicity's ear. "Is this your meet-and-greet time?"

"Yes." She nodded then stopped at an aisle and scooted past the first chair and took her place at the second one. "Dad, this is Will. Will, my father, Roy Edwards."

She leaned back, and Will offered his hand. Mr. Edwards cut an imposing figure. "Nice to meet you, sir."

"I'm glad you could join us today, Will." Mr. Edwards squeezed his hand. "Are you joining us for lunch afterward?"

Will's gaze slid to Felicity's in silent question. She bit her lip and raised her eyebrows in a plea.

"I'd like that, thank you." He'd go from one meal of inquisition to the next at Elliot's house. Today would be an interesting Sunday.

The service order mirrored the one at his church. The worship team led them in praise, singing songs from contemporary and Gospel artists alike. Then the preacher got up to preach the Word. The way he delivered the message riveted Will and had him reflecting on how the Word applied to his life.

It always amazed him how pastors could read one or two verses and then sermonize an hour's worth and leave him convicted and seeking to do more in his spiritual walk. He had to admit, Felicity's church went a little more in-depth in the Bible than his own. Definitely something to consider if and when the time came.

Will that time come, Lord? I hope this ease I feel with Felicity means good things for our relationship, for a possible future together.

Felicity had quickly slipped into his daily thoughts. Lately, while he cut his customers' hair, all he could think about was when he could see her again. Talk to her and share a smile or two over something that caught his attention that day. He loved how often she texted or just let him know she was thinking of him.

Their relationship was pretty perfect. Hopefully, she felt the same way.

Chapter Seven

Felicity placed the plates on the table as Tabitha followed behind her with the silverware.

"It's not fair that Junior doesn't have to help," her little sister grumbled.

"He is helping. He's outside helping Dad on the grill."

"He gets to do the fun stuff."

"You could always go in the kitchen and help your mom."

Tabitha rolled her eyes and blew out a breath. "I just want to eat the food. Not do all this."

Felicity bit back a laugh. Leave it to Tabitha to make things theatrical, in or out of the theater. "You don't complain when you help me bake."

"That's because whatever comes out of the oven is guaranteed to be better than something that was cooked." Tabitha raised her brows.

She sure had the teenage mood down pat. Felicity couldn't believe how fast her sister was growing. This fall she'd be going to high school since she had a summer birthday.

Felicity turned and hugged her little sister. "I love you, squirt."

"You just love that I love cake more than my mom's cooking."

Felicity laughed. "That's not it, but I am glad you like to eat sweets. I'd have to disown you if you didn't." She winked to let Tabitha know she was teasing.

"I actually believe that." Tabitha tugged her curls into a bun and slipped the hair tie from her wrist around her hair. "Felicity, could I ask you a question?"

"Sure, kiddo. What's up?"

"Have you ever liked a boy and wondered if he liked you back?" Tabitha shook her head derisively. "Dumb question, since you have Will here. But I mean, grown-ups probably just ask each other out without worrying what'll happen, huh?"

Felicity wanted to throw back her head and laugh maniacally. "Oh sis." She draped an arm around Tabitha's shoulder. "I wish being an adult made things easier. Sometimes I think it makes it harder."

"Really? But didn't Will just come up to you and ask you on a date?"

"No. His sister told me he liked me."

"What?" Tabitha's mouth dropped in shock.

Felicity pulled out a chair and sat, motioning for her sister to do the same. Then she told the story about how Will asked her for her number after being embarrassed by Olivia.

"But it worked out for you guys. He seems nice." Tabitha peered through the sliding glass door, watching the men standing in the backyard.

Felicity had been nervous when her father asked Will to join him and Junior at the grill. But Will had squeezed her hand and murmured he'd be okay and followed them to the deck. Heather had immediately headed for the kitchen, leaving Felicity and Tabitha to catch up on life.

But Felicity didn't know how much to share about the trials of dating. It felt wrong to inform Tabitha of her infertility, because then she'd have to ask her to keep it a secret from Will.

She sighed. "Just know that there's so much to dating that creeps up as an adult. There's more than just wondering if the guy likes you. You want to know if his values and beliefs are the same as yours. Because a lot of times, one is searching for marriage and one could be there just to have a good time. That causes heartache."

"Yeah, I get that. I guess I hoped I'd have confidence to look forward to. You know?" Tabitha played with her fingers as she stared downward.

"Of course, sweetie. And there's nothing saying you can't have confidence now. A lot of time, that's what attracts people. If you want, you could walk right up to this boy, tell him you like him and want to know if he wants to hang out with you." She held up a hand. "But I do think you're too young to date. Give that a few more years."

Tabitha nodded. "Mom says I can't date until I'm sixteen."

"That's a good age. How do you feel about that?"

She shrugged. "I don't know." Tabitha lifted her head, her brown eyes focusing on Felicity. "Thanks for listening."

"Anytime. I mean that, 'kay?"

Tabitha nodded and stood. "I'm going to go finish *Hairspray*. Call me when lunch is ready?"

"Sure thing."

Felicity headed for the kitchen to see if Heather needed any help. Her stepmother muttered under her breath as she added herbs to the food processor.

"Making dressing?" Felicity asked.

Heather jumped, placing a hand over her heart. "You scared me."

"Sorry."

"It's okay. And yes, I'm making dressing. Do you mind putting the salad on the table?"

"Sure."

Felicity did as she was asked then walked back into the kitchen. "Tabitha is watching another musical and said to call her when lunch is ready."

"That girl. If it isn't musicals, it's horses. Her latest obsession."

"As far as obsessions go, not so bad."

"True." A tight smile flitted over Heather's face before disappearing.

"Everything okay, Heather?"

"Actually. . ." Heather spun around, hand on her hip. She dabbed her forehead with a towel. "I'm feeling a little overwhelmed lately."

"Why? What's wrong?"

Her stepmother teared up, and her lower lip trembled. "I shouldn't be talking about this to you."

"What is it?" Felicity stepped closer and laid a hand on her stepmother's shoulder. "Please, you look so upset. You have to talk to someone, right?" And wouldn't a chance to be real bring them closer?

"I'm pregnant."

Felicity stumbled back and tried to breathe against the weight on her chest. "You are?" she whispered.

Heather nodded, tears spilling over her cheeks. She brushed them away, sniffling as they continued to fall despite her efforts. "I thought it was impossible at my age. My cycle has become erratic, and I thought menopause was coming."

"What did Dad say?" And what could she do to make Heather feel better through the fog of her own grief? The desire to sink to the ground and let her own tears go washed over her. She blew out a breath, fighting them back.

"I haven't told him yet," Heather covered her mouth as a sob rose.

Felicity went to her stepmother and wrapped her in a hug. Heather clung to her as her shoulders shook. Felicity wanted to ask all the questions bombarding her mind, but right now was the time for stillness. For Heather to know she wasn't alone and would have help and someone who cared.

Because even though they weren't as close as Felicity wished, Heather was still family. She rubbed her stepmother's back and continued to make soothing noises until the sounds of Heather's cries went silent and her sniffling ceased.

Heather drew back. "I probably look a mess now."

"No. You always look pretty." And she did. Her black hair fell to her waist in a straight curtain. She had some lines around her mouth and eyes, but she was approaching fifty in a dignified fashion. . .and apparently would be carrying around another life.

"When are you due?"

"Next year. January."

"Aww. You know I'll help out in any way."

"I really appreciate it. I know this topic isn't an easy one for you."

Felicity bit her lip. That was an understatement.

"Have you told Will about. . .?"

"No." She sighed. "I will eventually."

"If he's meeting your family, maybe the next conversation should be just that."

Felicity simply nodded, but inside she knew that it would be the toughest conversation ever. No guy stuck around once they knew. And she very much liked Will and wanted to see where their relationship would go.

What do I do, Lord?

Will placed his palm on the small of Felicity's back as he escorted her through the house. Elliot had decided to throw an impromptu get-together instead of just a family dinner, so Will had invited Felicity to join him.

Hopefully she wasn't sick of him yet. They had just spent the last few hours at her dad's house. Will had to admit, going from one house to the next felt a little surreal, but he wanted to see how Felicity would interact with his friends.

Would she and Olivia get along well outside a professional environment? Would Felicity like Elliot and think him a good fit for Olivia? And who knew who else they'd invited. The house was empty, so he and Felicity headed for the backyard, Elliot's oasis.

He pulled open one of the French doors, and a clamor of noise filtered in.

"Wow. I didn't expect this many people," Felicity murmured.

"Is this okay? We can leave before we go out there. They won't notice us."

"Will!" Elliot shouted. "Everyone, Will's here."

"You're right. They won't notice us at all," Felicity said with a chuckle. "I'm fine. Introduce me." She smiled.

He let out a sigh. They would be okay.

They walked outside, and Elliot came over and clapped him on the back. "Man, am I glad to see you. Liv's trying to get me to agree to a couples' party instead of doing separate bachelor and bachelorette parties."

Will stood frozen on the spot. He was the best man and had been planning on an all-day guys' outing. "Is that what you're going to do?"

"It's not what we originally planned. I'm not sure if she's worried what will happen or. . ." Elliot glanced at Felicity. "You know. . .sorry." He held out a hand. "I'm Elliot. I don't think we've officially met yet."

"Right." Will shook his head. "Elliot, this is Felicity. Felicity, Olivia's fiancé, Elliot."

"Nice to meet you."

"It's nice to meet you as well. Olivia said the cake design is amazing."

"You'll love it."

Elliot looked over his shoulder at Olivia, his affection written all over his face. "In the grand scheme of things, the cake itself doesn't really matter as much as who I'm slicing it with."

Will chuckled. "Sap. Which is why you'll do the couples' party."

Elliot groaned. "I would normally say *fine* and just do it. But this is probably the last time I'll hang out with the guys without feeling guilty if Liv wants to do something else."

"I'll talk to her." Will patted him on the shoulder. "But first I'm going to introduce Felicity to everyone else."

"Sure, man. Sorry for being a bad host, Felicity."

"No problem."

Will slipped his hand in Felicity's and guided her around the backyard, stopping to greet Elliot and Olivia's friends. Felicity seemed to join each conversation with ease. He knew she was a little introverted, but she handled herself well despite the constant *Nice to meet you*s.

Finally, Will made his way toward Olivia. She was perched on an outdoor sofa surrounded by a few of her girlfriends who would be her bridesmaids. He and Felicity sat down on a nearby love seat.

"Felicity, I'm so glad you made it." Olivia beamed.

Will's stomach twisted at the glint in her eyes. Maybe he should have given his sister the *behave* talk.

"Thanks for inviting me. I appreciate it."

"Oh, I had to. As soon as Will told me you two were going to church together, I figured it was time to get to know you."

Her words sounded right, but Will couldn't shake that she had something up her sleeve. He shifted and leaned forward. "Elliot told me about your couples' party idea."

"Isn't it the best?" She clapped her hands. "I can't wait."

"Well, Livie, I had something already planned for the guys."

"But people do men and women parties now."

"Not willingly," he muttered.

"What did you say?" Olivia folded her arms across her chest.

Will rubbed the back of his neck. He hated when his sister dug in her heels, and judging from the look on her face, she was ready to go full-fledged into this idea.

Before he could open his mouth to retort, the maid of honor's baby let out a squall just as her two-year-old came flying around the corner. Mercedes bounced the baby on her knee while trying to console her toddler.

"Here." Felicity held her arms out. "Give me one."

"Thank you so much." Mercedes passed the baby to Felicity, then settled her toddler on her knee now that her arms were free.

"That was nice of you," Will murmured.

"I need the practice." She settled the baby girl in the crook of her arm, crooning to her softly.

Something warm unfurled in his middle. Was it crazy that he could see them with children? Felicity holding a little girl that had her same complexion and curly hair? Or maybe even a child who had his eyes?

"You planning on having kids sometime soon?" His face heated. "Uh, forget I said that. Please."

She chuckled. "Heather's pregnant. But don't say anything. She was planning on telling my dad after we left."

"Oh wow. She happy about the news?"

Felicity nodded. "Just overwhelmed."

"Three kids, yeah that could be overwhelming."

"And the age difference."

"How do you think your dad will take it?"

"I don't know. He's in his sixties. He might worry about being there for the baby."

Will nodded at Felicity. "You're a natural."

She smiled, but it didn't quite reach her eyes. Did she not want children? That was something he definitely wanted in his future. He opened his mouth to ask but stopped at the tap on his shoulder. Olivia stood by his side and motioned for him to follow.

"Be right back," he told Felicity.

"All right."

"Will, I can't believe you approve of a bachelor party." Olivia started in on him as soon as the French doors closed.

"Livie, you know better. No one is going to be getting into any foolishness. We'll play a little touch football, probably go to a sports bar to catch a game and eat burgers. This'll be the last time Elliot will be able to hang out with the guys without first checking to make sure you don't have plans for the two of you. Do you really begrudge him that?"

She bit her lip. "Well, that makes sense."

"Exactly. You won't be going on all these girl trips and spa days once you're married. At least not without wondering if Elliot wants to do something, right? Marriage changes things."

She blew out a breath. "You're right. *This* time."

He laughed and hugged her. "You'll be fine. You'll have more fun at some spa than trying to get all the couples together."

They stood there, looking out into the backyard.

"Do you think Felicity would like to come?"

"I'm not sure." He watched her rocking the baby.

"She likes babies. You did good, brother. With my help, of course."

He squeezed her shoulder. "Thanks. I think lunch with her family went well too."

"Then enjoy the dating period. You'll be proposing before you know it."

Chapter Eight

Felicity smiled down at the picture of her and Will. They'd taken the photo when they'd gone to Chapungu Sculpture Park. Felicity had brought miniature cakes to share for dessert after they walked around. This last month, dating Will had been so. . .so easy. Almost too easy.

Don't think like that.

Will hadn't given her reason to fear that when he learned of her infertility he would bounce like all of the other men she'd dated and told in the past. The ones who were now firmly in the ex category. She blew out a breath. She desperately needed to tell Will, which was why she'd invited him over for dinner.

Felicity flicked the oven light on and peered through the window. The pizza crust bubbled, sporting a golden brown color. It should be done in a few more minutes, just in time for Will to arrive. She figured making homemade pizza would score her points in the food department. And if not, her dessert would seal the deal. The fruit tart she'd made looked more like a glammed sugar cookie but tasted just as delicious as the real deal.

The doorbell chimed, and Felicity's pulse tripled its beat. She wiped her hands on her apron, then hung the flowered fabric on the hook in the kitchen.

Lord, please let Will take the news with grace. I'm enjoying getting to know him, and I hope this doesn't change his opinion of me.

The crush she'd had on Will since high school had solidified into something real, tangible, and just within her grasp of happiness. If it were to be snatched away, Felicity didn't know what she'd do. She walked through the living room and opened the front door that was perfectly situated in the middle of the living room wall.

"Hey, pretty lady." Will brushed his lips against her cheek as he paused over the threshold.

"Hi. Come on in." She stepped aside and bit her lip.

She remembered the first time he saw the inside of her place. She'd examined the place as if it weren't her own and catalogued the cedarwood shelves lining her walls. They were decorated with various knickknacks and a few Bible study books she'd read. Denim-colored chairs flanked her reclaimed-wood coffee table and went well with the off-white sofa. She considered her apartment homey, but did he view her furnishings as dated?

Felicity shut the door and slid her hands into her jean pockets. "Dinner should be ready soon." The oven timer chimed. "Or right now."

Will grinned. "It smells great. Pizza?"

"Homemade. Hope that's okay."

He followed her into the kitchen. "Sounds perfect. Did you make the crust from scratch?"

"I did."

"Wow. You didn't have to go to all that trouble, but I appreciate it."

Felicity could feel her cheeks heating. Then again, it could be from the four-hundred-twenty-five-degree oven. She turned it off and opened a drawer to get her pizza cutter. "How many slices do you think you'll want?"

"How about two, so I don't feel like a pig. But I hope you'll ignore how many times I get up for more."

She chuckled. She loved his sense of humor. "Sounds good. I'm saving my repeat visits for dessert."

"Yum." Will rubbed his stomach. "I'll keep that in mind while I'm gorging on pizza."

She plated two slices on her light blue pottery plates.

"I'll carry these to the table." He picked up the dishes and headed to the left where an open doorway led to a closed dining room.

Felicity always fancied herself knocking down the wall and opening it to the living room, but that was a no-no in apartment living. Besides, she didn't mind the seclusion the space offered. She could just imagine, twenty years from now, home buyers would be wondering why there were no walls and hating the open concept of her generation.

Will sat across from her at the round table. "Mind if I say grace?"

"Please."

She stretched her hands across the table, sliding them against his warm palms. Tingles skittered up her arms, and she wanted to sigh at the comfort he brought and the excitement that unfurled inside her whenever he was around.

"Lord, bless the hands that prepared this wonderful meal." He squeezed her hands. "May it be nourishing for our bodies. Amen."

"Amen."

Will reached for a slice and took a huge bite. Felicity watched as he closed his eyes and chewed slowly. When he swallowed, his eyes opened and met her gaze. "This is amazing. How will I order regular pizza now?"

Pleasure filled her. "I'm so glad you think so. I wondered if it wouldn't have been safer just to order a pizza."

"Oh no. Now that I know you can cook, I say you do so for all of our dates." He winked.

She chuckled and bit into her own slice.

Conversation flowed between them as their food disappeared, including the extra serving Will grabbed after devouring his first two. When Felicity plated the tart awhile later, Will turned the conversation.

"Do you ever think of the future?"

"Sure I do."

She sat and tucked her knee under her chin, bracing her foot on the sofa cushion. Will's suggestion to eat dessert in the living room quieted her nerves over the upcoming conversation. "But do you mean something specifically?"

"Well, general and specific. I mean"—his face flushed—"do you ever think about getting married? Having a family of your own?"

This was it. The perfect segue to tell him her news. "Yes. Doesn't everyone?" Okay, so she'd chickened out. But the conversation wasn't over.

"I think so. I know I do."

"Do you want to get married?" She studied his face, took in the warmth in his light blue eyes.

"If I found the right woman, definitely."

Was she the right woman? His declaration hadn't exactly

loosened the band that had her chest in a vise. "What about children?" She swallowed, wishing she'd refilled her glass of water.

"I want a big family. As much as I gripe about Olivia, I loved having her around growing up. I actually wanted more siblings, but my parents had always planned on two, so that's what they stuck with."

"A big family?" she whispered. Her pulse thudded in her ears, making his voice sound farther away than it really was. Maybe sharing the vulnerable places of her heart wasn't such a good idea after all. Was their relationship solid enough that she could trust him with this?

"At least four kids." Will peered into her eyes. "You? How many kids do you want?"

How could she answer that? How could she tell him she'd never have biological children? And who could afford to adopt four kids? They were small business owners. They weren't rolling in piles of money.

"Felicity?"

She licked her lips. "I'm not sure." And she wasn't. She always imagined having a baby, but after her surgery, her dreams had turned to adopting. If she could ever afford the fees of the private agency she'd looked into.

"We have time. . .I mean, you have time to think about it. Nothing's set in stone, right?"

Wasn't it?

She couldn't tell him only to see the happiness erased from his features. Felicity could still recall the look when he'd found out Heather was pregnant. How he insisted Felicity was a natural with kids.

This is bad. Very bad.

If Will continued dating her, his dreams would die a quick death as soon as she revealed her medical history. But right now, she just couldn't bring herself to reveal it. Surely it was too soon. A month of dating was nothing in the grand scheme of things. Plus, they hadn't labeled their relationship.

Convinced she was right, she took a nibble of her fruit tart and ignored the fact that her broken heart rendered the taste like cardboard in her mouth.

—

Will dunked his tortilla chip into the salsa and popped it into his mouth. He wiped his hand and reached for the game controller. "I can't believe you didn't get any wings."

"Wings don't go with game night," Isaac said exasperatedly.

"Sure they do. Wings are man food, and we're men."

"Using controllers to beat each other in a battle doesn't allow a person to eat wings and keep everything clean."

Will kept silent, conceding to Isaac's point. The click of buttons echoed in the room as Will did a counterattack. He shouted in triumph as *K.O.* flashed across the TV screen, then set his controller on the table. Isaac grimaced as the screen tallied their battle and showed Will's wins of each round.

"You never win this much. What gives?" Isaac threw his hands in the air then reached forward to grab a jalapeño popper.

"I've got skills."

"Skills my foot. Something's going on with you."

Will shrugged. So what if he played a little more aggressively than usual? It was just a video game. Not like he walked around Loveland snarling at people.

"I mean, you don't *have* to talk about it, but maybe if you do, I'd be able to get some chips too."

Will paused, chip and salsa dangling in front of him. "Sorry," he mumbled. He pushed the bowl away.

"It's Felicity, isn't it?"

"You're just not going to let it go, are you?" Will turned and glared at Isaac.

"What? That's what friends are for, right?"

"We're not girls."

Isaac nodded. "True." He popped a chip in his mouth then a popper then another chip.

"Fine." Will dragged a hand across his chin. "She's been acting weird since dinner last week."

"How weird?"

"Her texts have all been one-word responses. When I took her on another picnic lunch yesterday, she seemed quieter than usual." He swallowed. "Do you think she thinks I'm too cheap? I mean, we haven't been on any extravagant dates."

"Come on," Isaac said. "She's not Jackie."

"Yeah, but I made this comment." He rubbed the back of his head. "Told her now that I knew she could cook, she could do it for all our dates."

"And you think that's what made her back away?"

"I mean, yeah." *Wasn't it?* "What if she thinks I don't want to spend money on her? Like she's not worth it, even though that's far from the truth."

"Why don't you just tell her you're frugal? If she can't handle that, then move on to someone better."

Will stared blindly at the TV. The problem was he didn't want to start over. He liked Felicity. . .a lot. What he felt for her now made any teenage crush he'd had on her pale in comparison. He didn't want her to be like Jackie. In every other area of life, she stood out as a good woman. But was it all a disguise?

"I don't know, man. I'm not ready to just call it quits."

"Then test her. Take her somewhere fancy—budget allowing— and see what happens. If she orders the most expensive item on the menu without blinking an eye, then you have your answer."

But did Will want to know the truth? "Definitely something to think about."

"Well, while you're thinking, let's start another battle."

Will picked up his controller and selected his characters. "How are things with you?"

"They're great. Clarissa's starting to hint about marriage. Bringing up conversations on how many kids we want, etcetera."

"Just now?" Will pressed start. "You haven't had that talk already?"

"Man, we've only been dating for ten months."

"So, guess I shouldn't admit Felicity and I had that convo last week?"

"Who initiated the conversation?"

"I did." Why did that matter?

"Bruh, that's why she's distant! You can't bring up marriage and family until you've been established as a couple. You know, the exclusivity label women always want to slap on a relationship."

Will winced as Isaac attacked with a thirty-hit combo in the game. "I don't know, Isaac. She didn't seem put off when I told her about wanting four kids."

The screen froze, and Will turned to fuss at Isaac. "What

did you pause it for?" He'd been in the middle of a super move that would've pummeled Isaac's character. Now his charge was interrupted.

"Kind of showing your hand a little fast there, aren't you?"

"Man, I don't play games. I like her, and I want her to know it."

"Humph." Isaac shook his head then faced forward in his recliner. "I'll be praying for you, man. Hopefully, you two are on the same wavelength. I'd hate to see you get hurt again."

"I'm good, but thanks." Despite his bravado, Will worried.

Maybe he should give Isaac's suggestion of testing Felicity a try. It only made sense to make sure he didn't fall for the same trick twice. Jackie had been sweet and nice until she hit that point where all she wanted was for Will to make more money and spend it on her. In fact, when she broke up with him, she straight-up told him, "You can't keep me in a lifestyle worthy of my attention. We're so over."

But thinking about that day didn't carry the usual sting. In fact, his nerves were more attuned to the possibility that Felicity might be who she appeared to be—well, who *he* wanted her to be. He wanted a future with her.

Lord, please let it be so. I don't want to see any other woman. I don't think there's someone better than Felicity. I like who I am when I'm with her. Is it possible she's the one? Could You smooth the way for me?

Chapter Nine

Something was different.

Today had started off pretty normal. Will had texted Felicity to see if she wanted to go out. Since both of their Saturday evenings were open, they'd scheduled a date for then. But even though arranging times to meet one another had become their new norm, the request that she dress her best had made her pause.

What did Will have planned? Surely it was way too early in their relationship to make any kind of declaration. But what other reasons did couples have for a fancy dinner? She and Will had never been anywhere super expensive together. For goodness' sake, their first date had been to the miniature golf course, which had more underage patrons than adults. Was the date to celebrate some obscure anniversary she hadn't thought of?

No, Will didn't seem like the type to celebrate minor milestones.

Felicity ran the flat iron through the last section of her hair. She smiled at her reflection in the mirror. Her hair gained a few inches in length after straightening the curls away. If they were going to a fancy restaurant, Felicity wanted to appear as polished as possible.

Her eyes stood out in the midst of her black eyeliner and mascara. And the emerald green dress she wore complemented her brown skin nicely. She grabbed her matching clutch and made her way to the front of the house. Any moment Will would arrive and, hopefully, Felicity would find out where exactly he was taking her.

The doorbell chimed, and Felicity twisted the knob open. Her heart pattered double time as she took in Will's appearance. He wore a black suit that fit his figure perfectly, emphasizing his broad shoulders and lean waist. And even more devastating was the blue shirt he wore. The color of his eyes popped, reminding her of a sunny Colorado day.

"You look amazing." A wide smile spread across his face.

Felicity returned the sentiment. "I didn't know you could look any better than you usually do."

He gave a low chuckle that sent shivers through her. He leaned forward, cupping her cheek and placing a soft kiss on her lips. She wound her arms around his neck.

Maybe different wouldn't be such a bad thing after all. Maybe he just wanted to solidify them as an exclusive couple.

Will pulled back and placed a kiss on her forehead. "You ready?"

"I am." Felicity locked the front door and followed him to the car.

The dark gray sedan gleamed, and not a speck of dirt could be seen. Apparently Will wasn't the only thing that had been cleaned up. She murmured her thanks as she slipped past the opened car door he held for her. She soaked in every detail to remember for later. The suit, detailed car, and gentlemanly manners were definitely something to share with her closest friends.

When Felicity told them about her upcoming date, Cassie thought Will wanted to make up for the simple dates he'd taken her on thus far. Ronnie thought he wanted to say those special three little words. Kiki thought they were all overthinking, and now that Felicity sat in the car and watched as Will drove, she had a feeling Kiki was right.

It was just a date. Nothing momentous would happen. Just two people who liked each other enjoying each other's company.

Tell him.

More and more often, she heard the whispered words. As if they wanted her to gather the courage to be vulnerable and share. But she couldn't. A fine-dining date wasn't the time to bare her soul. *Was it?* Then again, maybe sharing her history with Will in a public place would soften the blow.

Lord, what do I do? He wants a big family, and I can't give that to him.

Although she wasn't in love with Will yet, if he could accept her—infertility and all—she'd fall right into the emotion. *That's it. Just tell him tonight.*

"You're awfully quiet tonight."

She turned to him. "Sorry. I kind of got lost in my thoughts for a moment." She took a deep breath. "Forgive me?"

"Nothing to forgive. I can understand following a rabbit trail."

She chuckled. "It was definitely one of those." She twisted in her seat to get a better view of his profile. "Are you going to tell me where we're going?"

"You mean you haven't guessed already?"

"Not for lack of trying. But you haven't given me any hints." She poked his arm. "But I do like surprises."

He flashed a grin at her then turned to face forward. "I'll have to remember that."

After a few more turns, Felicity stared out the front windshield and searched for restaurant signs. "Will we be eating steak?" She knew this area.

"It would make sense, considering where we're going."

"I knew it." He was taking her to the best steak house in Loveland. She clasped her hands together. "I've never been there before, but I've heard wonderful things."

"Good. I want you to have a great time."

Felicity placed her hand on his forearm. "I always do when I'm with you, Will."

"Same here." He squeezed her hand.

Will held her hand as he led her through the restaurant, following the hostess to a booth made for two. After handing them their menus, the hostess went back up front and silence descended around Will and Felicity. Her heart drummed in her chest, the words on the menu dancing before her eyes. She could do it now. Blurt out everything.

"Would you like some wine?"

She blinked, and the wine list came into focus. The prices were exorbitant. "I don't really need any." She looked up from the menu and leaned forward. "Plus, it's a little pricey."

Something flashed in his eyes. Some mood she couldn't quite detect.

"It's fine. If you want a glass, get one."

"I'm good. Promise." She smiled, but Will didn't look like he believed her.

The server soon came and took their drink orders, relayed the specials, and left them to spend more time looking over the menu. Felicity's stomach twisted and knotted. The prices for the different cuts of steak were through the roof. Not to mention the additional charge if she wanted to add a side salad or baked potato.

She sighed.

"Is everything okay?" Will asked softly.

She met his gaze. "I really appreciate you taking me to a place like this. . . ." She bit her lip to keep from saying the rest.

"You're not enjoying yourself?"

"Oh, I am." She rushed to assure him. She didn't want Will to think she was ungrateful. He obviously wanted tonight to be special. So maybe she should just smile and enjoy herself without worrying. Save her news for another time and let him set the pace of their date. "This place is lovely, and the company's even better."

He smiled, but his jaw went rigid. What was wrong with him? Was he nervous? Surely he hadn't planned a proposal. No, that was crazy talk. They hadn't even said the three words. She couldn't even think them yet.

"Order whatever you like. I mean it."

She nodded, though the tightening of her stomach didn't loosen. The meal tonight could cover a whole week's worth of groceries. She didn't want to offend him by implying he couldn't afford it, but spending this kind of money on one meal made her uncomfortable. Even so, when the server stopped by with her pen poised over a pad of paper, Felicity squeaked out an order.

That done, she tried to focus on the quiet conversation between her and Will. Things had been strained between them the past week. She hadn't meant to pull back from the relationship, but she couldn't deny she had. Her mind seemed set on protecting her from his inevitable rejection.

No way Will would be happy that she couldn't have biological children. That his dreams of a big family would go up in smoke if he continued to date her.

"Do you guys have a wedding tomorrow?"

Felicity blinked Will's face into focus. "No. Fortunately, we don't do many Sunday weddings. I enjoy being able to go to church and relax the rest of the day."

"I can imagine."

"What about you? Do you ever make an exception and cut hair on Sunday?"

"No. I can't say I have. Not because I wouldn't, but because everyone pretty much understands I'm closed Sunday and Monday, and they work around that."

"Isn't it amazing how, if you take something out of the equation from the get-go, people are much more willing to accept that?" Her stomach dropped to her toes. *Gracious!*

Suddenly everything became clear. Felicity should have told him sooner. Now she'd made things more complicated by making her infertility some huge secret. No, they hadn't labeled their relationship, but for her, there was no one else she was interested in.

"Agreed."

She refocused. Maybe when he walked her back to her door at the end of the evening, she'd get up the nerve. That way if he said goodbye, she could go cry in the privacy of her own home. She just needed to stay present until then. "Do you think you'd get more clients and therefore more money if you were open six or seven days?"

His nostrils flared. "Why do you ask?"

She sat back. Apparently she wasn't the only one with something on her mind. "Oh, I was just making conversation. I'm sorry if that was taboo. It was something we discussed before opening our business, so I thought maybe you thought about it too."

He rubbed the center of his forehead. "I'm sorry. Let's just talk about something else."

"Is everything okay, Will?"

Confusion hammered his frontal lobe. He never should have taken Isaac's advice on "testing" Felicity. Were her comments about work purely for the sake of conversation, or did they hold a deeper meaning?

Not to mention her brow kept furrowing as if something bothered her despite her insistence that she was having the best time. He couldn't recall her mentioning having fun during miniature golf. Then again, that outing had been a complete disaster. But the picnic lunches since then and time at the park—she always thanked him for a good time. Was that different than how she was responding now?

"I think I'm getting a bad headache."

"Oh no." She riffled through her clutch. "And I forgot to bring pain meds. I usually carry at least ibuprofen." She bit her lip. "Should we leave?"

"No." He shook his head. He had to know how this evening would play out. "I'll live. Promise."

"If you're sure."

He couldn't help but be pleased at the concern in her eyes, the soft touch of her hand on his. He squeezed her fingers in gratitude. *You're imagining things, man. Just enjoy the evening.*

But the ball of tension that had been building since they arrived hit him. Maybe Isaac's other suggestion held merit. "I had an interesting conversation with Isaac the other day."

"Oh yeah? What about?" Felicity propped her chin in her hand.

"He said I jumped the gun talking about the future with you. About having a big family and whatnot." He swallowed down a bottle of stress in one imagined gulp. *Please let him be wrong.*

"Why would he say that?"

Was it him, or did her voice sound shakier? Had Isaac been right? Was this the true source of her distancing herself? "He said we haven't had the exclusivity talk yet, so I was premature in talking about the future."

A small grin tugged at Felicity's mouth. "Well, I may have wondered if you were thinking exclusively as well."

Was that it? He reached for her hand, ready to ease her fears. "The moment I asked you out, I ceased thinking about anyone else, Felicity."

"Oh Will."

Her eyes crinkled at the corners as her lips curved into a smile. That was it. The source of her distance. A weight fell off his shoulders. Felicity had simply been wondering about how he felt.

"I hope you know I consider you my girlfriend."

Her cheeks bloomed. "Do people our age say that?"

"I do."

"Then that works for me."

He wished they were alone so he could kiss her. Now that they'd solved the pesky little label problem, everything would be okay. He wanted to fist pump and praise God, but since the restaurant had a quiet atmosphere, he'd have to wait until he was alone to rejoice.

The conversation changed once their entrées arrived. A lightness filled the room. He couldn't believe his one faux pas had been the cause of all the drama. All he'd had to do was let Felicity know she was his girlfriend. He could kick himself for not having the conversation sooner. *Oh well, no harm done.*

Will cut a piece of his steak and looked across the table at Felicity. "What should we do for our next date?"

"How about something low-key?"

"Such as?"

"We could go to the movies."

That wasn't a bad idea. Actually, pretty standard as far as dates went. "What kind of movie?"

"I actually don't know what's out. I just thought it would be a nice change." She smiled and took a sip of her drink. "Plus, it's probably cheaper than here."

What did that mean? "Do you think I can't afford this place?" A few guests turned and glanced his way. He took a deep breath and lowered his voice. "I can afford to pay for your meal, Felicity." He didn't know whether to be offended she didn't think he could or thankful she seemed to care, unlike Jackie.

"Which I appreciate. But I don't expect you to plan something like this every week." She sat up. "Maybe we could even split who pays when we go out. Maybe that's something boyfriends and girlfriends do?"

He rubbed the back of his neck, trying to breathe through the resuming hammers to his skull. Finally, he met her gaze. "I'm kind of old-fashioned. I like paying, *really*."

"All right," she murmured.

Tense silence sat heavily as they finished the rest of their meal. Every piece tasted like dirt in his mouth. How had his feelings of euphoria faded? And why was he so upset?

Felicity wanted to save him money. Shouldn't he be celebrating the fact? Except he couldn't ignore the ding to his pride. Did she think him incapable of providing? If they were to marry one day, would she feel she had to work because quitting and raising a family wasn't an option? Not that she seemed like the type to stay home. She loved baking wedding cakes.

Too bad his brain didn't feel like being rational at the moment.

Dead air surrounded them all the way back to her house. By the time he walked up the sidewalk to her place, his hands were clammy and sticking to his suit pockets.

"Will." Felicity placed a hand on his arm. "I don't know what went wrong, but won't you talk to me?"

He blew out a breath. "Can I ask you a question?"

"Of course."

"Do you think I can't afford to take you somewhere nice?"

"Not at all. Did I give you that impression? Because if I did, I'm sorry. I always enjoy spending time with you, Will. I don't care where we are."

"And completely hypothetical, but if we got married, would you feel like you could stay at home and raise our children if you wanted to? I mean, not that that's what I would expect or anything. I mean, do you think I could provide for you and our kids on my income alone?"

All color drained out of Felicity's face.

His stomach sank like a stone. So, she *did* have a problem

with money. Just not like Jackie. She didn't think he could provide. "Look, maybe we should just step back and evaluate our relationship."

She gasped, and Will had to still himself against the wounded expression on her face. It was best for him to cut his losses now. Before his heart cracked beyond repair.

He took a step back and another, then turned and walked away. *It's better this way.*

But the widening chasm in his chest made him suspicious he was only lying to himself.

Chapter Ten

If her eyelids got any heavier, Felicity would need to tape them open. Kind of reminded her of an episode from one of her favorite cartoons. Unfortunately, there was nothing to laugh about in her life right now. Sleep had eluded her all last night in between time spent crying and ranting at her ceiling.

When she came into work today, she'd avoided Cassie's office and counted her lucky stars that Ronnie decided to cook at her house today. Kiki always seemed to be in another world when working on alterations and had no reason to come into the kitchen. The only person she had to worry about was her assistant.

Good thing Jill wouldn't be coming in for a couple more hours. Which meant Felicity had time to get herself together. Until then, it was just her and strains of Debussy's "Clair de Lune" filling the kitchen.

Felicity rotated the flower nail, squeezing the buttercream frosting onto the square piece of parchment. She continued to twirl the nail and watched as a chrysanthemum slowly took shape. The pink flowers would look gorgeous on the ivory fondant for the Chang wedding.

The couple had met online and had a whirlwind romance. Something that was now no longer in Felicity's future. She sniffed, widening her eyes to keep the tears from falling. There was no crying in wedding cake design. Besides, the Changs were such a fun couple. They deserved a cheerful cake baker.

Felicity removed the parchment from the flower nail and placed it on the cookie sheet. She'd already made ten blossoms and had many more to go before she could stop and freeze them. They would be easier to place once they were hardened and ready to stick to the fondant.

For once though, Felicity felt no joy in baking. She could still picture the look of hurt that had flashed across Will's features when he asked if she could be a stay-at-home mom. In that one moment, she'd realized how horribly wrong she'd been in keeping her infertility from him. But she'd been frozen in shock and couldn't respond fast enough.

And he'd walked away thinking she had a problem with how much he made. Money was the furthest thing from her mind when it came to being with Will Davenport. But it was all moot now. He didn't want to be with her.

"Why, Lord? Why did You bless me with a great man if it wasn't going to work out? There's no one better than Will Davenport."

"I'm glad you think so."

Felicity gasped and stared at the doorway to her kitchen. Olivia stood there, eyeing her warily.

"Olivia, what are you doing here?" Felicity glanced at the kitchen clock. "We didn't have an appointment, did we?"

"I came to talk to you about my brother."

Felicity bit her lip. "All right. Give me a few minutes, and I'll meet you in my office."

Olivia nodded then closed the door behind her. Felicity rushed to the sink and washed her hands then took off her white coat and put on a long-sleeve sweater over her tank top. Leaning closer to the mirror over the sink, she used a towel to wipe her face and winced at the red eyes and bags hanging underneath her lower lids.

When Felicity walked into her office, Olivia stopped midpace. "Oh wow, you look as bad as he does."

Did that mean Will regretted breaking up with her? "You've seen him?"

"I stopped by the barbershop earlier. Had to ask him a question about the bachelor party." Olivia shook her head. "That doesn't matter. What happened? Will said some craziness about you two breaking up?"

Felicity could feel her lower lip quivering. She inhaled, trying to steady herself as she sat down behind her desk. "If that's what stepping back means."

Olivia watched her. "Did you not want to break up?"

"No!" Felicity squeezed her eyes shut and took a deep breath to calm herself. "I'm sorry. No." She opened them once more. "Nothing could be further from the truth."

"Then what happened? You two are perfect for each other." Olivia held up a hand. "Wait. Never mind. I don't need to know."

"Thank you for that." Because if she had to tell anyone what went wrong, Will deserved to be the first to know.

"All I need to know is if you care about my brother."

"Very much," Felicity whispered.

"Then good. You two fix whatever this is." Olivia waggled her finger back and forth. "And before my wedding. I can't have you both moping around on the happiest day on earth."

Felicity chuckled then stopped as she thought about Will. "He didn't seem too keen on talking to me again."

"He will be. I'll make sure of that." Olivia paused, hand on the doorknob. "Are you good, Felicity? Do you need to talk?"

"Thank you so much." Felicity stood and neared Olivia. "But I really should talk to Will first."

Olivia nodded. "Maybe when everything is smoothed over, we could get together again? I'd like to get to know you better."

Felicity smiled. She'd like that too, but right now she had no idea of knowing how Will would take her revelation. "We'll see."

"Take care." Olivia left the room, and Felicity sank into the nearest guest chair.

She didn't even know what to pray for right now. If she hadn't let fear of being single overrule the need to be vulnerable, she wouldn't be in this situation. Either Will would have accepted her news and continued asking her out or they would have stopped seeing each other before either one of them got hurt. Now she had to wheedle through this heartache.

Felicity reached for her cell and sent a message to Will.

CAN WE TALK?

She waited for the three dots to appear. A minute passed. Three. Five. She sniffed back tears and set the phone down. She would try again later, after she finished making the buttercream chrysanthemums for the Chang wedding.

⌒

Will threw the golf ball in the air, caught it, and threw it back up again. When he'd paid for the broken window at the miniature golf place, he'd asked the guy if he could keep Felicity's ball. He hadn't had any plans for it other than to remember an awful first date that he hoped would turn into a lasting relationship.

Who knew she'd break more than a window?

The door to his office crashed open, and Olivia strode through. She stopped in front of his desk, hands on her hips.

"What in the world, Livie?"

"Go fix it."

"Fix what?" He gaped at her like she was a madwoman. Had she finally succumbed to the bridezilla bug?

"Whatever it is you broke with Felicity."

"Olivia," he groaned. "Please, stay out of my business."

She snorted. "I haven't yet, so why start now?"

Wasn't that the truth. He rubbed the back of his neck, searching for the words to tell her so she'd leave well enough alone.

"I just saw Felicity."

"You did what?" He shot to his feet. "You had no right."

"Oh calm down. I didn't spill your secrets or tell her you were crying in your soup."

"I'm not eating," he grunted through clenched teeth.

"I'm making a point. You're walking around here like a ghost even though you obviously regret breaking up with her. And that poor girl. . ." She shook her head.

Will studied Olivia. "Was she. . .upset?"

Olivia rolled her eyes. "What do you think? A guy breaks up with a girl for no good reason? Oh no, she was jumping for joy." She threw up her hands.

"I had a good reason."

"Do tell." She folded her arms, tapping her shoe against the tile.

Isaac stepped behind her. "Uh, boss, things are getting kind of loud in here."

"Could you close the door behind you?"

"Sure thing." Isaac shut the door and leaned against it.

"I meant for you to close it behind you when you *left*."

"Oh no, this info is too good to pass up."

Will wanted to growl. "Look, let's just say she failed the test, so I thought it would be best if we parted ways."

"What test?"

"You did it?"

The questions came simultaneously. Olivia's brow furrowed, and Isaac's jaw had dropped. Will sank into his chair. Obviously neither one of them would be leaving his office anytime soon.

"What test, Will?" Olivia repeated.

"Your big brother was worried that Felicity would turn out to be like Jackie." Isaac supplied.

Olivia snorted. "Puh-lease. They couldn't be any more different."

"That's what I thought," Will said.

"So, she really did fail?" Isaac asked.

"Can someone tell me what the test was?" Olivia groused.

Normally his sister's melodrama could be ignored, but each cry scraped his already raw nerves.

"Isaac told me to take Felicity to a fancy restaurant to see if she would act like Jackie."

"Of all the reasons to take a girl to a nice place." Olivia flopped into the chair in front of his desk. "Continue."

"If she ordered the most expensive item or made it seem like she wished I made more money, then I had a reason to worry."

"And she acted like Jackie?" Olivia asked, hesitation and a look of disappointment slowly creeping into her features.

"Not exactly."

"But you said she failed?" Isaac asked.

"She did, but in a way I wasn't prepared for. She seems to think I *can't* provide."

"Marriage talk again, Will?"

"Wait, you two were already talking about marriage?" Olivia's head swung between him and Isaac.

Will took a deep breath and relayed the whole evening's events. When he finished, he threw the golf ball back and forth between his hands, waiting for someone to say something.

Olivia placed her hands on the edge of the desk, leaned forward, and spoke. "You might be the stupidest brother ever. Go fix it!" Her voice ended on a yell as she pointed toward the door.

Will turned to Isaac. "You get it, right?"

"Bro, unfortunately, I'm going to have to side with Liv here. She didn't act anything like Jackie."

"But she doesn't think I make enough money."

"That's not the impression I got. Besides, you ever think maybe something else is bothering her?"

"Like what?"

"Isaac's right. Something is going on with her. She told me she had to talk to you. She was worried you wouldn't listen, hence my demanding you go fix it."

"But. . ." Will racked his brain for every memory of their interactions. For some clue that he was wrong, and money wasn't the issue.

He drew in a breath. There it was. His lightbulb moment.

Felicity had gone pale every time he talked about having a family. Did she not want a lot of kids and had been too afraid to tell him because he kept going on and on about it?

"I'm an idiot."

"Finally!" Olivia pumped a fist in the air. "Now will you go talk to her?"

"I will. After I figure out a way to apologize."

"Flowers," Isaac and Olivia said in unison.

Will laughed. "We'll see. Could you two leave so I can do some thinking?"

"Make it quick, brother. I expect her to be your plus-one at my wedding."

"She's your baker. She'll be at the wedding."

"And hopefully not out of obligation but because *someone* will—"

"Yeah, yeah, fix it."

Olivia beamed and waved goodbye.

Isaac raised his eyebrows "Good luck, man."

"Thanks."

Isaac closed the door, this time behind him, and Will sat in silence.

Lord, I messed up big-time. I was so focused on my insecurities and finances that I didn't stop to be present and hear what she didn't say. Please bless me with her forgiveness and whatever the issue is, open my ears to hear. And if You know a way I can apologize, that would be great.

He pulled up an internet browser and typed in "ways to say you're sorry."

Chapter Eleven

Felicity parked her car.

Her day had been long and exhausting. The girls had wanted to know if she was okay, but Felicity had asked for time to process instead of baring her soul. They'd respected her wishes, but she was no closer to knowing where to go from here. Will had never responded to her text the other day, asking to talk.

She climbed out of the sedan and trudged up the stairway toward her apartment.

Someone cleared their throat.

Her head flew up, and a startled cry left her lips. "Will," she exclaimed, pressing a hand to her heart. What was he doing here? Was this a good thing?

"Hi." He rose to his feet, a bakery box in his hand. "Sorry for scaring you."

"No, I'm fine." She cleared her throat. "Uh, do you want to come in?"

"Please."

"All right."

He stepped aside so she could unlock the door. Tension hummed along her skin as she tried to steady her hand to stick the key into the lock. Obviously, Olivia had done her part in getting

Will to talk to her, but what would he say once she came clean?

She twisted the knob, flicked the switch, and set her items on the table near the door. "Um, does that need to go in the fridge?" She pointed to the box, curiosity pricking at her.

"Actually, how about we just sit at your table?"

Felicity nodded and led the way. She sat and watched as Will set down the box. He cleared his throat, rubbed the back of his neck. . .and remained standing.

"Will, you can have a seat."

"No, uh, I think I should do this standing up."

"Okay."

He gulped. "Please hear me out."

She nodded. What could he possibly have to say? Olivia didn't know what Felicity intended to tell him. And there was no way he'd figured out the truth. Right? Her heart thudded with uncertainty.

"I dated a woman once who was overly concerned about how much money I *didn't* make," he began. "It's been a sore subject ever since, and I'm afraid I let that insecurity cloud my judgment and prevent me from listening to you."

Felicity's pulse raced.

"When I took you to the steak house, it was a test." He gulped. "I wanted to make sure you were happy with how things were between us. That you didn't think I was cheap or wished I made more money to spend on you. And instead of hearing you say exactly that, I overcorrected. You were offering to be a partner, and all I could focus on was the thought you believed I couldn't provide."

"Will—"

"I know that's not what you said. . .now. I admit I got tunnel vision and kind of tuned out. But when I took a step back to think. . ." He grimaced. "More like, Livie slapped me upside the head—"

Felicity gaped. "She didn't."

"I meant verbally."

"Hmm." She shrugged her shoulders.

Will continued his earlier thought. "It dawned on me that your problem might be regarding children and not finances."

Now it was her turn to swallow, but her mouth held no moisture whatsoever.

"But before I ask you to talk to me and I take the opportunity to actually listen, I wanted to apologize." He opened the bakery box, and Felicity peered inside.

A bunch of cupcakes had been decorated to resemble flowers in a bouquet.

"Wow."

"I know I'm not a baker, but I thought the apology should be fitting. I watched hours of some famous YouTube baker doing online tutorials."

"Jessica Baker?"

"Yes!" Will snapped his fingers. "Yes. Her videos were so easy to follow, and I thought it was cool that her last name really *is* Baker. Anyway"—he waved a hand in the air—"I watched her tutorial for making the perfect cupcake and for decorating them like flowers."

"What flavor did you make?" Her fingers itched to grab one and taste.

"Strawberry. Go ahead. Try one."

Felicity pulled a cupcake out of the box and peeled back the liner. She took a bite and closed her eyes. The strawberry cake married perfectly with the cream cheese frosting. She opened her eyes and found Will watching her with expectancy.

"You made the frosting from scratch?"

"I did. Used food coloring too, like she showed in one of her videos."

"This tastes amazing," she said, taking another bite.

Will's shoulders relaxed, and he finally sat down. "I tasted one and thought it was pretty good, but I knew the real test would be when you tried one."

"You did great." She looked at him. "And I'm sorry too. I withheld some information." She swallowed. "Lied by omission really. And I can't ask for your forgiveness enough. I should have told you what was bothering me."

"I'd like to listen, if you want to tell me now."

She drew in a breath, praying that God would give her the words. "You've mentioned multiple times that you would like a big family one day. Well. . ." She bit her lip. *Just say it. Blurt the news like you're ripping off a bandage.*

Will reached for her hand and gave her fingers a light squeeze.

"I can't get pregnant." Her heart thudded as she stared at their hands, too afraid to look into his eyes. "When I was seventeen, I had this awful pain. The doctors assumed I needed my appendix removed, but after the imaging results came back, it was clear that wasn't the source of the trouble. They ended up removing my ovaries and the tumors attached to them."

"I'm so sorry."

At the sound of sorrow in Will's voice, Felicity peeked at him from beneath her lashes. He didn't look disgusted. She straightened her shoulders. "I should have told you sooner, but I just didn't want to risk a breakup before we even decided if we would work. That was wrong of me. I should have told you up front and let you have all the facts to make an informed decision."

"I accept your apology."

Relief warred with uncertainty. Knowing what he did now, would he accept her? She wanted desperately to ask, but fear muted her. Telling him after knowing how much she cared about him, well, it was huge. To be even more vulnerable and ask how he felt about her now seemed too much to ask. But she needed to know.

"Does that change things between us?" She bit her lip and waited for his reply.

⌒

Did it?

Will had always imagined a big family, not because he thought he should populate the earth with a dozen kids, but because his childhood had been so great that, in his mind, having more kids would only increase the joy. The more he thought about it though, the more he realized it had been his parents who'd made life great. The love they had for one another. The love they showered on him and Livie.

If his parents had never married, that would have been a shame. If Felicity couldn't have kids, that didn't mean their life couldn't be full of happiness. And it didn't mean a childless house was their future either.

"The only thing it changes is that there aren't any more secrets between us."

"But your dream. . ."

"Has always been an extension of a love I imagined between me and my wife. That it would spill over into how many kids we have." He rubbed his chin. "And I have to admit, saying that aloud makes me feel very shortsighted. The amount of kids you have isn't a direct correlation to how much you love a person."

"So if, hypothetically speaking, we were to marry, you would be okay with not having biological children?"

"Yes."

Felicity looked down at their clasped hands as if weighing his response.

"Look, Felicity, I don't know the future. I have no idea what's going to happen tomorrow. But my hasty reaction last night taught me this—I don't want to face life without you. If you're willing to be my girlfriend, then I know we'll be able to face whatever comes our way."

"Really, Will?" She studied him.

"Really."

Her lips slowly curved upward, and then she laughed with delight.

He tugged on her hand and stood to his feet, sweeping her into his arms. "There's just one more thing I have to ask."

She pulled back and peered up at him. "What's that?"

"Will you be my plus-one to Livie's wedding?"

"I'd love to."

"Good. Livie would have been outraged if you said no."

"She does know I'll be making the cake, so I have to be there anyway, right?"

"I tried to tell her. Will you walk me out?"

She nodded, and he slid his hand in hers, thankful that they were back on track. He could have seriously messed up the best thing to happen to him in a very long time.

"Hey, I know you probably have to ride with the girls to the wedding, but can I take you home?"

"Definitely."

Will pressed a kiss to her cheek. "Then I'll see you later?"

"You'd better."

He pressed his lips softly to hers then whispered a goodbye.

As he drove home, he thought about what to tell Olivia. Then thought better of it. When he arrived at his place, he simply texted: My plus-one will be there.

Good job. I'd hate to have to stop talking to my favorite brother.

I'm your only brother.

Hence the reason it would be a pain.

Will chuckled. He would enjoy celebrating his sister's marriage. And dancing with his plus-one.

⁓

Two days later, Will strode purposefully toward the table that held the wedding cake. He couldn't believe how talented Felicity was. She'd gone from using software to sketch some ideas with Olivia to this masterpiece displayed for the guests to admire.

He caught her eye as she set dessert plates near the cake.

"Hey there." She smiled, walking his way.

"Hey, beautiful. I was wondering if you'd be able to take a break for a dance."

"Definitely. Just let me tell Jill."

He watched as Felicity informed her assistant of their plans.

Jill glanced at him then whispered something to Felicity, who blushed.

What was that about?

As soon as Will led Felicity onto the dance floor, he drew her close and asked her what Jill had said.

"Oh, she understood why I wanted to take a break."

He laughed. "Guess that's not too terrible."

"No, it's definitely not." She squeezed his waist as they twirled around the floor. "Olivia is a beautiful bride."

He stared over at his sister and his new brother-in-law. "She really is. We even got a great brother-sister photo."

"Aww. She told me we were going to be good friends."

"I'm glad. She was very insistent that I fix us."

"I think you guys have a great relationship. She's your champion."

"You think?"

"Mm-hmm."

Will rested his chin on top of Felicity's head. "How about we stop talking about my sister and just enjoy this moment?"

"You have the best ideas, Will Davenport."

As he tightened his hold around Felicity, he thought she might just be right.

Epilogue

One year later, June

Felicity couldn't keep from bouncing with glee. Finally, finally she was going to marry the man of her dreams. Oh sure, the very first time she'd laid eyes on Will Davenport she hadn't known he'd be that man. She'd only prayed for the attributes she desired in a husband. And hoped and prayed and hoped some more that she would meet a man who would fulfill her dreams and enrich her life.

And it was true what the Bible said. God was able to do exceedingly, abundantly, above all that one could ask or think. Will was more than the man of her dreams. He was a gift from God. A blessing she didn't deserve, but one she would give thanks for each day they had together.

"You look beautiful, Felicity," Heather said, dabbing her eyes with a handkerchief.

Felicity squeezed her stepmother's hand. Throughout Heather's pregnancy, the two had grown closer and bridged the awkward gap that had plagued their relationship for so long. When she'd asked Heather to help her dress today, her stepmother had been honored and overcome with joy.

"Will won't know what hit him," Cassie chimed from her spot by the window.

Felicity smiled at Cassie from the full-length mirror. "Thank you." She took in her wedding dress one more time before she prepared to walk down the aisle.

Her chiffon ivory dress with a sweetheart neckline, a picture of pure perfection. She couldn't believe how much like a bride she truly felt. Her pearl drop earrings went with the pearl bracelet Heather had loaned her as her something borrowed. She inhaled the perfume from the lilac-colored peonies.

"I'm ready."

Kiki laughed. "You have to wait for your dad to come."

"Oh yeah." Felicity could feel her face scrunch up in amusement. How could she forget she was waiting on him?

A knock sounded on the door.

"Let's hope that's him." Ronnie twisted the knob and peeked around the door. "It is."

Felicity exhaled in relief. Not that she was nervous. More like happy her father had finally walked into the room. That meant she could now float down the aisle to become Mrs. Will Davenport. She wanted to squeal but sent up a prayer of thanksgiving instead.

"I can't believe you're getting married," her dad said. He sniffed.

"Please, you love Will." She squeezed his arm. "And it's not like I'm moving to another city or state. You'll still see me for weekly dinners or when you need me to babysit." She adored her new baby brother.

"That's true. It's only because I know he'll take such good care of you that I can give you away."

Tears blurred her vision. "Don't make me cry, Dad. I'm saving that for when I see Will."

He laughed. "Let's go, baby girl."

They headed out of the room and to the spot to await her cue to walk down the aisle. The music changed to announce her arrival, and Felicity's eyes locked onto Will. She wanted to wait for him to see her before she strolled forward. Elliot nudged him, and Will looked up. His lips curved into a full smile, and he mouthed, "Beautiful."

A blush warmed her cheeks. She had to remind herself to keep the sedate pace of Wagner's "Bridal Chorus" instead of quickening her strides to get to Will faster.

Finally, finally, her dad let go of her and she slid her hand into Will's. "Hi," she whispered.

"You look gorgeous," Will murmured.

"Not as good as you."

"I doubt it."

"Shhh," the preacher whispered.

Felicity stifled a laugh as the preacher greeted the guests. Her gaze stayed fastened on Will's, soaking in all the love and affection that made his eyes appear a deep blue.

She didn't hear every single word the preacher intoned, but she focused in for the important ones. The ones she vowed before her God, her almost-husband, and the friends and families acting as witnesses to their love and devotion. Her heart melted when Will recited his vows, his voice strong and confident. The warmth in his touch as he slid her ring on her finger made her want to swoon and reach the "kiss the bride" portion of the agenda.

When the pastor proclaimed them husband and wife, Will's lips were on hers. Felicity wrapped her arms around his neck and cupped the back of his head.

Her relationship with Will wasn't without its ups and downs. But through it all, Will had shown her she was enough. Whether they chose to add kids to their lives wouldn't make or break their relationship.

He was hers. She was his. Life was good.

Toni Shiloh is a wife, mom, and Christian fiction writer. Once she understood the powerful saving grace thanks to the love of Christ, she was moved to honor her Savior. She writes to bring Him glory and to learn more about His goodness. Her Maple Run series published by Celebrate Lit Publishing (2016–19), has been immensely popular. She is thankful these books have been well received and have had staying power. In fact, she can't believe her titles are still in the Top 500 in African American Christian Fiction all these years later! Her newest series recently sold to Harlequin Loveswept and will be available in 2021.

Hemmed In

by RL Ashly

Dedication

To everyone who stitches a family together

Acknowledgments

Agent extraordinaire: Terrie Wolf, AKA Literary Management.
Barbour Publishing editors: Rebecca Germany
and Ellen Tarver for their expertise and encouragement.
Critique editors: Donna, Nancy, Dianne, Shawna, Michelle,
Linda, and Dan. Thanks for your insights for the manuscript.

You hem me in behind and before, and you lay your hand upon me.
PSALM 139:5 NIV

Chapter One

Kiki Bell unlocked the front door to Weddings by Design and froze. Where was the furniture? The gowns? Her sewing machines? She lugged three wedding gown garment bags across the main room then peeked into her coworkers' offices. Precisely as they'd left them on Friday. It must be some joke on her. She veered toward the kitchen. Were Felicity's baking supplies safe?

And Ronnie's high-end knives? Everything looked fine.

Had the business been burglarized over the weekend?

If so, the thieves took everything she owned. Not a stray thread or dust bunny remained on the floor of her workspace in the main room.

Kiki stepped into Cassie's office and draped the bags over the office chair. A door shut at the rear of the house. Goose bumps rolled down her arms faster than a flying bobbin. Maybe the robbers were hauling her stuff out the back door while she stood pinned like a pattern to the carpet. She grabbed Cassie's desk lamp. If she got close enough to throw it, she'd light up their lives. No one was going to get away with her sewing machines without a fight. Ever. *Never mess with a seamstress.* Shuffling quietly out of the office, she reached the door to the kitchen.

A woman dressed in a black pantsuit jumped out from behind

the cupboards. "Boo!"

Kiki screamed and hurled the lamp.

The stranger dodged to the left as it flew into the trash can with a thump. "Scared you."

Kiki stepped backward to the center of the room, inching toward the front door. "Who are you?"

"Tsk, tsk, tsk. I sure have my work cut out with you. No wonder you're not married." The intruder who looked to be in her midthirties stepped out of the kitchen and peered at her. "Wisps of gray hair and a couple of zits. You're plainer than the plainest Jane I've ever beheld."

Kiki's mouth dropped open. Of all the nerve. Her ability to turn men's heads was below zero on a scale of one to ten, but this person didn't need to state the obvious.

"That dress." The stranger shook her head. "And you call yourself a seamstress."

Kiki glanced at her blue sleeveless frock. Clean, crisp, modest, and comfortable. While she'd never grace the cover of a fashion magazine, she did try to look presentable and professional.

"Your teeth look like a picket fence." The woman stepped closer. "Braces are in order for you, my dear."

Kiki reached into her pocket for her cell phone. Gone. Patting her other pockets, she moved to the front door then grabbed the handle and wrenched it open. Braces. Every middle-aged woman's dream. "I don't know who you are or how you got into the shop, but you can explain that to the police." She bolted down the sidewalk to her vehicle. Where was her phone?

The woman followed. "Kiki, dear. I'm the new office manager."

"I have no idea who you are or how you got into my building."

Kiki unlocked her car. "There is no new office manager."

"It's obvious Weddings by Design needs a manager. The partnership's failure to communicate could leave your clientele with the impression you aren't professionals."

Kiki grabbed her cell phone from the front seat, where it must have slipped from her pocket. She and her best friends worked hard at keeping every branch of the business informed. This nosy woman could explain it all to the cops.

A silver Grand Caravan pulled into the space behind Kiki's car. Cassie Blackthorn slid out and walked to the sidewalk. "Oh, I see you two have met."

Kiki exhaled. She shoved her phone into her pocket. She'd give Cassie a chance to explain before she dialed 911.

"That's right. Kiki has seen part of the new order I've established in the office to create a pleasant experience for our clients. Come check out what I've done." The stranger walked back into the shop.

Kiki exhaled and whispered to Cassie, "Who is she and what has she done with my stuff?"

Cassie's eyes widened. "I sent out a text to all the partners about hiring my cousin, Camilla Parsons, as office manager, and you responded with 'Perfect.' Here, look." She swiped her phone a couple of times and held it up for Kiki.

Kiki read it, then opened her texts and showed them to Cassie. "I sent you a text about my purchase order for sequins and silk fabric, but I didn't get one about hiring someone."

"I'm sorry. I'm not the best at tech stuff."

Kiki gazed at her phone with its taped-on screen protector. "Come to think of it, when I sent the message about the purchase order, my phone shook and buzzed. Then your message came in saying, 'Thanks so much.' It was weird."

"I'm so sorry." Cassie placed her hands on her cheeks. "Camilla needed a job, and I couldn't tell her no."

"I apologize too." Kiki draped an arm around Cassie's shoulders. "It wasn't your fault. Seems my phone went on vacation without me. We'll figure it out as we go."

Cassie sighed. "While technology has its perks, I prefer paper and pencil."

Anyone acquainted with Cassie knew she had a heart of gold and would never intentionally hurt anyone.

But where was Kiki's sewing stuff? Was she supposed to create beautiful gowns out of thin air?

Once inside, Camilla hustled them through the back door and into the detached garage. "Ta-da! Your new sewing space."

Kiki glanced around the area. Her sewing machines rested in a corner, surrounded by boxes. The shelves on the walls housed business records labeled by year, while her worktables, ironing board, and other sewing tools lay strewn on the cement slab. The place looked like the aftermath of a sibling rivalry war on steroids.

She drew in a deep breath. Somebody had plopped her wedding dress projects in a heap resembling a Bronco-Patriots pileup on the two-yard line. Thankfully Camilla had spread a bedsheet on the center of the dusty floor first. Tossed over an exercise bike was the ball gown she needed to hem for one of tomorrow's appointments. Warmth flooded her face. Sweat drops formed on the back of her neck. "Cassie, this isn't—"

Camilla grabbed Cassie's arm and pulled her out of the garage. "Cassie dear, you have several urgent phone calls you need to return. Your brides are waiting."

Camilla popped her head back through the doorway. "One word of complaint, and I'll have you removed from Weddings by Design faster than a groom kisses his bride after the official pronouncement," she hissed through her teeth. "I have the power to fire you. I'm blood. Family. You're not." She jerked the door handle. "I heard you're responsible for two children. Single moms can't afford to lose their jobs, now can they?" She slammed the door behind her.

Kiki sat on a box. The woman's words cut like electric scissors on Chantilly lace. What was she to do? Ousted from her lovely sewing space in the shop to a dusty garage by one of her best friend's relatives. Who was this woman to think she could act unprofessional and threaten a partner in the business? She'd just have to catch her colleagues alone and discuss the situation.

It was nothing more than a simple misunderstanding.

Her phone buzzed.

A text from her nephew. FIRE.

Her breath caught in her throat.

CALLED FIRE DEPARTMENT. WE'RE SAFE.

She exhaled. Her fingers shook and she made several typos before succeeding in sending a text stating she was on her way.

Racing to her car, she hopped in and pulled into traffic. This was turning into her worst Monday in recent history. What had happened? She checked her side-view mirror then changed lanes. Did the kids knock something flammable over and accidentally ignite the piles of her aunt's belongings in the house?

Over the years, Kiki tried to convince her late aunt and uncle to declutter the house and outbuildings. They'd refused. Instead, they left the farm and a colossal hoarding mess as her inheritance. With soaring rent prices and two teenagers, she couldn't afford her apartment, so she'd moved her family into the old farmhouse over the past weekend.

Her knuckles stiffened as she clutched the steering wheel. At least the kids were safe. Was her new home burning to the ground? Glancing at the dashboard clock, she noted the time crawling like an endless messy seam. Why did she have to hit every red light in Loveland? Finally free from the last traffic signal, she raced down the country roads, accelerating as fast as she dared, not slowing until she turned into the driveway of the farm.

The tired white farmhouse stood sentry over the dilapidated barn, faded outbuildings, and exhausted corrals. Two fire trucks sat in front of an outbuilding, billowing clouds of smoke emitting from broken-out windows and a hole in the roof that wasn't there when she'd left this morning. Kiki blew a sigh of relief. The house and the barn were safe, along with her plan for their future use.

She parked the car and searched for the kids, locating them behind the house, watching the fire.

Kiki engulfed her niece and nephew into a family bear hug. "Glad you're okay. What happened?"

"We don't know." Fifteen-year-old Tressa freed herself and pointed to the fire. "We heard a loud bang. When we came out to see what it was, we saw the smoke."

Her younger brother, Jack, his face smudged with dirt and soot, nodded. "I tried putting it out with the garden hose, but it didn't help. So we called the experts."

Kiki hugged him again. "Smart move."

The fire crew put out the flames on the building she'd designated a she-shed for her veil making, and a larger nearby structure once used as a cattle loafing shed. She and the teens sat on the back stoop until the smoke diminished. Kiki brushed the hair out of her eyes. What a day. How was she to recover financially from a fire and build her vision for the farm? On top of that, she had to figure out how to deal with a problematic office manager. Tressa and Jack depended on her.

The beeping of a truck backing down the driveway forced her thoughts away from the fire scene. The trash company arrived to deposit the roll-off she'd ordered. That dumpster represented freedom. Freedom to relocate the insides of the house first, then the outbuildings. Freedom to begin some much-needed updating to the place. Freedom to design her dream.

She motioned the driver to place it close to the house and then rejoined her family.

A handful of firefighters huddled together at the front of a fire truck, surveying the smoldering mess and packing up equipment.

One of the men, clad in bunker pants with his jacket unzipped and his dark hair matted to his head, left the group and walked toward her, a sheet of paper gripped in one hand. "Ma'am, are you the owner of this property?"

Kiki stood and took a few steps forward. "Yes."

"We think rodents and faulty electrical wiring played a hand in the fire." Sweat dripped from his face. "Good thing the kids were here and spotted the smoke so quickly."

"Thanks for your help. I appreciate it."

He fidgeted with the form. "Is everyone okay?"

Kiki smiled. "The most important things are safe." She pointed to Tressa and Jack. "Those two."

He nodded, closed his eyes, and drew in a deep breath.

Kiki frowned. Had she said something wrong? Maybe the

smoke irritated his eyes. Eyes the color of dark chocolate.

Focus. Now was not the time to be thinking about eye candy.

His eyes flashed open and locked on hers. "M–ma'am," he stuttered. "Here's a written notice of violation requiring you to clean up the old chemicals in the outbuildings within thirty days. From a safety standpoint, if that's not done, you could have another fire on your hands."

He gave her the paper.

She stared at the black marks on the page, her blurred vision preventing her from reading the words. Just what she needed. Another project. Another deadline. "Look, I recently inherited this farm from my late aunt. I need time to bring it up to scratch. Last night was our first night here."

He bowed his head. "Understood. The fire department is only thinking of your safety. I—somebody will come by in a month and make sure you've cleaned up the place. Have a good day." He turned to walk away, paused, and stopped. He looked at Kiki. "I hope you won't be offended by what I'm about to say."

What could this man possibly say that would offend her? She'd already been called ugly, unnecessary, and negligent this morning.

And it wasn't even nine o'clock.

She waited.

"You are the most beautiful woman I have ever seen."

She sucked in a breath.

Wow. That was definitely unexpected.

And definitely untrue.

"Good pickup line," Kiki snapped. Maybe he said that to try and make her fix-it ticket seem less of a blow. "I bet you've said that thousands of times."

He wiped the sweat from his forehead. "I've only said it once."

Kiki gulped. When it came to men, she was usually invisible. They didn't notice her. Like ever.

Why would he say that to a stranger?

What was his angle?

Before she had a chance to respond, he walked back to the fire trucks and disappeared behind them.

Tressa laughed. "Maybe we should start calling you Beautiful instead of Auntie."

Kiki pointed to the back door. "Stop teasing and go do the dishes."

Tressa slipped away, leaving a trail of giggles echoing in the air.

Jack hung back. "He's right, you know. If you hadn't adopted us when our parents were killed in the car crash, we'd be in foster care." He gripped her hand. "That makes you beautiful to us."

The car crash seven years earlier that took the life of her sister and brother-in-law, Callie and Jeremiah Torres. A day that left a deep void in their hearts and two empty chairs at holiday dinners.

Tears welled in Kiki's eyes. She was having a terrible morning, but the kids made her life richer. "For a fourteen-year-old, you're pretty wise."

⁓

Bing Kelley bent over the hose. Why had he told the woman in blue she was beautiful? Hopefully, she wouldn't notify his boss and file a complaint against him. He'd never had a professional reprimand, and he didn't want one now. Yet somehow the words slipped out.

Probably because they were true.

He folded the bundle hose in accordion-style four-foot lengths. He didn't want his coworkers to know. In his forties, with two broken engagements, the last thing on his mind was courting a woman. His career and his music kept him busy enough. He positioned both coupling ends of the hose on top of the folded bundle then grabbed the straps to stabilize the hose.

His friend, Henry Vega, bent down to help him buckle the hose together. "Hey, Bing. I'm having a cookout on Sunday if you want to come over. I invited most of the station."

"I'd love to, but I have a gig and then a family dinner." Bing hoisted the bundle hose on his shoulder. "Thanks. Maybe next time."

"Sure thing." Henry clapped Bing's back. "I'm holding you to that."

Bing nodded and put the hose away in its compartment then turned to repeat the process for the next one.

Once the equipment was packed, the firefighters hopped into the trucks. Bing chose a backward-facing seat. He wanted to be alone with his thoughts. The trucks pulled away from the scene and down the driveway. Bing looked to see if the beautiful woman remained on the back steps.

She was gone.

When they rounded the front of the house, he gazed at the windows. There she stood, a lovely vision in blue. He exhaled. She was certainly out of his league. Besides, he was a busy guy. A song for his gig this weekend needed more work, and he'd picked up an extra shift at the station.

Work was a balm for the heart and music food for the soul. But women were beautiful, complicated. He needed to throw a flame retardant on his thoughts and focus on the pleasant life he'd created for himself.

No sense in dwelling on the impossible.

They would never see each other again.

Chapter Two

In the church auditorium, Kiki sat in her favorite place, the back row. It was fun to people watch before the service. And she enjoyed the option of resting her head against the wall as she contemplated the sermon. Jack and Tressa joined her after the youth class. The row in front of her filled up with the usual back-of-the-room crowd. The old theater, repurposed as a church, had a sloped floor to the small front stage. She smiled at the memory of Tressa and Jack's first youth group activity, where the teens held relay races down the incline on wheeled office chairs. Someday when she was here alone, she'd have to try that.

Kiki had left Loveland Community Church a couple of years ago for West River Road Chapel when Tressa was old enough for youth group. LCC was a friendly, accepting congregation, but she knew that her Latino brother-in-law would have wanted his kids to go where the pastor looked like them.

Pastor Otero walked onto the stage and began the service. "Good morning. Our regular song leader is ill, and his brother has agreed to substitute today. Please welcome Brother Bing Kelley."

A tall man with dark hair entered the stage from behind the curtain and approached the podium. Dressed in business casual attire and carrying a guitar, he introduced the first song as he smiled and gazed around the room.

No. It couldn't be. Kiki bent forward and peered at him. It was. He sure cleaned up well. He strummed his guitar. She looked for a place to hide. If she raced out the door, maybe she could escape before he spied her.

Too late.

His pearly whites froze as he focused on her. Or at least she thought he did. Kiki slid down in her seat. How could she avoid this one?

Jack leaned in, "Auntie, is that the firefighter who gave you the fix-it ticket?"

"Yes."

"What are you doing?"

"Hiding." She continued her descent.

Jack covered his mouth with a hand, stifling a laugh. "You're hiding from a man?"

"Keep a lookout," she whispered. "Let me know when it's safe to reappear."

Tressa snorted. "This is going to be epic."

During the song service, while everyone stood, Kiki slumped behind the man in front of her. When the congregants sat for the special music, she bent over and pretended to adjust her shoe.

Accompanying himself on the guitar, Bing sang an original song. His rich baritone voice floated over the room. She sat up faster than a prairie dog standing guard over its underground abode. Wow! He was good. Maybe she'd heard him on the radio.

Still, she couldn't take any chances. Time to adjust her hideout position. Squatting in front of her chair, she pulled out her purse and shuffled through it, looking for a pen. She could not deny his musical ability. By the time he finished, her legs hurt.

Jack glanced at her. "It's safe. He sat down."

"Thanks."

She pulled herself up and slid onto her seat. Stretching her legs, she scoped out the crowd, noting his presence on the center aisle seven rows ahead of her.

While Pastor Otero spoke, she took notes and kept an eye on Bing lest he got up and walk past. If that happened, she'd have to hide again, but he remained in his seat. Kiki relaxed and crossed her legs. She slipped her foot out of her shoe, dangling it on her toes as she rocked her leg back and forth, keeping time with the pastor's cadence.

At the end of the sermon, she swung her leg a little harder than usual. Her heel flew like a helicopter over the rows in front of her, floated for a second suspended in midair, then succumbed to gravity.

Kiki's mouth dropped.

No, it couldn't be happening.

The airborne shoe plopped right into the crooner's lap.

Tressa squealed, and Jack guffawed. She tossed them *the look,* but they were losing it. And fast.

Pastor Otero raised his hands. "Let's stand and pray."

Tressa and Jack raced through the doors and into the foyer. Their howls of laughter reverberated like thunder.

The congregants turned and stared.

Everybody. Including Bing.

Those kids. Kiki limped after them.

"Auntie. . ." Jack sucked in a breath. "I've never. . ."

Tressa held her side and giggled. "Seen a shoe fly like that."

"Shhh. Be respectful. Pastor Otero's praying." Kiki plopped down on a bench and bent over. If she took off her remaining heel, she could sneak back into the auditorium, grab their things, and race out of the building before the service ended.

A shadow in front of her.

She held her breath.

"I think this might be yours."

She couldn't look.

Bing knelt beside her and cupped her foot in his hand. Her face and heel burned like a Colorado sunset. She forced herself to glance at him.

He slipped her shoe on with the ease of an old-school shoe salesman.

Kiki managed a half smile. "My glass slipper has a crack in it."

"This is one church service I'll never forget." He grinned. "Not only my first time leading worship but also my first time playing Prince Charming."

Jack's and Tressa's peals of laughter echoed through the empty foyer.

Jack gave Bing a high five. "Me neither."

Kiki slipped past them, retrieved their belongings from the auditorium, and returned to the foyer where Bing chatted with the teens about school and youth group.

She'd had enough for one day. "We need to go."

Jack grabbed his things from Kiki. "Aww, can't we stay? I wanted to ask a firefighter question."

"Some other time. We have a dinner to attend." She hustled the teens out the front doors then stopped and glanced back. "Thanks for helping me with my shoe."

Bing bowed. "Anytime."

Kiki followed her family to the car. Well, that was that. Their regular worship leader would be back next week, and her church haven would return to normal.

After a quick trip to the grocery store for a pie from the bakery, she drove to her pastor's home. The brick ranch smiled as daisies and sunflowers waved in the wind.

Mrs. Otero answered the door and ushered them into a cozy great room. "Lunch is almost ready."

Kiki spotted a picture of a younger Mrs. Otero in a football uniform. She picked the frame up from the side table. "You played tackle football?"

"Yes. We had a mom's league." Mrs. Otero laughed. "It was a good outlet."

Pastor Otero snorted. "She's tough. In the championship game, her team won."

Mrs. Otero brushed hair out of her face. "We were up by seven when my teammate accidentally broke an opponent's arm. That ended the game. Both ladies became the best of friends."

Kiki smiled. "You look good in football pads."

The doorbell rang.

Pastor Otero opened the front door. "Bing, come in. Hope you're hungry."

Kiki rolled her eyes. Not now. She'd never live down the flying shoe incident.

"I am, Uncle Ben." Bing stepped into the living room.

Mrs. Otero rushed over. "We don't see you enough."

"I know. My bad, Auntie Valerie." Bing wrapped his arms around her in a big bear hug then released her. He spotted Tressa and Jack, then Kiki.

Kiki sucked in a breath. First the man showed up at her church, then she propelled her shoe into his lap, and now she had to face him at lunch. She set the frame back down. This home was one of her favorite places to visit, and now he'd ruined it for her.

Mrs. Otero turned to Kiki. "This is Bing Kelley, our nephew."

Kiki grabbed Bing's hand, squeezing hard. "Nice to meet you."

He coughed, stifling a laugh. "Likewise."

Pastor Otero carried a large soup tureen to the dining table. The teens claimed chairs on one side, forcing Kiki to sit next to Bing. After the blessing, Mrs. Otero filled each bowl with savory potato soup while Pastor passed around the crusty rolls and salad.

"Auntie, this smells so good." Bing filled his glass with lemonade and set the pitcher on the table in front of him.

Kiki placed her hand on Mrs. Otero's. "It does. Thanks for having us over."

Mrs. Otero passed Kiki the salad dressing. "My pleasure. How's the farm cleanup going?"

"Better." Kiki poured dressing on her salad. "The bedrooms are decluttered, and we're painting them. My aunt and uncle saved everything for decades, so it'll take awhile to sort through it."

"You'll get it done."

Pastor picked up his spoon. "How's the progress after the fire?"

Tressa blurted out, "We're going to fix the old barn and turn it into a wedding venue. We don't have any money, but that's not a problem. We're resourceful."

Jack nodded. "Aunt Kiki has a dream, and we're going to make it happen."

Kiki's toes tightened. While those two were her world, they

didn't need to announce her private desires in front of everyone. "That's a long-term goal. It might not happen for a while."

"Well, we'll pray that it does." Mrs. Otero buttered her roll. "Thanks for sharing. Perhaps we can help when you're ready."

"I'll let you know."

Pastor glanced at Bing. "How are things at the fire station?"

"We're gearing up for our July Fourth fundraiser," Bing said.

"How'd you get into firefighting?" Jack wiped his mouth with his napkin. "Do you let teens help out?"

Bing grinned. "Want to help with the petting zoo on the Fourth?"

Jack looked at Kiki, brows raised. "Can I?"

"We'll talk about it." She turned to Bing. "May I have some lemonade?"

"Sure." He reached for the pitcher.

Kiki held her glass in front of her. He was a feast for the eyes.

Eyes locked on Kiki, he poured but didn't notice he missed the glass.

The lemonade gushed toward Kiki faster than the Colorado River rolling over a cliff. Her skirt turned into Lake Lemon. She shrieked and stood, bumping the pitcher out of his hand, juice pouring down her legs.

He bent and tried to catch the container, but it landed with a thud on the floor, backsplash baptizing his face.

Mrs. Otero rushed to Kiki's side. "Come, dear, let's get you cleaned up."

She led the way to the bathroom down the hall, where she pulled a towel, washcloth, and soap from the closet. Her eyes twinkled. "My nephew is a confirmed bachelor-till-the-rapture, and he can't keep his eyes off you."

"I'm sure you're mistaken." Kiki turned on the water. "I don't turn heads."

"You gave him whiplash. His head hasn't turned away from you." Mrs. Otero chuckled as she shut the door behind her. "It's a sight to behold."

There had to be a mistake. Kiki dabbed at her drenched skirt and looked at a piece of framed handiwork hanging beside the mirror. Embroidered on silk was Psalm 139:5–10.

You hem me in behind and before,
and you lay your hand upon me.
Such knowledge is too wonderful for me,
too lofty for me to attain.
Where can I go from your Spirit?
Where can I flee from your presence?
If I go up to the heavens, you are there;
if I make my bed in the depths, you are there.
If I rise on the wings of the dawn,
if I settle on the far side of the sea,
even there your hand will guide me,
your right hand will hold me fast.

Mrs. Otero was good with her needle.

Kiki placed the towel on the sink and turned off the water. *Lord, please guide me and hold me fast, because I'm a fossil and invisible, and I'd like to keep it that way.*

Chapter Three

Kiki parked in the alley, loaded her arms with bolts of fabric, and entered the garage sewing studio. She flipped on the lights, plopped the fabric on a chair by the door, hung her purse on a hook, then glanced around.

Was that someone's art décor or a sculpture on the cutting table? She sucked in a breath and walked around the worktop. She stepped back. Not artwork. A car bumper painted silver chrome. Discarded aerosol paint cans lay strewn on the cardboard covering most of the wedding dress project she needed to cut out and stitch together this afternoon. She lifted the corner of the cardboard. Silver paint created an outline around the pattern pieces. The muscles in her arms quivered. Heat flashed through her body. She'd have to start over. No bride wanted to smell like paint on her big day.

She glanced at the bumper, and her image glared back at her like a distortion mirror from a carnival. Her colleagues' bumpers were happily attached to their respective cars. Or were they? There was only one person Kiki could think of who would be capable of this level of selfishness. She snapped photos of the "bumper on silk" to use as evidence when confronting said person.

Ugh, she'd have to crank out a dress faster than expected. She grabbed the bumper and hauled it out the back door, struggling not to throw it against the garage. Then she pitched the cardboard and cans into the trash outside.

After being banished to the garage via Camilla's business experiment, Kiki had spent several days scrubbing the room and creating a studio. She'd draped yards of colorful, lightweight fabric from the ceiling to hide the cinder block walls and strung holiday lights around the room. Her sewing area took one half of the building. Several chairs and an end table created a waiting area by the back door while a curtained-off corner served as a dressing room. Mirrors flanked the wall outside the changing area. Not as pleasant as the shop, but it would do.

Now everything smelled like paint. She opened the back door and the windows. After she unpinned the pattern pieces, the silk joined the cardboard in the trash. What a waste of all that time, not to mention the cost of fabric. Who would pay for that?

After Kiki scrubbed the table and turned on a fan, the studio smelled better. Classical music filtered across the room as she stitched along to a Mendelssohn piano concerto. Old school music for sure, but it calmed her nerves. Her industrial machines made sewing a dream. Much faster than a turtle-speed home machine. She could whip up a simple dress in a day. An elaborate design with ornate beading or lace required many days of Mendelssohn, Bach, and Brahms. But never Johnny Cash. Or any country music. Ever.

At 12:50 Kiki turned off the machines and hung the dress on a rack. If she hurried, she could eat lunch before her bride showed up at one. Leaving the back door open, she pulled a sandwich and a banana out of the cooler in the car and sat on the trunk. Apart from the paint fiasco, it was a beautiful spring day.

She glanced at her watch. Two minutes to go. She peeled her

banana and stuffed half of it in her mouth.

A man with dark hair popped his head out of the garage door. His eyes blinked, then stared. "Kiki?"

She did a double take. How did he get here? He wasn't her bride. She chomped on the banana that now threatened to choke her.

He stepped outside. "Do you always eat lunch in the alley?"

She shook her head and chewed faster. Did she look like a chipmunk?

"I'm really sorry about pouring lemonade in your lap yesterday. I can't seem to keep my eyes off you." He scratched his chin. "Since we keep running into each other like this, do you want to join me for dinner and a movie?"

"She isn't going on a date with you, Bing." Camilla emerged from the garage like a disturbed bull in a pasture. "She doesn't have time."

Kiki swallowed her banana. Who was Camilla to dictate her private life? "Bing, I'd—"

Camilla interrupted. "Your bride is here. Hurry up."

Kiki slid off the car. "Is that your bumper?"

Camilla glanced at the car part resting against the garage. "No. Now move it."

"I will if you will."

"What's that supposed to mean?"

Kiki pointed. Enough was enough. "You're blocking the door."

Camilla stood aside. "Oh."

Kiki stopped beside Camilla and whispered, "Remember, it is unprofessional to dictate what a partner in the business can and can't do. Last I checked, you're the hired help. Something you've forgotten."

The woman's nostrils flared. "We'll see about that."

Bing exhaled. The tension in the air was thicker than smoke at a four-alarm fire. He appreciated Kiki's stance with Camilla. It was another thing he'd discovered about her. She could stand up for herself. At least she was no pushover. He followed the women inside. Why was the sewing area in the garage? Seemed like it would be better inside the main building. A faint odor of paint lingered in the air. Or maybe it was his olfactory devices working overtime. Perhaps they were remodeling.

Bing joined his buddy and stood against the wall. He was out of his element. Fabric, lace, and a host of sewing things he knew nothing about were organized better than his fire truck.

Kiki hugged Henry's fiancée, Ana Yee. "Good to see you. Who'd you bring with you?"

Ana stepped back, flipping her long black locks over her shoulder. "This is my fiancé, Henry Vega, and his best man, Bing Kelley."

Kiki shook hands with Henry. "How do you know Bing?"

Henry grinned. "We go way back, and now we work at the fire station together."

Camilla stepped into the middle of the group. "The guys are here for measurements for custom ties and vests."

Kiki looked at Ana. "Do you want your fiancé to see you in your dress before the wedding?"

Ana shook her head. "Definitely not."

"Fellas, that means I'll take your measurements first, and then you'll have to leave." Kiki picked up her clipboard and tape measure. "Henry, we'll start with you."

A wonder of competency, Bing marveled as she moved into

seamstress mode. From what he could tell, she was good.

She pulled a fresh sheet of paper to the top of her clipboard and turned to him. "Bing, your turn."

He stepped forward, pulse racing.

"Raise your arms."

He complied. Her wish was his command. When she measured his wrist, butterflies shot through his torso and straight to his head, confounding his brain.

She quickly took his measurements and made notes on her sheet. "Thank you. I'll consult with Ana and Henry. They'll keep you updated for a final fitting. Does that work for you?"

He stared at her.

"Bing?" Her voice was like a slow-moving river where the fishing was perfect. "Is that okay?"

He scratched his head. "Sure."

He needed to get a grip on things or Henry would tell the guys at the firehouse, and he'd never hear the end of it.

Camilla draped her arm through Bing's, crowding his personal space. "Why don't you and Henry come with me and have a cup of coffee in the kitchen? Felicity has freshly baked cookies waiting. That way Ana can have her fitting in private."

He looked at Kiki, but she didn't glance up from her notes. "Kiki, do you have a business card?"

Camilla pulled him forward. "I can give you one in the office."

How would he get rid of this clinging vine? He followed Henry.

In the kitchen, Camilla introduced Felicity to the men. "She's our baker extraordinaire!"

Felicity's smile was as warm as the plate of cookies she passed him.

"Thanks." The smell was intoxicating. He took one and handed the platter to Henry, then bit into the warm goodness. Mmm, old-fashioned sugar cookies fresh from the oven. The best. Bing grinned and punched Henry's shoulder. "These are amazing. We should try this at the firehouse."

Henry took one and set the plate on the counter. "I doubt we can bake as well as a professional."

"Agreed, but we can practice and maybe have a baked goods table at the fundraiser this summer."

"Now you're talking. Options to make money for the fire station and lots of taste testing."

Camilla sidled up to Bing. "Maybe we can help with that. Felicity would be glad to donate to the cause. So would Ronnie. She can make dinner for the station to sell."

Blood rushed from his arms down to his feet. This woman hadn't changed a bit. She still hovered like a gnat over a rotting banana. "We'll have to discuss things at the station then ask Felicity and Ronnie if they'd be interested in helping. We can't just assume they'd volunteer without asking permission."

"I call the shots around here," she cooed.

His phone buzzed. Perfect. An excuse to slip away.

She ran her hand down his arm. "Honey, what I say goes."

He pulled his phone out of his pocket and read the text from a volunteer at the station. Toilet running away. Help.

He'd have to thank the volunteer for the perfect timing. He tugged himself from Camilla's death grip and raced to the door. "Emergency. Gotta go."

Henry's footsteps echoed behind him.

Outside he turned and faced his friend. "Look, I gotta get

away from Camilla. No need to take you away from your plans."

Henry wore the typical firefighter's face. Focused, intent. "Emergency at the station?"

Bing grinned. "Yeah. A toilet that won't stop."

Henry laughed and slapped him on the arm. "Gotcha. See you later at headquarters."

Back at the station, Bing put new innards in the toilet tank then went to the vehicle maintenance bay. Might as well do a little cleaning on the fire engine the mechanic worked on. He grabbed rags and a bucket of soapy water and concealed himself behind the vehicle. He wrung out a rag and attacked the bumper with a vengeance while reflecting on Camilla's first visit at the previous Fourth of July fundraiser. She'd sure made a nuisance of herself since then too.

He scrubbed faster. Camilla's unexpected appearances at the station annoyed him, but he dodged her the best he could. Until the day she showed up at Loveland Community Church and followed him around enough that he finally sought spiritual refuge someplace else.

He dipped the rag back in the water, wrung it out, and moved farther down the bumper. One good thing that came out of his fitting—he now knew where Kiki worked. He'd just have to figure out a way to sneak her out of that garage and away from Camilla's clutches.

As he polished the bumper, a determined face stared back at him. His rescue of a damsel in distress would not involve a fire truck, but he would come up with something to conduct covert operations under the nose of hawk-eyed Camilla.

Chapter Four

Kiki stopped raking and stretched. Would she ever have a day off? While it was nice to take a break from the never-ending decluttering of the house, yard work did not qualify as rest and relaxation. She mulled over the problem of overflowing closets, drawers, and boxes piled shoulder high in rooms she still couldn't access. Little by little, she and the kids were making progress. She had to focus on that. Otherwise, she'd be overwhelmed with the volume of work yet to be accomplished.

She surveyed the grounds. Tressa mowed while Jack weeded the flower beds. Maybe she could pick up some flower seeds tomorrow after work. She resumed raking. It would be nice to have something pretty to look at in the front yard.

A black lab, the size of a coffee table, ran across the grass. He sniffed a few trees and lumbered to Jack, who laughed as he wrapped his arms around the big dog.

Tressa stopped the mower. "Where'd he come from?"

"It's a mystery to me." Kiki leaned her rake against a tree, grateful for the break. "Any tags?"

Jack nodded. "One. From a veterinarian. Probably proof of vaccinations."

Tressa walked to the dog. "Good boy."

Jack hugged the animal. "Can we keep him?"

The lab plastered Jack's face with kisses, his tail beating a silent rhythm against Tressa's leg.

Kiki bent and scratched the dog behind the ears. He wriggled with delight. She inspected his collar. "There's an address. The number is close to ours. He must live in that farmhouse up the road."

Tressa knelt beside the lab, and he slathered her with dog licks.

Kiki laughed. "I'll find something to use as a leash. Then we'll walk him home."

Jack smirked. "Take your time. I like watching my sister's face washing." He giggled. "Dog drool looks good on her."

Kiki chuckled as she walked to the barn. She'd love to have a dog. Maybe one like this friendly intruder. He seemed like a jolly giant. She grabbed a short rope and rejoined her family. "Here." She handed Jack the cord.

Tressa held the lab while Jack tied it to his collar. She jumped up. "I'll take him."

Jack passed the rope to her. "Lead on, oh great one!"

Tressa rolled her eyes. "Boys."

The lab pulled her down the driveway while Kiki and Jack followed.

Jack peered at Kiki. "I'm excited to meet our closest neighbor."

"Hopefully, they'll be nice." Kiki picked up her pace. "Tressa, do you need help?"

"Naw, I got him." She looked back. "He's strong."

Kiki chuckled. "Looks like it."

They walked past the piles of debris she'd raked together. Good thing tomorrow was trash day. At least the thick grove of trees provided some cover from anyone passing by.

Out on the dirt road, the lab sniffed a hole in the ditch, his hindquarters shaking. He yipped and dug like an excavator in high gear.

"Get 'em, dog!" Jack yelled as he raced to the culvert. He jumped into the ditch, egging the animal on.

The lab whined and plowed faster.

Kiki sighed. They needed to drop off the dog and finish the yard work by dark. The teens laughed as they played with the lab.

Maybe just a few more minutes.

A rabbit shot out of another hole. The dog yelped in hot pursuit, the kids racing after him.

Jack yelled, "There's no way he can catch it."

Tressa snorted. "I know, but it's fun watching him think he can."

Kiki giggled. She walked briskly, admiring the wildflowers and weeds that grew in the ditch.

The rabbit disappeared.

The dog's ears drooped, and then he exhaled and moved on. Stopping at the next mailbox, he lifted his leg.

Kiki caught up. "This is the address from the pup's collar."

They turned onto the dirt driveway that wound past a grove of trees similar to those growing on their own farm. However, whoever owned this place sculpted the trees after the fashion of lawn and garden shows Kiki watched on television. Who had time for that? She'd be happy to get the yard waste into the trash cans for tomorrow's pickup.

The dog whined and tugged against his restraint.

"Hang on, boy." Tressa soothed the animal. "You're almost home."

When they rounded a bend in the drive, the perfect yard spread before them. An immaculate green farmhouse. Cream-colored outbuildings.

The perfect abode.

The one every farmer strives to own.

Kiki gulped. Great. Just what she needed. Her nearest neighbor had created a place that could grace the cover of the finest farmer's magazine.

The perfect neighbor.

Almost.

She tipped her head as music reached her ears. Johnny Cash tunes blared over the airwaves.

Who in their right mind listened to that kind of music?

An old pickup guarded the garage, the hood propped open with an old broom. Two tires lay on the ground beside the truck.

A man standing on the bumper was bent under the open hood.

The dog whined as he pulled Tressa to the vehicle. Then he barked.

The man startled and straightened, thunking his head on the underside of the hood. The broom snapped in two as the hood crashed down, leaving his legs swimming in the air.

Johnny Cash continued to wail.

Kiki raced to the truck. She and Tressa lifted the hood while Jack pulled on the man's legs and helped him slide to the ground. The lab broke free. With a joyous yelp, the dog dove for the man, knocking him into Kiki. With a momentum known only to labs,

Kiki fell backward, her new neighbor tumbling on top of her. They landed like a pile of dominoes on both tires.

Kiki groaned. She should have stayed home.

The dog alternated between kissing her and her neighbor. Nothing like communicable germs via stinky dog breath.

"Ox, stop." The man rolled off Kiki, his eyes wide. "I'm so sorry. Are you okay?"

She sucked in a breath.

No.

It couldn't be.

No way. No how.

Bing Kelley was not her closest neighbor.

He was just a figment of her imagination. A mirage. He'd go away as soon as she turned to go home.

He scratched the stubble on his chin, leaving a greasy smudge. "Kiki?" He held out his hand. "Let me help you."

She stared up at him. "First, you give me a ticket. Then you show up at my church. Now your dog tackles us to the ground like a Bronco linebacker."

Kiki sat up. Why did she keep running into him? What had she done to deserve this?

"I regret the ticket and will take care of that tomorrow." He knelt. "I apologize about that and Ox. He's everyone's friend."

She closed her eyes and counted to ten. He sounded sincere. She'd have to forgive him. Plus, she did not like holding grudges against neighbors. Boy, was she in a pickle.

"Can I make you dinner?"

There he was talking again.

She opened her eyes. "Why?"

"We're neighbors. That's what neighbors do."

"Thanks but no thanks. I have a lot of work waiting at home." She scrambled to her feet.

He grinned. "I'll tell you what. I'll challenge you to a game."

Jack sidled up. "What kind of game?"

Bing stood. "Soccer."

Tressa scratched Ox behind the ears. "I like soccer."

"Ah, but this kind of soccer is played on tricycles." Bing winked at the kids. "How about a challenge? Lads versus lassies. If the lads win, you stay for dinner."

Jack nodded. "I'm in."

Tressa laughed. "Me too!"

Kiki folded her arms. If Bing thought he could get her away from her duties and her dream, he'd just have to learn to play solitaire.

"Please, Auntie." Jack wrung his hands. "You always work. Take a night off."

"I agree. You need a break." Tressa grinned. "I want to see how soccer's played on trikes."

"Ugh," Kiki groaned. "It's a conspiracy."

Tressa hugged her. "Thanks."

"Deal." Bing hitched up his pants. "We'll play a full match."

Kiki shrugged. "Looks like I'm outnumbered."

While Kiki and Tressa planned their strategy, Bing and Jack went into the barn and rode out on two recumbent trail trikes. They returned to the barn and produced two adult tricycles painted cherry red, four mismatched helmets, four road cones, and a tired soccer ball.

Bing pointed at the transportation. "Ladies first."

"We want the ladylike trikes." Tressa laughed. "You boys can get dirty in the low riders."

"Score!" Jack roared as he raced to the recumbent trikes. "These things are sweet."

Kiki shrugged. "Kids."

Bing nodded toward the children. "You've done a nice job with them."

"Thanks." She sat on the trike and stared him straight in the eyes. "Prepare to die a slow, painful death."

He chuckled. "Challenge accepted."

He trotted across the yard and arranged opposing goalposts with the large orange cones. Then he hopped on his bike and explained the rules. "This is like regular soccer, only instead of running we ride our trikes to the ball, take our feet off the pedals, and kick it. No picking it up and tossing it to a teammate. Any questions?"

"Nope." Jack pulled on his helmet. "We'll take the goal by the truck."

"Deal." Tressa pointed. "Our goal is by the cherry tree next to the house. It matches our trikes."

"That's right." Kiki laughed. "Matching a tree is rule number one in trike tournaments with the neighbor."

Bing tossed the ball at her. She matched his tree and his life quite nicely.

Kiki kicked it to Tressa. "We're off." She pedaled toward the goal. "In more ways than one."

Tressa responded with a hard kick, sending the ball toward the goal faster.

Bing chased after her, trying to intercept the ball before it rushed between the cones. Too late. The gals were good.

"Score!" Tressa yelled. "We're up one, little bro."

Bing picked up the ball. The lassies were competitive. He'd have to up his game if he wanted them to stay for dinner. Back at center field, he tossed the ball to Jack.

Jack turned on a dime, stopped, and pelted the ball toward their goal. The lassies pedaled hard to stop the lads from scoring. Tressa managed a good save. She kicked the ball to Kiki, who moved it closer to the cherry tree.

This wouldn't do. Bing pedaled faster than a startled jackrabbit toward the goal. When Kiki stopped to kick the ball into the end zone, he flew past her, blocking the ball and keeping the gals from scoring. Somewhere behind him, Jack cheered.

Kiki drove straight at him with the speed of a gazelle, and a pretty one at that. If he wasn't careful, she'd T-bone him. He tapped the ball out of the way and moved just in time. Jack raced to him and kicked the ball far down the field toward the truck. All four trikes raced forward with Ox chasing after them.

Jack sped to the front of the pack and whacked the ball through the end zone.

Bing winked at Kiki. "We're even now."

"Enjoy." She raced past him. "It won't last long."

Tressa put the ball back into play. For an hour, they pedaled and kicked until Bing's legs screamed for relief. His neighbors did not complain but seemed to enjoy themselves, especially the teens.

He yelled, "Sudden death. Next goal wins the game!"

Jack and Tressa duked it out at center field. Tressa broke free and kicked the ball to Kiki. She pedaled to the goal. Ox lumbered across the grass and picked up the ball.

"Come here, Ox." Tressa coaxed the mutt with clicks and finger snaps. "Drop the ball."

Jack whistled. "Here boy, come here, Ox."

But when he pedaled closer, Ox jumped and trotted down the field toward the truck, his four humans trailing behind.

Jack waved his arms. "Catch him, Auntie."

Kiki operated her trike like she did her tape measure, with speed and accuracy. She closed in on the dog. Ox gave her a long side look and a happy bark as he raced through the goal post.

Jack cheered. "We won! We won!"

Tressa stopped beside him. "No you didn't. Dog goals don't count."

Jack challenged Bing. "You said the next score was sudden death. Now we cook."

"Gentlemen's honor." Bing saluted. "We cook and the lassies rest." Ox raced to Bing and dropped the ball at his feet. He bent down and scratched the lab's ears. "Oxford saves the game."

Tressa laughed. "You named your dog Oxford?"

"Yeah, I was hoping for a smart dog and named him after a university." He picked up the ball. "But his best talent is eating."

"And scoring goals," Jack piped in. "Trike soccer is fun. You should add it to the Fourth of July lineup."

Bing looked at Kiki. "Will you stay for dinner?"

She hesitated.

"I make a mean grilled cheese."

"Please, Auntie," Tressa pleaded. "This is the most fun we've had since school let out."

Oxford trotted to Kiki and licked her hand. She patted his head. "Sounds like I'm outnumbered."

Bing chuckled. "Jack, we have work to do. Ladies, we'll get a fire going in the pit. You relax while we cook." He led them to the yard behind the house. "There's a picnic table, chairs, and a horseshoe pitch to keep you entertained."

"Cool." Tressa walked to the horseshoe game. "Auntie, wanna play?"

"Sure." Kiki joined her.

"Jack, there's wood by the fire pit." Bing walked sideways. "The matches are on the shelf in the porch by the back door."

Bing turned, ran into the house, and gathered supplies for salad and fruit for dessert. Grabbing a cookie sheet, he quickly buttered bread and assembled cheese sandwiches, lining them up in rows on the pan. He tossed his secret cooking tool, plates, cups, and silverware into a basket and carried everything outside to the picnic table.

"Kiki, if I can make you a grilled cheese in a very unconventional manner, will you go on a date with me?"

She held a horseshoe in midair and peered at him. "Define unconventional."

"Not over a fire, not on a stove, and not in a source of heat."

Tressa tossed her horseshoe. "How are you going to do that?"

Bing rested his hand on the basket. "Kiki?"

"Oh, why not." She pitched her horseshoe, which landed close to the stake. "My crazy niece and nephew will want to see how you do that. They'll outvote me anyway."

Dare he hope?

He laughed. "Tressa, would you like to help?"

Tressa nodded and followed Kiki to the table.

He pulled out the pan of prepped sandwiches. "My secret tool is a culinary blow torch. Go ahead and grab it, and I'll show you how to use it."

Tressa picked up the torch, while Bing provided instructions on adjusting the flame and toasting the bread. He set the table, and when the sandwiches were ready, he motioned for Jack to join them.

"Food." Jack plopped down on the bench. "I'm starving."

Kiki laughed. "You have hollow legs."

"Auntie, you have to go on a date with Bing." Tressa passed Kiki a sandwich. "He said grilled cheese could be made without a stove or over a fire."

Kiki took one. "They were still made with a fire."

"Yup." Jack grabbed two sandwiches. "Think about the prepositions he used."

"And since these were made *under* a fire and not *over*, you have a date, Auntie." Tressa turned to Bing. "What day and time are you picking her up?"

He chuckled. "You sound like a dad." Would Kiki play along with this strategy? He eyed her. "Saturday?"

Jack nodded. "Saturday's perfect. We don't have anything going on."

Kiki stared at Bing. "I warned you about these two."

Tressa piped in. "Auntie, you haven't had a date in, like, forever. Go."

Kiki's face turned a dark shade of pink. "Announce it to the world, why don't ya."

Bing winked at her. She was adorable when she blushed. "Six on Saturday?"

"We'll make sure—" Jack began.

"That she's ready," Tressa finished.

Bing's smile faded. "No one is going to make your aunt do anything against her will."

"We know." Jack bit into his sandwich. "She just needs encouragement," he said through his mouthful.

"We're excited she has a prospect." Tressa helped herself to the salad. "Auntie, he's nice. You should go if you want, not because we think it's a good idea."

Smart girl. Bing kept his gaze focused on Kiki. "Is six on Saturday okay?"

She nodded.

Score. He had a date with the prettiest woman he had ever met. He'd have to figure out a way of thanking the kids and Ox. Especially Oxford. That dog instigated one of the best evenings Bing had the pleasure of enjoying in recent memory.

He sat back and bit into his sandwich, the gooey cheese melting his insides. Or perhaps the sensation originated with the first woman in a long time who caught his attention and filled his every waking moment.

Was he falling in love?

Chapter Five

K iki looked down at her soft pink shirt and matching knee-length split skirt she'd stitched from a favorite pattern. Bing said he'd pick her up at six and suggested she wear something comfortable. If they were going someplace nicer, she would be presentable. Her toes peeked through her 1940s-style heels. She draped a sweater over her arm then stabbed a few more hairpins into her messy bun. After slipping out the back door, she trotted to the front yard.

Plopping down on the bench under the cottonwood by the house, she envisioned the possibilities the evening held. Maybe he'd take her to the new restaurant she heard the gals at the office raving about. She fidgeted with her skirt.

Would he kiss her?

Warmth crept over her face like the wind playing with the treetops. She sighed. It was silly to let emotions get the best of her. She checked her messages. Nothing.

What was keeping him?

A meadowlark whistled from the branches above. Kiki followed the sound, searching for the bird. She spied his yellow breast in the canopy of leaves and the object of his symphony, his mate.

A baritone voice belted a country tune up her driveway. She grinned. Her fireman had arrived. Turning her head to his musical number, her smile melted faster than chocolate in a double boiler. Bing sported a neon-yellow shirt, lime-green shorts, argyle socks, and a brown checked tie.

She had a date with a bug.

What inspired this grasshopper outfit? And what in the world was that contraption he pushed? Not a tandem bike with one rider in front and the other behind, but a bicycle with two seats side by side with double handlebars and pedals.

Someone pounded on the front window. Kiki glanced back. Engulfed in the drapes, Tressa and Jack stood in front of the big window, laughing. She'd hear about this night for the rest of her life.

Bing's song and red contrivance stopped in front of her. "Found a tandem bike in a shed and converted it to this." He stepped around the bike, his dad sandals crunching the gravel. "Do you like it?"

"Um. . ." She raised an eyebrow. A metal milk crate welded to the front of the frame held a brown picnic basket. "Why the changes?"

He gazed at the ride. "Women shouldn't be pedaling behind men. They should be beside them as equals."

Tears welled. She could ignore his lack of fashion. "That's beautiful."

"And so are you." He winked. "Ready?"

Kiki folded her sweater and tucked it on one side of the picnic basket. "Is this easy to ride?"

"Yup."

She glanced at the front window. The teens were still laughing while Tressa recorded the events on her cell phone. Lovely. After years alone, the entire social media world would see her leave on a date with an insect.

Kiki positioned herself in front of her seat and placed her foot on the far pedal.

"On three." Bing did the same. "One, two, three."

They pushed forward, mounted their seats, and pedaled, wobbling down the driveway.

Kiki laughed. "Where are we going?"

A smile crossed Bing's face. "On an adventure." At the end of the driveway, they turned left and pedaled down the dirt road. "We're going to a place few know about. It's called Frog Pond."

Kiki adjusted her shoe on the pedal. As a general rule, she avoided amphibians. "Frog Pond?"

He eyed her. "It's shaped like one. At least that's what my dad told me when I was a kid."

High heels and water critters were not a combination she considered for a romantic date. She sighed. Oh well. If anyone showed up unexpectedly, she would look good.

They stopped at a wooden gate along the Kelley pasture fence. Old tire ruts constituted a path in the tall grass.

Bing slid off his contraption. "I'll open the gate if you don't mind holding the bike."

A green SUV raced past, sending a swirl of dust in the air. Kiki coughed and covered her mouth. The vehicle's backlights shone as the driver slammed on the brakes. "Someone you know?"

"Haven't a clue." Bing pulled the gate open enough for Kiki to push the bike through, then closed it.

She kept her eye on the car. Who would stop on a dirt road in the middle of nowhere to watch two people go through a pasture gate? Did they need help?

The vehicle inched away.

"It's okay." Bing reached her side. "Let's go."

They mounted the bike and pedaled down the trail. She glanced over her shoulder. The vaguely familiar car disappeared.

He cleared his throat. "Hope you like what I made for our picnic."

"It'll be a treat to be relieved of cooking duty for an evening."

Kiki faced forward. If that car was whose she thought it was, why was the driver out here?

They pedaled through a grove of trees and down a hill. Nestled at the bottom was a small pond.

She squinted then laughed. "I guess if you use your imagination, it looks like a frog."

"When I was a kid, we used to come here for family picnics. It's one of my favorite places. Quiet. Away from people." Bing pointed to a homemade dock at the edge of the pond. "If you don't mind, let's go there."

After coasting to a stop, Kiki dismounted, and Bing leaned the bike against a cottonwood that shadowed part of the pier. He grabbed the picnic basket and offered his arm to her. She slid her hand through the crook of his elbow, and they strolled to the dock.

He adjusted the basket. "Thought we'd sit at the end of the dock and eat our meal."

She glanced at her pretty skirt. "Perfect."

What was a gal to do? Dress for a night on the town only to

party at a pond. Being alone with a firefighter in the middle of nature had its advantages. Absolutely no competition or interruptions whatsoever.

The dock squeaked and swayed with their steps. Kiki stopped. "Are you sure this is stable?"

"Firefighter's honor."

They walked to the two tall support poles at the end of the ramp, and Bing set the picnic basket down to his left. "Let's soak our feet."

When he peeled off his socks and sandals and sat, Kiki hesitated, not really wanting to slide pond-soaked feet back into her favorite heels. Yet the lure of the water enticed her.

"Come on." Bing tapped the wood beside him. "You'll never know what Frog Pond has to offer without trying it."

"True."

She slid out of her shoes and placed them carefully in the center of the pier close to the shore. Nothing could harm them there.

Bing held up a hand. She grabbed it and sat beside him. Following his example, she dipped her feet in the water. Ooh, that felt good. Her worries over her shoes, skirt, and Kermit's brothers and sisters slipped away as she dangled her toes at the end of a dock in the middle of nowhere.

They sat for a while, basking in the solitude of nature. The breeze tickled the water into a gentle motion that massaged her feet. This would be a great place to bring the kids. She'd have to ask his permission though.

Bing opened the picnic basket. "Hope you like Italian." He handed her a plate and fork. "Nothing but the best for you."

She smiled. "Impressive."

He pulled out a pan and scooped a piece onto her plate. "I can bake frozen lasagna with the best of them."

"I do that too. Especially on those mom-taxi days when the kids have their activities." She took a bite. "Yum. Thanks."

He helped himself then tossed a piece of garlic bread on her plate. "How's work going?"

Kiki chewed. Should she tell him what it was really like or keep up a professional front? No need to bother him with the details of lace, sequins, and a demanding coworker.

"Well. . ."

A woman's voice yelled from the top of the hill. "Bing dear, sorry I'm so late. I got here as fast as I could."

It couldn't be.

Kiki sucked in a breath. What was she doing here? This was supposed to be Bing, Kiki, and Kermit's secret place. Not hers.

Kiki glanced at Bing. His mouth hung open, a bite of noodles hanging out like a dog's tongue on a hot day.

"Sorry, honey. I got lost." Camilla trotted down the hill.

Bing swallowed his noodles and coughed, then set his plate on the picnic basket.

Camilla reached the dock and pirouetted on the wood. "So glad I found the place."

She stepped on the same board where Kiki had placed her heels. The panel shot up like a teeter-totter.

Camilla tripped.

The heels slid toward the water.

Kiki thrust her plate in Bing's lap and scrambled to her feet. Faster than a Rockies shortstop, she raced toward her heels. Dodging the office manager, she dove. The pier swayed like a ship at sea while the heels twirled over the water and plopped into Frog Pond. She landed with a thud on the rigid boards.

Bing hurried to her. "Kiki, are you okay?"

She sat up and surveyed her dusty outfit. "I'm fine. Not sure my shoes are though."

He jumped into the knee-deep water. "I'll find them." He moved his feet along the bottom. Locating the shoes, he fished them out and turned them upside down on the grass near the dock.

Kiki stood. Maybe she should put on her wet shoes and leave.

Bing reached her side. "I'm so sorry. This dock isn't as strong as I thought. Obviously, repairs are needed." He pointed to the end of the pier. "Please, let's finish our meal."

She nodded. His apology seemed heartfelt.

He escorted her past Camilla and sat beside her at the end of the pier then handed her plate to her. "Now, where were we?"

"Bing, my love, when are we going to work on another fundraiser at the fire station? I need to help you." Camilla's voice poured from her mouth sweeter than caramel fondue. She slipped off her shoes, pushed her way between the pair, and sat down. "Excuse me. A little room, please."

Kiki slid away from Camilla and hung on to the side of the dock, precariously balancing her plate on her lap. Of all the nerve. Would she never get a break from this woman?

So, they worked at the fire station together, and according to Camilla, Bing invited her on their date. Did that mean Kiki would be included? Always a third wheel?

"How about some of that lasagna?" Camilla batted her eyelashes. "It smells so good."

"Uh, sure." He scooped out a piece, plopped it on the lid of the baking pan, then pulled the garlic bread out of its package and gave her a serving. The remainder he placed on top of the basket. "Here's a fork I saved for dessert. That should work."

Bing leaned back. "Kiki, shall I refresh your plate?"

She turned and shook her head. "No, thanks. It looks like your cup runneth over."

"I can explain."

"No worries."

What to do? What kind of guy would invite two women on a date? Unless Camilla overheard something and assumed it meant her. No surprise there.

Kiki needed an exit plan. "How deep is the water here at the end of the pier?"

"Four to five feet. Why?"

"Just wondering."

A pair of geese swam over from the other side of the pond. Maybe they would scare Camilla away.

"Bing dear, what about the Fourth of July fundraiser?" Camilla cut her lasagna with her fork. "Any new ideas?"

Bing's eyes rested on Camilla's face. "Uh. . .the usual. Cookout, booths for the kids, a petting zoo."

"I want to contribute to the fundraiser and also volunteer to help our incredible firefighters."

"Call the office and get on the volunteer list."

"I did that. Hoping you'll give me a specific job."

Kiki held on to her plate with a death grip. If it were up to her, Camilla would not be the office manager at Weddings by Design. The woman's strategies involved whatever was in her best interests. Were her intentions to shift Bing's growing affection to herself?

Bing scratched an ear. "I'm not in charge of that."

Camilla wrinkled her nose. "I thought since you were such an important member of the squad, you could find something special for me to do."

"Can't do that. Call the office."

Camilla slid closer to him. "Your eyes shine nicely against the backdrop of the pond."

He slithered away from her and closer to the pole. The pier swayed.

She grabbed his checked tie and pulled his face close to hers. "Mmm, you smell so good."

Kiki set her plate down on the dock. Enough. She had more important things to do than watch Camilla sabotage their date. Right now, laundry at home seemed like more fun.

"I have to go." She stood. "Thanks for dinner, Bing. I'll see myself out of your pasture."

"Wait, don't go." His face reddened. "I can explain."

He scrambled to his feet. The dock shifted.

The geese swam next to the pier. Frogs croaked in the shadows of the trees hanging over the water.

Kiki walked backward. "I'm sure you have your reasons. I just consider a date an event between two people. A party of three makes it a bit crowded."

She reached the section of dock closest to the shore. The geese took flight and landed in the spot Kiki had vacated. The gander nibbled on Camilla's plate while the goose surveyed the garlic bread.

Camilla screamed as she tossed the dish in the air then struggled to her feet. She rushed away from the geese and flung herself onto Bing. The momentum pushed them hard against the end post of the pier.

The dock swung to the left. Kiki raced to shore, glad to feel solid ground once more.

The pier snapped like a mousetrap as each section folded under the next. Bing crashed into the water. Camilla flung her hands over the top of the post and hung in the air for a few seconds. Bing surfaced. The pole toppled into the water, and Camilla landed with a *splat*.

Kiki stifled a laugh as she slipped into her soaked shoes.

Camilla emerged in the chest-deep water. Weeds hung from her head like a droopy bridal veil. Lasagna scraps resting on her shoulders reminded Kiki of the braid on a high school band uniform. The goose floated next to her, nibbling on garlic toast. The gander rose from the water and landed on Camilla's shoulder, searching for dinner.

Camilla screamed and ducked underwater while Bing shooed the geese away.

She stood and clung to Bing. "There's tadpoles swimming around us."

Kiki couldn't hold it in any longer. She laughed as tears pooled in her eyes.

He helped Camilla move around the dilapidated dock. "Come on. Let's get out of the water."

Kiki turned and walked up the hill, past the wooded area, and slipped through the gate, still giggling. Her first date with Bing couldn't have ended better if she'd planned it.

Chapter Six

On his next day off, Bing polished the old motorcycle and sidecar until it sparkled, dents and all. He knew that what he planned to do was a gamble, but he needed to try. He tossed two deli sandwiches, a bag of chips, and two bottles of water into a lunch bag and placed it on the seat of the sidecar. On the drive to Loveland, he rehearsed his response if Kiki refused his apology. Couldn't say he blamed her. If only he'd known Camilla planned to crash their last date, he would have done something else.

He timed his trip to park behind the garage of Weddings by Design at noon and keep out of sight. So far, so good. No Camilla. He knocked on the door.

Kiki answered. "Oh, it's you."

He held up a hand. "Look, I understand you must be angry, but I did not expect Camilla to crash our date. I had no idea she was coming."

Kiki froze.

"She must have overheard me talking about my plans to Henry at the station. Camilla shows up there all the time." He scratched his chin. "I stopped in to apologize. I'm very sorry it happened. Disturbed, in fact."

"Apology accepted." Kiki nodded. "It was strange."

He let out a breath. "Agreed. I packed a lunch. Would you care to have a bite to eat?"

She tossed her hair over her shoulder. "Why not? It would be nice to step away for an hour."

He waited while she shut down her machines, turned out the lights, and grabbed her handbag. "You might want a sweater or a hat."

Kiki grabbed a sweater and followed him out the door. She locked up and turned around. "Another interesting mode of transportation."

Bing laughed. "My ancestors were tinkerers and created with what they had on hand. Guess I'm kinda like that too."

She smiled. "It's a good way to be."

His pulse raced. "Shall we?"

He made sure she was safely stowed in the sidecar with the lunch bag at her feet. She slipped her sweater on and tied her hair back. He liked a woman who could adapt and take a chance at enjoying herself.

He eyed her. "Here are the rules. We're going to take turns deciding which street to go down. Ladies first."

Kiki pointed to the end of the alley. "Take a right when you come to the street."

He started the bike, backed up, and coasted past the back of Weddings by Design. Camilla stared daggers at them as they drove by the kitchen window. She looked madder than he'd ever seen her. Hopefully, she'd stay away from the station and leave Kiki alone. He doubted that would happen, but he could wish. Still, he was with the woman of his dreams and about to embark on a new adventure.

At the end of the alley, he turned right and then left at the next street. They took turns giving directions until they ended up at a small park with a seating area under a gazebo encircled with pink flowers.

He parked the bike and helped Kiki out of the sidecar. Not that she needed it, but he wanted to show her he cared. He grabbed the bag, and they walked to the pavilion. "Here's to a disaster-free meal."

Kiki chuckled. "How's the dock on Frog Lake?"

He placed the insulated tote on the table. "A complete disaster. I'll have to start from scratch and build something new."

"Holler if you need help." She sat on the bench. "The kids and I can do something."

"Will do." He sat across from her, opened the bag, and passed her a sandwich, napkin, and water. "How are your projects going?" He understood fire, engines, and water pressure, but thread, sewing machines, and lace were entirely beyond him.

"I cut out a veil this morning and worked on adding sequins and trim according to the bride's design."

Bing opened the bag of chips. He'd purchased a plain kind since he didn't know what she liked. "Are all your orders what the bride wants, or do you have the freedom to create your own designs?"

"Both." Kiki opened her sandwich and used the wrapper as a plate. "I prefer designing something original and working with a bride who allows me to do so. The creativity part is fun for me."

He held the bag out to her. "May I ask how the barn is coming along?"

She took the bag. "The kids and I began cleaning it out, and I made a list of repairs."

"That's a good start."

"It helps to know what I'm up against." She poured chips onto the plastic wrap and handed the bag back to him.

Bing helped himself to chips. "What's the biggest obstacle?"

"Time. Money. The usual issues with a building project." Kiki bit into her sandwich.

"How can I help?" He popped a chip into his mouth and waited for her to finish chewing. The way her mouth curled when she ate was cute.

She swallowed and wiped her mouth with her napkin. "I don't know."

"You don't know, or you're unsure about me?"

"Both."

He shrugged. At least she was honest. "You intrigue me, and I like you."

Color seeped across her face, matching the pink flowers behind her. Maybe he spoke too soon.

She opened her water bottle and took a sip. "I can guess on supplies. The plan is to recycle wood from the farm. Spend as little as possible but make a nice venue."

"Can you pull wood from the destroyed loafing shed?"

She nodded. "And from the piles of materials my uncle never got rid of. It'll have a rustic flair, but it's the best I can do."

"That's brilliant."

Kiki wrinkled her nose. "You think so?"

Bing raised one eyebrow. "Definitely. Lights made from upcycled farm products would add to the charm."

She picked up a chip. "There will be strings of lights hung from the rafters. Love that look."

"Me too. Great idea."

"After the barn, I'm going to put in restrooms and renovate

two of the outbuildings as changing rooms for bridal parties."

He took a swig of water. "You've thought through your vision well."

"I try." She smiled. "What are your plans for the broken dock?"

He laughed. "It'll include materials stored in my barn."

"The geese enjoyed the lasagna." Kiki snorted. "So did the frogs."

Bing tossed his head back and laughed until his eyes watered. He could use a daily serving of her sarcasm.

After they finished their meal and cleaned up, Kiki suggested they try the swings. He didn't mind. Once he was in flight, he found he'd forgotten how much fun it was. He burst forth in song. Couldn't help himself. A date with a beautiful woman would do that. Especially this one.

She winked at him. He melted.

Kiki slowed her swinging and jumped off. "I have to go back to work."

"Your wish is my command." He flew from the swing and landed like a frog with one leg. So much for trying to impress her with his mad skills. He would have preferred to land like an Olympic champion.

All too soon, Bing parked the motorcycle by the back door of the garage. He offered her his hand and helped her out. "Can I come over tonight and look at the barn?"

She shrugged. "I guess, though there's not much you can do about it."

He disagreed with her assumption but kept his thoughts to himself. "Seven?"

"Sure."

He winked and returned to the bike. She waited by the door. The last thing he saw as he drove off was her quick wave. He squared his shoulders and puffed up his chest. He'd use the barn as an excuse to continue to see this lovely lady.

⌐⌐

Kiki unlocked the garage door and hesitated before entering. Trouble would be waiting.

Camilla stood by the big table. "If you think you're going to get away with my man, you better reconsider your lot in life."

"What are you talking about?" Kiki turned on the light and dropped her sweater and purse on the chair by the door.

Camilla picked up a metal yardstick and tapped her palm. "Go near him again, and I'll see to it you never—"

Cassie burst through the side door. "Meeting in my office. Hurry."

Camilla stared needles into Kiki then followed Cassie to the main building.

Kiki grabbed her clipboard and a pen and took a deep breath. Was this job even worth it anymore? Since Camilla came on board, the shop was no longer her happy place. She stepped into Cassie's office, where the other business partners waited. She knew she should talk to Cassie about it, but she didn't want to hurt her feelings. If things became worse, she'd say something. Maybe she was overly sensitive, because if she was honest with herself, she was falling for Bing.

Cassie appeared as if she could burst. "We've got a 911 contract that pays exceptionally well, which means bonuses for each of us. Only problem? We need to leave Monday at dawn."

Kiki grimaced. Monday? What about her kids? The barn? Her blood pressure?

Cassie continued. "We have a bride who is marrying a military officer, and he's deploying in three weeks. The wedding has been rescheduled, leaving us less than two weeks. That gives the new couple time for a quick honeymoon before the groom ships out."

Felicity straightened her skirt. "Am I baking the cake?" With a sparkly diamond on her left hand, she oozed the happiness of a loved woman.

Cassie nodded. "Yes, and Ronnie, they'll have a fully stocked pantry for the rehearsal dinner and wedding meals."

Ronnie tucked a strand of her hair behind her ear. "Good news."

Kiki sighed. Her three coworkers and best friends were so beautiful inside and out. She was blessed beyond measure. And then there was Camilla. What was she going to do about her?

Cassie continued. "Kiki, you're on the wedding and brides-maids' dresses. Nothing for the groom's party, so that will help, but they don't have any fabric."

Wait. What? Kiki scratched her head.

Cassie grimaced. "And the bride doesn't know what she wants."

Kiki stiffened. A custom gown meant creating a custom pattern and whatever detailing the unknown bride wanted. And the bridesmaids? How many did that entail? Sleep would not be on the agenda for the week. Talk about a ticking time bomb. She'd have to plan carefully and make sure she had everything she needed to rise to the task.

Cassie opened her desk drawer and pulled out a notebook. "I've got some leads for limousines."

Kiki forced a smile onto her face. "Is there a fabric store in town?"

Cassie shook her head. "No, sorry. You'll have to bring fabric with you. The venue is on private land in the mountains."

Kiki gritted her teeth. Great. Instead of working on the barn, her weekend now entailed sourcing fabric, appliques, and supplies just so she could travel to the unknown on Monday morning. Her bride and the bridal team would need to be patient and understanding.

Camilla opened her laptop and typed in a document. Kiki glanced at the spreadsheet of customer names and contact information. Camilla quickly closed her computer and fidgeted with her hands.

Was Camilla stealing from their customer base?

Kiki bit her tongue. She didn't have enough facts to call her on it at the meeting and didn't want to make a fool of herself if she was wrong. After all, maybe Camilla was updating the files of Weddings by Design.

She spent the rest of the meeting with her face downward, focused on her clipboard. She started a list of items she'd need to bring and a list of tasks she must do before Monday morning. This gig had its advantages. She could work on her part of the project and avoid Camilla.

Camilla monopolized the rest of the meeting, and Kiki felt the fight seeping out of her. From now on, her main long-term goal would be to create a wedding venue on the farm.

Entrepreneurs ran in her family. Weddings by Design would pay the bills until then. She was leaving the business as soon as she could. In the meantime, she'd bite her tongue. This bonus would pay for repairs to the barn.

She managed to make it through the day alone. The garage had its benefits. She packed everything on her list in boxes to take with her on Monday. Then she locked the garage and hit every fabric store in Loveland and the surrounding area. Finishing late, she grabbed a cheap pizza and drove home. After dinner, Tressa and Jack were cleaning the kitchen when a sudden knock on the back door startled them.

Kiki pulled the door open and forced a smile on her face. "Bing, let me show you the barn."

The old barn, with its faded paint and mismatched boards, had seen better days. Piles of rusty farm equipment and implements lay in disarray across the farmyard. Reminders of an earlier agricultural era where one kept everything in case it came in handy someday. Only problem with that plan? Someday never came.

She slowed in front of a rusty two-ton dump truck parked next to the barn and leaned against its wooden sides. She couldn't fight it anymore. Bing, dressed in a firefighter T-shirt and jeans, perched on the tailgate, sure looked agreeable. She closed her eyes and held her breath. How could she focus when he resembled something off a calendar? It didn't help. She stumbled.

He caught her arm, averting a disaster. "You okay?"

Her arm tingled. "No."

"Wanna talk about it?"

She squinted. "You are a major distraction."

A hurt expression spread across his face. "Sorry, I can—"

"Don't go. You're just so good-looking," Kiki opened her eyes the rest of the way. "I lose my focus."

The corners of his mouth twitched. "You think I'm good-looking?"

Her cheeks grew warm. "Have you looked in the mirror recently?"

Bing scratched his chin. A grin the size of Colorado stretched across his face. "You think I'm good-looking?" he repeated.

She nodded. Might as well admit it. "You're handsome in a sweet teddy bear sort of way. You know, the kind of guy they put on a firefighter's calendar."

He squared his shoulders. "I'll take that."

She gave him a tour of the barn, showing him the salvaged materials she and the kids had set aside. "We've only taken a small bite out of this project."

The dumpster outside the front door of the barn rattled.

He picked up a post. "I'd say you've done quite a bit."

The trash lid slammed shut. It sounded like Jack had followed them.

Kiki grabbed a toolbox and moved it out of Bing's way. "At the rate we're going, it'll take until eternity to make this venue ready."

A grunt echoed from inside the dumpster.

She placed the toolbox on a makeshift workbench. "What do you think that is?"

"Definitely not a teenager."

"Some probably grunt like that if they're hungry."

Bing laughed and set down the post. "Men too."

Kiki slid quietly to the barn door. Peering around the wall, she spied no teenagers or other signs of humanity. She felt Bing's warm breath on her neck.

"See anything?"

"Not yet." She walked over to the dumpster, lifted the lid, then slammed it down. "Bear."

He followed her. "Come again?"

She turned and stared at him. "There's a young bear in the dumpster."

He stared back.

The animal grunted.

Bing opened the lid, and the bear jumped up.

He screamed, dropped the lid, and ran away. "Flying gargoyles."

Kiki bent over. She couldn't hold it in. A belly laugh the size of the Rockies erupted from her lips.

The bear garumped.

She laughed even more. "A. . .firefighter. . .afraid of"—she fought for breath amid her giggling—"a bear."

Bing placed a hand on his hip, cocked his head, and gave a sideways grin. "If you stop laughing, we can come up with a plan to get the animal free."

Bear flatulence echoed inside the metal chamber.

Kiki leaned against the barn wall and giggled. "Did you hear that?"

Bing chuckled. "He has gas."

She clutched her side. "A bear with gas and a firefighter without a gas mask." She laughed as she slid down the wall and plopped on the ground. "I can't take anymore. My side hurts."

The odor wafted from the waste receptacle.

As funny as it was, the situation needed a remedy. Kiki hopped up. "I'm going to open the dumpster. This guy is young, but he should be able to crawl out. Cats climb trees, and we don't need to rescue them most of the time. So I'm in favor of seeing what he can do before we intervene."

After grabbing a long stick, she pushed one lid and flipped it over the back of the dumpster. Good thing it was mostly empty. The bear sniffed the bottom. She hurried to toss the other lid open then trotted to the rusty truck.

"It's probably best to be out of the way when the critter lands on the ground." She climbed onto the flatbed then moved the tailgate to enclose the sides. "You might want to join me."

"Naw, it'll be fine down here." He dodged behind a tractor. "He'll run away."

Kiki had her doubts. But what could she do? He was a grown man, and she was not going to mother him.

The bear rose on its hind legs and surveyed the area. He stared at Kiki then Bing, his long snout and yellow, beady eyes lingering on each in turn. He lunged, landing with his front limbs over the ledge of the dumpster, claws scraping against the metal.

"You have to admit, he's kinda cute." Kiki slid backward until she rested against the rear window of the cab. "I'm going to call him Crusher."

Bing raised an eyebrow. "Crusher?"

"Yeah, when he's grown, he could crush anything."

Growling, the bear fell back into the receptacle, the thud echoing across the farmyard.

Bing glanced at her. "He might be cute if he were a panda."

With a finesse known only to bears, the animal vaulted from the depth of the dumpster and balanced on the corner, grunting.

Bing remained frozen behind the tractor.

More bear toots emanated from the creature.

Kiki yelled from the truck bed. "Come on, boy."

Bing gagged. "Bear gas is disgusting."

She giggled.

The doglike omnivore descended to the ground next to the dumpster, glanced around, and trotted toward Bing's hiding spot.

Bing moved backward toward the barn.

Crusher slowed then inched closer.

The firefighter reached the barn door and disappeared. The bear stopped to scratch his belly then walked into the barn. A loud crash sounded from inside the building.

"Need help?" Kiki moved to the edge of the dump truck. Her shoulders tightened. Was he okay?

Bing raced out of the barn and into the farmyard. "I got this." He slipped into an old car and closed the door.

Crusher eventually emerged from the barn, bawling like a lost heifer.

"What'd you do to offend that animal?"

"He acts like I'm his mother." Bing rolled down the window a bit. "Bet he hates firefighters."

"He'll probably give up the chase."

The young bear wandered around the farm then disappeared.

A few minutes later, Bing stepped out of the old vehicle and climbed onto a tractor. "Looks like he's gone."

"You might try the dumpster," Kiki said. "Looks like Crusher wants to visit."

Bing jumped down on the opposite side from the bear, leaving the tractor between them. "If the guys at the station saw this, they'd be laughing harder than the monkeys at the Denver Zoo."

Kiki smiled. "You gonna tell them?"

"I'd never live it down."

"Thanks for giving me blackmail material." She laughed. "I'll jump down and distract him."

"Stay put. I'm a firefighter, and your safety's paramount."

"So is yours."

Bing trotted toward the dumpster. Crusher peeked around the tractor.

Kiki pounded on the cab roof. The bear looked at her. "Now's your chance. Jump in." Kiki yelled. "He's not going to want to go back in there."

The bear trotted around the farmyard then moved toward the trash container.

Bing heaved himself up onto the dumpster and slid in hands first. "If I die at the paws of this wild creature, just know that I love you."

She swallowed. Did he mean that, or was he simply caught up in the spur of the moment?

While Crusher sniffed around the trash receptacle, Kiki pawed through the junk in the dump truck's bed and located a broken shovel. Grabbing a bent metal bucket, she pounded them together like cymbals. If the bear was considering dumpster diving, she needed to thwart his plans.

Crusher sniffed the air then glanced in Kiki's direction before sauntering off like he had better things to do with his time than visit the Bell farm.

"It's clear. He's heading toward the road."

Bing climbed out of the trash receptacle, scoped out the bear's location, then helped Kiki down from the truck.

His ears turned red as he held her hand. "I was going to tell you I loved you later, but Crusher forced it out of me. Sorry, claiming my love from the floor of a dumpster is not very romantic."

She squeezed his hand. "Depends on who you ask."

He bent and kissed her on the cheek.

She'd never wash her face again.

Chapter Seven

Kiki followed the caravan of cars into the parking lot of the private resort owned by the bride's parents. High in the mountains, the log-built lodge enveloped by pine trees and rock outcroppings exuded a grandeur she could get used to. She met her partners at the front door.

Cassie handed out housing assignments. "All cabins have two bedrooms. Felicity and Ronnie, you're in Piñon, which is closest to the lodge. That should help with access to the kitchen. Kiki and I are in Conifer, and Camilla is in Walking Stick, which is the farthest from the lodge."

Camilla stomped her foot. "No, I'm not walking all over the place. I have to be closer to the lodge to fulfill my duties and help you all stay organized."

"Camilla, I thought you'd enjoy being closer to nature."

"Give it to Kiki. She can use it as an excuse to keep the bride's gown a secret."

Cassie sighed. "Kiki, do you mind?"

Kiki shook her head. "Not at all." Having a cabin to herself in the woods would be better than a strawberry sundae. No Camilla was the cherry on top.

"We need to park in the side parking lot behind the lodge."

Cassie motioned behind the building. "Let's get settled and convene in an hour in the great room to meet the wedding party and formulate a game plan."

The team moved to their cars. Cassie caught Kiki by the arm and pulled her aside. "Thanks for being a good sport about the cabin assignments. I wanted to share it with you. Camilla can be a force to be reckoned with sometimes."

Kiki shrugged. "As long as I don't have to cook this week, it will be vacation enough."

Kiki parked her car, grabbed her suitcase, and followed a dirt path a quarter mile from the lodge to a small log cabin enclosed in a grove of trees and bushes. Perfect. Alone from prying eyes would help her create a custom gown more efficiently, even if it meant lugging supplies. At least she would get her workout in.

Walking Stick Cottage boasted a front porch and back deck. She climbed the wooden steps, opened the door, and entered the main room. A nice-sized dining table took up most of the space in the middle of the room, with a love seat shoved into a corner. The kitchen nook included a small stove and mini fridge with a few cupboards on the walls. Clean and efficient worked for her. Two small bedrooms flanked each side of the great room.

She chose the room with a double bed. The bunk beds in the other room would have done nicely for her kids. She missed them already, and she'd only been gone a few hours. It was kind of Pastor and Mrs. Otero to step in and take care of them while she was gone. She'd set aside some of her earnings to pay them. They wouldn't want to take it, but she would still offer. Maybe she could purchase a gift card for dinner and a movie.

Kiki opened the back door to discover a hot tub. Score! It'd be worth keeping that one a secret from Camilla. Work all day, soak at night.

She made several trips from her car to her cottage, then joined her team in the main building.

Cassie began the meeting by introducing Jeanette Floyd, the mother of the bride.

"Welcome to our lodge. Please be seated." Dressed in a navy pantsuit, Mrs. Floyd commanded their attention. "Thank you for coming to our aid so suddenly. My new son-in-law deploys in a few weeks, and the happy couple wanted to exchange vows before he left."

Kiki sat in a rocking chair and propped her clipboard on her lap. Cassie and Camilla claimed the love seat while Felicity and Ronnie curled up in squishy armchairs.

Mrs. Floyd brushed her dark graying hair out of her eyes. "We have six days to put this event together. The wedding is Saturday. Then Weddings by Design has agreed to clean the lodge and cottages after the wedding."

Camilla interrupted. "Jeanette, I can take over."

"I'm sure you can, but always remember, I'm paying you. So please wait your turn."

Cassie placed her hand on Camilla's arm. "Shhh."

Kiki bent over her clipboard to hide a grin. She'd never seen Camilla put in her place.

Mrs. Floyd pointed to three young women sitting on the couch. "My daughter Edith is the bride."

Edith's smile stretched from ear to ear. A younger version of her mother, she radiated excitement and happiness. Kiki looked forward to working with her.

"My other daughter, Ava, is the maid of honor."

Ava's red hair and cheeky grin gave Kiki the impression that this daughter fought the status quo of the more well-to-do society.

Mrs. Floyd continued. "Edith's best friend is a bridesmaid. Meet Emma Mason." Emma's mousy brown hair and demure stature stood in stark contrast to the Floyd women.

The partners of Weddings by Design introduced themselves and shared their specialties.

Mrs. Floyd suggested breaking into groups. She wanted to focus her attention on Felicity and Ronnie but insisted Kiki work with the bride first. "Whatever gown you two come up with will need to be started today."

Kiki stood. "Agreed. Edith, is there another room we can work in?"

Edith sprang up. "Yes. A den down the hall."

Kiki followed her. "Tell me about the groom."

Inside the cozy den, Edith shut the door and spoke in a low tone. "His name is Liam James. My parents would prefer I marry a rising genius in the financial world rather than a soldier."

"But you love him. I'm sure you'll be happy."

"Can't imagine life without him. Maybe my parents will come around when we give them a couple of grandkids."

"I hear grand-sugars are fun."

Edith smiled. "They will make amazing grandparents."

Kiki pulled a blank piece of paper to the front of her clipboard. "Tell me about your dress."

"I'd like something simple but elegant with pearls. Lots of pearls."

Inwardly Kiki groaned. The sewing would keep her hopping.

Pearls meant late nights and early mornings. With her seamstress smile plastered on her face, she sketched out the bride's dream gown. Together they formulated a plan for fabric choices and fittings, agreeing to meet at Walking Stick to keep the gown a secret.

After meeting with each bridesmaid and the bride's mother, Kiki retreated to her cabin to check on patterns she'd brought with her to create the new garments. She could use skirt pieces from some of her original creations then draft new bodices for each lady for a custom fit. That would save a lot of time. What the bridal party didn't know wouldn't hurt them.

As she created sample muslin bodices for the clients, Cassie walked in.

"Cassie, you're as white as a snow-covered mountain peak." Kiki pulled out a chair from the table. "Have a seat."

Cassie sat. "She's done it."

"Iced tea?"

She nodded.

Kiki pulled two glasses from the cupboard, spooned tea mix into them, then filled them with ice and water. She handed one to Cassie. "What happened?"

Cassie took a sip. "Camilla signed me up as a guest on a local talk-radio show to advertise the business. It's on Friday."

Kiki took a seat across from her. "Why'd she do that?"

"She thinks it'd be good for me."

Kiki shook her head. "Forcing you to do something contrary to the way you're wired is dumb."

Cassie nodded. "I agree. To make matters worse, that's the day of the dress rehearsal and dinner. It upset Ronnie and Felicity."

"Can't blame them. What are you going to do?"

She rested her hands on the table. "Advertising the business sounds great, but I'll freeze up. It feels like she's trying to sabotage me."

"Maybe we can come up with an alternate plan."

"It gets worse."

Kiki groaned. Camilla and her ways. "What else did she sign you up for?"

"To speak at the Wednesday night newlyweds' class at the community church down the road."

Kiki's mouth dropped open. "You're not even married."

"Tell me about it." Cassie pulled her glass to her lips. "What can I tell a room of star-gazed sweethearts? How to remain single forever?"

"You and me both. There has to be a way to make this work for the business and keep you off center stage." It was one thing for Camilla to make Kiki's life miserable, but not sweet Cassie's. Felicity and Ronnie didn't deserve the added stress either. "Can we cancel the appointments?"

Cassie took a drink then set her glass on the table. "It's already on their websites."

"I'll figure something out if you can help me sew a bazillion pearls onto the bride's dress."

"I planned to help you anyway, but this will give us time to plot."

Kiki grinned at the thought of foiling Camilla's plans. Maybe the woman would learn to respect other people by asking permission first before volunteering them for events. "Perfect. What's up with the cleaning after the wedding?"

Cassie smiled. "Mrs. Floyd agreed to pay a nice sum for us to stay so they wouldn't have to arrange cleaning or do it themselves. The extra cash will be nice. I figure we can relax on Sunday from the wedding and do the cleanup on Monday."

"For sure."

Cash for shingles and wood. Cash to move the dream of owning her own wedding venue one step closer to reality. Cash from cleaning toilets and mopping floors to create a better future for her kids. She was grateful for the work even if it meant she would get home later than she would have wanted.

Cassie stood. "Most of my arrangements for limos, music, and decorations are finished. How can I help?"

"If you can find the bridal party and send them down, I'd like to have an earlier fitting with them."

Cassie moved to the door, then glanced back. "Camilla is all right most of the time. I don't know what's come over her."

"It's going to work out in your best interest. Don't worry about it. We've got your back."

Cassie nodded then left.

If it were up to Kiki, Camilla would have been fired a long time ago. She couldn't change the woman's narcissistic personality, but she could get creative with her responses to the office manager's demanding ways.

Let the games begin.

⌒

Bing climbed a ladder and addressed the crowd of volunteers, the late afternoon sun beating down on the Colorado prairie. "Thanks for coming out to help a single mother of two fulfill her dream of restoring this old barn. We have three team leaders: Henry is overseeing construction, Tressa and Jack are heading up decluttering the inside, and Pastor and Mrs. Otero are in charge of food and rest. Uncle Ben, will you please lead us in prayer before we begin?"

Pastor Otero removed his Rockies ball cap and bowed his head. "Lord, we thank You for this opportunity to help a sister in need. Please bless our efforts and keep us safe. Amen."

Bing divided the volunteers into groups based on their interests and skill level. He took his role as project manager seriously. He'd assembled a small group from the fire station, Kiki's church, and the neighbors. Though the volunteers would help at the site in the evenings and on the weekend, he was using his vacation days to work on the barn full-time until he returned to his job. He put most of the teens with Tressa and Jack. They'd have fun cleaning out the rest of the junk from the barn. The teenagers laughed and chatted as they entered the old building. Tressa barked orders like a boss, commanding each teen to sort clutter into piles of scrap metal, wood, and recycling.

Bing laughed. The apple didn't fall far from the tree. By now, Kiki should have arrived at her jobsite and set up shop, working on her projects. He admired a woman who stepped up to the plate.

He enjoyed the challenge of repurposing something old into something new and serviceable. A labor of love in two ways—the building and the heart of the woman whose hand he wished to win. He joined Henry's team to assess the foundation, walls, and roof.

Henry knelt by the north corner of the barn. "This section needs a few repairs, and I found another spot on the other side of the barn. Otherwise, the foundation is in good condition."

"Will it take long?"

"We'll finish before dark."

"That's the kind of news I like to hear."

Bing retrieved a wheelbarrow from the cargo bed of his truck. Behind the barn, he loaded farm tools and trash and added to the piles Tressa supervised. He needed the area clear because it had the easiest access to the roof. That done, he grabbed his ladder from the pickup and climbed onto the roof. The view of the Rockies, surrounding farms, and a never-ending blue sky distracted him. Next time he came up here, he'd bring a cup of coffee and sit.

Surveying the roof yielded better results than expected. A few shingles needed replacing, but overall it was in good shape. He planned on using materials onsite as much as he could, then pay for supplies himself as needed. Come to think of it, he could raid his farm too. He'd inherited troves of paint, lumber, and materials. The older generation of farmers never threw anything away. Ever.

With Kiki away, he should manage to pull the build off without her taking offense. She was a proud one and needed to pay her own way, from what he could tell. He respected that. Admired it, in fact.

Admired her.

After making a list of repairs, he climbed down and found two guys to help him. By nightfall they'd made sufficient progress to keep him happy.

As the workday ended, Bing joined the group assembled at the barn's front, when Jack tapped him on the shoulder. "Bing, what should we do with the Slug Bug shell?"

He laughed. "You found a Slug Bug in the barn?"

Jack nodded. "Come see." He led the way to a corner of the

almost empty barn where the front half of a '60s-era faded blue Volkswagen rested against the wall. "Scrap it?"

Bing scratched his head. "Let's put it on the side of the barn. Since it's devoid of a motor or parts, I have an idea. Might be eccentric but fun."

"Okay."

"If you run across any old barbeque grills, put them there too."

"Will do."

Jack waved the teens over. "We need to move this out. No scrap pile for this baby."

The youths pulled the shell from the wall, surrounded it, and carried it outside. Bing surveyed the emptying structure. How many tons of junk had they hauled out in a few hours? Kids were sure good these days.

He pulled a piece of paper and a pen from his shirt pocket and added fire-engine red paint to his list. His plans for the VW would surely impress Kiki. Especially if it meant she didn't have to cook. Maybe when he gave her a tour of their handiwork, he'd have his VW surprise ready for her. It would take planning, but he could pull it off. Sleep wasn't on the list either. After everyone left, he hauled out two broken water heaters, old ladders, and rustic boards.

Early the next morning, he drove a tractor to Kiki's and extricated two dilapidated tractors from the barn's back corner. Since he had no idea what she would want to do with them, he moved them out of sight. Tressa and Jack were staying with his aunt and uncle. He smiled when they drove into the yard, teens in tow. He needed a daily dose of Kiki's kids and his family.

Uncle Ben, Aunt Valerie, and Tressa grabbed paintbrushes

and rollers to paint the barn red with white trim. Traditional and classy.

Bing taught Jack how to use a grinder to smooth out rough spots on the VW shell. Might as well teach the kid a new skill and let him take charge of the surprise. Next came primer and paint.

Jack pulled up his face shield. "Why did you become a firefighter?"

Bing knelt and scanned the car front for any sharp spots they'd missed. "I like the extremes. Mopping in the station, then the alarm rings. The adrenaline rush from putting out a fire is addicting."

The young man wiped his brow. "Was your dad a firefighter?"

"Yes. It runs in my blood."

Jack checked to make sure the grinder remained plugged into the extension cord. "What about helping people?"

"That's why most people join the station. To serve." Bing ran his hand along the hood of the VW. "There's nothing like having someone grab my hand and say thank you for saving a life. I can live off those moments for weeks."

"I've been thinking about it as a career. Is riding in the fire truck kinda fun?"

Bing grinned. "Never gets old."

Jack held out his hand. "I hope you marry my auntie. You'd make a good dad."

He rubbed the back of his neck. In his thirties, the dream of a family had died like a smoldering ember. Now a young teen wanted him for a father. Moisture teased at the corner of his eyes.

Bing shook Jack's hand and enveloped him in a bear hug. "I hope so too. You'd be every man's dream of a son."

Chapter Eight

The howl of an animal in pain woke Kiki. She jolted and rolled off the bed, landing on the floor in a tangled web of sheets and blankets. Was a wild donkey warding off a cougar? She crawled to the wall then sidled up right next to the window. If something threatened an animal, maybe she could help.

She wiped her eyes then moved the curtain and peeked through the edge of the window. Illuminated in the shadow of the yard light stood Camilla, playing a bagpipe.

Except playing was not the operative word.

Foghorns made better music. At least that sound fit the setting of waves, water, and wind. Camilla's piece resembled a herd of goats attempting their first trombone lesson.

The woman removed her mouth from the blow stick. "Kiki, rise and shine. It's time to get back to the grind of sewing pearls on the wedding gown."

Kiki slid away from the window and glanced at the alarm clock. Five a.m. Her alarm was set to go off at six. Who was Camilla to tell her she needed to get up and begin stitching?

Footsteps echoed toward the front of the house. Kiki slid along the wall to the corner of the room.

Camilla pounded on the window. "Kiki, get up. Now!"

At their business meeting yesterday, no one mentioned a five o'clock wake-up call.

The office manager hit the side of the cabin as she made her way along the building, culminating with a rousing kick on the front door. She jiggled the doorknob.

Kiki slipped into the main room. Last night she'd buttoned up the cabin tighter than a high-collared shirtwaist from the Victorian era. Good thing too.

Camilla knocked on the front window. "Get up, or you'll be sorry."

If Camilla's screams reached the main lodge, Weddings by Design would be sent packing. They couldn't afford to lose the contract. Kiki couldn't afford to let Camilla win. If Camilla wanted to play summer camp, Kiki would gladly oblige.

A few minutes later, the world's most annoying office manager left. Kiki crawled back in bed, plotting her revenge. When the alarm sounded, she rose and prepared for the day, then stitched pearls on the wedding dress until she joined her partners and the wedding party for breakfast in the lodge at eight.

After breakfast, Kiki spoke with Ava in a corner of the great room. "I need some help."

Ava tossed her red hair over her shoulder. "Of course. What can I do?"

Kiki filled her in on Camilla's talk-radio appointment and her disrespect of Cassie's dislike for being in the limelight. "Is there any way we can get Camilla out of cell phone range on Friday afternoon?"

"Maybe. I know a mountain road accessible by Jeep that holds some possibilities."

"She'd need to get there without any of my partners."

Ava picked a piece of lint off her skirt. "After her bagpipe solo this morning, the bridal party would be happy to assist you."

Kiki winked. "I have a plan for that too."

"Good. My mother wouldn't stand for a repeat of her theatrics."

"Camilla takes a fancy to firefighters."

Ava's eyes widened, and then she giggled. "Leave it to me. This is going to be rich."

"Can you make sure she leaves by one thirty Friday afternoon?"

"My mother can."

"Perfect. Bring her back around four."

"Will do."

"Is there an animal feedstore nearby?"

If Ava considered that a strange request, she didn't show it. "Five miles west. Right on the highway."

"Thank you."

Camilla's voice screeched across the great room. "Felicity, if you think this is a professional groom's cake, you'd better rebake. Crooked lines, bleeding icing, fondant stiffer than a boulder. Pathetic."

"Thanks, Ava." Kiki turned. "I'd better throw some water on the fire."

Ava nodded. "Good luck."

"Oh, one more thing. I love to watch birds. Would it be okay to hang a couple of environmentally friendly birdfeeders in the trees?"

"Sure."

"Thanks."

Kiki walked past the main table where Camilla's laptop

displayed two windows. One with a marketing proposal and another with event planning. Only problem—they weren't for Weddings by Design. Not only was the woman hard to get along with, but she seemed to be stealing clients from the business, and all on company time. The screen faded dark as the machine automatically shut down from lack of use.

Kiki sucked in a breath then joined her friends. "Felicity, dear, this is the best groom's cake I've ever seen. You're exceptional at your job."

Camilla stomped her foot. "Who are you to interrupt our conversation?"

"Please keep your voice down," Kiki hissed. "If you keep this up, we'll lose this contract."

The office manager lowered her voice. "I'll get you for this."

"No doubt you will. But in the meantime, we have a wedding to plan."

Camilla turned on her heel like a drill sergeant. She approached Ronnie. "What are you making? It smells like dirty laundry."

Blood rushed to Kiki's temples.

Ronnie closed her eyes. "Coconut curry lentil soup for lunch."

Camilla gagged. "Yuck."

Ronnie exhaled and returned to chopping vegetables.

Cassie carried dirty dishes from the table to the sink. "Cousin, it smells delicious. Maybe you should apologize for offending the ladies from the firm."

"Well, I never." She spat out the words. "I'm just trying to make things perfect for the bride."

Kiki filled the sink with water. "There's a big difference between perfection and good enough."

Camilla stormed out of the building, slamming the door behind her.

Cassie shivered. "She's going to get us fired. I'm trying to help her. She's turned her life around for the better. Hopefully her personality will catch up soon."

Felicity draped her arm over Cassie's shoulder. "Maybe she didn't sleep much last night."

Kiki shut off the water and turned to her colleagues. "I have some concerns. At the office, I saw Camilla compiling a customer base, and I couldn't tell if it was for our company. Then when I walked past the table just now, her laptop showed a marketing proposal and an events planning document that weren't ours."

Cassie looked around at her friends. "I'll keep an eye on her and report back to you."

"Fair enough." Ronnie placed the knife on the cutting board. "We need to keep her away from the family."

"How?" Kiki pulled a dishcloth out of the drawer. Camilla was everywhere. Like a bad smell.

Felicity picked up a small offset spatula. "We can send her on errands to Denver."

"That would work. It'd take all day." Ronnie tossed the vegetables in the pot. "Maybe I don't have some exotic ingredients for the wedding dinner that I can't make do without."

Kiki laughed. "If we send her to Denver today for food, she can run back down tomorrow for a scavenger hunt for lace while battling metro traffic. I'll even pitch in for her lunch."

Cassie swallowed. "On Friday morning she'll need to make a deposit for me at the bank in Loveland. We do have to pay our bills."

Felicity nodded. "We're not going to let you speak alone at the service for the newlywed group tonight either."

"Agreed." Kiki washed a plate. "What should we do?"

Felicity waved the spatula. "Ronnie and I've been discussing that. We think we should teach the class how to make coconut curry lentil soup and homemade cupcakes. I can share Bible verses as we cook."

Cassie sighed. "I'll introduce you. We can tell Camilla that much."

"Brilliant." Ronnie stirred the soup. "Now, what about the talk show on Friday?"

Kiki placed the clean plate in the dish rack. "Ava and company will take Camilla away, and our two expert chefs can discuss cooking. That should draw a crowd."

A smile raced across Cassie's face. "I have the best friends any gal could ask for. You three make coming to work so worth it."

Ronnie stirred as she added seasonings to the pot. "Feeding a crowd is a topic newlyweds would appreciate."

After she finished the dishes, Kiki pulled Cassie aside. "By the way, which side of Conifer Cabin are you on?"

"The south side. Camilla's room faces north. Why do you ask?"

"Just curious as to the layout of the cabins. Wonder how old they are?"

Cassie grinned. "I overheard Mrs. Floyd say everything was built early in the twentieth century."

"Old places are so interesting." Kiki left her pals to their duties in the lodge. She drove along the road Ava mentioned, located the feedstore, made her purchases, then returned to the Floyd property. She spent the remainder of the morning working on the bridesmaid dresses.

At lunchtime, Kiki carried the shopping bags from the feed-store and hid behind the trees until Cassie and Camilla entered the lodge. She pulled out two large birdfeeders and hung them in the tree next to Camilla's window. While not a bagpipe, the menu should collect the interest of nature. Preferably critters to serenade Camilla in the predawn hours.

After the midday meal, Ronnie sent Camilla to Denver with a list of herbs, spices, and other ingredients needed to tweak the wedding banquet. With Camilla occupied until bedtime, Felicity, Ronnie, and Cassie attended the newlyweds' gathering while Kiki remained at Walking Stick, stitching pearls onto the train of the bridal gown.

Cassie joined her after the midweek service. "Kiki, you should have seen the newlyweds. They loved Felicity and Ronnie."

Kiki handed her a needle and thread. "And you too."

She shrugged. "I guess."

They chatted and sewed until ten, when Cassie received a text from Camilla saying she had returned. As Kiki locked up after her friend's departure, she hoped Camilla's business errands by day and her nature visits by night would render the office manager busy and tired enough for extra naps.

One could only hope.

⌒

Bing swept the cement floor with a push broom. Tressa and Jack strolled into the barn joking about something in a language only teenagers understood.

"How're my favorite teens?"

Tressa slipped on her work gloves. "We're up."

Bing laughed. "Forgot you were on summer hours since school got out."

Jack yawned. "At least I got the last bowl from my favorite cereal box."

"That's a win."

"We're going to get rid of those dead office chairs." Tressa pointed to a pile of junk in a battered stall. "Jack, let's race them across the floor, through the side door, and down the vehicle ramp."

Jack wiped his eyes. "Winner doesn't have to do dishes tonight."

"Deal."

After pulling two heavy wheeled chairs out of the pile, they lined them up.

"Bing, you be the judge." Tressa dusted off her seat then gave her younger brother a superior stare. "That way, there's no cheating."

Bing chuckled. "What if I want to join in?"

"Suit yourself. You'll just end up last."

Youngsters. He found a chair without a back and took his place at the starting line. "Ready, set, go."

Tressa and Jack scooted themselves toward the door. The wheels on Bing's chair refused to move forward. Rather than succumb to Tressa's prediction, he turned the chair around. Pushing hard, he looked over his shoulder, directing his way to the ramp. The kids had a good head start.

Oxford raced in front of him, hampering his progress. "Ox, move."

He did. Right to the edge of the ramp, where he stretched out for the beginnings of what looked like a long nap.

Jack reached the ramp right after the dog. He bent over and lifted Ox's head. "Excuse me, puffy puppers! I have to beat my sister."

The dog shifted slightly, leaving room for one chair to pass. Tressa followed her brother but failed at beating him down the ramp. Jack whooped and hollered while Bing scuttled around the dog and coasted down the ramp backward. When the wheels hit the dirt, he crashed, landing on his back.

Jack doubled over laughing.

Oxford barked as he raced down the ramp then pelted his human with kisses.

Tressa giggled. "Jack won the first round."

Bing rolled over and stood. "That he did. Round two. I need to redeem myself."

They raced up the ramp and back to the stall to pull more dilapidated chairs from the pile. Round two went to Tressa while Jack won round three. Bing took the honors for four, but Jack sealed the battle by winning the fifth and final contest.

Jack heaved his chair onto his head and walked toward the dumpster. "Who would keep so much dead office equipment?"

Tressa followed him. "You make a good point, little bro."

After they stowed away the chairs, the racers returned to the stall.

"Looks like everything else needs hauling out with a wheelbarrow." Bing indicated where the hand vehicle waited. "Think you can handle what's left?"

"Yup." Tressa drove it into the stall. "I wonder how Auntie is fairing with that bossy woman. What's her name?"

"Camilla." Jack tossed a conglomeration of used baling twine and tin cans into the cart. "She's an interesting one. The kind of woman a guy needs to run from."

Bing pulled an old window from the stack leaning against the wall. Smart kid. "You're wise beyond your years."

Aunt Valerie joined them and swept the floor. The kids cleaned out the stall then kicked down the dilapidated fence partition, widening the open space, while Bing climbed into the loft and ripped out a broken window. The replacement window was slightly larger, so he chiseled against the frame until it fit. After securing it in place, he foamed and caulked the cracks. At lunchtime, they returned to the house for tacos, salad, and fruit.

After the meal, Bing pushed back his chair from the dining room table. "Auntie, that was delicious. You spoil us."

She smiled. "You're worth spoiling."

A green SUV pulled into the driveway and parked by the house. Jack walked to the window and peered out. "I think it's that Camilla person."

Valerie stared at Bing. "Hide."

"Why?" Bing rested his arm on the table. "She's annoying, but I can deal with it."

She pointed her finger at him. "You're not going to be a confirmed bachelor-till-the-rapture. You and Kiki belong together. This woman means trouble for your eligible hubby status. She wants you for herself."

Camilla pounded on the back door. "Hello, I need to pick up some lace for Kiki."

His aunt stood. "Now."

Jack raced to Bing and pushed him under the table. "The tablecloth will hide most of you. I'll sit in your chair."

"Why hide?" He saw no point. He'd dealt with Camilla more than they had.

Jack insisted. "You have to let us help you marry our aunt."

Outvoted, he slipped farther under the table and sat on the floor.

Aunt Valerie's phone buzzed. "A text from Kiki."

Tressa's shoes disappeared from view then returned with Camilla.

"Mrs. Otero, this is my aunt's coworker." Tressa sounded annoyed.

"Yes, I just received Kiki's text about lace in her stash. Tressa. Camilla. Follow me. She keeps it in a bedroom."

Jack pulled up the tablecloth. "Betcha anything my aunt sent her down here on a wild goose chase to keep her out of the partners' business."

Bing chuckled.

"Jack, pumpkin, we need you to move some boxes." His aunt's voice rang out. "We're in the sewing room."

Jack sighed, dropped the cloth, and joined the search.

Bing adjusted his seating position. Over forty and hiding under a table. This was not his idea of a fun experience. Still, his aunt always had his best interest in mind.

Camilla's loud voice echoed to him. "I'll just run to the kitchen and grab a glass of water for myself. You all are much better at finding what she wants. You know her organizational system."

Footsteps echoed close, then Camilla's brown heels clipped to the kitchen. Several cupboard doors opened and shut. The faucet turned on and off. A minute later, Camilla returned to the sewing room.

"Score." Tressa's shouts of triumph filled the farmhouse. "Found it."

The search team filtered into the dining room.

"Thanks for your help." Camilla's heels stopped next to the dining table. "Wedding prep keeps us hopping."

Jack's foot kicked backward, touching Bing's leg. "How's our auntie?"

"She's doing everything I tell her, which means she'll be finished on time."

His aunt coughed. "I suspect she can manage on her own just fine."

Camilla shuffled her feet. "Why's Bing's pickup outside?"

"I drive it occasionally."

"You?"

"Yes, me. He's my nephew."

"I didn't know that," Camilla cooed. "Is he here?"

Auntie Valerie moved toward Camilla, and they walked toward the kitchen. "If he is, I doubt you'd be able to find him."

Tressa giggled.

Jack's feet appeared by the window.

The back-porch door squeaked open and shut.

"She's walking to her car." He pulled the tablecloth up. "You can get up now."

Good thing too. Bing's legs cramped, and his neck hurt. He crawled out from under the table and stood, stretching his muscles.

Auntie Valerie returned, hands on hips, and stopped inches from him. "You'd better propose to Kiki soon, or I'll do it for you."

Chapter Nine

Friday morning Camilla rested her head on the couch's arm-rest in the great room of the lodge. "I'm exhausted. Between running to town every day and the wildlife that howl, chirp, or claw at something outside my bedroom window, I've not been able to sleep properly."

Cassie handed her an envelope. "Sorry, dear, but we all knew it would be a stressful week. I need you to run to town and make a deposit at the bank."

Kiki bent over to adjust the strap on her shoe, hiding her smile. Wildlife enjoying the birdfeeders had accomplished their intended purpose—no more bagpipe screeching in the predawn hours.

Camilla pulled herself off the couch. "I can tell I'm not appre-ciated for my leadership skills. Run for this, run for that. This is stupid."

Ronnie opened the oven door. "Don't forget it's payday. If you don't make that deposit, none of us will get paid. Including you."

Camilla rolled her eyes. "You're all plotting against me."

Cassie patted her on the arm. "No, Cousin. Mrs. Floyd paid her bill, and we need to meet payroll. You excel at your job. You're already done with your part. The rest of us need to finish last-minute things before the rehearsal dinner tonight and the wedding tomorrow."

"Since you put it that way." Camilla waved as she left the lodge.

Felicity smoothed frosting on the top layer of the wedding cake. "I'm almost done. What time are we leaving for the radio station?"

Cassie glanced at her itinerary. "Around one thirty. Edith will make sure Camilla gets into her car. As soon as they drive off, we can head to the station."

After lunch, Kiki held the door open as Edith, Ava, and Emma led Camilla from the lodge to Edith's Jeep. "Camilla, we need you for a photo shoot."

Camilla stopped. "I planned to stay here and supervise to ensure everything is finished before the rehearsal dinner this evening."

Edith unlocked the vehicle. "My mother will deal with any last-minute details."

"No."

Ava winked. "It involves a firefighter."

Camilla's eyes glinted. "Bing?"

Emma opened the back door. "I don't know if that's his name, but he's handsome."

Edith snapped her seat belt into place. "Let's go see Bing or whatever his name is."

Camilla climbed into the back seat with Ava while Emma sat in the front. Kiki waved as they left.

A few minutes later, the partners of Weddings by Design drove to the radio station in Cassie's minivan. A two-story wooden building with a steeply slanted roof so typical in the mountains greeted them. Surrounded by high peaks, the usual rock outcroppings, and a blue sky, the renowned C. C. Gil had chosen a beautiful location to conduct one of the country's most famous talk-radio programs. A receptionist escorted them down a hall to a studio. She directed them to take a seat at a high-topped round table.

Kiki noted the sound-absorbent squares that hung on the walls. The consoles held more controls and knobs than she would know what to do with.

A middle-aged man, wearing a partially unbuttoned shirt that revealed more hair on his chest than on his head, entered the room. "Welcome. I'm Mike, the producer. Please put on the headphones and make sure the microphone is positioned in front of your mouth."

C.C. joined the group, her red dress showing off her lithe form, her hair perfectly coiffed. She smiled at the partners, exposing a flawless set of pearly whites against her caramel skin. She was stunning.

Kiki covered her tea-stained teeth with a hand. How was she supposed to discuss topics related to the bridal industry when her own appearance left room for improvement? She made a mental note to pick up teeth-whitening strips from the drugstore. She grabbed the headset and placed it on her head, checking to make sure the mike rested at attention in front of her mouth. Not that she had anything brilliant to add to the conversation.

Mike provided instructions then slipped into the control room next to the studio. He put on a headset and did a sound check.

Kiki watched C.C. for clues as she listened to the theme

music playing in her ears.

Their host opened the show. "Welcome, listeners. Today we have a special treat for you. The four partners of Weddings by Design from Loveland, Colorado, are in the studio to discuss weddings. Please welcome Felicity Edwards, Ronnie Fare, Cassie Blackthorn, and Kiki Bell. Ladies, why did you get in the wedding business?"

"Cassie here. I excel at organization." Cassie adjusted her headset. "Years ago, I attended a friend's wedding. Her planner quit at the last minute. The bride's deer-in-the-headlights look said it all. So I jumped in to help, and the rest is history." She raised her eyebrows, then the sides of her mouth pulled down.

Kiki gave her a double thumbs-up signal. That must have cost her to step out of her comfort zone and into the fire.

"We've been best friends for years. During one of our ladies' nights out, we tossed around the idea of starting a wedding business." Felicity smiled. "Rather than enjoying dinner and a movie, we spent the night writing out business plans on napkins and receipts from our handbags."

Ronnie laughed. "I remember that night. You all encouraged me when I suggested creating delicious dinners, appetizers, and specialty coffees. I was so excited I couldn't even sleep."

"Me too," Kiki interjected. "For me, it was about having a creative outlet to design gowns, veils, and headpieces without corporate management breathing down my neck."

Right now, the only hot breath down her neck was Camilla's, and she was off on some unknown adventure deep in the mountains out of cell range. That did provide some satisfaction.

C.C. glanced at her notes. "What trends do you see in the

current bridal industry?"

The partners looked at each other. Cassie raised her hand. "We use social media to interact with potential clients. Most of the time they bring us their ideas, and we figure out a way to implement them."

"Food is a common denominator in all societies. It's one thing that binds us together," Ronnie commented. "I love trying new recipes the bridal party requests for their dinners."

"Desserts as well." Felicity leaned forward. "Once I baked a wedding cake for a Brazilian couple. They held their wedding in a two-bedroom apartment overlooking a lake. They knew how to entertain, and it was amazing how many people they crammed into such a small space."

C.C. interjected, "What fun."

"Fun and heartwarming."

Mike waved at C.C. from the control booth. After a quick commercial break, they accepted calls from listeners.

C.C. smiled into the microphone. "Hi, Catherine from Greeley. What's your question?"

"How much time do you need to come up with a plan?"

Ronnie nodded. "We've pulled off an event with four attendants on each side in as little as two weeks. And I think our longest contract was just under two years. Most are in the six- to nine-month range."

Their host punched up another call. "Aria from Cripple Creek. What's on your mind?"

The questions kept coming, fast and furious, until C.C. directed a call to Kiki, who up to this point had little to say.

C.C. rested her arms on the table. "Our next guest has

questions for our seamstress."

Bing's voice floated over the airwaves. "Thanks for taking my call. Kiki, what is the worst project you've ever dealt with?"

Kiki swallowed. How did he know she'd be on this particular program? "I enjoy most sewing projects. Recently, I pinned the pattern pieces for a beautiful wedding gown on an expensive cut of silk then left for the day. The next time I returned to the office, I discovered a car bumper on my worktable. Whoever painted the bumper silver put some cardboard down but not enough. They sprayed silver paint onto the uncut gown. That was a costly oversight that tried my patience."

Cassie's face grew pale. Kiki's heart thumped in her ears. Did she just offend Cassie?

C.C. cleared her throat. "How frustrating. Did you ever find out who did that?"

Kiki shook her head. "Nope."

Bing whistled. "Wow. Question number two. If a bear chased you and you dove into a dumpster, would you reciprocate terms of endearment if you thought your life was in danger?"

"Yes. Most definitely."

"What if it wasn't in danger?"

Kiki closed her eyes. "I'd probably find a different way of doing that."

"But you would definitely say it?"

"Yes, but I think you already know that."

"I do. Your eyes twinkle."

She opened her eyes but avoided her partners'. The last thing she wanted them to know about was her growing relationship with Bing. He'd told her he loved her from the bottom of a dumpster, and she'd just blabbered to the world her love for him. Why couldn't things be more romantic? Dinner, roses, and a stroll along the Riverwalk under a canopy of brilliant stars?

Quizzical expressions from Felicity, Ronnie, and Cassie floated across the table.

She raised her hands and shrugged. Maybe if she acted like she had no idea about the caller and his unusual discussion topics, they wouldn't catch on.

Bing's voice held tones of joy. "One final thought. Your dream is in progress. If you build it, they will come."

What was he up to?

The theme music signaled the close of the program. "What an unusual way to end, but a good reminder to all of us." C.C. glanced at her notes. "Work on your dreams. Build them." She raised her head and smiled at the partners. "Thank you, Felicity, Ronnie, Cassie, and Kiki, for an insightful glimpse at creating beautiful weddings for your clients. This closes out our program for this week."

The Off-Air sign lit, and the women removed their headsets.

C.C. shook their hands. "Thank you so much for coming on the program."

Kiki's voice squeaked. "I'm such a huge fan of yours. Can we get a photo with you to hang in our offices?"

She chuckled. "Of course."

Mike played photographer as the partners flanked C.C. for a picture. Kiki smiled through closed lips. No need for a permanent record of her tea-stained smile.

As they left the studio, Cassie pulled Kiki aside. "Why didn't you tell me about the bumper?"

"I didn't know who did it and decided to bide my time and figure it out." Kiki pulled her sunglasses out of her purse. "You can tell how good my sleuthing skills are."

"The bumper on my van was so scratched and rusty that Camilla offered to paint it for me."

Kiki slid her glasses on. "I suspected she instigated the paint-on-silk event. I know she's your kin and all, so I kept quiet."

Cassie placed her hand on Kiki's arm. "But what good does that do our friendship if we hold frustration in and don't resolve issues?"

"True. Sometimes it's best to take one for the team and keep quiet. However, I'm not going to lie. Camilla has gotten on my nerves quite a bit."

"Promise me you'll at least tell me if something affects the business. Or our relationship."

Kiki nodded. "Will do."

"Good. She challenges team morale. I'll talk to her."

Maybe Camilla would take a positive pill every day after Cassie confronted her. She was undoubtedly qualified to be an office manager. Her services were excellent, but she lacked people skills. She also wanted a certain fireman, and if Camilla had heard the radio program, she'd be furious. Who knows what kind of revenge she'd plot?

Chapter Ten

Edith and Liam wed under the Colorado sun in the meadow behind the lodge. Kiki and her partners watched the beautiful ceremony from the back row. Edith's gown with lace sleeves and an A-line skirt fit her perfectly. The bridesmaids wore floor-length dresses constructed with lace over chiffon.

Kiki wiped her eyes. Weddings were special but emotionally draining. *Always a bridesmaid. Forever a wedding planner.* Over the years, her friends married and moved on. How many dresses had she purchased or stitched for herself? She had her family and a role to play at Weddings by Design. At least for a while. Kids grew up and moved on. She'd adjust accordingly, but she wasn't ready to give Tressa away or make a groom's tie for Jack.

After photos and appetizers, Ronnie's delicious dinner and Felicity's beautiful wedding cake not only satisfied the guests, but Cassie booked appointments for several new clients. Kiki pitched in and served food, carried dirty dishes, and even stitched a guest's button that had come loose. Busy and fulfilling, but she missed her kids. Texting and calling weren't the same as sitting around the farmhouse kitchen table swapping stories. She wanted to go home but had a couple more days left in the mountains to wrap up the contract.

On a return trip to the kitchen, Edith, Ava, and Emma cornered Kiki.

Edith hugged her. "Thanks so much for making my gown. I love it."

Kiki smiled. "You're welcome. You look lovely."

Ava winked. "Want to know how our trip with Camilla went?"

"Of course."

Emma laughed. "We took her out of cell range to a shack nestled between two mountains where an eccentric fireman lives. He's the same age as Methuselah!"

Ava's eyes twinkled. "Camilla couldn't wait to meet him."

Edith adjusted her veil. "As soon as we stepped inside the hut, Fireman Dave kept Camilla right beside him for several hours telling her all about the glories from his fire days back in Indiana and how his kidneys and heart don't work so well now."

"He gave an organ recital." Ava coughed. "You should have seen Camilla's face after she realized she'd be spending her afternoon in a geriatric unit."

Kiki chuckled. "Thanks for doing that."

Edith touched her arm. "After her bagpipe recital, it was the least we could do."

Mrs. Floyd claimed the young women for pictures, so Kiki slipped out the front door and located an empty bench under an enclosure of aspens. After kicking off her shoes, she curled up to soak in some quiet. In the silence, she contemplated the words from Psalm 139. Just like when a bride adorns herself in a beautiful gown that is hemmed and finished, so God encircles his children with His presence and care. Where can a believer go on earth or in the heavens that God is not already there?

Nowhere.

God is in the hemming business. His stitches are perfect. While her imperfect hems did the job, they also served as a reminder of the Lord's omnipotent presence and love.

"Aha, I finally found you." Camilla's voice broke the calm. "I know what you were up to yesterday."

"Come again?" Kiki swung her legs off the bench and searched for her shoes.

"You tried to ruin my appointment for the business on the radio program."

Kiki kept her silence while she slid her feet into her heels. No need to acknowledge the obvious. Camilla's plan to humiliate Cassie on national radio didn't sit well with her.

"You think you're so smart. Well, you're not. I'm the best at my job. Quit trying to manipulate my hard work."

Kiki sighed. She had no energy for yet another battle with the office manager.

Camilla continued. "Furthermore, Bing is mine, so hands off. I'm prettier, more intelligent, and have an incredible personality."

Kiki stood and raised her hands. "Fine. He's all yours. You love drama." She turned to walk away. "Enjoy your theatrics with someone else."

Camilla grabbed her arm in a viselike grip.

Kiki spoke through gritted teeth. "Take your hands off me."

"I know your type. Manipulative, sneaky." She shoved Kiki's arm away. "If you so much as look at Bing, I'll start my own wedding business and take your clients."

Wowzers.

"Shall I tell Cassie? Especially after she's done so much for you?"

Camilla stepped so close their noses touched. "He's mine. Lay off." With a turn, she disappeared from the grove of aspens.

Kiki sat on the bench. She was done. Done with Weddings by Design. Done with Camilla. The hassle wasn't worth it.

What about Bing? Perhaps she needed to keep her "always a bridesmaid" status intact.

She bent over and pulled the hem of her long skirt up enough to wipe the tears she could no longer hold in check.

No. She needed to move on and start a new career. Maybe she could get a job in a restaurant. Keep working on the barn until she could host smaller weddings and events. With her love life and brides-maid gigs as extinct as the dinosaur bones in the Denver Museum of Nature and Science, her old maid status solidified her plans.

Over the next two days, Kiki avoided Camilla as best she could, while wearing a seamstress smile in the partners' presence. She pulled her weight with the cleanup. Then on Monday she packed up her equipment and suitcase. Time to head for home.

Home. Her family.

By Friday, she'd hand in her notice.

Peace at last.

Someone knocked on the back door of her cabin. She sucked in a breath. The last thing she wanted was another encounter with Camilla. She peeked out the window.

Bing.

Holding a pizza box and a small cooler.

What was he doing here?

He grinned as Kiki opened the door. She'd never looked more beautiful.

She raised an eyebrow. "How did you know where to find me?"

"My auntie. She's pretty determined to get us together." Heat sprinted up his neck and to his ears. Maybe she wouldn't notice.

A look of alarm rushed over her face. "Are my kids okay?"

"Having a good time. Though they miss you."

She stepped aside. "Please come in. I'm packing up and ready to go home."

He raised the cooler. "Thought you'd like to have a bite to eat. I came to help you load up. Parked on the other side of the property, out of sight."

She sighed. "Thanks. I've been avoiding a work pal. Planned to find a drive-through and grab a sandwich for the trip home."

Bing placed the pizza on the table. "Five guesses, and they all start with the name Camilla."

The corners of her mouth fought to create a smile. "Nailed it."

Camilla made a pest of herself at the fire station. He could only imagine the level of stress working with her full-time could cause. Why the partners didn't fire her was beyond him.

"Take a quick lunch break." He pulled out a chair for her. "You'll feel better after you've been fed and watered."

She chuckled. "Spoken like a true farmer." She grabbed the cooler. "Let's eat out back."

He followed with the pizza as she led the way to the back deck and the picnic table. "Nice setup. Pines, aspen, wildlife. Hot tub. Bet you spent every second you could out here."

Kiki sat on one side of the table. "Tried to. It worked well for hand sewing on small pieces of my project."

He handed her several napkins and a piece of pizza. "Sorry, the restaurant only offered napkins. No plates."

She shrugged. "I don't have to cook. It's perfect."

"Perfect indeed. Great setting." He opened the cooler. "Lunch with the most beautiful woman in the world. Now, what else did you do out here?"

She unrolled several napkins and placed them in her lap. "Unfortunately, most of my work kept me inside. Loved coming out here for breaks. Enjoyed the hot tub."

He stared at it. It'd be great to relax in there after his crazy schedule renovating an old barn. "Care if I soak in there after we eat?"

Kiki chuckled. "Go for it." She helped herself to a tea from the cooler. "I have to finish packing anyway."

It made him feel good that she felt comfortable enough with him to grab her beverage. "So, about that radio program."

Her face turned many shades of pink. "Who told you I'd be on the show?"

"Tressa spilled the beans. She can't keep a secret very well." He chuckled. "Love that girl."

She bit into her pizza. Was she avoiding discussing her radio proclamation? After waiting a few seconds for her to respond, he ate a few bites. Maybe she needed to relax before he popped the question.

She opened her tea as he grabbed another from the cooler, pulled the tab, and took a gulp.

It was no use.

Bing plopped his pizza slice on top of the box. "I love you. Do you love me?"

Kiki nodded.

His stomach turned over like a fire engine racing down a hill.

"Can I kiss you?" He could reach in and kiss her like they did in the movies, but it seemed more fitting to ask this lovely woman for her permission.

She froze then nodded again.

He moved to her side of the table and put his arm around her. His heart beat faster than the wings of a hummingbird. She'd said yes.

He bent over, slowly memorizing this moment for all of eternity. His nose only centimeters from hers. Their lips almost touching. This would be one of the best moments of his life. He just knew it.

"Kiki," Camilla screamed from the front door. "I know you're in there."

Kiki groaned.

"Woman, I know my man is here. I can smell his scent. If you so much as try and take him away from me, I'll see to it that you'll forever regret thinking he belonged to you."

"Is she always this pleasant?" Bing whispered.

Kiki nodded, pulled away, and tossed his slice in the pizza box. "You'd better hide."

Camilla banged on the door. "Let me in. Gonna stop this once and for all."

Bing looked around. "Where?"

Kiki threw his open tea into the cooler and slammed the lid down. "Jump into the hot tub."

The front door burst open, rattling the windows like empty railroad cars dashing across the prairie.

"We've got seconds." Kiki snatched a broom leaning against the deck's railing, raced to the hot tub, and opened the side farther away from the back door. "Hop in and keep the lid propped up with this. She won't be able to see you."

He resisted. "I should just tell her to go away."

Kiki shook her head. "I'm not up for all that drama. Please?"

He wouldn't push the issue. "Okay."

He had to admit, the lid's positioning would make it hard for anyone to see him unless they walked over to the tub. He handed Kiki his phone and wallet, then slid in. Water seeped through his clothes. Warmth soaked his tired body as he rested his head on the ledge, avoiding the broom. This would be interesting.

The back door slammed open. "Where are you?" Camilla's voice echoed against the hot tub. "There you are."

Kiki's voice sounded angry. "How dare you burst into my cabin like a mad bull?"

Bing covered his mouth with his hand, suppressing a belly laugh. Comparing Camilla to a bull. Well, if the shoe fit. . .

Camilla stomped her foot. "Where. Is. Bing?"

"Why don't you ask him?"

"Where'd you get that pizza?"

"Venus," Kiki said. "It's hot enough there to bake pies."

Camilla blew out a frustrated breath. "You're not even remotely funny."

"And your point?" The back door creaked open. "You need to go."

"Not until I rescue my hunk of a man from the likes of you."

Footsteps echoed away from Bing's hiding spot then closer.

Camilla kicked the side of the tub. Her voice sounded away from him. "You got him in the hot water?"

Bing's eyes widened. So much for relaxing. He slid to the cover, ready to duck underneath if needed. He could hold his breath for a minute or so while he came up with a plan to put

Camilla in her place.

Kiki snorted. "Camilla, do you store spare men in a hot tub?"

"You keep your pins and needles off him. He's mine."

Camilla's voice drew closer.

Quietly, he slid beneath the half of the closed lid. He'd give Kiki a few seconds to get Camilla away from the tub. When he couldn't hold his breath any longer, he pushed his head out of the water, exhaling through clamped lips.

Camilla and Kiki sounded farther away. Someone else had joined them.

"Camilla, I could hear you from our cabin."

Kiki coughed. "Cassie, she's demanding I produce Firefighter Bing."

He smiled as he heard his name pronounced formally.

"I don't see any firemen around here," Cassie said. "Come on, Camilla. I want to go home."

"I need to find my man."

"You can find him after we get home." Cassie's tired voice floated to him. "Then you can try the fire station. He's probably polishing trucks."

Footsteps moved away, and the front door shut.

Several minutes later, Kiki's head appeared next to the broom. "I watched until they left. Have you simmered enough?"

Bing shook his head and crawled out of the hot tub. Water dripped from him like a waterfall. So much for creating a romantic memory. "I'm sorry. This isn't turning out the way I wanted."

Kiki winked. "I think you were going to kiss me."

He wrapped his arms around her, bent down, and kissed her. It was hotter than a five-alarm fire.

Chapter Eleven

Bing led a blindfolded Kiki from the back seat of his aunt's car and past the Bell farmhouse, then steered her to a position right in front of the barn. His heart thumped faster than water coming out of an unattended fire hydrant. Would she be upset or happy at what he'd done?

He nodded at the crowd of Kiki supporters who had assembled for an impromptu barn party then whispered in her ear. "Just so you know, this was a community project, and a lot of people love you."

"Bing, what did you do, burn the barn down?"

"Not quite. You can take off the blindfold."

She did and stared at the grinning crowd. Many phones were videotaping the moment. People from her church, the kids' youth group, the few neighbors she knew, his aunt and uncle, the partners from Weddings by Design.

And Camilla.

Always Camilla.

Kiki's eyes wandered from the people to the barn behind them. She froze, then rubbed her eyes.

"What?"

Tressa and Jack raced forward. And always down for a

party—Oxford yapping happily on their heels.

Tressa waved her arms. "We fixed the barn for you."

"To help your dreams come true." Jack beamed.

Tressa nodded. "Well, mostly to help you pay for our college."

The crowd laughed.

Kiki enveloped the teens in a big hug. "How did you manage to keep this a secret?"

Jack grinned. "I did okay, but Tressa struggled. She wanted to drop hints all the time."

"Who plotted this?"

Jack kissed her on the cheek. "Bing got stuff rolling, and we wanted to do something about it. So did the Oteros."

"Thank you." Kiki released her kids then hugged everyone present.

Bing pulled her away from the group and led her inside while the crowd followed. "Come see the barn."

Her eyes widened. "Wowzers. This is amazing. Look at all that space."

Jack yelled, "Watch this." He flipped the switches by the door, and light filtered through upcycled farm gadgets turned light fixtures. "Isn't it cool?"

Kiki's eyes darted upward. Silence.

Was she angry that he'd spearheaded the renovation without her permission?

Bing tapped her shoulder. "Is it okay?"

"Okay?" She gazed at him. "It's wonderful."

Jack and Tressa slipped to either side of Kiki.

Tressa tugged at her arm. "Come on, Auntie. I want to give you a tour and tell you what each person did."

Kiki nodded and allowed herself to be pulled around by the teens.

Bing sighed. Kids. They had a right to recollect their impressions of the project and give her a detailed account of the week she missed.

Aunt Valerie slipped her arm through his. "She's pleased."

"I hope so." He glanced down at her. "Thanks for all your help with the teens and everything else you did."

She winked. "You're welcome. Anything to get you married off."

He chuckled. "This one is different. Real."

"Agreed."

Bing joined the men flipping burgers on the new grill Jack created from the VW Bug's front. Kiki and her kids reached the cooking area at the same time.

Jack's face lit up when he told his aunt about the grill project. "I did the welds that hold everything together. Don't look too close, 'cause they aren't very good."

Kiki reached in and planted a kiss on his forehead. "It's perfect. You are so clever."

Jack stood tall the rest of the evening from the power of his aunt's words. Bing appreciated her even more. Her devotion to her niece and nephew made him love her beyond words. The rest of the evening passed quicker than a fire truck headed to an emergency. It was like that whenever he was around her. Hopefully, she felt the same way.

Bing stayed until the very end. After the guests left, he walked around the barn with a large bouquet, looking for Kiki. When he entered from the back door, a rustle in the loft caught his attention. From his vantage point, he couldn't see who or what was up there. Probably critters. The Bells needed a barn cat.

A shadow crossed the front doors when Camilla moved into the barn. She strutted toward him, acting like she was hotter than a prancing dog's toenails. He steered away from her as he headed toward the front door.

"Bing, dear," she cooed, "you did such a nice job on this project. I love your compassion for the poor and downtrodden."

He closed his eyes. Kiki and her family, enveloped in the love they had for each other, were richer than anyone who lived in a mansion where strife was served daily on a golden platter. His patience decreased to the consistency of paint thinner as he moved to the doors and freedom.

He opened his eyes.

Camilla rushed toward him. "We're finally alone. I've waited for this moment all evening."

She threw her arms around him with enough momentum to send them backward toward a weight-bearing support post. He coiled away from her as best he could, but his back crashed into the column.

Camilla wrapped one arm around the flowers and yanked them free. "For me?" She reached up and planted a kiss on his cheek. "You're the best. We need to set a date for our wedding."

Pain shot through his back as words squeaked from his mouth. "I got those for—"

"There you are." Cassie slipped into the barn. "Ready, Camilla?"

"Bing and I were discussing dates for our wedding. I'll be along shortly."

"Oh, I didn't know you all were an item."

Bing twisted free and placed his right hand on his back. He'd need some kind of pain killer from his medicine cabinet before the night ended. Right now, his greatest desire entailed getting rid of another type of discomfort.

"Cassie, she'll be along shortly." He stepped away from Camilla.

Cassie nodded and left.

Bing whispered, "Leave me alone. Kiki alone. Her kids alone. And while I'm at it, don't come back to the fire station."

Clutching the flowers in one arm, Camilla slipped closer and clung to him. "Bing dear, escort me to my car."

He complied just to get her off Kiki's property. He marched to the group of cars parked on the other side of the farmhouse, Camilla trotting to keep up as Cassie's minivan pulled onto the dirt road.

Bing stopped beside Camilla's green SUV. "Let's get one thing straight. You and I are not an item. We never were and never will be. I love Kiki."

Camilla's face reddened. "How dare you? We're getting married."

"In your strange world, perhaps, but not in mine." Bing pointed to the road. "Please leave."

She stomped her foot. "Well, I never. There are plenty of hot men out there who want me."

He clenched his fists and walked backward. "Then go find one."

Camilla raised the bouquet of flowers as high as she could and slammed them onto the ground. After grinding them in the dirt with her heel, she climbed into her car and sped out of the driveway and into her future somewhere else.

And good riddance.

Bing searched the yard and outbuildings but couldn't locate Kiki. Back at his vehicle, he picked up the flowers, his perfectly planned evening spoiled by a conniving woman.

Ox approached and sniffed his hand.

Bing scratched his head. "Let's go home. We can come back tomorrow."

The dog grabbed the mangled bouquet and tore off, vanishing behind the house.

"Oxford, come back here."

With speed known only to labs, the flowerless dog reappeared with a satisfied look on his face.

Bing opened the car door. "What kind of mischief are you up to now?"

The dog wagged his tail then jumped onto the front seat.

He sighed. Time to go home. Maybe tomorrow would garner him an opportunity to pull the small box out of his pocket and pop the question.

Tonight demanded pain pills and ice packs.

~

Kiki backed against the wall. When she'd climbed the ladder to inspect the hayloft, she hadn't expected a balcony seat overlooking a theater of dramatics. She'd heard much of the conversation between Camilla and Bing. Through the cracks in the floor, witnessed their hug. Heard Camilla's declaration of marriage. Even though she'd strained to listen, she didn't hear Bing's whispered response after Cassie left. No doubt, loving words of affirmation.

Then Camilla demanded Bing escort her to her car as she clung to him like melted cheese on a burger. Witnessing them walk arm in arm away from the barn and disappear behind the farmhouse was the final straw. She slid to the loft floor, tears streaming down her cheeks.

Always a bridesmaid.

Never a bride.

Why had she ever let herself get involved with a two-timing firefighter?

Wiping her nose with her sleeve, she peered through a crack in the wall, keeping an eye on the barnyard and the back of the house. Darkness fought for equal time as the sun slipped behind the mountains.

A few minutes later, Bing rounded the corner from the barnyard and poked his head into several buildings. Was he looking for her? He'd be out of luck. There was no need to talk to him again.

Ever.

He disappeared behind the house. Good. Maybe he'd take the hint and leave.

Ox, with something large dangling from his mouth, ran to the back porch and dropped whatever it was onto the steps. At least the dog loved her.

Waiting was easy. She'd done that her entire life. She moved to the side of the barn closest to the road and peered out the window. After the lights from Bing's vehicle exited the driveway and moved along the road, she climbed down the ladder and left the barn.

What started out as a great day turned sour faster than homemade buttermilk forgotten in the trunk of a car.

She reached the back steps and discovered what the dog had left.

A mangled bouquet. Leftovers from Camilla's claim on Bing.

Kiki tossed the flowers aside and entered the house, where the teens were watching a funny movie. She said nothing about her broken heart but slid in between them, grateful for their presence. They laughed together in all the right places. At bedtime she hugged the kids then said good night. She returned to the kitchen for a glass of water then decided to check on a recipe for dinner the next day.

Retrieving her cookbook from the cupboard, something slipped off it and onto the floor. She picked it up then gasped.

A photo of Camilla and Bing's faces stared back. Cut into the shape of a heart with pinking shears.

Further confirmation she needed to move on with her career and her heart.

She shoved the cookbook back into the cupboard then opened a drawer and drew out a piece of stationery and a pen. Sitting at the table, she composed a letter of resignation from Weddings by Design. She couldn't take it anymore. Her time there? Over. Her friends might not like it, but she had to do the healthy thing for herself and her children.

Once finished, Kiki knocked on Tressa's door then Jack's. "I'm going to make several trips from the house to the shop in town. No need for alarm. Just wanted you to know in case you wake up."

Jack hopped out of bed. "I'm coming. Maybe I can help."

Kiki shook her head. "No. It's just a simple thing I need to take care of."

She locked up the house and left.

Once at Weddings by Design, she unlocked the garage and loaded the car with her equipment and supplies. Not quite as simple or as quick as she'd told the kids. The sun peeked over the horizon as she left her resignation on Cassie's desk, looked around one last time, locked up, and left.

After sleeping away her heartache, she'd have some chocolate and formulate a plan.

Create something new from the ashes.

Chapter Twelve

Bing rested his head on the bumper of the fire engine. The trucks shone more now that he had been unable to get ahold of Kiki. He'd stopped by her farm multiple times and frequently called, but his messages went unanswered. She hid well.

It'd been a month since the barn incident. Why, oh why, had he spent so much time and energy fixing up the building? Especially if it went unappreciated. Surely some explanation was in order for the sudden no-contact. But what?

His aunt had texted him, asking for a meeting at his place that evening. Seemed Tressa and Jack had a plan. With the kids involved, an opportunity may well arise to talk to Kiki.

Might as well call it a day. After he finished his duties, he left the station and went home and changed. He swallowed a microwave dinner that threatened to stick to his throat. He couldn't keep living this way.

Six thirty on the dot, his doorbell rang. He kissed his aunt on the cheek and hugged Tressa and Jack as they entered the living room.

He pointed to the couch and recliner. "Please, have a seat."

"No thanks." His aunt shook her head. "I'll get straight to the point. The kids have a plan."

Tressa spoke first. "Weddings by Design is supposedly hosting a party in the barn tonight."

Bing's eyes widened. "Well, at least the building is in use."

"The partners have invited Auntie Kiki back to the firm." Jack shrugged. "She'll let them know tonight. Even though she's quiet about it, I can tell it bothers her not to work in the business."

"So that brings us to you." Tressa pointed at him. "We'll take you to her."

Jack nodded. "Everything else we've tried hasn't worked. I know she needs space and all, but when is enough enough?"

Tressa slugged his arm. "Exactly, little bro."

"Remember." His aunt pushed him toward the front door. "If you don't propose, I'll do it for you."

Bing chuckled. "Hang on." He rushed to his room, pulled a small box out of its hiding place behind a stack of books, and shoved it into his pocket. Maybe he'd need it after all.

Tressa, Jack, and Auntie Valerie led him through his farmyard and across the road.

Tressa turned to him. "My aunt walked into the woods behind the barn. She's been taking out her frustration working on a project for the venue business."

Jack nodded. "Wait until you see it."

"Nephew, you crawl through that wire fence and locate your damsel in distress." Auntie Valerie forced him to the fence. "You'll know what to say."

As much as he loved his auntie, he didn't want to approach Kiki without the blessing of her kids.

"Tressa. Jack. Do I have your permission to propose to your aunt?" Bing looked at the teens. "If she says yes, I'll become a parent to both of you. Have you seriously considered that?"

Tressa gave him a hug. "Promise me you'll walk me down the aisle when I get married in ten years?"

He swallowed. Never in his life did he think he'd be asked that question. "I'd be honored."

Tressa wiped tears from her eyes then stepped back.

Jack held out his hand. "You'll be a good dad."

Bing shook his hand, then engulfed him in a man hug. "You two kids are her world. Thanks for inviting me into yours. If *Dad* isn't the right word, I'd settle for Uncle Bing."

Jack playfully pushed him to the fence. "Uncle Bing has a nice ring to it."

Bing slid through the opening.

His aunt nodded at the teenagers. "We've got work to do." She ushered them down the road toward Kiki's driveway.

What were they up to?

After they disappeared, he turned and walked toward the wooded area, his heart thumping in his ears. What if she said no?

He took a few breaths then moved through the pine and aspen trees until he emerged into a small meadow. Wildflowers bloomed in the tall grass. A meadowlark whistled him forward.

There she stood, the woman of his dreams, knee-deep in a moat with some wooden contraption used as a bridge. She had created an island on the Colorado prairie. In the center stood a freshly painted green 1929 Ford Model-A tow truck. He had to admit the lady had class.

But a moat around an old truck? What a zany idea.

Too bad he hadn't thought of it.

He grinned as he got closer. She had painted BELL FARMS on

the driver's door. The towing apparatus sported a freshly minted red color. Polished black tires completed the look.

Kiki stood in the water, adjusting a rock that held a plastic water barrier in place.

"Amazing." Bing chuckled. "Did you do this yourself?"

She looked up, then stiffened. "What are you doing here?"

"I've tried to talk to you for a month, but you avoid me. Your kids and my aunt held an intervention and told me to slide through the fence and patch things up."

She sighed. "Those kids." She sat on the island edge, feet dangling in the water.

"May I join you?"

She shrugged. "My island is probably stronger than your dock."

He chuckled as he crossed her homemade bridge. After kicking off his shoes and socks, he sat beside her and placed his feet in the water. The chill calmed his nerves.

"Just so you know, I haven't seen Camilla since the day you got back from the wedding in the mountains."

Kiki looked at him. "You two seemed pretty chummy."

Bing shook his head. "We're not, nor will we ever be, chummy."

"The night of the barn reveal, she threw her arms around you and pronounced the two of you engaged." She stared at the water. "You even gave her flowers."

"Camilla came after me and pushed me against the support beam, hurting my back." He scratched his head. "How did you know that?"

Kiki fidgeted with her hands. "I climbed into the loft to investigate the repairs. Heard everything and saw your amorous embrace."

"Did you see me try to get away and her snatching the flowers out of my hand?"

She shook her head. "I saw enough though."

Bing gritted his teeth. "She grabbed the bouquet that was meant for you."

Kiki stared at the trees across the meadow. "When Cassie came in, Camilla announced the finality of an upcoming wedding. Are you planning on postcards or pompous stationery for the 'Save the Date' announcements?"

She sucked in a huge breath and continued. "You told Cassie that Camilla would be along shortly, then you escorted Camilla to her car."

Bing stiffened. "You missed the other half of the conversation. I told Camilla her chances of marrying me were zero. She threw a fit when I told her to leave."

Her shoulders slumped. "I've got proof you two are together."

"Show me."

She pulled a small heart-shaped photo out of her pocket and handed it to him. "Here."

He took it, looked at it, then shook his head. "That conniving woman. She got this from the group photo from last year's volunteer appreciation night. Camilla sat next to me in the front row." He retrieved his phone from his pocket and pulled up the same photo from the station's website. "See."

Kiki took the phone, stared at the web page, and compared it to the heart-shaped picture. "Did she print this off then cut out your heads?"

Bing nodded. "Looks like it."

"But how did it get into my kitchen cupboard?"

He scratched his head. "I bet she planted it the day she came for lace for your project. My aunt and your kids implemented a plan to keep Camilla away from me, so I ended up hiding under the dining room table. While the others searched your sewing stash, she slipped into the kitchen for a glass of water."

"Where she hid the photo." Kiki gave the phone back to him. "She's difficult to work with. I handed in my resignation at the shop. It's not worth the stress."

"Can't blame you there."

He placed the phone on the ground beside him. "She's wrong, you know." Retrieving the small box from his pocket, he opened it, then knelt in the trench, facing her.

"You're getting all wet."

"No matter. Kiki Bell, I've been waiting my entire adult life for you. Will you marry me?"

The question she'd waited for her entire life floated to her from a moat.

How was she supposed to answer and breathe at the same time?

"Kiki?"

She nodded. "I accept."

Bing slipped an old ring on her finger. "My grandmother wore this. She would have loved you."

Kiki gazed at the solitaire diamond set in a gold band. "How beautiful."

Next to a vintage wrecker, standing in a homemade moat of water, he pulled her into an embrace and kissed her.

Nothing could be more romantic.

"Told you." Tressa's voice echoed from the trees.

Kiki and Bing pulled apart.

Kiki located her niece in the woods closest to the barn.

Jack stepped out into the open and gave Tressa a high five. "We did it!"

Ox burst through the trees, happy-barking.

"Yes, little bro." Tressa grinned. "We did."

When Kiki looked at Bing, he winked at her.

"Auntie. Uncle Bing. We've got an engagement party in full swing in the barn." Tressa waved at them. "Don't keep the guests waiting."

Bing took Kiki's hand and helped her out of the moat. He slipped on his shoes and walked beside her as they followed the kids and Ox to the barn. "We have remarkable kids."

She nodded. "Instigators."

"For good."

They joined a large gathering of friends from church and the fire station inside the barn. The partners of Weddings by Design waited inside the entrance.

Cassie sidled up to Kiki. "Camilla has something to say to all of us."

Kiki stiffened as Camilla slipped from a corner and stood before her.

"Felicity, Ronnie, Cassie, Kiki, and Bing, I want to apologize for my behavior. See, I decided to go back to college to finish my major in hospitality, tourism, and event planning. I've been doing homework at the office and subsisting on caffeine and sugar with little sleep. It's made me do and say stupid stuff. I'm really sorry."

Walking in forgiveness wasn't always easy, but Kiki tried. "You should have told us. We would have worked things out."

Cassie rested her arm on Kiki's shoulder. "Will you come back?"

"Please?" Camilla asked.

"Not gonna lie, missing my best friends and my job has made me miserable. So yes, I'll come back."

The four best friends congregated for a group hug. And then they reached out and included Camilla.

Felicity grinned. "From now on, we communicate better."

Kiki sighed. "Agreed."

Jack climbed onto a chair and rang an antique dinner bell. "Gather round, everybody."

Tressa joined her brother on the chair and placed her arm around him.

Bing reclaimed Kiki, and they stood next to the kids.

Tressa spoke first. "Psalm 139 tells us, 'You hem me in behind and before, and you lay your hand upon me. Such knowledge is too wonderful for me, too lofty for me to attain.' "

"When our parents died, Auntie Kiki snapped us up. It wasn't easy for her to take on two grieving kids," Jack continued. "God hemmed the torn fragments of our lives."

"One stitch at a time." Tressa looked at her brother, tears streaming down her face. "She made us a family."

Jack wiped his eyes. "Auntie said yes. We kinda helped with that, and now God is sewing another member into our family."

Tressa raised a hand. "A confirmed bachelor-till-the-rapture is no more. Uncle Bing is engaged to our beloved Aunt Kiki. Let's party!"

Cheers rose to the barn rafters.

Those kids.

Kiki rubbed her eyes with her sleeve.

Bing bent down and kissed her, his tears mingling with hers. "May our love know no bounds."

"And may we always marvel at being hemmed in."

The inspiration behind this story lies with my uncles who married my aunties and raised my cousins as their own. Their legacy lives on long after they moved to heaven.

RL Ashly is a master seamstress with a master of arts degree in literature. A mother and grandmother, she is active in her local writing community, never says "never" to a home improvement task, and strives to one day write the great American novel. This is her first novella.

The Worst-Kept Secret

by Leeann Betts

Acknowledgments

First and foremost, to God the Father,
Jesus the Son, and the Holy Spirit.
Without them, no story is worth telling.

To my husband Patrick. My biggest fan
and the light of my life. Thanks, honey bear.

To Terrie, my agent extraordinaire, who goes
above and beyond the call of duty on every project.
You are a special gift from God in my life.

To the ladies of the Word Crafters critique group.
You've stuck through my stories for many years
now. Your books are next. Thanks, Nancy,
Shawna, Dianne, and Ms. Rose.

*"For nothing is secret that will not be revealed, nor anything
hidden that will not be known and come to light."*
LUKE 8:17 NKJV

Chapter One

Cassie gritted her teeth and huffed as she stared at her calendar for the next few weeks.

Ronnie—Saffron, the wedding planning company's chef—peeked in through her doorway. "You look like you have the world on your shoulders."

"Seems like every time I turn around, somebody—"

She clamped her lips shut. No way she wanted to air *that* particular piece of laundry. If her partners knew how much she hated her job right now, they'd—well, she might be out of said employment in a flash.

Instead, she smiled at the woman who always smelled like vanilla and exotic spices. "Just a lot of promotional events coming up."

Ronnie perched on the chair across from her. "You amaze me all the time. How organized you are. How you manage to get your work done and still speak to all these groups."

Cassie shrugged. "Part of my job. Speaking to groups of giggling girls about planning the perfect wedding. Nervous couples. Remarrieds."

One-on-ones she could handle. No, her nemesis was gatherings numbering anything over ten.

"I think I hate my job."

Ronnie, always so perky and positive, grinned. "You know that's not true."

I hate talking to people.

Except wild horses wouldn't drag that confession from her. And the assessment wasn't exactly right.

Herds. Flocks. I don't like crowds.

She sighed as she snapped the appointment book closed and turned to her partner and friend. "Have you ever wondered if you could do this job?"

The chef shook her head. "Not without great friends like Felicity, Kiki, and you. I mean, what more could a person ask for? Pals strong in their faith, confident in their abilities. Capable women, secure in their careers." She leaned across the desk. "I'm so glad I joined the singles group at the church. That's where I met y'all."

Cassie nodded. Totally true. She didn't even want to think about how much poorer her life would be without these three ladies. Without this business. And wasn't Loveland, Colorado, the perfect setting for a wedding event company? An old Craftsman bungalow at the edge of the downtown business section, the ideal headquarters.

But she couldn't disappoint. Letting the team down wasn't in her. Her father's voice still rang in her head. *"If you don't know what to do, just do something and figure it out as you go."*

Maybe she could talk to Camilla and ask her not to say yes every time somebody called and asked for a speaker for their group. Not that the woman ever did anything asked of her. As office manager, Camilla was a whiz, but her people skills—Cassie struggled to come up with something positive. Nothing came to mind. Snap. Cousin or not, she'd get her point across on this issue.

No. More. Speaking.

At least, no more dates added to her calendar until after Labor Day. Or else she might have to fess up to her partners what a disappointment she was.

She smiled at Ronnie. "Thanks for the pep talk. I have a lot to be thankful for. And you and the others are tops on my list." She exhaled. "Back to work."

The chef stood. "I get the hint. I just came in for a couple of ingredients. I'm headed home."

Cassie selected the office manager's image from the favorites list in her cell phone and waited. Voice mail. Where was the woman? And why didn't she have her phone with her? She pasted on a grin. Somebody said folks could hear a smile in a voice. Maybe Camilla wouldn't notice how false this one sounded. "Camilla, it's Cassie. Call me when you get a minute. Thanks."

After disconnecting, she sat back in her chair. A slow day loomed ahead. They'd had a big wedding Saturday night, Sunday busy with church, then today. Somebody should come up with a calendar with no Mondays.

A stack of papers cluttering her inbox caught her eye. Then again, maybe not so slow. She leafed through the contents, sorting each into a pile. Invoices to pay or send for approval. Deposits to record. Phone calls to return.

What was she most in the mood to do?

She shoved the phone message slips back into the inbox and opened the accounting program on her laptop. Always paperwork over personal contact.

Sure, she could coordinate an event, set up transportation,

manage the project. And by the time the initial consultation ended, she knew what the bride and her mother really wanted. Colors. Flowers. Reception hall. How many guests. Who not to invite.

She sighed. An empathic nature might be helpful had she chosen counseling or medicine, but as a wedding planner? Well, it had served her several times. But really. She'd take being able to speak in front of groups any day over knowing whether the bridesmaid dresses should be teal or emerald green.

Her phone rang, displaying a number she didn't recognize. She groaned, then pressed to answer. "Hi, this is Cassie with Weddings by Design. How can I help you?"

"Hi, Cassie, it's Amanda Walker? We talked on the phone last week?"

Yes, Amanda with the irritating habit of turning every statement into a question. "How are you?"

"Well, I wondered if we might get together? I checked out some other event planners, and honestly, they didn't click with me the way you did? I'd love to come over and meet your partners, see samples, maybe talk about colors and numbers?"

"Sure. When?"

Please don't say today. Please, not today.

"This morning, if it works for you? We're in town today? My mother is excited to meet you too?"

A chuckle in the background confirmed the young woman's assertion. "That I am, Cassie. That I am. Can't wait to see the ladies who will pull this one off."

Well, there hung a challenge if ever she'd heard one.

"How about eleven?" That gave her two hours to get other

work done. And to steel herself for the meeting. "Do you have the address?"

"Yes, we've driven by a couple of times? If the garden and the outside of the house are any indication of your firm's skills, then you'll be perfect? Love what you did with the rose garden?"

Cassie's mind struggled to recall what the front of the bungalow looked like. She always came through the back entrance. Maybe she should take a wander out and see what greeted clients. "Uh, thanks. But I can't claim any kudos. I'm hopeless with that stuff." Her word meter had just about reached its limit. No point in running out when the small hand on the clock hadn't quite reached nine. "See you at eleven."

She disconnected and sat back, shrugging the kinks out of her shoulders. Was she getting worse, or had the busy weekend not replenished her introvert's need for time alone? If talking on the phone for—she glanced at the clock again—for less than ten minutes wore her down this much, the prospect of a presentation at Girls of America to aid future brides in deciding whether they needed a wedding planner loomed too large to contemplate. Maybe she needed a vacation.

No. Coffee. She needed coffee. With enough caffeine, she could talk to a stadium full of folks and come away with enough energy to do the same the next day. Not that she'd enjoy the experience, but she'd be jazzed enough to complete the task.

After exiting her office, she headed for the kitchen, enjoying the quiet of the house. Felicity was working from home this morning, whipping up another batch of delectable treats, no doubt. She and Ronnie—who usually worked from home—loved experimenting with ingredients. Cassie glanced into the client meeting area then into Kiki's office—newly returned from Camilla's banishment to the garage—strewn with fabric samples, headpiece netting and tiaras, and a beautiful bouquet from the wedding on Saturday. Display cases and mannequins lined the wall, making the room feel comfortably full even without its usual occupant.

She chuckled at the memory of Kiki's face when she caught the flowers, then a familiar ache filled her chest.

Always a wedding planner, and never a bride.

Then again, Felicity and Kiki thought the same thing just months before. And now they enjoyed relationships that made her jealous.

A holy jealousy, of course.

The closet in her small apartment overflowing with dresses worn to friends' weddings didn't help. As far back as high school. College. Church. Cousins. Girls she barely remembered from grade school who recalled a pledge they'd made at ten to be bridesmaids for each other.

She snorted as she entered the kitchen. Not that *she* kept any of these distant friends busy buying dresses they'd never wear again. Cassie checked the water in the one-cup brewer, turned on the machine, then selected her favorite coffee flavor—hazelnut—and popped the canister in the brewer and her cup under the spout. While she waited, she peeked into the refrigerator for a snack. Good—a chocolate donut with her name on it. And the cream.

Back in her office, she dealt with the paperwork then looked up at a knock on the front door. Goodness! Eleven already? She hadn't consumed nearly enough caffeine for this meeting.

Pushing her shoulders back and lifting her chin a mite, she

headed to meet their new client. She could do this. Yes, she could.

Cassie opened the door, her smile already in place. This one a tad more sincere than the one she'd communicated to Camilla. "Hi, Amanda. Mrs. Walker. Come in."

The bride's mother nodded and stepped in. "Oh, it's as lovely on the inside as on the out."

Amanda gushed. "Must be a dream to work here?"

Cassie gestured to the meeting area to the left. "Let's sit in there. Would you like coffee or tea? Water?"

Mrs. Walker shook her head, then chose the chair at the head of the table. Cassie's spot, complete with her presentation binder and notes. "No thanks, dear. We just had breakfast."

This woman's take-charge attitude could intimidate others, but not me.

"Great." Cassie sat to Mrs. Walker's left and slid her binder of forms and checklists away from the older woman, then opened to the first page. "So let's start with getting contact information, date of the wedding, and so on."

Amanda, sitting across the table, squirmed in her chair like a three-year-old. Or a soon-to-be bride. "We know exactly what we want?"

Cassie filled in the blanks as the two women answered her questions. After about fifteen minutes, she sat back. "Okay. We've plenty of time to get everything in order but none to waste." She tapped the binder. "You're months ahead of most brides who come here." She stood. "Let's look at samples. Do you plan to have us create your gown and the dresses for the bridesmaids?"

Mrs. Walker crossed the hallway to the display cases along the far wall. "Yes. Each of the girls is so different in body shape that we didn't want to pick something off the rack."

"Makes sense. And what about the wedding dress?"

Amanda clapped her hands. Again, like a little girl. "We have that already? My mother's?"

"Good. Perhaps you could bring it in so our seamstress can see the style. She might like to incorporate a corresponding design piece, such as beading or lace into the bridesmaids' dresses." Cassie pulled a dress rack from the corner. "This is one style that might work. If you see several you like, we can mix and match them together. You could have the same fabric for all the dresses and still have different styles according to your preferences and the bridesmaids' shapes."

The two discussed every dress on the rack, what they liked or didn't. Finally, two outfits remained: a peach-toned frilly A-line gown, and a seafoam-green strapless tea-length cocktail sheath.

The first, Mrs. Walker's choice, and the second, her daughter's.

Wow, talk about a contrast.

Cassie held the peach gown in front of Amanda. "Here, look at this one in the mirror, and try to imagine each of your three bridesmaids wearing it."

As Amanda did so, two deep creases formed between her eyebrows just above the bridge of her nose. She glanced at her mother, who fairly purred her approval. The worry disappeared from the younger woman's face, and she nodded. "This one?"

Cassie took the first and handed her the second. "You haven't even tried—"

Amanda shook her head. "No, this is the one I want?"

She doesn't. Not really. She simply wants to please her mother.

In that moment, Cassie determined that this girl would get

the dresses she wanted.

⌐

Brady Millman grunted at the state of his recent purchase—the newest limo he owned. Financed with his favorite payment plan—cash. Yes siree. Business had been profitable this year. Lots of folks getting married, graduating high school and college, or wanting to arrive at a special function in style.

And he was the guy to do it.

He opened the rear door of the limo and sniffed. Smelled like booze, sweat, stale perfume, and—what? Sour, rank—nasty. He dialed a familiar number. "Joe, Brady here. Man, I was just getting ready to polish and prep the limo after your party last night."

Joe's bass voice, perfect for the church choir—if he attended, which he didn't—boomed through the phone. "What a great time, bro. Thanks for the deep discount. We had a blast."

"Man, if one of you turned my new car into a puke bucket, I'll—well, you know."

"Hey, down off your high horse, bro. Just a few of your friends out for a bachelor party."

"Still—"

"Come on, Brady, old buddy. Step down out of the pulpit and give us a break here. Chill out, man."

Chill out? Chill out?

He'd chill them out. "This is my livelihood we're talking here."

"Well, we paid you for the use of the car. Don't sweat it."

"Which didn't even pay for the gas. You didn't tell me you were driving to Rocky Mountain National Park."

"Hey, I said a tour of town. The park is practically inside the town limits."

"The next time you want a car—"

"Sure, I know. Give you a call. Bye."

That wasn't what he meant at all. Maybe he should change his phone number. And his name. He fetched a trash can to gather the empty cans and bottles littering the interior.

He followed his sniffer around the interior, gingerly poking his fingers into nooks and crannies until the smell told him he'd come too close to use his hands. "Yuck."

Brady fetched a bucket of water, a handful of rags, and a can of disinfectant spray and cleaned the mess. Good thing he checked. If that fermented in the summer heat, he'd never get rid of the stench.

He tossed the water on the concrete and the rags onto the porch for washing, then slipped into the driver's seat. After rolling down the windows to air out the car, he got out and wheeled the trash can and overflowing recycle bin to the curb. Next on the list: wash the interior, clean the carpeting and headliner, restock the bar.

Mrs. Green, his neighbor on the left and normally an amiable woman, walked past with her poodle. She eyed the trash dumpster and the bin of bottles and cans and wrinkled her nose. "Looks like quite the party."

"Appears so. I wasn't there myself."

The poodle sniffed at his leg then growled. He sidled away in case the creature had caught a case of unneighborliness from its owner.

She harrumphed. "Well, maybe your sort of business isn't suited to this area. This is a quiet neighborhood, and we want it to stay that way."

That's not how he'd describe the Fourth of July fireworks that started in May and didn't end until Labor Day. The police never appeared to put a stop to those shenanigans. But there was no point arguing with her.

Besides, the way that dog snarled, it could have rabies.

Or worse.

His cell phone rang. Perhaps a booking? He glanced back at the neighbor woman. "I've got to take this call. Thanks for stopping by." He turned his shoulder toward her and punched to answer. "The Wheel Deal. Brady speaking."

"Hi, Brady. This is Cassie from Weddings by Design. I have a client and her mother who'd like to talk to you about cars for her wedding. We're on our way. See you in about five minutes."

Five minutes? Yikes. It'd take him thirty to finish cleaning. And the smell—still, a booking was a booking. "Sure. No problem."

He hung up and hurried around to sniff the passenger area again. Some deodorizer, and the car might prove ready. He sprayed his favorite odor remover around then topped it off with a little lilac air freshener. Time to change out of his grungies and pray nobody wanted to look—or, Heaven forbid, sit—inside the limo.

Two minutes later, he exited the house, his company driver's cap, complete with the embossed and tasteful logo he'd designed, completing the picture of a successful businessman. He'd impress this bride all the way to the border and back. No problemo.

Maybe he'd even have time—oh no. Two women headed straight for the car.

The younger raised herself on the balls of her feet. "Oh, it's beautiful?"

The older woman patted her arm. "Calm down, child. It's just a limo."

Only a limo? What planet did these ladies come from?

He scooted down the steps and planted himself between them and the vehicle. "Hi, I'm Brady." He gestured to the car. "I can see you have good taste. This is my newest model. Top of the line."

The petite young lady's brow pulled down. "I'm Amanda? Can I see inside?"

No, no, no.

He lifted a shoulder and let it drop. "Sure. But your mother is right. It's just a car. A magnificent car. Leather seats. Carpeted. Fully stocked bar."

Behind this pair stood Cassie. Arms crossed. Toe tapping. Not looking at the car.

He followed her gaze. Oh no. The overflowing recycle bin.

A sniff.

And the distinct smell of beer and cheap wine.

Doomed.

Maybe he could still pull this off. "I have pictures from previous gigs in my office that show how many we can pile into a car like this for the bachelorette and bachelor parties, the rehearsal dinner, and the event itself."

The blond shook her head. "I want to sit in it?"

The older woman joined her daughter. "Is there a reason we can't open the door?" She chuckled. "Or have you locked your keys inside?"

He held out the fob and clicked the unlock button. "I was cleaning it when Cassie called. Not quite finished."

As if he'd stayed mute as a ventriloquist's dummy, Amanda

pulled on the handle, stuck her head in, then jumped back as though burned. "It stinks?"

Her mother leaned closer and inhaled. "Like a brewery." She turned to him. "Is this how you allow your clients to treat your vehicles?" She peered at him. "Or how you treat them?"

He glanced toward Cassie again. Could she get him out of this? Would she? Likely not, if her expression showed anything.

Cassie's brows pulled down, marring her otherwise beautiful face. Too bad. He thought her the best looking of the partners. Sure, each of the other three ladies had their own kind of good looks, but Cassie—well, down to earth just about covered it. The girl next door of every boy's dreams.

And she seemed to think him lower than a snake. Why, he couldn't fathom. So far as he knew, he'd done nothing to insult her. Always gave a good discount. Cars in pristine condition.

Usually.

He leaned closer to the car and sniffed. Amanda's assessment proved correct. Spilled liquor soaked into the carpets, splashed on the seats, and—he leaned in to check the headliner—even on the ceiling.

Amanda's mother stepped back. "I think we should look elsewhere. You know how your father detests even the odor of alcohol."

The bride's bottom lip jutted out. "I at least want to try it?" She batted her eyelashes at him. "I bet it cleans up nice?"

"It does." He gestured to the pair—correction, three. "Have a seat, ladies. See how comfortable the genuine leather is. And I'll crank up the AC. This is my finest model for the most beautiful bride and her mother."

Cassie unfolded her arms from over her chest and nodded to her clients, and the two slipped into the car.

Brady smiled at the wedding planner, but she ignored him. Or pretended to, at any rate. He edged closer to her and kept his voice low. "Have I offended you?"

She stepped back, her head tilted to one side. "What makes you think that?"

He shrugged. "I figure I must have, because if you treat all your suppliers this way, I wouldn't think you'd stay in business long."

A smile tickled her lips, and then she narrowed her eyes at him. "You might as well stop trying to butter me up. I know all about you."

Chapter Two

Cassie bit back a chuckle. The look on Brady's face? Priceless. If only she had a camera, she'd be sure to win the Candid Photo contest in the Loveland paper. Maybe she needed to give him some grace. Wasn't that what the pastor always said?

"Give what you want to receive."

He gulped and his cheeks flamed. "You do? Is my secret out?"

Maybe a little more razzing wouldn't hurt. Much. "Both Saffron and Felicity texted me about your party. And the cops showing up on your doorstep."

His lips pursed, and then he held out his hands, palms up. "A party got out of hand."

He looked so sincere. For a flash, she looked at him like a man and not simply her limousine driver. Did he have a girlfriend or significant other? Would that two-day smudge of growth on his upper lip—would a kiss—tickle? She shook off her thoughts. No point in going there. This man? Not right for her. A party animal by all accounts. A playboy to boot. Footloose and fancy-free, she'd heard from a few sources. And a secret life he shared with few.

Granted, all combined in a very attractive package. Not good-looking in the Fabio sort of way. No, his six-pack was more likely a three. Or a four. Not that she claimed to be an award of any sort, unless a booby prize. Midthirties. Never married. As the saying went, all the best ones were already taken. So what did that make her? And Brady Millman too, for that matter?

Off-limits. As her father used to say, no smoke without a fire. Meaning that even if word around town didn't get the story completely right, enough smoke resided there to warn her away. Not that she was interested anyway. For that, she'd have to talk to him. Get to know him. Share her deepest secrets. Open herself up to scorn and criticism. And if she couldn't share honest thoughts with her three closest friends and business partners, how could she even think about a romantic relationship?

Still, he stood as the best—and the cheapest—limo service in town. But what about Amanda? And more importantly, her father?

She glanced at the two women relaxing in the seats as though born there. The smell couldn't be too bad. And no doubt he'd finish cleaning up the car. Her call probably came out of the blue.

After stepping around him, she stuck her head in. A deep inhale. No skanky smell like was usual with marijuana, just that prevailing stink of alcohol. Like Amanda's father, she didn't drink and didn't like what spirits did to those who imbibed. Did that make her old-fashioned? Or sensible?

Hopefully, both. Which meant she needed to rein in her thoughts about kissing—or being kissed by—Brady Millman, here and now. Word around her circle of acquaintances claimed he came to Colorado because of legalized marijuana. If true, another reason to steer clear. That stuff rotted the brain and stole people's souls.

Cassie addressed the two in the limo. "Well, ladies, are you satisfied?" She straightened. "I'm sure the next time you see this car, it will be in showroom condition." She turned to Brady. "Right?"

He nodded. "Uh, right. Absolutely. I wasn't expecting anybody to come looking for a car today." He held her gaze. "Usually they give plenty of notice."

Heat crept up her neck. Snap. She hated that the blotchy effect would likely tickle his funny bone. Time for a distraction. "Amanda, Mrs. Walker, let's go back to the office. My partners should be in now, and you can get more information."

She herded her charges down the driveway like a hen and her chicks—she needed to stop thinking of herself in these terms—and into her minivan. On the return drive, she kept her eyes on the road and one ear on the chattering conversation going on behind her. Amanda assuring her mother she loved the peach dress. When Cassie knew for certain the bride wanted the seafoam green. Agreeing two hundred guests was perfect. Again, untrue. Amanda wanted a smaller, more intimate gathering. Fifty, Cassie estimated. And shrimp cocktails? How retro.

Cassie sighed as she pulled back into the driveway at Weddings by Design HQ.

She had her work cut out for her.

⌐

Brady stood back and surveyed the limo. He had his work cut out for him. Well, he'd show Miss Snooty Cassie that she had him all wrong. He'd have a word with his friends and remind them how they reflected poorly on his business. Not to mention on any potential to make inroads with Cassie. Or any other woman, for that matter.

Not that he had the time or the interest right now. He had a business to run, a house to maintain, and his second line of work—or rather, his true calling—that took up most of his free evenings. A calling which he preferred to guard from the lime-light for client confidentiality. Keeping anything anonymous in a small town like Loveland proved a Herculean task.

Despite his good intentions to complete the process quickly, the time flew past faster than expected. Late afternoon came and went, but finally his best girl shone from grille to tail, inside and out. He tossed his waxing glove into the bucket for laundry. Now what? Maybe he should take the car and show Cassie how he really operated. Professionally.

He clapped his chauffeur hat on his head and slid into the driver's seat. After easing onto the street, he made a left, then a right, heading toward downtown. The light traffic made travel easy this time of day. Just before the evening rush hour. Many of the town's residents migrated toward either Fort Collins or the suburbs of Denver for work and then the return trip each day. Right now, Loveland streets resembled a ghost town.

Perfect time to pick up a couple of coffees and drop in unexpectedly.

What's good for the goose is good for the gander.

He stopped at Fourth and Adams to allow a family to cross in front of him, and movement from the pub on the corner to his left caught his attention. Could be somebody he knew. Some-one who needed his intervention, particularly if he caught them before they went in. Much easier to help a sober person than one already drunk.

He swiveled his head.

His pastor.

Coming out of a bar?

And staggering like he'd had six too many. Wobbling from side to side. Feet tripping over each other. Accompanied by an equally intoxicated man.

Brady waited for a break in oncoming traffic then pulled into a handicapped spot. A ticket—even a hefty one—meant nothing if his friend was in trouble.

He pocketed the keys and trotted over to the pair. "Pastor Rick. Are you okay?" When he got no answer, he slipped an arm around the preacher's back and glared at the stranger who held a beer bottle in one hand and Rick in the other. "What's wrong with him?"

The unkempt man, reeking of alcohol and sweat, grinned. "Too much to drink, I guess. I'm just helping him."

Brady pulled his friend toward him. "Well, I'll take him now."

The beer sloshed down Brady's arm when the stranger resisted. "No, he wants me to help. Said he'd give me five dollars to get him to his car over yonder."

Something didn't sit well with this story. Or fabrication. First, he'd never even seen Pastor Rick consume alcohol. Second, the man was too responsible to drink and drive.

Then again, that's what so many of his clients said. That they knew when they were drunk. Knew when they couldn't drive safely. Or legally.

And how many paid the price for their stupidity?

His pastor raised his head, his facial muscles slack. "Help. Me."

His eyes rolled back, and he mumbled something Brady couldn't make out.

Brady caught the other guy's gaze. "Help me get him into my car."

The stranger released his hold on the pastor, and Rick fell into Brady's grasp. "He's all yours. Don't want my help, that's fine with me. But I want my ten bucks."

Brady glared at him. "You said five."

"Yeah, well, I spoke wrong. Ten. Or I'll make sure your pastor's face is plastered all over the news."

Brady knew Rick well enough to know that was the last thing either he or their church needed. He dug into his pocket and pulled out a bill, which he crammed into the man's hand. "There. Now get lost."

The man tossed the beer bottle on the ground, where it shattered and splashed on Pastor Rick's pants legs. Then he backed away, hands held at shoulder height as if in surrender, before pivoting and turning down the alleyway.

Brady, unable to give chase for fear of his friend dropping to the ground, held tight to him instead. "Okay, Pastor, I'll get you in my car and take you home in style. We'll come back later for your car."

Somehow, he managed to goose-walk-side-step Rick toward his limo. He leaned him against the side and held him in place with one hand while fumbling with the fob until the doors unlocked. Pastor Rick's legs buckled beneath him, and Brady ended up sliding him across the seat where he sprawled, half on the floor, half upright.

What happened to the leader of his church to put him in such a publicly untenable position? Why hadn't he called somebody for a ride? Did Pastor Rick feel his secret sin so unforgivable that he feared exposing himself to correction or rebuke?

Brady started the car and continued down Fourth Avenue, toward the subdivision at the edge of town where the pastor lived. He didn't know what to do once he got him there. Hopefully Rick's wife, Nancy, was at home. Or he could find a key in Rick's pocket. Get him inside and into bed. Or a cold shower.

Or both. Maybe strong coffee too.

As he neared Weddings by Design, he sighed.

Proving his worth to Cassie would have to wait until another time.

He grinned, feeling like Clark Kent. A mild-mannered limousine driver by day, Superman by night.

Who'd ever believe him, even if he could tell them, what he really did for a living?

Chapter Three

Cassie glanced at the clock in the corner of her computer screen while shrugging kinks out of her shoulders. A long, stressful day. Not made a whit easier by the near-fiasco with Brady Millman first thing this morning.

She shut down the computer, tucked her cell into her purse, and headed out the door. Rustling in the kitchen caught her attention, and she headed in to see who still worked at this late hour.

Felicity pulled a pan out of the oven and set it on the counter. Something golden and warm, smelling like summer sunshine and heaven all wrapped in flour.

Cassie's stomach growled, reminding her she hadn't eaten lunch. And dinner still waited on the distant horizon. She sighed. Another meal to prepare. And eat. Alone.

Fliss hummed under her breath, her back to Cassie. What had she baked now? Better make her presence known so their *baker extraordinaire* could invite her to the tasting.

Cassie backed up a few steps to the door opening, tapped on the wall, and breezed in as though she'd just arrived. "Hi, Felicity. Didn't know you were still here."

Happiness oozed from the woman's every pore and bubbled

up to her face as she turned and leaned against the counter. "Hi, Cassie. Trying out a new recipe." She gestured to the pan. "Well, an old one, really. Found it in my grandmother's diary. One she tried at a garden party about seventy years ago."

Cassie sidled up next to her partner and inhaled. Yummy. Vanilla. Sugar. Cinnamon. And something else? "What's it called?"

"She called it Delish. I'll need a better name than that." She pulled two side plates from the cupboard. "Want a taste?"

Cassie chuckled. "I suspect I'll want more than just one. This calls for a heaping helping."

Felicity deftly cut the concoction into generous portions and scooped one onto each plate. "Hold on. That's not ready yet." A quick trip to the fridge, and she returned with a bowl of macerated berries and a can of whipped cream. She topped each slice with the oozing strawberries, raspberries, and blueberries along with two layers of cream. "Now it's ready."

Cassie eyed the coffeemaker. Dare she? Decaf. "Coffee for you?"

"No, thanks. Get yours, but hurry before the fresh-out-of-the-oven effect wears off."

Cassie slid a mug under the spout and pressed the brew button then sat. "First bite needs nothing to adulterate it."

Fliss laughed. "Let's give thanks first. It's a miracle I found the recipe, and if it's as good as my grandmother suggests by the name, could be a year-round hit for smaller events like bridal showers."

Cassie resisted praying aloud as much as she did talking to groups. "You go ahead."

Her partner's prayer, short and to the point, meant that within ten seconds Cassie forked a portion of dessert into her mouth. She closed her eyes to experience the sensation without distraction. Her taste buds exploded with the myriad of flavors. Holding the food in place, she reveled in the sweetness. The tantalizing spiciness of—what? The cushiony delight of the whipped cream.

Next she squeezed the berries with her tongue to extract every morsel of their sunshine and soft rain. The top crust of the cake, just the teensiest bit crunchy but not hard, finished the sensation, providing great juxtaposition for the tender berries and fluffy cream.

Regretfully, she swallowed and opened her eyes. Fliss stared at her, eyebrows raised, waiting for her reaction, her own forkful uneaten.

"Well?"

"What's in it besides the vanilla and cinnamon?"

"A touch of fresh ginger." Felicity sniffed deeply of her portion. "Do you think it's too much?"

"Not at all. In fact, you could use a little extra. Maybe candied ginger."

The baker nibbled at the edge of the cake then included a berry and a generous dousing of cream. "Yes, you're right." She set her fork on her plate while Cassie dug into her own. "Maybe I'll serve this at all our own bridal showers."

Cassie snorted. "That might take another fifty years at the rate I'm going." Oops, her partner's smile slipped away. "But you and Will. And Kiki and Bing."

Felicity's smile reappeared. "Will and I plan to go for a walk tonight." She sighed. "He's the best thing since—since—"

When she paused, searching for the right words, Cassie

laughed. "Sliced bread?"

"Yeah, that too." She quirked her chin toward Cassie's now-empty plate. "Another?"

Cassie wanted more but restrained herself. She'd never have Fliss's svelte form nor Kiki's athletic shape, and definitely not Ronnie's long and lean athletic build. No, at five feet ten, she already stood taller than most women and many men, but convincing herself she was large-boned so she could consume more calories wouldn't whittle down these few extra pounds.

She shook her head. "Nope, but thanks. I'll take my coffee to propel me home. Then I'll eat a healthy dinner to offset this indulgence." She snapped her fingers. "Indulgence. That's a great name for this. Implies richness, forbidden treats, exquisite taste, and a discerning palate."

"Great idea." Felicity stood and cleared their plates while Cassie poured her coffee into a to-go mug. "I'll put this away. I have enough time before meeting—before—I have plenty of time."

Cassie appreciated her friend's sensitivity to the not-so-small difference between them now that hadn't existed before.

As a woman in love with a great man, Felicity exuded joy, while Cassie—well, not.

She sighed. Sticking around here until all hours wouldn't change that. Maybe she'd take Fliss's lead and go for a walk around her own neighborhood this evening. See who else ventured out and about. Pet a dog. Smile at a child.

Maybe meet Mr. Right.

Sure, and perhaps she'd win the lottery while she was at it.

Except she hadn't bought a ticket.

Cassie headed for her car, which reminded her of another

conundrum that required an answer. Should she hire the limo contract out to Brady Millman, or should she look elsewhere? Sure, he offered the cheapest rates in town, although not a decision point for the Walkers. Judging by Amanda's comments, they were willing to overlook the present state of the vehicle. Except, a party-wrecked car would be a big thing if it happened on the wedding day. Could she trust him?

She definitely didn't want to mess up.

Pausing beside her van to listen to a pretty songbird in the tree between their property and the next-door business, a squeal of tires caught her attention.

She whirled and faced the road.

Well, if it wasn't the man himself, as though her thoughts had conjured him up.

His limo—the one she'd seen earlier today—turned the corner faster than the posted speed limit. Harrumph. Another X in the *choose another company* column. Still, a single sharp turn shouldn't completely disqualify him.

She lifted a hand to wave but got no response.

Other than the back passenger window rolled down and a man stuck out his head.

Gripped the doorframe.

And puked.

She gasped as the liquid struck the asphalt at the end of the driveway.

Their driveway.

Like a dog leaving a calling card on a fire hydrant.

Yuck.

She unlocked her vehicle and slid in, making certain the doors locked around her. Cocooning her in safety. Protecting her from *that man*. And his friends.

Brady Millman proved exactly who and what rumors said. A party boy. Party *animal*, more like.

Her mind made up, she started the car. He'd made the decision easy for her.

Tomorrow she'd find a new limo contractor.

⌒

Brady groaned as he turned the corner on two wheels. Well, it felt that way. This car could not maneuver narrow streets at higher-than-prudent speeds.

But that wasn't really the problem. Not the whole one anyway.

That look on Cassie's face just now. In fact, her entire body language—slumped shoulders, one hand dropping to her side, smile sliding into the abyss of disappointment—spoke volumes. Pastor Rick's upchucking hadn't earned Brady any points with the wedding planner.

Or with the woman herself.

If he could, he'd go back and park across the driveway so she couldn't escape until he explained the circumstances.

But he didn't have the time.

Pastor Rick doubled over, groaned, and fell onto the floor of the passenger area.

Brady glanced in the cabin-view mirror. His friend wasn't moving.

"Rick. Rick, wake up, buddy. We're almost there."

Still no response.

"Come on, Rick. Quit fooling around. This isn't funny."

Nothing.

Two more sharp turns, and then Brady pressed the accelerator as he hit the straight run down Eisenhower toward the hospital. Four-way flashers signaled a situation to other drivers, but several either didn't notice or didn't care. He careened in and out of lanes, once crossing over into the center turn lane, hoping no other vehicles wanted its use.

Finally, the blue-and-white sign indicating the last turn from Highway 87 and into the Emergency entrance.

This one he took on two tires.

He laid on the horn, attracting curious stares from several pedestrians, and hopefully, also from the staff inside. Uh-oh, maybe not the right kind of attention, since first out the door was a woman attired in a dark blue security uniform.

He slowed then stopped the car, hopped out, and opened the back door.

The officer held up a palm and strode toward him. "You can't park here, sir. This is—"

He paused. "I need help. My friend is unconscious."

"You can leave it here for ten minutes. Then you'll have to move it." She snapped her fingers toward the medical person following her. "Get a stretcher. Now. Stat." She laid a hand on Brady's arm. "Help is coming, sir."

"We can't wait."

He hoisted Rick over his shoulder, following the moves Bing, his firefighting buddy, taught him one Saturday afternoon. How was he to know he'd need that today for one of his best friends? He staggered under the pastor's weight, regained his balance, then turned from the car.

The dead weight draped down his back groaned, then a warm

liquid slid down Brady's back. Well, at least whatever was inside his friend that needed to come out was doing so.

This time, not on his car door, but on his back.

Rattling wheels and scurrying footsteps signaled that help had, indeed, arrived.

The officer directed him away from the car. "Step aside and let them do their job."

He relinquished his hold on his pastor and stepped out of the way. The two medical personnel and the officer lifted Rick onto the stretcher, strapped him in, and wheeled him into the hospital, with Brady close behind.

Rick was so pale. So white against the sheets, as though striving for invisibility.

But the staff treated him as very real.

"Pulse forty."

"Respiration sixteen."

That was good, wasn't it? He shoved his hands into his pockets to keep from reaching for Rick's hand. His foot. Something to reassure him his friend was still alive.

He had to be.

The security officer barred his way as they wheeled Rick through double doors that swung shut, blocking his view. "Move your car first, then come over here and answer a few questions while they assess your friend."

He stared into her eyes. Was she speaking to him? In English? Why couldn't he understand her? Her mouth opened and closed, but with his ears filled by a roaring wind, he couldn't hear.

He glanced around. Several people sat in chairs, nobody talking to anybody else. A child played in the small area set aside with blocks and books. A man in a suit came out of the treatment area and tapped a woman on the shoulder. He whispered a few words to her, and she crumpled like a deflated balloon. Bad news. The worst.

Would that be him soon?

The officer—Romero by the name on her tag—steered him toward the door. In less than three minutes, he returned, having moved his limo to the visitor parking lot. At the admissions counter stood a large man with ebony skin who smiled at him. Brady's legs carried him, but he had no idea how.

Ahiz—again, the name tag—spoke with a thick accent, lyrical in its cadence, gentle in its tone. "You brought this man in? You know him?"

"Yes." One-word responses he could manage. "Rick. King. Pastor."

Ahiz nodded. "Take this form and fill out as much as you can, please. Particularly next-of-kin, medical conditions, how he came to be in this state."

Brady stifled an inappropriate chuckle. More like a giggle. Pastor Rick drove to this state, of course. Colorado. About ten years ago in response to his call to the Loveland Community Church. "Sure."

He took the clipboard and sat in the first empty chair. Next-of-kin. Nancy. He had to let her know what was going on. He pulled his cell from his pocket and dialed. Nothing. He checked the bars. No coverage. He crossed to the desk. "Ahiz, can I use a phone? I need to call his wife."

"Please, sir, let us do that. We know how to make that connection."

Made sense. He'd probably bungle it. Sound too calm. Or get all hysterical. Although, right now, he felt nothing. Numb. He returned to his chair and continued answering what he knew. Ten minutes later, he looked up when a shadow darkened the form.

Ahiz. With a steaming cup of something hot. "For you, sir. Your friend is in excellent hands. You must remain strong for him. Hot tea with plenty of sugar."

Ah. Jamaica, perhaps. Or Barbados. One of those formerly British-owned islands. Where tea laced with sugar solved most ills. He forced a smile. "Thank you." He handed over the form. "That's all I know."

The ward clerk scanned the paper. "You know a great deal more than most do in these circumstances, sir."

Seemed a pitiful small amount given their close friendship over the years. So far as he knew, Rick had no medical conditions. Saw a doctor once a year for the mandatory health plan checkup. Went to the dentist twice as many times. Brushed and flossed. Worked out. Didn't drink or smoke. Lived a healthy life.

So why was the pastor staggering out of a bar like he was on the back end of a weeklong bender?

And who was the man with him?

He had no answers, but he knew the One who did.

He bowed his head, closed his eyes, and prayed.

A tap on his shoulder roused him from beseeching the throne of grace for his friend's life, and he looked up, stiff and sore from the prolonged position of reverence.

A man—this time in a white lab coat—smiled down at him. "Mr. Millman? You brought Mr. King in?"

"Yes." Unable to sit any longer, he stood, his mind clear and his spirit at peace. "Have you called Nancy? His wife?" He looked around. "She isn't here."

"No. She's at a women's retreat in Colorado Springs. We talked to her, and she'll head this way tomorrow morning."

"Tomorrow?" This made no sense. Unless Rick was already—no, it couldn't be. "He's not dead, is he?"

The doctor shook his head. "No, but since it's late in the day, and Mrs. King knows you're here, she decided to wait and drive safely in the daylight. He's being admitted, and you're welcome to sit with him for a while if you like."

"What happened? I've never seen him like this."

"And you likely won't again. Somebody drugged him, and he's having an adverse reaction." The doctor peered into his eyes. "You've heard of the date rape drug, right?"

"Well, sure. But—"

"Not only used by men on women. Sometimes used to knock a person out before they get mugged or robbed. Did you see anybody with Mr. King?"

"A man. Smelled bad, looked worse. Told me he was helping him, but Rick said he wanted me to help. Guy got miffed and took off."

"Most likely hoping to take your friend down an alley and roll him for his wallet." The medico checked his phone. "Room 2212. Second floor. He'll likely sleep through your visit. And don't stay past ten. The head nurse on that ward can be a tyrant." He offered his hand, which Brady shook. "Good night."

Brady waved to Ahiz then headed toward the elevator. After getting lost just the one time, he found Rick's room and settled into the recliner beside his friend, who, as the doctor said, slept soundly.

Tubes ran from a pole containing a bag of clear liquid. Several lines came from beneath the sheets and signaled a box with a screen. Brady squinted in the dim light. Heart rhythm, pulse, respiration, oxygen, blood pressure. He glanced around the room. Nothing to read. He checked the table beside the bed and smiled.

A Bible placed there by the Gideons.

As thankful as he was for his friend's positive prognosis, he could think of nothing he wanted to read now other than words of praise and reverence for the God who saved his friend. Who created the men and women operating under His direction, using medicine and wisdom to diagnose and treat Rick.

He flipped to the middle, to Psalms, paged back to Psalm 1, and read about this mighty triune God.

By the time he reached Psalm 150, darkness covered the parking lot outside the large plate-glass windows. Brady paced the room to stretch out his muscles and get the circulation flowing again, pausing at a light tap on the door.

An older woman in a traditional nurse's cap and wearing pale pink scrubs stuck her head in. "Doctor Farmer probably told you I'm an ogre, but visiting hours are long past."

"Actually, he used the word *tyrant*." He glanced at his friend in the bed. "I hate to leave him alone."

The nurse stepped back out of the doorway and gestured for him to follow. "He's not alone. There are three nurses and nursing assistants on duty all night. The doc is just a call away." She smiled at the book he still held. "And he's already in the Great Physician's hands."

Brady nodded. "The best place to be. Let me put this back, and I'll go."

He replaced the Bible on the bedside table, prayed a quick entreaty over his sleeping friend, then left.

The clock over the nurse's station told him the head nurse wasn't as much an ogre as she admitted or a tyrant as the doctor claimed.

Half past two.

Chapter Four

Cassie tossed and turned, refusing to look at the red digits on her clock radio. No, she wouldn't calculate how many hours until her alarm went off. She wouldn't—arrgh—less than four. And she hadn't closed her eyes for more than ten minutes since giving up on a senseless movie and crawling into bed at eleven.

And all that was after a pathetic microwave dinner of purported mashed potatoes and meat loaf, although she doubted whether the spuds had ever inhabited a field. More likely a mishmash of chemicals and factory floor sawdust.

As if that weren't enough excitement for one night, she'd then spent two hours going over—and over—her limousine contacts. Making calls. Getting line-disconnected messages. Fully-booked voice messages. And one who rudely hung up on her.

Served her right for depending on one company for the past couple of years.

Everybody else had moved on without her.

Leaving her stranded.

She'd even called a company in Denver that rented stretch vehicles, thinking she could drive if needed.

No joy. Chauffeur's license required.

She turned and fluffed her pillow. Again. Just thinking about limousines brought Brady Millman's face to her mind. She wanted to like him. He seemed personable enough. Turning that blinding smile on Amanda and her mother. Hoodwinking them with excuses and promises.

But not her. No siree. Sweet words wouldn't fool her. No matter how much she needed to use his services, he wasn't bowling her over with his charm.

Of which he had plenty. And charisma.

But that wasn't all he had, was it?

He also had a reputation. And while she didn't subscribe to the gossip mill, she had ears. Heard what others—mostly women—said about him. Flirtatious. Well, that probably served him well in his business. Nobody ever complained he crossed the line. She thought back to her social interactions with others. Few and far between. At work. At church. The occasional casual conversation with the cashier at the grocery store. If the checker forced her. Otherwise, she didn't talk to many.

Will seemed to like Brady. Will said he and the chauffeur knew each other through the men's group at Loveland Community Church.

Cassie smiled. She'd like to be a fly on the wall in that room.

She kicked off the covers. Why hadn't she seen through the veneer to the real man beneath? She was so empathic about her clients, knowing their deepest thoughts, their dreams, exactly what they wanted their weddings to look like. Why did that gift—or curse, truth be known—evade her in her personal life?

Unable to bear one more minute of this pointless activity, she swung her legs over the side of the bed, searching for her slippers. Finding only one, she paused. Better yet, get dressed and go for a short walk. If she didn't feel tired after that, well, she'd clean the house. Heaven knew it needed it. Between work and—well, nothing except work and church—she'd neglected both laundry and housework far too long. She needed the exercise. Surely that would count as a workout, right? A hundred calories for every fifteen minutes of cleaning? And if that didn't work, she had a boring romance sitting on the bedside table as a last resort.

She slipped into a pair of sweatpants, a hoodie, socks, and shoes, grabbed her keys, and headed outside. Down the quiet hallway of the apartment building, down two flights of stairs, and she stood outside in the courtyard. A couple of half-hearted leg stretches, a jumping jack or two to limber up the tense muscles, and off she went.

The residential neighborhood lay quiet as a cemetery at this hour of the morning. Three o'clock. Except to go to the bathroom in the middle of the night, she rarely saw this time of day. Two houses down, a dog barked once from a backyard as though doing its duty but not really interested in a full-scale alarm. She smiled as she pumped her arms, enjoying the rush of cool air in and out of her nose.

At the next block she slowed, walking in place as she considered whether to turn around or continue. Streetlights cast pools of illumination onto the sidewalk and curb area. No cars went past. The neighborhood was safe. Quiet. Walkable day or night.

Across the empty field and down over the hill, the city lights, pinpricks in the inky night, twinkled back at her. Somewhere she'd read that singing while walking burned more calories. And if she wore a hat, she'd burn a few more. She could use all the help she could get. She tugged the hood of her sweatshirt over her head and drew a deep breath to prepare for singing the first tune that came to mind.

"Twinkle, twinkle, little star. How I wonder what you are."

She stepped off the sidewalk to cross the four-lane street. At the next major intersection, she'd turn around and head home. Hmm. A cup of hot chocolate and a boring book might be just what the doctor ordered to send her off to la-la land.

And then, for the second time that day, squealing tires froze her in her tracks.

⁓

Brady jammed on the brakes. What the—?

A large floppy doll lay across the hood of his car.

Had some kid thrown it at him?

He blinked. Hard. Several times. If so, from where?

Here he was, cruising down the road, minding his own business—okay, struggling to keep his eyes open—and suddenly this doll jumped out at him. His mind intent on getting to his bed—how had this happened?

He gripped the steering wheel, and his heart plummeted to his toes.

No, not a doll.

Man? Woman? Child? He couldn't tell. Definitely a hoodie.

And then the thing—the person—slid over the fender of the car. As if in slow motion, one sleeve catching in the turn signal indicator, impeding their flow over the edge. Leaving two trails of smudges in his freshly waxed fender as they went.

Oh no. Oh no. Oh no.

Because it was definitely a woman.

And one he knew.

Cassie Blackthorn.

He shut off the engine and pocketed the keys, then jumped out and trotted around the front of the car. She lay on her back, staring up at the sky as though counting stars. Except her eyes were closed. Well, that was good, wasn't it? Didn't all the mystery shows on television always have the eyes of the dead wide open, staring into eternity?

He knelt beside her and poked her arm with a finger. Was she hurt? Maybe only stunned. She didn't move.

"Cassie. Can you hear me?"

Trust this obstreperous woman to be the exception to the eyes-wide-open rule. No, she couldn't be dead. He wasn't going fast enough to kill her. Was he? Then again, the limo was a big, heavy car.

"Oh God, please don't let her be dead. Please."

Should he move her? No, those TV shows said not to. She could have a head injury. Spinal cord damage. Internal bleeding. Fractures waiting to puncture a lung or a spleen. Or worse.

Considering all the possibilities made him nauseous, and he fought the urge to puke.

Okay, Millman, think back to first aid class.

He drew a couple deep breaths and ran shaky hands down her arms and legs. Couldn't feel any broken bones. Seemed she was out for a walk. Dressed for it, anyway. But at three in the morning? And crossing a street without looking for oncoming traffic? Had to be her fault, right?

Couldn't be that he fell asleep at the wheel.

He groaned. His insurance would go through the roof if it was his fault. And even if it wasn't, he'd still want to be certain she had the best of medical care.

Medical care. Right.

He pulled his phone from a pocket and dialed 911. He gave his location, his name, and the details of the accident. Dispatch assured him help was on the way.

For the second time today, he needed help.

He was unable to bring himself to check for broken bones in her torso—much too personal, and if she came to, she'd probably break his arm and pin *him* to the ground. Instead, he covered her with his jacket then hurried to the trunk, where he extracted reflector triangles and placed them at strategic locations front and back of the car to alert other vehicles and the ambulance on its way.

Back at her side, he leaned close to check her breathing. Seemed okay, but what did he know apart from a two-hour high school class on simple bandages and splinting a broken bone? Thankfully no blood gushed from her head or anywhere else, and she appeared as peaceful as if she were in her own bed.

Not that he knew what she looked like when she slept.

His cheeks grew hot at the way his mind skipped around like a chicken on LSD. Not a good comparison, either, given his sideline as a drug counselor.

He sat back on his haunches, close enough if she roused, yet not too near that she'd feel crowded if she did.

Then he sought help in the only place he knew he could trust.

He bowed his head and prayed.

Chapter Five

Cassie grunted and struggled to open her eyes. Yuck. What was that smell? Beer? Vomit?

She wrinkled her nose then peeked through slit lids once more. Where was she? Why was she lying on the floor? Had she fallen out of bed? A small turn of her head to the left. Shiny. Round. The sun? No. The moon? Nope. A hubcap.

Hubcap? She rolled to her side, and her world rolled with her. Hands to her temples kept her brains from rocking around inside her skull but failed to alleviate the feeling that she was in an open boat on a stormy sea.

She had to get out of here. Wherever here was.

Pushing with her arms, she managed a hunched-over seated position but found she needed to grip her knees to steady herself. At least she had no broken bones from whatever she'd landed herself in the middle of.

Because it wasn't her bedroom floor.

Or anywhere in her apartment.

Eyes wide, trying to pierce the darkness, she saw a form huddled near her. Not quite close enough to touch. Smelling like a brewery, no less.

She studied the top of his head. Did she know him?

Oh no. The last person she wanted to see right now. Or maybe ever.

None other than Party Boy.

Swiveling her head slowly so her vision kept up with the movement, she scanned her surroundings. And her physical condition. Her palms stung from road rash. Along with her knees. Had she fallen while crossing the street? And Mr. Chauffeur just happened to be going past?

She didn't think so.

Which meant only one other possibility.

He'd deliberately run into her with his limousine.

That made little sense.

He loved the car far too much to risk damaging it by running her over.

Then again, it was a big car. With a huge chrome bumper and front grille. It could probably run into a moose and not even need a new waxing.

She shivered, rubbing her arms to warm herself. Ooh, that was going to be black and blue tomorrow. She ran her hands through her hair. No blood, thank goodness. But her nose was tender. No wonder. She'd mashed it into the car. If her proboscis remained intact, she'd still surely have two black eyes tomorrow. And likely a crooked nose for the rest of her life. Which meant her chances of finding a husband had dropped to minus ten. With millions of beautiful women in the world—with perfect noses—why would a man look twice at her?

Tomorrow. Oh no. She had clients to meet. A job to do. And now look at her.

She turned back to her would-be assassin. What exactly was

he doing? Head bowed. Mumbling something. Maybe he was a victim here too.

Cassie cleared her throat. "Excuse me."

His head snapped up, the whites of his eyes bright in the dark. "You're awake."

She grunted. She was the one injured, and he made it sound like she wasn't doing him any favors by not dying on him. Or maybe her scraped elbows were telling her that. "You don't sound as if that makes you happy."

"No, it does. I mean, yes, it makes me happy." He scooted forward. "I checked for broken bones."

She peered at him. "You checked—"

"Yeah. Ran my hands up and down your arms and—" He glanced at her lower extremities as if just now realizing what an intrusion into her personal space that might seem to her. "Cursory only, mind you."

"What are you? A doctor or something too? Besides being a chauffeur?"

He straightened. "Business owner. Not just a driver."

She sniffed. "Whatever." She looked around, grateful this was a quiet stretch of road. Nothing worse than somebody driving past and seeing her on the ground. "So what happened? And if you try to tell me you found me like this—"

He shook his head. "No. I didn't. I mean, you ran into my car. Or something like that."

Cassie jabbed a thumb into her chest. "I ran into—" Now she pointed at him. "Your car?" She laughed, then wished she hadn't. Her ribs and back ached. "Don't make me laugh."

"Well, what I mean is, I was driving along, minding my

business, and you—"

Her memory snapped into place. "I was walking. Crossing the street. Nothing coming."

She paused. Well, usually she checked for traffic. And rarely saw any vehicles out this late at night. Or early in the morning. Had she been so deep in thought she'd neglected to look both ways this time?

He shrugged. "I don't know. One second you weren't there. Then the next you were. I jammed on the brakes, you hit the hood, then you dropped over the edge like—"

Was that a smile tickling his lips? How had she ever wondered what it might be like to kiss him? What had she been thinking?

"Like what?"

"Sorry. Nothing. You slid over the fender to the ground. I jumped out. Checked for broken bones. Called 911." He paused and tilted his head. "I hear a siren. Must be them. You'd better stay there until they arrive."

"No such thing. I don't need medical attention. I need a hot shower and my bed."

The driver—correction, chauffeur—extended his hand to her. "Let me help you."

She scooted out of his reach. "Are you kidding me? You're drunk as a skunk. I saw you earlier with your equally drunk party car. Now you're out by yourself mowing down hapless pedestrians with your land yacht. I should call the cops."

"You're wrong about most things, but you're right about the police." He pulled out his cell phone. "Here, use my phone."

He placed the device into her hand as gently as if it were a newly hatched chick.

What did that say about his level of intoxication? That he could carry on this conversation without slurring a single word. Have the sense to call an ambulance. And now, without a tremor visible, pass her his cell.

Had she jumped to conclusions about Brady Millman?

Perhaps yet again?

⌒

Everything within Brady wanted to hop into his car and speed away into the night. But common sense—or perhaps that still, small voice that kept telling him things would be all right—kept him there.

How could he have messed things up so badly? The one woman in the entire world whom he'd even given a second glance in years, and he almost killed her with his car.

At least, that's what she believed.

And it wasn't the only thing either. She'd said he was drunk, but he knew different. So why—he sniffed his clothes—oh right, Rick had thrown up on him. And that stranger had tossed most of a bottle of beer at Pastor Rick too.

The siren neared. He had but a few minutes to plead his case before she told her version, which, in this case, wasn't true.

"Please, Cassie. Hear me out."

She shook her head. "I've heard enough from you for one night." She gripped the limo's bumper and struggled to her feet. "I don't need medical help. Let me go home. I live just over there."

He opened the passenger door. "I could drive you."

"Are you kidding? After trying to kill me? No, thanks."

"Well, that's just it. I didn't try to run you down. It was an accident."

Rescue sounded like it was only a few blocks away. If they smelled alcohol on him, they'd run a portable breath test. Or they'd call the police and have him arrested. He'd test negative, but still—too embarrassing.

Why wouldn't she let him drive her home? She had to be sore. "Are you worried about letting me know where you live?"

She wouldn't meet his eyes. Of course. That was it.

"It's not like I'm going to stalk you or something."

Her brows lowered. "Funny you should be the one telling me all the bad things you won't do to me. Wasn't mowing me down enough? Do you have other plans?" She pivoted. "Go away."

"But what about the ambulance?"

"You called them. You explain. I'm out of here."

She checked both ways for traffic then crossed the road, turned down the first street, and disappeared into the black night.

She was so wrong about so many things, but she was so right about one: he'd have to explain to the EMTs why their patient got up and walked away.

A long night would be even longer.

⌐

Thank You, God.

When the fire truck pulled up, his friend from the men's group at church, Bing Kelley, hopped down, his brow pulled low and his mouth surrounded by worry lines.

"Hey, Brady, didn't realize you were our call for service." He quirked his chin toward the limo. "What happened? Heard there was a potential bodily injury."

Brady scuffed his toe on the asphalt. "She got up and walked away. Not hurt as seriously as I thought."

Bing laid a hand on Brady's arm. "What do you mean, not hurt as badly as you thought?"

Brady filled him in and explained how he checked for broken bones before calling 911. "Then she came to, said she was fine, and walked home."

Bing scanned the dark neighborhood around them. "Do you know where she lives?"

"No."

Bing sniffed. "Do I smell alcohol? You don't drink."

"A drunk threw a beer on me tonight." Keeping their pastor's situation to himself seemed the best bet right now. "And somebody else vomited on me."

His firefighter friend nodded as though everything he said made perfect sense. "Sounds like another night in the party car." He leaned closer. "Or was this a client from your *other* line of work?"

"No, it wasn't like—"

An ambulance pulled to the side of the road behind the fire truck, and a paramedic trotted toward them, medical bag in hand. "Where's the injured party?"

Bing laughed and stepped away. "You're on your own for this one."

The medic glanced at each in turn. "Don't think you're hurt. What's going on?"

Bing clapped the medic's shoulder. "This is my good friend Brady. He goes to Loveland Community too." He turned to Brady. "Mike Snow. He and his wife and kids come to LCC. Known him for years." Back to Mike. "And Brady I know inside and out. We've been mentoring partners over the years. He's a good guy.

You can believe what he tells you."

Mike nodded. "I hear you. Be safe, Bing." The two shook hands, and Bing got back in the fire truck and pulled out. Mike leaned against the rear fender of the limo. "Want to start at the beginning?"

Leaving Pastor Rick's name out, Brady did just that, culminating with the woman leaving the scene. "And that's how it happened."

"She didn't ask for your insurance information?"

"No, why should she?"

"In case she wakes up tomorrow with a severe case of whiplash or back pain or the like."

Brady groaned. He hadn't even considered that. And he doubted Cassie had either. Well, if that happened, she knew where to get in touch with him.

If she didn't burn the telephone lines between her phone and his.

In less than twenty minutes, Mike decided there was nothing more for them to do, and Brady got in his car and drove off, wondering if perhaps he should have had Mike check him out.

The ache in his chest every time he thought of not seeing Cassie again overwhelmed him, threatening to cut off his breathing.

He was probably better off without her. She was high maintenance, right?

He didn't need her—or anybody like her—in his life now.

So why didn't that make him feel better?

Chapter Six

Cassie gritted her teeth against the pain in her skull, her back, her shoulders, her knees—in fact, everything from the top of her head to the tips of her toes hurt. Maybe she should have accepted a ride from Mr. Party Animal. No, at least she arrived home in one piece.

With how that man drove, she had no such guarantee if she'd gotten into his car.

After a hot shower, she patted herself dry with the thickest and softest towel she could find in the linen closet, then headed to the kitchen for an ice pack. As she passed the mirror in the hallway, she wondered if she had a steak in the freezer. Wasn't that a recommended treatment for black eyes?

Not an hour after hitting the pavement, already she noted purple-and-blue circles beneath her eyes and around her nose.

She rooted around the tiny freezer. No steak, but plenty of ice. Cubes, a freezer gel pack, and a thick layer lining the walls of the compartment. She sighed. Something else to do on her day off. If she felt like it, which she doubted. Not with these aches and bruises.

Maybe a hot pad for her back. Now, when did she last see— Oh yes, also in the linen closet. On the top shelf. Along with a set of electric curlers, a gift from her mother about twenty years ago. She pulled down the pad and retreated to her recliner. After plugging in the hot and wrapping the cold in a tea towel, she eased into the chair and raised her feet.

Ah, much better. Easing the gel pack onto her nose, she winced. Despite not being broken, it hurt like the dickens. Mr. Brady Millman should thank his lucky stars—or whatever he believed in—that she wasn't lying in the ER right now, racking up his liability insurance dollars by the minute.

And what did he believe in? She'd never gotten into any discussion with him beyond their business relationship. She didn't know his marital state, although she suspected, by the rumors she struggled to ignore, that they shared the same status. Parties seemed to be what he lived for. And what a perfect business to fall into—the kind where folks rented his vehicles to go to lavish and extravagant and out-of-control parties.

Which made him sound very shallow. Did she really know him well enough to judge him that way? What was it Felicity's beau said one time? When they watched that politician on the television, the one who got himself into trouble with his secretary?

"Don't judge a book by its cover."

Cassie snorted. She wasn't like that. Brady Millman and his ilk were well-known to her, right through to the epilogue in his story. High school. College. They were all the same.

And they never changed.

She wriggled in her chair for a more comfortable position, sighing when she found the magic spot.

Magic, that's what she needed right now. A potion or incantation to erase this evening. And the aches and pains that went along with the memory.

She closed her eyes, and the accident flashed across her mind. Crossing the street. Nothing in sight. Then wham! Slam! Down on the ground.

And Brady Millman, kneeling beside her, head down. Mumbling?

Or praying?

No, surely he wasn't a believer. A real Christian man wouldn't drink and drive. And when she'd accused him of being drunk, he hadn't denied her words. But did she give him a chance? Or had she flung those hateful words so hard and fast he didn't have the opportunity?

Funny how she had no problem talking when it came to running her mouth.

If her father were here, he'd say a genuine believer in Jesus wouldn't consume alcohol period. No siree. No spirits. No smoking. No cussing. No bad habits. That last one brought her up short. What about her? Well, she didn't do any of those things. Except maybe her habit of retreating within herself when around others. Nothing new there. As the youngest of three, the baby of the family, she'd felt invisible all her life. An afterthought. The girl that messed up the perfect family photos of her beautiful mother, handsome father, and two almost identical brothers, even though they were eleven months apart.

And her. The gap between her front teeth that even braces couldn't correct. Sure, Lauren Hutton had the same look, but she also had everything else. Cassie herself wasn't so blessed.

Nope, she'd overheard that conversation between her parents when she was about six. About how it was too bad Cassie wasn't a boy so her brothers' hand-me-downs could be used. Talk about making a girl feel good about herself. Not.

She closed her eyes, willing the replay of the accident to go away. And it did, replaced by the message at church the previous Sunday. About the consequences of not trusting in God. Another of her bad habits, if she could call it that. Trying to make herself feel better about herself. Reminding herself of her attributes, her strengths, her accomplishments. Not trusting in God working in her and through her but, instead, relying on herself. Not leaving room for Him.

Or worse, comparing herself to others. At least she wasn't as bad as—as bad as Brady Millman, who drove while intoxicated. That had to be a lot worse than—wait a minute. What else did Pastor Rick say? God doesn't grade on a bell curve?

Cassie slid her hand into the pocket of the recliner, her fingers searching for—there it was. The little orange pocket testament she received in middle school. From that older man in a suit jacket and tie. A lifetime ago.

She opened the book to the front section and ran her finger down the list until she came to the heading of TRUST. There, one she recalled from a Bible study at church from a few years ago. *Trust in the Lord with all your heart. . . .*

Well, she'd trusted Him with her salvation, hadn't she? With erasing her sins? With saving her? Was there more?

What about that one from Philippians? *And I am sure of this, that He who began a good work in you will be faithful to complete it.*

A good work? In her? Was it possible?

She returned to the list and read each verse, ending where she'd begun. Tears blurred her vision and trickled down her cheeks, and she stifled sobs. But after a couple of minutes of the ache in her heart and throat matching that in her battered body, she gave up, succumbing to the realization she'd fallen woefully short in her relationship with God.

She returned the chair to its upright position and slid—for the second time today—this time to her knees. To ask God's forgiveness.

After kicking off his shoes, Brady collapsed onto his bed, his body and mind numb. But when he closed his eyes, begging for sleep, Cassie's face filled his vision. First the look of disgust from this afternoon when Pastor Rick puked out the car window. And later, after she hit his car and then came to, fear. Of him. Of who he was. What he might do to her next.

Then, when she smelled his clothes and realized who he was, disgust mixed with something else. Pity?

Why did she dislike him so much? Surely she didn't have a vendetta against limousine drivers in general? Against chauffeurs in Loveland in particular?

Him, specifically?

And if him, then what? He was a nice guy. Called his mom every Sunday. Didn't kick dogs. Helped little old ladies across the street. Nice to everybody he met. Okay, not everybody. For example, not the drunk trying to roll his pastor in an alley, for that certainly was what he intended.

Could he have handled that situation better? Offered the guy a cup of coffee? A free session at his clinic? What did Jesus say? When you're asked to go a mile, go two. But how did that apply to his situation? He'd given the man twice his original asking price to keep quiet about Pastor Rick. He'd offered Cassie a ride home.

Why did her failure to like him cause him so much grief? It wasn't like she was the only woman in the world. Or even in Loveland. No siree, there were plenty of fish in his particular pond. He could have his pick.

So why was she the only one who caught his attention? Her witty repartee? Unfortunately, usually aimed at him. Her quiet thoughtfulness that implied she was a deep subject? One he'd gladly study.

He rolled over, stifling a chuckle. Maybe he needed to enroll in a "Master of Cassie Blackthorn" program.

He thought back to his morning devotional reading. The verse in Romans. *That is why his faith was counted to him as righteousness.*

He longed to experience the level of righteousness that warranted commendation from his Savior. Brady slipped to the floor, determining to start anew, here and now. "Lord, please forgive me for taking You for granted." He swallowed hard. "Please show me how to live for You in all areas of my life. Help me to please You and only You. In Jesus' name, amen."

He rose and sat on the edge of the bed as a weight the size of his limo slipped off his chest and his shoulders. He breathed deeply, reveling in the newfound sense of purpose.

Number one on his list: mend fences with Miss Cassie Blackthorn.

Chapter Seven

At five till seven the next morning—correction—the same morning, Cassie strolled into the Weddings by Design building. She flipped on the lights in the kitchen and made a quick cup of coffee to get her brain working. Then she hurried to her computer, on a mission.

After checking her notebook for the bridesmaids' measurements called in by Amanda the previous day, she ordered the dresses Amanda *really* wanted for her wedding: the seafoam green in three styles to suit the girls' body shapes.

That accomplished, she checked their computerized records for names of other limo services in the area. She had eliminated all but one—and rumors suggested that company was out of business—when the back door opened and an explosion of business partners filled the kitchen with their laughter, chatter, and early morning energy. Kiki mentioned an article in a magazine about ways to promote their agency. She groaned. Promotions meant photographs, which usually meant dolling up for a camera. Wouldn't she look a treat?

Kiki, their seamstress, poked her head in Cassie's doorway. "Saw your car in the driveway." Her eyes widened. "Wowzers. What happened to you?" She stepped back. "Felicity, Ronnie, come quick."

Cassie swiveled her chair to turn her face from the door, but it was too late. The baker's flats and the chef's trademark heels click-clacked across the kitchen and hallway, stopping outside her office.

Ronnie bounced on her toes from the rear of the group. "What's going—oh my."

Oh my indeed.

Felicity pushed past the other two and swept into the room, bringing with her the mouthwatering smell of orange peel and cinnamon. She tipped Cassie's head toward her. "Oh girl. Did you have that looked at?"

Cassie scooted her chair away. "It's nothing."

But Felicity wouldn't let up. "What happened?"

Ronnie and Kiki stood their ground in the doorway, Kiki with her arms crossed over her chest.

The seamstress tilted her head. "We aren't leaving until you tell us."

Ronnie's eyebrows shot up. "Not a bad date?"

Kiki snorted. "I'd hate to see what *he* looks like if that's the case."

They weren't making this easy. "Not a date."

Felicity laid a hand on her arm. "Were you mugged?"

"Would you believe me if I told you I fell down the stairs?"

Kiki's brow lowered. "At your apartment building? Then I hope they have good insurance. You'd better see a lawyer."

They would not let go. She sighed. "Okay. Not stairs. I ran into a car. Sort of."

Kiki shook her head. "I saw your van. Not a mark on it. Well, except for the dent in the door where you rapped it on one of those concrete thingies at the gas station."

"Not *my* car. *I* ran into another car."

Ronnie perched on a chair opposite Cassie's desk, propped her heels on the edge, and wrapped her arms around her legs. "Start at the beginning. I haven't had coffee yet, and my brain is still asleep."

Kiki flopped into the other chair. "What she said."

Cassie shrugged. She *really* didn't want to get into this discussion. Way too much work to do. Time for the abbreviated version. Maybe if she recited her activities quickly enough, their caffeine-deprived minds wouldn't truly grasp the meaning. Which meant they'd leave her alone. To commiserate over her sorry condition alone.

She drew a breath. "I couldn't sleep last night, so I went for a walk. I guess I crossed the street without looking, and a car was coming, and I sorta ran into it. Knocked myself out for all of about three seconds. Skinned my palms and knees." She waved her hands in their direction to prove her point of not making a big deal about it. "Did a face-plant. Got up and walked home. By myself. End of story."

She exhaled in a whoosh. That had to be the longest one-inhale speech she'd ever given.

She surveyed the room. Fliss, perched on the corner of Cassie's desk, peered at her. Oh no. *The Look.* Ronnie, chin resting on her knees, looked ready to spring into action, like a kangaroo poised on its tail to kick some butt with its hind legs. And Kiki—well, that was a surprise. The girl acted like the toughest chick on the block, but were her eyes actually filled with tears?

Time to change the subject. "My nose isn't broken. Thankfully. Not even as bruised as my ego."

Ronnie unfolded her legs and planted her feet on the floor before leaning forward. "And who was driving this car you just happened to run into?"

"Wasn't the driver's fault. All mine." Cassie tapped in a password, intent on moving on with her day. "Can we drop it, please?" She sipped her coffee. "What was the chatter about an article somebody saw? And should Camilla be here? To take notes or something?"

Kiki smirked. Apparently not completely over their office manager's harsh treatment of her yet. "Or to get the coffee." She held up her insulated cup. "Or iced tea."

Cassie chuckled. "I'm sure she'd be thrilled to hear you suggest that."

Kiki shook her head and tossed her a mock frown. "Are you kidding me? We just narrowly averted World War III. Not pushing that atomic button."

Felicity stood. "I don't think we need her here for this discussion. Back to business. But I don't think you can change the subject so easily, Cassie. You're not off the hook yet. There's more to this story." She glanced at the other two. "We'll weasel it out of you or figure it out between ourselves, won't we, ladies?"

Ronnie nodded and settled back, crossing one knee over the other. "We will. They don't call us the Three Sherlocks for nothing."

Cassie frowned. "Somebody actually calls you that? I had no idea."

Kiki laughed and slapped her thigh. "No, she just made that up. But it's a good moniker."

Felicity pulled a periodical from a file folder. "Saw this article last night in *Foothills Business*." She leafed through several pages. "It's a great article on boosting business." She scanned the group. "With four of us on board, I think we can take on more clients."

Glad for the change of subject, Cassie nodded. "Go on."

Their baker scanned the article. "They start with the simple and well-known stuff. Excellent customer service for repeat business and word of mouth."

Ronnie smiled. "Well, hopefully none of our clients come back again. But I think we do pretty well on personal recommendations."

Kiki held up a hand. "I need an iced tea before we really get into this discussion. And something to sustain our mortal bodies?"

Felicity set the magazine on Cassie's desk. "How about we convene in the conference room in ten minutes? We can think better in there."

Cassie stood, easing her aching muscles into a different position. A touch of a headache threatened at the base of her skull. Perhaps caffeine and sugar would stave off a full-blown migraine.

Eight minutes later, the foursome settled around the oversized worktable they lovingly called the conference table, beverages and cinnamon buns in hand.

Felicity continued as moderator. "Another suggestion was a mailer. Perhaps offering a discount on services booked within thirty days, say. Urgency is key for those to really work."

Kiki's nose wrinkled. "I don't think a wedding is something we want to push somebody into choosing simply to save money."

Ronnie nodded. "I agree."

Felicity turned another page. "This is the one I'm most excited about. With all the advances in technology, it can be easy and cheap to produce a short television ad, say thirty seconds or so. Using our smartphones, we can edit, do music, voice-overs, whatever we want."

Oh no. That didn't sound like anything Cassie wanted to do. Not now, for certain, because of her facial injuries. And not in the long term either. She'd die if she had to stand in front of a camera and talk to people she didn't even know. "But we're not actors."

"Well, that's the point. The person writing this article says customers like to feel that they *know* who they'll be working with. Feel they can trust them." Felicity looked to Ronnie and Kiki. "What do you think?"

Ronnie wriggled in her chair. "I already have some ideas for what we could say."

Kiki nodded. "And I took two film classes in college."

They outnumbered her. And out-enthused, judging by all the ideas that flew back and forth between the three. Nobody seemed to notice she contributed nothing else to the conversation.

After almost an hour, Felicity shut the magazine. "We've got a splendid start here. Let's get together again in a day or so and hash out the details."

Ronnie drained the last of her coffee. "I should have a draft script pounded out by then."

Kiki licked icing from her fingertips. "I'll practice shooting you in candid situations. You know, natural-like."

Cassie groaned to herself. There was nothing natural about her distaste for the camera. Or the sick feeling she always got when looking at images of herself, either stills or video.

But the others were so excited. There was no stopping them. Somehow she had to perfect her avoidance technique. If they shot enough good footage of themselves, they wouldn't need her.

She followed Kiki out of the room. "I have three dresses coming in tomorrow, different styles, along with the preliminary measurements. Will you have time to do alterations?"

"Sure. If I get them by nine, I can have them ready by noon.

Will that work for you?"

"Perfect. Amanda and her bridesmaids are coming in the afternoon, and I'd like to surprise them."

Camilla occupied her cubbyhole at the junction of the hall-way near the kitchen. Cassie paused at her desk. "Did you get my voice message?"

Her cousin and office manager smiled up at her, feigning her innocent-as-a-newborn-babe look, all eyes and raised eyebrows. "I did. You needed something?"

Cassie stifled a groan. "I asked you to call me."

"Didn't want to interfere with all the important work you're doing."

Ever since her showdown with Kiki, Camilla had been irritatingly pleasant and gracious.

Funny how fake that persona made her seem. Still, she managed the phones, fetched mail and office supplies, and spoke politely to clients.

"My calendar is full enough. Please don't accept any more speaking engagements on my behalf. Instead, send them through to me."

"Hunky-dory. Your wish is my command."

Refusing to react to Camilla's bottomless vat of passive-aggressiveness, Cassie headed for her office, wishing she could close the door and crawl under her desk. But she had a lot to do first.

Like find a new limousine service.

Seated in Pastor Rick's home office, Brady unburdened his soul. His friend lounged in an easy chair across from him, close enough to touch. Still pale from his ordeal, the pastor nodded as Brady described his experience of the late night before, once or twice asking a question for clarification.

When Brady finished, Pastor Rick leaned forward, elbows on his knees, hands clasped. He stared at him, holding his gaze. "I believe you had a very real encounter with the living God. Something that happens to those truly seeking a deeper relationship with God. It's obvious you have a special calling on your life."

Brady sat back, his arms and legs weighing him down like anchors. "That's one of the scariest things I've ever been told. Special calling?"

"I know what your next questions will be. What will that look like? Why me? Why not somebody else?"

He chuckled. "You've read my mail."

Pastor Rick nodded. "Been there. Got the T-shirt." He relaxed again. "So let's talk about what this might look like in your life."

"I guess that's my biggest question. I don't know where to start."

"What this means is that you must treat your business, your calling, and everything you do as though God is the CEO. He calls the shots. You're the guy at the end of the line who does what the Boss says when He says. Without question. Like you're in the army. Which you are. The Lord's army."

"Where do I begin? I mean, I've been a believer for a lot of years, but I never understood here"—he tapped his chest—"that God wants to be the center of everything."

"It means you must take every decision to the Lord in fervent prayer. Whether to devote your time to the limo business or make the leap to full-time counseling ministry. What clients to take on in either line of work. Which woman to date. All the important stuff."

That familiar ache lodged in Brady's chest again at the

mention of dating and women. Unlikely he'd stand a chance with Cassie now. Not after this morning's fiasco. Which meant he'd have more time to devote to the other areas of his life. "I'm out of my depth."

Pastor Rick tossed him a half smile. "We all are. Our nature wants to be in control. We're impatient. We want it now. Waiting on God can be infuriating. Not choosing our own path can make us feel like children. Which we are." He picked up his cell phone. "I can give you the names of a couple of guys who might work as mentors."

Brady shook his head. "I can't think of sharing this with anybody but you right now. Would you have time in your schedule?"

"Had time for you today, didn't I?"

"Because I brought pizza and soda."

The pastor chuckled. "There is that. How about we meet each week for a month and see where it goes from there? And you can always call or text if you have questions."

"Expect tons of those." Brady gulped his soda, his throat dry. Nerves? "How are you feeling?"

"Like I was dragged through a knothole. But much better than I was."

"Any idea how you ended up drugged?"

Pastor Rick shook his head. "I went into that pub because a parishioner's wife called, suspecting her husband fell off the wagon. That was one of his hangouts, she said. He usually showed up around six there. I ordered a soda and waited for him."

"You don't think the bartender—"

"Nope. I went to the restroom once. A fellow at the end of the bar tried to chat me up just before that, but I told him I was waiting for somebody." He slapped his forehead. "Stupid. I shouldn't have left my drink on the counter. But I thought he was harmless."

"Did the man you were waiting for show up?"

Another shake of the head. "I started feeling groggy, and this same guy came over and offered to drive me home. Didn't feel right, but I wasn't in any shape to resist." He smiled. "I'm so glad you showed up when you did. What were you doing, cruising the downtown bars?"

The speech he'd prepared to apologize to Cassie, to impress her with his suave demeanor and perhaps work his way back into her good graces, flashed across his mind. "Just on my way home."

The pastor's brows pulled down a moment then relaxed. "Roundabout way, but I guess God was in control. I don't know what might have happened if you hadn't been there."

"At the least, he could have mugged you. Glad I could help. Did you call the police?"

"I don't have any evidence that was the man's intention."

"Well, I'll keep an eye out for him. I'm sure he was on something more than simple alcohol."

"You'd know the signs, for sure."

"From personal experience and from training."

Brady left the pastor to recuperate and headed toward his second job, his own words ringing in his ears.

How he wished his knowledge of the pull that drugs had on a person's life wasn't so up close and personal. His brother's battle in that particular arena still filled his thoughts, spurring him to do what he could to ensure no others fell victim to its evil influence. Not the addicts themselves and not their families.

Chapter Eight

The next morning, Cassie answered the business's front door before eight thirty. The parcel express driver handed over the box containing the bridesmaids' dresses, and she practically skipped down the hallway, despite his lifted eyebrow, no doubt wondering about the bruises around her eyes.

Still, she wouldn't let that spoil her day. Amanda would be so surprised when she saw the beautiful gowns, each specially chosen with her bridesmaids' builds and preferences in mind.

Kiki, already knee-deep in an ocean of veil fabric, looked up from her worktable. "Dresses here already?"

"Yep. I don't think it's going to take much to alter them. The girls were almost perfect sizes six, ten, and fourteen. Maybe a tuck here and there."

"No worries." She accepted the form Cassie handed over. "Looks good."

Kiki, a master seamstress, worked magic with a needle and thread. Plus four sewing machines, each a little different from the others, that apparently served special purposes.

Cassie skirted Camilla's desk, but the woman wasn't present. She peeked at her computer screen. Solitaire. Why didn't that surprise her? Seemed her commitment not to do her college assignments to the negligence of her work duties didn't extend to finding something more productive than playing online games.

At her own desk, Cassie researched online about other limo companies. The one she'd selected proved out for the count—of business, that is. The person who answered said she'd had that number for at least three years and knew nothing about Classy Cars.

Checking out pricing proved more difficult. Nobody gave quotes over the phone.

Unlike Brady Millman, always glad to estimate an upcharge when she called.

Nobody wanted to give her a straight answer about liability. Background checks. Drivers' records.

Unlike Brady Millman, always happy to fax over that information without hesitation.

She gritted her teeth. Why did nobody else measure up to that man?

At least in the customer service department?

But in his driving? Mario Andretti in a chauffeur's cap.

Except not as good a driver as the classic race car champion.

She wanted to like him. Really, she did. So why did he go out of his way to ruin his business? And any chance of a friendship between them.

Just under an hour later, Cassie's intercom buzzed. She pressed the button to answer. "Cassie here."

"Dresses are ready. Want to see?"

Cassie disconnected the call, rounded her desk, and bolted across the hallway and into the living room, ignoring her protesting muscles. Sure enough, in the far corner, the gowns robed three mannequins with shapes similar to the three girls. Subtle. Breathtaking.

Perfect.

Amanda would be thrilled.

⁓

Brady sighed and pushed away from the desk in his home office. Enough paperwork for one day. He shut down his computer and stood. Now what? No assignments lined up for today. And a definite drop in business if he didn't patch things up with Cassie.

The mere thought of her made his breath quicken. What could he do to mend fences? Pastor Rick's words of the previous day echoed through his mind. "*Pray first.*" Well, he could do that on the way to Cassie's. Didn't the Bible say not to let the sun go down on his anger? He wasn't the one who walked away. He should help her by going over there with a peace offering and asking if they could start again.

What to bring? Flowers? Nah, wedding planners likely had enough of those, free samples and all. Coffee? What woman could resist a man bearing coffee? That was it. He'd head down there midafternoon. Coffee in hand. A little pick-me-up to get her through the rest of the day. After the minor mishap with his car fender, she'd need that.

He paced the floor of his office while he thought. Then he stopped, snapped his fingers. How did she like her coffee? He had no idea. No worries. He'd bring cream and sugar.

Brady glanced at his cell phone. A little after twelve. Was that too early? How could a coffee-carrying hero be too early? Not possible. In fact, he had another brainchild. He'd get coffees for her partners too. Overload her with his generosity and thoughtfulness.

Which drive-through? Hot, strong, and expensive franchise brew? Or the local drive-up espresso with fourteen flavors? He went with local, resisting doctoring the java with the Italian syrups. Stick with regular old Joe until he got to know her better.

Five cups in a cardboard tray sat on the floor on the passenger side of the car as he eased out of the drive-through. No point wasting even a single precious drop.

But the cars ahead of him weren't moving. What the—? Not rush hour, surely. And the last chance to turn off this street lay behind him. He could back up—nope. Two more cars filled his rearview mirror. He craned his neck to look out the window and up the street.

An orange sign ahead warned of the construction zone and lane closures.

Just his luck.

The coffee was getting cold, and his mood turned sour as he fumed at the delay.

Then his pastor's words came to mind as surely as if the man sat beside him. *"Pray first."*

Maybe he should have listened. He jammed the limo into Park and closed his eyes.

This could take awhile.

Chapter Nine

Cassie led Amanda and three delightful and giggling girls into Kiki's area, stood before the mannequins, and did her best Vanna White impression. "Ta da!"

The bride-to-be's eyes filled, and she wavered in place, held up by a bridesmaid on either side. "Oh no?"

This didn't sound good. She glanced at the notebook in her hand. Had she fallen down the rabbit hole and ended up in the wrong wedding party? Nope. Walker. Three attendants. Seafoam green.

It's what Amanda wanted, despite her weak protests of joy at her mother's choice of frilly peach, all the same style.

Or had she been completely wrong? No, not possible. While she sometimes thought her ability to know what others wanted was a curse, in most cases, her empathy enabled her to help brides reduce stress and anxiety when making the dozens of choices needed to pull off a successful wedding.

"Isn't this the color you wanted? I was certain—"

Amanda swallowed back a sob. "No, it is? But I wanted my mother to be happy? She was just diagnosed with cancer? The doctor says she has three to six months?" A hiccup and another sob. "She might not live long enough to see me married?"

"Oh, I'm sorry to hear that." Now what? Because of the

alterations, she couldn't return the dresses. And selling them in their current condition—wait a minute. Thinking about her own troubles wasn't very empathic. Or supportive of Amanda and her mother. "We'll work this out. Somehow."

Rose, a bridesmaid, patted Amanda's arm. "Yes, we'll figure something out. Is it too late to get married sooner?"

Amanda sighed. "I already talked to Peter, and it's the first thing he said?" She clasped her hands to her chest. "He's so understanding? He'd marry me tomorrow at the justice of the peace office?"

Cassie swallowed. The direction of this discussion did not bode well for an event successfully planned and carried out by Weddings by Design. Not that she'd interfere for a second, given the circumstances. "We can check with the venue and see if they can move the date up. And the mini orchestra. I'm sure our chef and baker will be fine."

Kiki looked up from a veil she was sewing. "If our regular venue isn't available, I know one that is."

Cassie lifted her gaze from her paperwork. "Oh? I hadn't heard of another company other than the approved list we always use. Are they on that?"

"Uh, no." Kiki averted her eyes. "I don't think they would be."

She chuckled. "Don't tell me you're offering that great big barn of yours?"

"Well, I—never mind."

Cassie glanced at her partner. They always selected vendors from the approved company list. Was Kiki trying to branch out on her own? Break up their partnership? Her stomach flip-flopped at the thought of not only losing her friend but perhaps of competing with her. In her experience, that arrangement never worked out. Friends couldn't be rivals.

And rivals couldn't be friends.

She guided Amanda and her bridesmaids to the conference room. "Everything will be fine. Those gowns are so lovely, I'm sure they'll sell quickly. Don't give it another thought."

Because I'll be doing enough thinking for both of us. No return. No refund. Well, she'd have to eat the cost until they sold them to somebody else. At a deep discount, no doubt.

"And I'll order the other dresses right away. They should be in tomorrow. We'll get the alterations done, and you should be able to come in after noon for a fitting. We'll forget today ever happened. Okay?"

Amanda brightened, and her three attendants smiled and assured their friend everything would be fine.

Zoe, another bridesmaid, sighed. "They were so beautiful. Maybe I could purchase the one you had for me. Can I look at it again?"

Well, that was a pleasant possibility. "Sure, let's go back to the sewing room."

When they returned, Kiki was removing the last dress from the third mannequin. She turned when they entered. "Thought I'd pack these away until we decide what to do with them."

Amanda held out her hands. "Let me hold them for you, Zoe?" Kiki handed over the dresses. The bride-to-be melted, landing on the floor in the midst of an ocean of fabric. The three dresses layered themselves around her like a single unit. "Oh, I really love them?" She held the straight sheath toward Yvonne. "This one was yours? You'd look so tall and fit?"

Zoe sank to the floor beside her friend and selected the off-the-shoulder version with the shorter skirt, full enough to disguise but not magnify her round curves. "It's lovely. But probably way beyond my price range."

Rose sat next to Yvonne and tentatively touched the material of her dress. "I'm sure the peach ones will be just as lovely."

Young Miss Walker shook her head. "They're exactly how I envisioned them?"

Sobs escaped as her face crumpled. She covered her eyes with her hands and rocked in place, groaning out her grief at the loss of her dream.

Cassie longed to scoop her into her arms and somehow produce the other gowns. But she couldn't. They were an online order and a plane flight away.

First the face-plant and resulting bruises.

Then the prospect of acting in a TV ad.

And now the dress fiasco.

Could anything else go wrong?

The bell over the door tinkled an arrival, and she half turned. *Oh.*

She closed her eyes. *God, are You kidding me?*

Just what she didn't need.

The playboy.

Brady had spent almost an hour stuck in traffic, distracting himself from his painfully slow progress by creating a video—more than one, actually—in his mind of how this scene would pan out. He'd step into the house, smiling, coffee in hand. Cassie would receive his offering with joy and gratitude. She'd call her partners and extol all his many virtues, including thoughtfulness and good looks. Then the two of them would go for a walk, let bygones be bygones, and start again.

Well, his part in this little production hadn't changed. Much. He stepped in. Gift in hand. So far, so good.

But instead of happy partners, four young women sat on the floor, surrounded by a heap of green dresses, crying their hearts out. Cassie, her face white, perched on the corner of a desk.

He glanced from the group to Cassie and back. Thankfully the girls ignored him, caught up in their own little drama circle.

He could still do this.

He stepped to close the distance between him and Cassie, then held out the coffee cups in the cardboard tray. Which promptly crumbled like cheap paper towels in a hurricane. In slow motion, the five cups of black coffee tumbled top over end and smacked the floor with a sickening thud.

Splashing coffee in all directions.

Including onto the sea of green.

He stared at the outcome of his gesture.

An oil well erupting in the middle of the office wouldn't have made more of a mess.

The huddle of four screamed, jumped to their feet, and shook off the frothy material, fading toward the wall as if they hoped to distance themselves from the devastation.

The pallor of Cassie's skin now matched the whites of her eyes.

Another woman at a sewing machine gasped.

His eyes flitted from the dresses to the spreading stain to Cassie and the woman behind her, not knowing where to land.

Could things get any worse?

Chapter Ten

Amanda and her bridesmaids fled quickly after more desperate apologies from Cassie and Kiki—enough devastation for one day. Cassie stared at her nemesis. Just when she thought maybe Kiki could salvage the gowns by undoing the alterations without anybody knowing the difference, now this. She'd already envisioned hanging them on the sale rack and at least recouping her investment. Or selling them to the Walker bridesmaids.

But no. Brady Millman, Lover Boy to half the single women in Loveland, comes striding in where not invited and dumps coffee all over the gowns. And the fact he offered to pay for them meant little right now.

He'd walked into her life when she wasn't looking, making a nuisance of himself. Almost killed her with his car. Proving the rumors true about himself.

And now this.

And to make matters worse, Camilla stuck her head in. "Sorry, I was away from my desk. Did I hear the door open?" She glanced around the room then backed away. "Never mind. I see you're all *very* busy with your *very* important work."

How like her.

Kiki hurried around the table and gathered up the gowns. "I'll see if I can do anything with them." She tilted her head toward Brady. "I'll leave you two alone."

Cassie permitted a tiny, tight movement intended for Kiki's eyes only. "No. Leave them. They're ruined."

"But—" Kiki shrugged. "Whatever you say. Gotta go." She tossed Brady a smile. "See you later."

With that, the master seamstress beat a hasty retreat to somewhere else. Where she suddenly needed to be.

Well, she wouldn't see Brady Millman later. Because *he* wouldn't be *here*. No matter that he was the only limo service in Loveland with something better than a C-minus rating at the chamber of commerce *and* Better Business Bureau. No matter that he was the only chauffeur with a car available for the Walker wedding.

Or not. The date just changed, didn't it?

She allowed a smile to tickle her lips. Maybe he was already booked elsewhere—perhaps Siberia—on that date. Whatever it was.

And in the meantime, she'd set him straight.

She pointed at him and opened her mouth to speak her mind. Then she stopped. To accomplish that, she'd have to talk to him. Just her and him. Nobody else as a buffer.

Alone. The two of them.

Well, she didn't have to stay. She scooped up the gowns and crammed them into the fifty-five gallon industrial-sized trash can Kiki kept near her worktable. Then she pivoted on one foot, brushed off her hands, and headed for her office, where she firmly closed the door before sinking into her chair. Then she laid her head back, succumbing to the headache she'd held at bay for hours.

She was done.

~

Well, that didn't go as planned.

Brady slid into the driver's side of the limo, gripped the steering wheel in both hands, and laid his forehead against the back of his hands.

Any hope he'd held of getting another contract with Weddings by Design lay crammed in the bottom of that garbage container. As was the second chance he wanted with Cassie. No way would a classy woman like her forgive him for making such a blunder. Not that it was really his fault. How could he know the tray couldn't hold five cups? Or that one of them leaked.

Just like the accident was exactly that. An accident. Not. His. Fault.

Nobody to blame.

He started the engine and pulled out of the driveway. Where to? To work. Not his limo company, which provided his living. No, to his work as an addiction counselor, his calling and his passion. He headed toward his other office.

When his cell rang, he pulled over to the side of the road before answering. "Hi, it's Brady."

"Hey Brady, old buddy. It's Bing. How're things going?"

"Fine."

"Doesn't sound fine. Sounds downright miserable. What's going on?"

"Can't talk now. On my way to my other job."

"Sounds like you're the one who needs counseling, brother."

"Marriage counseling, for sure." His attempt at humor rang hollow and fell flat. "Not that I'm likely to marry soon at the rate I'm going."

"Ah, matters of the heart. A treacherous path, to be sure."

"Did you and Kiki have trouble on a mammoth scale?"

Bing chuckled. "There was a month when she didn't return my calls."

"Right. I remember you asking for prayer at men's group." He hesitated, unsure he really wanted to know the answer to his next question. "So it's kinda normal?" The minutes ticked away on the dash clock. He had to get to work. He had a client scheduled in an hour, and he needed to pull himself together. "When does the trouble end?"

"It doesn't, brother. You and the woman aren't perfect. You won't always get it right. Don't fool yourself about that. Kiki and I still have some discussions we'd never share with friends or family."

Brady sighed. "Doesn't give me much hope."

"No, brother, it should give you all the hope in the world. Everybody goes through this. Don't despair. If she's the woman for you, she'll come around. Pray."

Brady thanked his friend and hung up. Pray. Pray. Seemed to be his mantra today. Well, fine. He'd get to the office and spend extra time talking to the Lord—and listening—before his client arrived.

Hopefully God had more answers than he had questions.

Chapter Eleven

Cassie looked up from her computer screen. Everything ached from spending too long in one position. Or from being slammed to the road by a land yacht. The quiet office reminded her that the workday had ended, and she should too.

She scanned her planner for the next day. A couple more tasks to complete before she called it quits. She stretched and yawned.

I need coffee. A small one, so I don't stay up the entire night. Just long enough to catch up for tomorrow.

She grabbed her billfold and the office keys, then headed out the front door to the diner a few businesses down. What a day this proved to be. The fiasco with the dresses. Then the disaster with the coffee— She slowed. Maybe she should forgo the java and stick with water. *Nah.*

As she neared the intersection, she glanced around. Not a lot of foot traffic this late in the day. Seemed like the downtown core buttoned up each evening then burst into a song and dance as the restaurants and bars filled up long into the night.

She wrinkled her nose. She saw no benefit in doing drugs or drinking alcohol to the point of losing control. Or humiliating one's self. Which is what usually happened when folks overindulged.

Movement in a parking lot at the rear of a small office building across the street caught her eye. Strange. She rarely saw anybody in that area at this time of day. Was that— No, it couldn't be.

Brady.

Climbing the steps and going inside. Not just strange.

Bizarre.

What was he up to? Why would the Party Boy enter that building? As far as she knew, a tattoo parlor, a hospital staffing company, and another business that moved in within the last few months operated there. And she only knew that because of an announcement in the local chamber of commerce newsletter. Get to know your fellow business owners.

Like that would happen anytime soon.

She'd rather have a root canal.

Well, she'd take the long way around and see why he was still in the area. She waited for the light to turn in her favor, and then she crossed the street and through the near-empty parking lot, following his steps.

She peered up at the sign on the door he went into. HOPE ARISING ADDICTIONS COUNSELING.

So, she was right about him. Drugs and booze. Booze and drugs. Didn't matter where the problem started. Not a good combination for a guy who ran a chauffeur and limousine service.

And definitely not for one that might interest her.

Not that she was interested.

And if she had been, she sure wasn't now.

Cross him off her list.

Not that she had a list.

But if she did, he wasn't on it anymore.

⌒

Brady's last client of the evening bid him good night, and he walked the disc jockey to the door, watching until he rode off on his bicycle. So many clients were dropped off by a friend or concerned relative. Seeing one who retained his independence gave him a flicker of hope.

He returned to the small waiting area, tidied the magazines on the table, and shut off the coffee machine. In his office, he typed up notes of the counseling session, saved the document, printed a copy for his paper file, then shut off the computer.

Brady exhaled and leaned back in his chair. What a day!

After turning off the lights and locking the door, he descended the steps and got into his car. As he eased onto the main street, he kept a close eye out for pedestrians. Particularly those on foot and wearing dark clothes. No way he wanted a repeat of the accident. Although still convinced the incident wasn't his fault, he couldn't be too careful.

At a red light, he checked his cell for messages. Maybe she'd found it in her heart to forgive him. Or at least to give him a second chance. Or third. Or whatever he was up to now.

Nothing.

Looked like he had nowhere else anybody wanted him to be. Not even a particular wedding planner anybody. Which meant he was free as a bird.

The light changed to green, and he checked the intersection before starting out again. No, not quite free. He needed to spend time before the Lord. Maybe a drive into the country tomorrow. He had a few hours. He'd pack a picnic, find a rest stop, and read his Bible.

Sounded like a great idea.

When he got home, he'd check in with God and see if He thought so too.

Chapter Twelve

The next day, while Cassie listened to the phone ring and ring as she tried to call Amanda, she scrolled through her email to check the tracking information for the frilly peach gowns that Mrs. Walker preferred. A series of clicks in her ear indicated that voice mail was her next destination, when her worst nightmare popped up on her computer.

Her order had been cancelled. The dresses wouldn't be available for at least three months. Had she missed her window of opportunity by presumptuously ordering the seafoam-green gowns?

She tore her eyes from that piece of bad news when the beep on the phone told her to leave a message. "Hi, Amanda. It's Cassie. Please call me when you get a minute."

She disconnected then called her contact at the dress company directly.

Five minutes later, she hung up, shoulders slumped.

No getting around it. The dresses were a special order, fulfilled in China from a company located in an area that recently experienced a series of earthquakes, flooding, and landslides. Closed for six to eight weeks.

No frilly dresses.

Maybe Amanda could delay her wedding until the new gowns arrived.

Cassie's stomach lurched. From what the bride-to-be said, Mrs. Walker might not live until then. How could she suggest such a thing? How coldhearted did that make her?

Perhaps she could convince her to use another style. Other companies could send the order via overnight express. She could offer a deep discount. Cost, even. Just so long as Amanda chose another gown.

Her eye caught sight of the small plaque on her office wall.

When nothing goes right, could it be you're the one going wrong?

Possibly. She'd made some less-than-stellar decisions lately. At least in her life right now. Seemed everything she touched, unlike King Midas and his gold, turned sour. To mush. To dust.

Hadn't she heard something once about God closing doors and opening windows? Well, she needed an escape hatch.

Was God trying to get her attention? Couldn't He simply come out and say what He wanted?

Maybe she should drive over to Amanda's place. Talk to her. Make sure she wasn't avoiding her. Screening her calls.

She checked the Walker wedding file for the young woman's address. Estes Park. Yes. She could use a trip out of town. Out of the office. Maybe even out of this state. A few hours could make all the difference to her attitude. And her outlook.

Cassie stuck her head into Kiki's sewing area. "I'm taking a run out to see Amanda in Estes Park."

Kiki looked up, straight pins tucked between her lips. She retrieved them and jabbed them into a pin cushion. "What's up?"

"Don't know. I can't get the dresses her mother wants for at least three months." Cassie perched on the edge of Kiki's table and recounted the whole sad tale. "So, I hoped if I saw her in person, I could talk her into another dress."

"Maybe."

"You don't sound so certain."

Kiki smoothed the satiny fabric she worked on. "Color and style and fabric are a mysterious combination. It's either what she wants, or it isn't."

"But that's the whole thing, isn't it? Mrs. Walker wants the peach and frills. Probably because that's what she had at her own wedding. And Amanda wants it because her mother does." Tears blurred her vision. "But deep down, I know she wanted the seafoam-green gowns."

"Love makes us do strange things."

"Huh?" Her friend wasn't making sense. "What do you mean?"

"Amanda loves her mom and wants her to be happy. She's even willing to sacrifice. And now that she knows her mother's health situation and grim diagnosis, she's even more determined her mother will have what she wants."

"But this is Amanda's wedding. Mrs. Walker has—"

"Has given Amanda over twenty years of her life. It's what mothers do. And while I'm not a birth mother, having the kids live with me has made a difference in how I view a lot of life. I'd do anything for them. And that's probably what Mrs. Walker modeled for her daughter. Now Amanda has that chance to do the same for her." Kiki set the fabric aside and came around the desk. "See, by knowing her mom is dying, Amanda has a gift few of us ever experience. She has the chance to make her mother's dying wishes come true."

"You're such a romantic."

Kiki swatted her hand. "Am not. Although that might be the nicest thing anybody's said to me in a long while." She shooed Cassie away. "Now leave before I start to cry. And you go talk to your bride. But don't tell her what she wants. Don't try to talk her into anything. Let her know how sorry you are for the way things are turning out. And let her make her own decisions."

Cassie stood and hugged her friend. "That's probably the wisest thing anybody's said to *me* in a long while."

Kiki shrugged. "Hey, occasionally I surprise even myself."

"Do you do relationship counseling too?"

A slow smile eased the crinkles around her friend's eyes. "Are you asking about that cute chauffeur?"

Cassie passed a hand over her eyes. "I don't know. You sound like you know something about him."

"He's in the same men's group as Bing. Seems like a decent guy. We've had a few meals with him. Loves the Lord, no doubt about it."

"Then why does he—"

"What?" Kiki pulled out a couple of stitches. "Has something happened?"

"It's just that—well, I've heard he's a party guy. And I think he drinks."

"Hmm. Doesn't sound like the Brady I know. Maybe you need to look a little closer. Don't judge without all the facts."

"The facts? So far he's run me over with his car. Dropped coffee on the gowns. And one of his friends puked at the end of the driveway. It's not like I'm jumping to conclusions here."

"He did offer to pay for them." Kiki gave her a Mona Lisa smile. "Give him another chance. I think you'll be pleasantly surprised." She returned to her sewing machine. "Now, off with you. I have work to do, and you have a client to see."

A few minutes later, Cassie headed down the highway, feeling lighter than she had in days. No matter what happened, she had grand friends like Kiki, Fliss, and Ronnie to back her up.

Even when she did something stupid.

Brady slowed the car when he spotted a couple of picnic tables alongside the road, then sped up again. Too close to traffic. Too much distraction from the real purpose of his time out here today. He patted the small picnic cooler on the front passenger seat. Egg salad sandwiches. A cold soda. An icy cold green apple.

Mmm. Heaven in an insulated tote.

So where to? Maybe Estes Park. Should be quiet during the week. He'd avoid the downtown drag where all the tourists congregated. Although there was that great bookstore. And the ice cream shop—maybe later. First, a secluded spot where he could focus on the real reason for taking a few hours out of an otherwise dull workday. Time with the Lord.

And lunch.

The library might be just the place. Tables under the trees. Just the ticket.

As he rounded a curve and went up an incline, his cell phone rang. He glanced at the caller ID. One of his addiction clients. He flicked on his right turn signal, eased off the gas, and pulled over to the side of the road before answering the call.

"Brady here. What's up, Michael?"

The recently separated banker launched into a litany of complaints against his employer, his landlord, and his wife. Brady let him rant on for several minutes, but when he circled around to the beginning and started in again, Brady interrupted him. "Michael. Michael, wait a second there, buddy. What are you doing?"

"I'm telling you—"

"No. You're rehearsing the problem. Remember, we talked about this? Once is information. Twice is propaganda. So what's really going on?"

"Man, you see right through me, don't you?"

"It's that special x-ray vision course we do in seminary."

Brady settled in and let the man begin again, this time addressing the real reason he called: he'd bought himself a six-pack, and while he hadn't opened them yet, the cans waited on his kitchen table, calling out to him.

Brady reminded Michael how good he said he felt when he woke up with no hangover. How he'd worked hard for a recent promotion. And how his last three dates with his wife went well. "So what set you off to buy beer?"

"Karen canceled dinner last night."

"Did she say why?"

"She had to work."

"Any reason not to believe her?"

"No. I drove by, and her car was there."

"Wait a second, buddy. You drove by her office?"

"Well, I—"

"No excuses. That's not right, and you know it, and now you're looking for a reason to punish yourself by destroying how far you've come. Stop it."

"But—"

Brady shook his head and glanced in the rearview mirror. A silver minivan in a long line of traffic raced toward him, head-lights blinking. Horn blaring. Weaving in and out of the lanes. Between other vehicles that swerved over the center line to avoid a collision. What was that driver doing? This road was narrow. Winding. With a steep downgrade coming.

As the vehicle passed, he turned to give the driver *the Look*. The driver stared at him, eyes wide.

Cassie.

Chapter Thirteen

Cassie's breath hitched in her throat. She pounded on her horn as she wove in and out of traffic, gaining speed on the downward side of the mountain.

Have to let them know to get out of the way.

Signal that I'm in trouble.

Oh God.

She swallowed back a lump the size of Mount Elbert as she wrenched the steering wheel to avoid the vehicle in the next lane. As she screamed past the other cars, most leaned on their own horns. Or stared at her as if she'd lost her mind.

Well, she hadn't.

She'd simply lost her brakes.

Cassie gripped the wheel in the ten and two position. Isn't that what she learned in driver's ed? And what to do during brake failure? What did they teach about that? Nothing, that's what. At least nothing she could remember right now.

Keeping her eyes glued to the road ahead, she prayed aloud, the words easing the tension knot building between her shoulders. "God, please send help. Or fix the brakes. Send an angel who can stop the car. Or a giant pillow I can crash into."

Was this another one of the Divine's practical jokes, intended to get her attention?

"Okay, God, I hear You. Please hurry my guardian angel along. I haven't asked for much lately."

Is that how it worked with God? Did she get a certain number of prayer requests a year? A month? A week? And if so, what was her limit?

Maybe she'd already used them and didn't realize it.

No, if she had to guess, she'd gone over her credit limit with God. They hadn't been much on speaking terms lately.

She yanked the wheel hard to the right to regain her lane as a truck barreled toward her. In its own lane, but too close for comfort as she couldn't maintain her own space in the curve.

Would she die on this mountain road today?

Brady started the engine and indicated his intention of pulling onto the highway. "Michael, I gotta go. Emergency. I'll call back."

He disconnected and tossed the phone onto the seat, next to his picnic lunch. As he sped to catch up with Cassie, his mind raced through the possibilities. Maybe she was on her way to an emergency of her own. Unlikely. From the little he knew about her, she wouldn't put others at risk.

So why was she driving like a maniac?

He flicked on his four-way flashers and, using his horn liberally, got within a couple of cars of her. A semi coming from the other direction flashed its headlights and blared on its air horn. Brady held his breath as Cassie's silver minivan jerked back into her lane of travel with mere inches to spare.

A break in traffic in the oncoming lane gave him the time and space to race past the two cars in front of him until he drew abreast of her. She glanced over, and then her eyes widened in recognition.

She looked forward again, and then quickly at him, and although he couldn't hear her, he knew she yelled, "I can't stop!"

No brakes?

A car approached, and he pulled around the compact car ahead of Cassie's vehicle, which seemed determined to maintain the speed limit. This wouldn't work.

He held his breath as Cassie weaved onto the shoulder, passing the compact on the right. Whew. Another close call. The driver of the two-door squealed his tires to get out of the way.

Brady slowed to let Cassie catch up to him, tapping his brakes. Praying she'd understand what he was about to do.

If not, this could be disastrous.

⁓

Cassie's heart threatened to push past the lump in her throat while she held her vehicle steady. Her arms trembled with the prolonged exertion. Or lack of oxygen. Or nerves.

Breathe, girl, breathe.

The front passenger tire dipped over the edge of the asphalt onto the gravel, and she resisted the urge to yank the steering wheel hard to the left. Instead, keeping her eyes on the shoulder and the cars behind her, she eased the wheel until the tire hummed along on the solid surface again.

She exhaled then focused on the rear end of Brady's SUV. What was he doing? Didn't he know she couldn't stop or even slow down? Which part of *no brakes* didn't he understand?

The vehicle's brake lights tapped on and off several times. A pause, then a repeat.

A signal? Oh, she should have paid more attention in Girl Scouts. He probably knew Morse Code. Wasn't that a guy kind of thing?

Then the brake lights lit and stayed on. Was he crazy? She was going to run— Her front bumper connected with the rear of his vehicle for an instant, and then he accelerated just out of range. She lurched forward into the seat belt. Ooh, that would leave a bruise.

She closed the distance between their vehicles again. Another *thunk*, this one harder than the first. But instead of speeding up again, he maintained that pace so their vehicles stayed in contact.

Her minivan slowed with the weight of his SUV as a barrier.

He was her guardian angel. An answer to her prayer.

Brady eased his car onto the shoulder, and she followed. The line of cars behind her passed, several tooting their horns or flashing their lights in acknowledgment of the success of the maneuver.

She drew several deep breaths when her van finally stopped. Then she rammed the gearshift into Park and shut off the engine.

Seemed God listened to her after all.

And He sent His answer in the most unlikely package. A druggie and drunk.

Then again, Jesus wasn't exactly what the people of His time wanted. Or even most of the folks of the current time either. Yet He was the perfect gift at the perfect time.

What a sense of humor the Lord has.

Brady pocketed the car keys then trotted back to check on Cassie. Her white knuckles on the steering wheel matched the pallor of her face, but otherwise she looked okay.

Beyond okay, in fact.

Beautiful. He tapped her window, and her head snapped to face him.

No, beautiful was an understatement. Despite the yellowing bruises and the redness around her nose, *stunning* was a more apt description.

When she opened the door, he stepped into the opening and offered his hand. She planted her feet firmly on the gravel as though glad to feel solid ground beneath her once more, then stood. But her knees wobbled, and she pitched forward.

Right into his arms.

He held her close as she laughed and cried, shaking and quaking, against his chest.

Which he didn't mind in the least. In fact, they could stand here on the side of the highway, cars whizzing past in both directions, for the rest of the day, and he'd enjoy every second.

She pushed away but not so far that he couldn't keep his arms around her waist. "You're my guardian angel. Did you know that?"

Serving in that capacity—particularly in this situation—both thrilled and exhilarated him. "I'm just glad you're safe."

She swiped away tears. "You're also an answer to prayer." A hiccup. "Look at me. I must look a mess."

You're gorgeous. Don't you know that? But he couldn't say those words. Not aloud. Not yet. "Well, if you're making a fashion statement, it's a new one on me."

Much better. Make light of it. Isn't that what she expects from the party animal?

She rested her cheek against his chest. Listening to his

heartbeat? Sniffing for drugs or alcohol? Well, hopefully the old ticker didn't betray his real feelings about her. And she sure wouldn't find anything on him today. No vomit. No spilled beer.

But this wasn't the time to take advantage of her fragile emotional state. Not that he was *that* kind of guy anyway. No siree. Knight in shining armor to the rescue. Nothing more.

He cleared his throat and then stepped back. "I'll drive you home if you want."

She stiffened. "I can call for roadside assistance."

The tender moment vanished like a vapor on the wind. "What is your problem with me?"

"Who said I have one?"

"Hmm. Let's see. Your body language when I offered a ride. Your response to my kind offer to go out of my way and help."

Now she stepped back, crossed her arms, and leaned against the van. Typical avoidance body language. Using her body as a barrier. The vehicle as a bolster. "Well, if it's such a bother, don't worry. I'll find somebody else to rescue me from the side of the road."

Aha, and her words as a weapon of attack.

Sometimes he hated that he knew so much about resistive communication.

Chapter Fourteen

Cassie couldn't believe that what began as a mini-celebration of answered prayer and Brady being in the right place at the right time disintegrated so quickly into—into what? Why was he so defensive? He'd been on the way somewhere. Well, he could just go on, continue like none of this happened.

Just because he saved her life didn't mean she had to trust him. And why should she? He'd already proven himself over the past few days.

Still, she hadn't detected even a whiff of alcohol or drugs on him when he held her. So close. For so long. Catching her before she did a face-plant on the side of the road. That wouldn't have done her already tender nose any favors.

Perhaps she'd misunderstood his words.

She drew a deep breath, held it an extra heartbeat or two, then exhaled and held out her hands. Maybe she could take a chance. Just this one time. He cleaned up nice. "I'm sorry. Whenever you and I are in the same time zone, things happen."

A smile teased his mouth, and she yanked her focus away. "I don't know why that is."

"Me either." She shook her head. "Yes, I do. I've heard stories about you. All over town. That you came to Colorado because of legalized marijuana. The party king. Want a good time? Call Brady."

He lifted one shoulder and let it drop. "It's my business persona." He gestured to his car. "Let's get in my vehicle where it's safer than standing on the side of the road. We can talk and figure out what to do next."

Once in the car, she turned in the seat to face him. Some conversations simply *had* to be face-to-face. "That time I saw you, the night you—you ran—I ran into—well, you smelled like booze. And you staggered out of a bar downtown earlier that afternoon. Along with two other equally drunk friends. And you got into your car and drove in that condition. Last evening you went into the addiction center. I commend you for working on your problem, but I'm not prepared to take on a project like that right now. Maybe never." She twisted her fingers into knots. "For me to be interested in a man, I need him to love God more than anything else."

She studied his face for a reaction, but he remained still. Didn't speak. Had he even heard her?

Oh yes he had. The veins in his temples throbbed. His jaw clenched and unclenched then tightened again. His fingers clasped into fists, flattened on his thighs, clasped again. And he wouldn't look at her.

This man was a ticking time bomb, ready to explode.

Maybe she should get back in her car and lock the doors. Call for help. And if he made a move to get out of his own vehicle, call the highway patrol too.

She slipped her phone out of her purse.

Great. No service.

Brady couldn't believe his ears. No wonder, since his pulse just about drowned out her words.

Cassie thought he was both an alcoholic *and* a drug addict. Where did she get her information?

Count to ten, Millman. If you don't, she'll run like a frightened deer, and you'll lose any chance left to mend these fences.

Seven. Eight. Nine. Ten.

He turned his entire body in the seat so he faced her squarely. "The night we. . .ran into each other, I was on my way home from taking a friend to the ER. I started that afternoon to come to your place to show you how nicely the car—and I—cleaned up. I saw my pastor in trouble. Turned out somebody drugged him. That other person was probably going to mug him. I spent the rest of the evening until early morning at the hospital, not sure he'd make it. I closed my eyes for an instant, and there you were." She turned her eyes away, but not before he noted that they were wet. "So I wasn't drunk. Or on drugs. Because I don't do that. I'm an addiction counselor. I came to Colorado because of the marijuana, but not to smoke it. To help with the increase in drug abuse. My younger brother died of an overdose when we were in high school. So it's a personal mission of mine."

Now the tears trickled down her cheeks. "I'm sorry. I was wrong."

Well, isn't that what he wanted? To make sure she knew how wrong she was? To prove that she shouldn't listen to gossip and rumors?

Then why did he feel no joy?

He reached over and gripped her hand. "Can we pretend we just met?"

Her tentative smile touched his heart in a deep corner that hadn't seen daylight for a long time. "I'd like that."

"Good. I'll forget that you jump to conclusions if you'll erase all the mischaracterizations you've heard about me."

She laid a hand on top of his. "And I'll forget how you ruined a thousand dollars' worth of dresses if you'll forget how I judged you based on rumors and misconceptions."

"Deal. And don't forget to send me the bill. I really do want to make this right. And not just to get into your good graces." He straightened and shrugged back his shoulders, breaking their contact again. But only for a moment. He held out his hand. "Hi, I'm Brady. And I love Jesus more than anything."

⌒

When Cassie and Brady returned to the office, Kiki, Ronnie, and Fliss were hard at work in the conference room. Camilla manned the phones in her nook in the hallway.

Cassie turned to the limousine chauffeur-turned-counselor. "Hang here a minute, will you?" She stuck her head in the doorway as her partners bandied about words like *campaign, producer,* and *camera angles.* "Hey, what are you doing?"

Kiki waved her in. "Planning our promotional strategy. You arrived just in time." She frowned. "How did it go with Amanda?"

Cassie sat across the table and explained about her brake malfunction. "So I didn't have the chance to explain to her about our problem." She held up a hand. "I have a confession to make. And I need to ask for your forgiveness." She exhaled. "I have a gift of knowing what people want. It's called an empathic gift. But sometimes it's a curse. Like with Amanda. I knew she wanted the green gowns. I went ahead and ordered them. In doing so, I committed the firm to the cost of the gowns, which I shouldn't have done without the bride buying in. That won't happen again."

Kiki smiled. "No worries. Problem solved. Amanda called. They're moving the wedding to next month, so she plans to use the dresses you ordered."

Cassie's tongue stuck to the roof of her mouth. "But they're—they're—"

"Going to be fine." Kiki rounded the table and rubbed Cassie's shoulder. "I have them soaking in a foolproof stain remover solution of white vinegar. And I checked with the current venue while you were taking your racing circuit through the mountains. It isn't available, but the one I have contact with is."

Cassie blinked tears out of the way as she looked up at her friend. "So it's not your venue?"

"Mine?"

"Of course yours, silly. Your barn is a beautiful venue since Bing and the others worked on it."

Kiki laughed and sat beside her. "Not a chance. And yes, while a lot of work is completed, it's not ready to host a wedding. Besides which, I wouldn't go behind your backs and steal business."

Brady leaned against the doorjamb and cleared his throat. Cassie smiled up at him then at each of her partners. And friends. One and the same. What a blessing. "You all know Brady Millman, right? Our chauffeur and limo service."

Felicity turned and nodded toward him. "Sure. We've met before." She swiveled back and faced Cassie, lowering her voice. "So, no doubts about using him?"

"Oh no. He's our only limo guy from now on. So long as he is available for the Walker wedding next month?"

He tapped his cell screen and opened the calendar app. "What date?" When Kiki provided it, he nodded and entered it into his phone. "Done deal. I'll be there with bells on."

Cassie steeled herself for the next thing she had to bring up with these sweet ladies. What did the Bible say? *"For nothing is secret that will not be revealed."* Well, now was the time. If they didn't want her as a partner, she—and they—would be better off if she left now. "I have another confession to make. I'm an introvert. Which means I don't like to put myself out there in front of people. Doing so taxes me emotionally and physically, and I need more time to refresh and renew. In other words, being around people exhausts me."

Ronnie set down her pen. "We already knew that."

"You did?"

The chef nodded. "Sure. But explain what that means to you, because, you know, we think you're cool the way you are. Always avoiding the camera. The microphone. Stuff like that."

Cassie's shoulders relaxed. "I'm fine one-on-one. Okay with you because I know you. But I can be socially awkward when it comes to meeting people. I never know what to say. How to stand. Every day I go home wishing it was Friday. If we have an event on Saturday, I don't get the time I need to recover. Even church adds to my overload."

Felicity reached across the table and patted her hand. "I suspected as much the first time I met you in singles class. You really made an effort to look like you had fun, but I knew. My stepmom is like that."

Cassie's head dipped. "I'm sorry that I'm a burden to the company and to you, but I can't do the television ad. The thought of standing in front of a camera paralyzes me. I can't breathe. I can't think. I can't talk. Please don't make me do it. And if you prefer that I leave the company, I completely understand. You need somebody who won't be a burden."

Fliss and Ronnie jumped up and surrounded her, creating a circle of support along with Kiki. They hugged and patted shoulders and hugged some more.

Kiki finally broke the group apart and sat beside her. "We've known that all along about you, but you're so good at what you do, we figured we'd let you work it out. Take an extra day whenever you need it. A long weekend, if that's what it takes. We're partners here. You work just as hard as we do, and you accomplish way more when you're rested and refreshed." She waggled a finger at her. "And no more talk about leaving. Hear me?"

Cassie smiled at her friends. "Seems mine was the worst-kept secret in town." She glanced at Brady and gestured for him to sit on her other side. "Well, almost."

Ronnie returned to her chair. "Oh, you mean there's another one?"

"Brady here might have a playboy reputation, but he's also an addiction counselor." She met each friend's eye. "So whatever you've heard—from whoever, including me—he's an okay, straight-up guy."

Felicity smiled and toyed with her engagement ring. "Well, as one who is happily engaged, I hereby pledge to do whatever I can to make sure that everybody I know is happily matched. I think you guys need to go on a date. Soon."

Cassie turned to Brady. "And since I blackened your name with these ladies, I need to apologize to you in front of them."

He blinked several times. "Didn't we just agree to start out brand-new? We haven't had time to have a misunderstanding yet. But I'd like to change that. Want to come for coffee?"

"Good idea. Outside the office." She smiled. "Yes, I'd like that."

Felicity tapped her notebook. "And don't worry about the ad. We'll figure it out. Sneak around with a camera and get you in candid shots. Like chewing the end of your pencil. Or sweeping the front step."

"You wouldn't." Cassie stood. "If you do, I'll post on social media the secret ingredient in your grandmother's lemon bars."

Felicity's eyes widened. "You wouldn't dare."

Cassie headed for the door. "I won't if you won't."

Ronnie and Kiki laughed, and Felicity joined in. "See you later. Enjoy your date."

Date? Is that what this was? Well, maybe that was a good thing. Feeling like the weight of the world was off her shoulders for the first time in weeks, she linked arms with Brady as they strolled down the sidewalk toward the diner. Maybe now she could relax and trust God to take care of all the minor details. Like how to fit this godly man into her life. She was fairly certain he would be a full-time job.

Which was fine with her.

Epilogue

Six months later

Cassie sat across the table from Brady in their favorite diner in downtown Loveland. The tantalizing smells of fresh bread, bacon, and coffee pervaded, and the fifties theme with battered chrome tables, hubcaps on the ceiling, and black-and-white-checked linoleum on the floor served as the balm of Gilead to her soul and her senses.

She drained her coffee, good to the last drop, as the old television commercial said. She'd already ordered a second cup.

The waiter delivered a fresh serving of joe and quickly retreated. Cassie caught a flash of light from the mug's saucer—gasping as she reached for the object.

A sapphire and diamond ring.

He lifted it from her grasp, dropped to the floor on one knee, and held her left hand in his. "Will you do me the honor of marrying me? Of being my wife? Best friends forever?"

She stared at him. Was he losing his mind?

No.

She'd lost her heart.

"Yes."

He slipped the ring on her fourth finger, stood, then pulled her to her feet and into his arms. Then he closed his eyes and planted his lips on hers. They'd kissed many times over the past months, but nothing like this. Urgent. Demanding yet gentle. Full of promise.

Finally, no longer only a wedding planner.

Now a bride-to-be.

Leeann Betts writes contemporary romantic suspense, while her real-life persona, Donna Schlachter, pens historical romantic suspense. Her first cozy mystery series, By the Numbers, recently concluded with the release of the twelfth title, and her newest series, Mysterious Ink Bookstore, boasts two titles with more to come. Together she and Donna have published more than thirty novellas and full-length novels, devotionals, and books on writing craft. They ghostwrite, judge writing contests, edit, facilitate a critique group, and are members of American Christian Fiction Writers, Writers on the Rock, Christian Authors Network, Pikes Peak Writers, and Sisters in Crime. Leeann travels extensively for research.

Taste and See

by Davalynn Spencer

Dedication

*To Amanda,
whose gifts of beauty, discernment, and service
reveal God's hand and leave this
mother's heart thanking Him.*

Acknowledgments

Thank you to all who aided and supported me in telling
Ronnie and Ty's story, particularly former Executive Chef
Hidemi Sakamoto, professional special events coordinator
Amanda Beck, chef and caterer Dietrich Ackermann,
and our creative Lord, who blessed us with the
incredible senses of taste and smell.

*Oh, taste and see that the LORD is good;
blessed is the man who trusts in Him!*
PSALM 34:8 NKJV

Chapter One

People were nuts.

Well, maybe not all people, but for sure Saffron Fare's neighbors, the Pixleys, who stood in her front yard, waving their arms at the Loveland Gas Company employee planted firmly on the dying grass.

Ronnie parked at the curb. She should have rented a condo or an apartment downtown above a Main Street business. Or accepted her mother's invitation to move into the family home.

But then she wouldn't have had her kitchen and she *had* to have her kitchen.

She pushed her floppy sun hat up and rubbed her forehead. Besides, she and her mother would eventually have a meltdown, so that would never work.

Too bad the lawn sprinklers didn't pop on right about now.

She cringed inwardly at the uncharitable thought, though she wouldn't mind a cool shower herself on this unseasonably warm September afternoon.

What was going on?

Stepping out of her Subaru, she pressed turquoise sunglasses against the bridge of her nose, hoping for anonymity.

But shoot. Mrs. Pixley would recognize her faded gray car, so whatever. She adjusted the umbrella-sized sun hat and approached the threesome.

"I'm suffering a raging headache," Mrs. Pixley told the man with a gas company patch on his shirt. "The smell is making everyone at this end of the block sick. You *must* do something about it."

Smell? Ronnie didn't smell anything. And who was *everyone?*

"It's either a gas leak or Fare's eggs are all rotting and about to explode." Mrs. Pixley paused for dramatic effect and pressed her fingers against her temples. "Either way, my head is *killing* me."

Ronnie would match the brick in her sinuses against Patty Pixley's headache any day of the week. Except today. She simply wanted these people to leave. They were trespassing, weren't they? And there were no rotten eggs in the kitchen. She'd disposed of anything perishable before leaving for her mother's birthday cruise. The milk as well, and anything else that would spoil her spotless, commercial-class kitchen, other than the fish and chicken she had in the freezer.

She didn't smell one single rotten thing other than Mrs. Pixley's theatrics.

"Excuse me." Ronnie stopped in front of Gas Man and pressed her sunglasses tighter against the bridge of her nose. "Why are you here?"

Unaffected by her arrival, he gave her a deadpan once-over from straw hat to flouncy skirt to strappy sandals. "Is this your property?" He glanced at his clipboard. "Fare?"

The glasses slipped, and she shoved them higher. "Yes."

"Your neighbor reported a gas leak, and our readings indicate she is correct."

He ripped a paper from the clipboard and handed it to her. "The leak must be repaired ASAP, but it's on your property—on *your* side of the meter. That means you repair it, not us."

"With what? Duct tape?"

Mrs. Pixley snorted.

Mr. Gas Company didn't even twitch. "You don't smoke, do you?"

Ronnie blinked. "No."

"Good. I've turned off your gas, but wait awhile before turning on electrical switches, lights, or appliances. And don't light any matches. Give the gas time to dissipate."

Ronnie needed her quiet pajamas. Not the shorty set covered with brilliantly plumed macaws, but the pale pink set with a matching sleep mask. She needed rest. Quiet. Solitude. After a crowded seven-day cruise, which her mother had insisted on paying for, she needed all three.

Her mother needed a sedative so she wouldn't call Ronnie to plan their next vacation.

No, that wasn't fair.

Her retired schoolteacher mother needed a husband so *he* could accompany her on the next trip. Widowed when Ronnie was thirteen, Francine Fare had put herself on life's back burner while teaching school and raising a headstrong, heartbroken teen who didn't understand why her daddy had died.

Ronnie still didn't understand the whys of cancer, but her mother and grandmother had faithfully demonstrated God's love and care over the years.

Now, with a Western-themed wedding to prepare for in the next four weeks, Ronnie had a tasting menu to finalize, complete with appetizers and entrées suitable for meat-and-potatoes guests. The groom had insisted on beef and, well, beef. But her training wouldn't allow her to do anything less than offer a few vegan samples as well. Covering the food and beverages branch of Weddings by Design wasn't exactly a piece of cake.

Ronnie's turn to snort at the insider joke.

Mrs. Pixley whipped her head around in a dramatic neck-snapping move and stomped down the sidewalk. Her husband followed. Poor man.

Right on cue, the sprinkler system semi-surged, demonstrating why the lawn was dying. Ronnie couldn't afford an extravagant water bill. Nor could she afford to finish renovating her Victorian home, not until business picked up. Way up. Every penny from her small business loan had gone into the kitchen. And that commercially licensed kitchen required a licensed plumber to check out the so-called gas leak, followed by inspections from the fire and health departments—each one a potential time sink for holding up her end of Weddings by Design and the last-minute wedding booked in her absence.

In the world of wedding planning, four weeks out was last-minute.

Not that she wouldn't be able to complete the menu. But preparing everything at the WBD house would mean an extra step in the process. And Felicity used the kitchen there for her wedding cake masterpieces. They both needed workspace, and if Ronnie was honest with herself, privacy. She didn't like having an audience while she was cooking, and she suspected Felicity didn't either.

Returning to her car, Ronnie parked in front of the antiquated garage. Desperate for a coat of paint, it sat close-mouthed and silent while she got out and hefted two overstuffed roller bags from her trunk and up the front porch steps.

Gas Man hadn't hinted at where the leak might be, though he'd made it clear it wasn't on *his* side of the meter. Welcome home.

The screen door whined its usual hello, and she let it slap behind her, waiting for a waft of stale air. The old house had been closed up for ten days, but stale didn't make an appearance. Neither did mercaptan, the sulfur-smelling chemical added to natural gas.

Patty Pixley had the olfactory glands of a basset hound, not to mention—

A sharp pang in Ronnie's conscience jerked her up short.

Okay, Lord. Sorry.

In spite of no stuffiness or rotten-egg odor, she opened windows in the kitchen and laundry room, then dragged her luggage upstairs to the closet, formally referred to by the Realtor as a cozy bedroom. Opening a sash window, Ronnie wedged in a box fan but didn't turn it on, just in case Gas Man was right. She didn't want to go up in a blaze of glory. Hopefully, the shade lingering beneath the honey locust tree outside would seep into her bedroom. It had to be ninety degrees in here.

She hoisted her suitcases onto the bed, kicked off her sandals, and freed her hair from its sun-hat cage before unzipping her bags and dumping everything into the wicker laundry hamper. A smarter, less-distracted woman would have saved herself a little work by taking her luggage straight to the laundry room downstairs. Sheesh.

At the landing, she paused and looked over the railing,

tempted to drop the basket over the edge. Instead, she once again lugged it down the aging carpet runner that protected the golden-oak staircase. The runner's replacement held the last slot at the bottom of her Hopeful Renovations list pinned to a corkboard in the kitchen.

Sunflowers greeted her from a side table at the base of the stairs, and her heart lifted by a degree. The giant silk faces never drooped and always looked bright and happy in their vintage cowboy boot. The soft-as-doeskin boot with a yellow tulip inlay was one of her better flea market finds. In fact, the sunflowers had cost more than the antique boot—the only thing even remotely Western in her entire house and heart. She had some serious research to do before prepping samples for the Gardner-Mitchell wedding in October.

Cool kitchen floor tiles set off a rippling effect that worked its way from the soles of her feet, up her legs, and into her back and arms. Life was good, mostly. She had a job she loved, appliances that worked, and sunflowers to cheer her. A glance at the black-lettered barnwood board over the marble counter reminded her of the greatest blessing in her life:

O Taste & See that the Lord is Good.

So was being home, in her own house, anticipating a relaxing bath in the old claw-foot tub upstairs.

But first, an arctic blast from her reach-in freezer.

She pulled the door open and stopped. Pale-pink water pooled beneath dripping packages of chicken, fish, beef, and pork—none of which bore signs of being frozen.

No frosty breath. No ice crystals glistening from stainless steel shelving.

No smell of rotting meat. *How can I not smell this?*

Something was definitely wrong and had been for quite some time.

She'd paid the electric bill before she left for the cruise. *Hadn't she?*

Not prone to tears in the face of disaster, Ronnie swiped at eyes that were brimming as quickly as the pools collecting on the bottom of the freezer.

She slammed the door shut and ran back upstairs for her phone. She not only needed to call the power company, but she needed a plumber—and pronto. She needed her appliances and what had been stocked in the freezer—all of which must now be replaced. Dollar signs pushed more tears between her lashes.

Thirty minutes later, she lay in the middle of her quilt-topped brass bed, shell-shocked over the prices quoted by every licensed plumber she could find in Larimer County.

"Lord, please," she whispered. "Help me."

From atop his horse, Tapper, Ty Ellicott backed the gelding into the roping box. The horse's eyes and ears fixed on the 260-pound calf waiting to run from the automatic, spring-loaded roping chute. Ty bit down on the piggin' string between his teeth and tucked its tail in his belt, hit the remote control, and squeezed his boot heels into Tapper.

The calf ran out and the gelding leaped from the box, hard on its heels as it ran for the opposite end of the arena. Ty swung his loop, and it settled over the calf. Bailing off Tapper's right side, he ran down the stiff line pulled taut as his horse backstepped against the calf at the other end.

He grabbed the calf by the neck loop and flank, laid it on its side, and yanked his piggin' string from his belt for a quick wrap and a half hitch around three legs.

As if a timer awaited his signal, he threw his hands in the air and stepped back from the calf.

Not the fastest gun in the West, but it wasn't about a quick time. It was all about the poly-nylon ropes and piggin' strings he made and how they handled. He wasn't in business to win a rodeo buckle or a world championship. He was in it to make the world's best ropes for those who did.

His belt buzzed.

He set the calf free, and as it trotted off toward the turnout gate, he walked back to his horse, mounted, and coiled the rope. It felt good in his hands. Good weight, good strength. His phone buzzed again.

Flipping open the hand-tooled case on his belt, he checked the caller ID.

Casey Lander. It'd been awhile.

He swung up in the saddle. "She finally kick you out?"

Lander laughed. He'd married his high school sweetheart in February and had been disgustingly happy ever since. Ty didn't know whether to throw up or throw a punch at his friend, but either way, late afternoon on a Thursday was out of character for a phone call from him.

"Cindy's got a friend who needs a licensed plumber and is cash-strapped."

Of course.

"Since you helped us out last spring with that leak in the basement, she insisted I call you. New wife and all—you know how it is. I promised I'd ask if you could help."

No, Ty *didn't* know what *new wife and all* was like. He turned Tapper back and let the other two calves out, then rode to the end of the arena and opened the turnout gate.

"Handyman" wasn't a title he'd choose for himself, but he seemed to have a knack for it. Even as a kid, he'd fixed things for his folks, grandparents, aunts, and neighbors, which all led to a plumber's license and a tidy side business. Between twisting ropes, feeding calves, and living on his own time schedule, life wasn't too bad.

It was just lonely.

"What's he need, and where does he live?"

"Thanks, man. I owe you."

More than you know.

"Ronnie Fare, on Fifth Street. Gas leak on the property, so the utility company is no help."

"I can check it out in the morning and leave an estimate. But it'll cost you a pan of Cindy's lasagna with a side of spumoni ice cream."

"Deal." Casey let out a happy sigh—that disgusting sound made by a man who knew his wife would be pleased.

⌒

Friday morning, Ty grabbed an Ellicott Ropes ball cap, set his toolbox in the back of his '65 Chevy pickup, and headed for the other side of town.

The driver's door moaned when he climbed out on a shady neighborhood street, but the solid *thunk* of the door reaffirmed his faith in the old beauty. Someday he'd paint it. Fix it up right or pay somebody else to do it. He was no car guy. Poly-nylon ropes, cattle, and a good horse were more his speed. And homeowners who could pay for his services.

A solid look at the half-dead lawn made him wonder how things were going for Ron Fare.

Wide steps led to a deep porch with a swing. The guy had to be married, judging by the wicker table with a tin pail holding potted red flowers.

A dim view through the antique screen door revealed the home's interior and foyer, typical of so many old houses Ty had worked in. An oak staircase shot up to a second floor. Ten-foot ceilings and hardwood floors. Wallpaper that had seen better days.

He rang the doorbell and reset his cap. An old buzzer sounded from somewhere deep in the house.

Rather than lean on the button, he gave the yard a second look. Needed work and water. The chipped-paint porch could use a coat or three, and a couple of balusters in the railing needed to be replaced.

"Yes?"

He turned at the voice, not surprised that a woman answered the door. The messy-haired beauty triggered a microflash of envy. Ron Fare shared his home with a lanky palomino, complete with holey jeans, oversized white T-shirt, and Converse tennis shoes. She pushed open the squeaky screen with a rubber-gloved hand.

He pulled off his cap, suddenly conscious of the hat ring he knew circled his head.

"Ty Ellicott, ma'am. I'm looking for Ron Fare. Casey Lander gave me this address and said there was a gas leak on the property."

She dipped her head and zeroed in on him with gray-green eyes. "Are you a licensed plumber?"

"Yes, ma'am." He swallowed like he had when his granny challenged his childish boasting.

The right corner of the gal's pretty lips tucked up. He mentally kicked himself for thinking another man's wife had pretty lips.

She held out a hand, then jerked it back, pulled off the glove, and offered it again. "I'm Ronnie Fare."

Without his permission, his gaze slid from the top of her golden head to her Converse and up again. "How'd you get a guy's name?"

She arched an eyebrow.

"Ron. I mean Ronnie. Is it short for Rhonda?" He was dying, and he knew it.

"Saffron."

His jaw tightened. "Isn't that some sort of spice?"

He wasn't dying, he was dead.

"Yes." She crossed her arms. "But it actually means 'yellow flower.'"

His jaw relaxed, and he cleared his throat. "It fits. I mean, nice to meet you, ma'am."

Her eyebrow flattened out but not her eyes. They were almost laughing. "Please, call me Ronnie."

Chapter Two

Ty Ellicott didn't exactly look like a plumber. Ball cap. Jeans. Cowboy boots.

Ronnie glanced over the guy's shoulder, checking for a horse.

But then, she probably didn't look like a culinary school graduate and professional chef.

When she'd approached her open front door and found him surveying the yard, she'd wondered if he was just someone at the wrong address—broad shoulders, trim waist, and all. But clearly not. Who had Cindy Lander lined up—the Lone Ranger?

Instead of saying "Hello" or "May I help you," she'd answered the doorbell with "Yes?" and a little hope in her voice. *Hope* was the operative word here. *Hope*fully, her comment wasn't some unintentional response boiling up from her subconscious. Sometimes she felt that wearing a white chef's coat to countless weddings rather than a bridal gown was affecting her psyche.

Then he turned and faced her, coffee-colored eyes taking a long draw on her ability to respond like a rational adult. Which, she reminded herself, she was. All twenty-eight years of her.

Then his assumptions began: *Ron Fare*—had to be a man, of course. Husband, most likely, which was twice wrong. And *ma'am*—what was this, 1880?

The annoying flip of her heart didn't help either. She needed a gas leak fixed, not a spur-of-the-moment flirt with some cowboy wannabe.

She brushed loose hair off her temple. "The gas company said the leak was on my side of the meter, but they didn't say where."

Cowboy walked down the steps and out to the biggest brown patch on her lawn.

She followed like a puppy.

"See this circular area in the grass?" He waved his arm over it like he was stirring a large kettle of soup. "I'll bet your leak is right here."

He looked at her, dousing her with another splash of hot-coffee brown.

Now that he mentioned it, the dead grass did take on a some-what circular pattern, though more of a crescent roll, she thought. "Is that normal? For a gas leak, I mean."

"Yes, ma'am." He lifted the brim of his cap and jiggled it back down. "There's a faint smell, but I'll get my meter and a shovel to be sure."

While he was gone, she moved closer and sniffed. She didn't smell a thing, which, come to think of it, she hadn't since she got home. *Strange.*

When he returned, he set his shovel dead center in the brown grass, and with one shove of his booted foot, drove it to the hilt. Handle, one would say. But hilt sounded more gallant.

What was the matter with her? "They turned the gas off already."

"Yes, ma'am." A couple more shallow scoops, and he bent down and brushed dirt away from a rusty-looking pipe.

He straightened and stuck the shovel in the ground. "Do you have a gas stove and oven? Hot water heater? Clothes dryer?"

All she needed was cream and sugar, and she'd be swimming in coffee.

She tipped her head in a universal "this way" indicator. Opening her mouth could prove deadly.

He wiped his boots on the sunflower doormat, but he didn't thud across the hardwood as she'd expected. Instead, from a polite distance, he trailed quietly to the laundry room where she pointed out the dryer in case he couldn't tell which of the two brushed-steel, boxlike appliances it was.

She headed for the kitchen and sensed him taking in the place, stealing side glances at the oak staircase railing in the hall and original wooden architrave and overdoor moldings. As they breached her sacred space, her expansive commercial setup came into view, and she heard a soft whistle.

"Boy, you must take your cooking seriously."

Pride preceded a fall, her mother had always warned, and Ronnie's was galloping at the moment. But she was nothing if not proud of her stainless steel, six-burner gas range with infrared broiler, convection air baffle, and halogen lights. Not to mention her oversized refrigerator and reach-in freezer, granite countertop, deep stainless steel sink, and butcher block island.

In spite of what she considered culinary splendor, he stopped in front of the white barnwood sign with black script lettering.

" 'O taste and see that the Lord is good.' " He read it under his breath. Stared at it for a solid sixty seconds without comment, then moved to the stove.

Did he catch its clever contradiction, the play on words?

Typically, taste and smell went together, not taste and sight, though presentation of food was nearly as important as taste. People were highly influenced by the appearance of a meal or hors d'oeuvres, particularly at a wedding. Which was why she needed her gas-powered appliances up and running ASAP. The wedding was twenty-eight days away.

Cowboy checked connections and approved every appliance with a single nod of his ball-capped head.

Stopping near her workstation, he spread his stance and folded his arms.

Boy howdy. Or whatever a girl said in situations like this. She didn't have a clue, because she'd been too busy planning other brides' wedding dinners to give the unending parade of grooms-men a second glance.

"You'll be out of commission for a few more hours, but I can fix your leak and get you up and running by tomorrow afternoon. Will that work?"

"Um, okay. I mean, yes, thank you." It would probably be perfect based on the amount of time it would take the fire and health departments to come out and label her good-to-go. She'd call them today.

He quoted a ridiculously low price for his time and labor, and she wondered if he knew what other professional plumbers were charging.

Doubt climbed her neck like buttercream roses on a wedding cake. Was he safe? Would her house blow up because she couldn't afford a *real* professional plumber and she let some cowboy who *said* he was licensed work on her gas line?

She glanced at her own business license framed near the

corkboard and asked the most critical question.

⁓

Ty cranked up the old truck, careful to check his side mirror before pulling into the traffic-free street, grateful that he carried a copy of his plumber's license in the glove box.

His newest client wanted a look at it.

She leaned against a support post on her front porch, one slender leg crossed over the other, nothing like what he'd been expecting when he agreed to help out a friend of a friend.

He had to get out of there fast, but without spinning his tires like a sixteen-year-old high school kid.

"Ronnie" Fare hadn't been wearing a wedding ring, but she cooked a lot, so maybe she didn't wear one when she worked. No woman like that would be unattached. There had to be a man waiting in the wings. A very lucky man.

Once out of her neighborhood and on the main road, he shoved the accelerator down. Thanks to his dad and older brother, he knew how to drive the old standard transmission—three on the tree—a skill most people his age didn't have these days. Modern vehicles were automatic, smooth, and challenge-free, and people wanted life to be the same. So did he if he was honest with himself. But that hadn't been his world since his dad's single-engine plane went down with his parents and brother on board.

One stormy, ice-filled night left Ty the sole owner of Ellicott Ropes.

Pulling the business out of a financial nosedive had kept him focused at first. Friends from church like Casey Lander helped him get his footing, his bearings. But that had been five years ago. He was finally making a go of it but still wondering if God had been looking the other way.

Until he walked into Ronnie Fare's kitchen and saw the barn siding on her wall.

"O taste & see that the Lord is good."

Was that God's idea of a joke?

The board wasn't your run-of-the-mill kitchen decoration. He'd been in enough homes to recognize outdated as well as current cutesy signs.

This one was neither, and it had cut through him like the knife lying on her countertop.

His mom used to quote that verse.

The drive out Highway 34 was slower than usual with late-season tourists and motorhomes, most of them headed to Estes Park before the highway closed for the winter. But he didn't begrudge the tourism industry. It helped keep Loveland humming a good part of the year, and when things slowed in February, the post office made up for down-time, with out-of-towners sending Valentines and love letters to be postmarked *Loveland.*

Love-*land*—not like the locals said it. The city's remailing program drew letters from around the world for Loveland's special stamp cancellation.

Ty turned in at his private drive and parked next to the rope barn. Living near the Sweetheart City hadn't done him much good in the heart department. With thirty-five staring at him from the rearview mirror, his chances of finding a woman to share his life with were growing slimmer by the year. But he didn't have what it took to date. Or see someone. Or whatever they called it these days.

The current girls in his life ran up to the truck yapping, and

Ty opened the door to Dally and Short-Go. Best cattle-bunching dogs he'd ever seen, in spite of their short corgi legs.

He hand-signaled them out around his roping-dummy straw bale and tossed them each a treat on their return.

"Taste and see. . ."

He repeated the visual order, and the pair responded with amazing agility, stopping at his feet for their reward. He delivered.

". . .that the Lord is good."

Was He? Was He good the night his dad's plane went down with every member of his family aboard?

The old question festered inside him like a deep rope burn.

His phone buzzed.

Pulled up from the pit, he read Casey's name, then recoiled at his friend's abrupt question.

"How'd it go at Fare's?"

Ty scoffed. "Tell me you didn't know *he* was a *she*."

A throat cleared on the other end. "Cindy said the gal was desperate for help. Ronnie's the chef for that Weddings by Design outfit that handled our ceremony and reception dinner."

Memory of the beef brisket and sweet baked beans Ty had enjoyed at their celebration circled the back of his brain, dragging his taste buds with it.

"Cindy's serving lasagna tonight, and your name's on one of the plates. Be here at six."

The line went dead.

Casey hadn't been so bossy before he got married. Maybe his new wife was getting the better of him.

Chapter Three

The benefit of getting up at five in the morning, driving to the Weddings by Design house, and baking a loaf of pumpkin bread was having something for Cowboy to munch on while he worked on Ronnie's gas line.

The downside was solidifying the fact that, no, she couldn't smell or taste a single thing. She'd wanted to try the new recipe since a fellow passenger on the cruise ship gave it to her, and she'd imagined how it would signal autumn as it baked, filling her kitchen with a cozy cinnamon scent. But imagination was as far as it went. With her gas stove as out of commission as her nose, cooking wasn't nearly as satisfying as it had been before.

"Smells good in here."

Felicity came in the back door with her satchel and binder, concern tugging her brows. "You're here early. Is everything all right?"

Felicity Edwards baked the most beautiful wedding cakes this side of the Rocky Mountains and helped earn the business rave reviews. If she said the kitchen smelled good, it smelled good.

"Thanks, and no, everything is not all right."

Her friend and business partner unloaded her arms and gave Ronnie her full attention. "What's wrong, girl?"

Tempted to spill everything, Ronnie tamped down the frightful emotion and opted for the obvious. No way could she let one of her three partners know that the Weddings by Design chef couldn't smell the difference between a skunk and a scallop.

"I have a gas leak at my house, and my stove and oven are down until it's repaired, which will hopefully be by this afternoon."

Felicity let out a commiserating sigh and opened her binder. She flipped through pages of cake photographs and options for flavors, colors, and presentation.

"That must have been fun to come home to." She looked up. "You have someone working on it?"

Ronnie flushed at the thought of the cowboy and turned away, hoping Felicity's eagle eye wouldn't detect it. "Yeah—a local plumber who said he would have everything up and running by this afternoon."

"Well, this kitchen is yours as well. I'm baking a few sample cakes this morning, but I won't be here all day."

Ronnie pulled her bread pan from the oven and set it on a trivet in the basket she'd brought. Slinging her bag over her shoulder, she picked up the basket.

Felicity opened the door for her, dark eyes roaming Ronnie's face, looking for chinks in her armor. "You sure you're all right?"

True to character, Felicity's tenderness nearly undid Ronnie, but she managed to dodge the question and dash down the back steps. "Good luck with your cakes."

⌒

Ronnie didn't know what time Cowboy would show up, and she wanted to be prepared. She'd been eating various appetizers since six-thirty, unsatisfied with everything. It all tasted the same.

No—scratch that. Nothing tasted at all. As if she were eating cardboard.

Frustrated, she sliced a piece of Romano and popped it in her mouth. Thank the Lord, her electricity had been turned back on. Surely the cheese would stimulate her sleeping taste buds.

Nothing. Nada. She couldn't even smell it.

Panic fired up the back of her neck, and she downed a glass of cold water. How would she know if her creations were any good if she couldn't taste them? Memory?

Was this how Beethoven felt when he wrote his Ninth Symphony after losing his hearing?

She assembled a platter of cheese, grapes, and other sliced fruits, mixed a pitcher of orange and cranberry juices, and set the platter atop a square of bright blue-and-yellow plaid on the sideboard next to generous slices of pumpkin bread. If Cowboy was hungry before he got started outside, she could watch his facial expressions.

Her eyes squeezed shut and a chill ran down her arms. She'd not thought of it like that before. He'd be tasting while she watched. *Taste and see*—a team effort. She didn't even *know* him.

Her cheeks flamed like Greek fried cheese. Wait—perfect.

Romano would do in a pinch. White. Firm. She cut a few more slices from the small block. No time to prepare a spicy tomato sauce—he'd have to settle for plain fried cheese.

She pie-sliced a large tortilla, turned on an electric hot plate she kept for emergencies, and dropped the pieces into olive oil for a hot second, then drained them on a paper towel. Next she dipped the cheese slices in warm water and flour, laid them gently in the oil, and turned them after a minute or two.

Perfect, golden brown slices topped the tortilla wedges. She set them out in a pinwheel design on a pale green plate.

The front buzzer rang.

Wiping her hands on her apron, she went to the door.

"Good morning." He was earlier than she expected, but she forced a smile. She needed his taste buds not his ire. "Come in."

"What smells?" His nose wrinkled.

At least it worked.

As she'd hoped, he followed her to the kitchen.

"I mean, uh. . ." He eyed the sideboard. "Quesadillas?"

"Not exactly, but along the same lines. It's called *saganaki*—panfried Greek cheese. I thought you might like a little something before you got started on the gas line."

He didn't look so sure. "Do you always cook this early?"

"I have a wedding in a month, so I'm starting my countdown for appetizers. After those are locked down, I'll prepare three or four entrées for tasting, and then decide on the beverages. Please, help yourself."

She pushed the pumpkin bread forward and poured him a glass of juice. Nothing like being obvious. But she wanted to know what he thought by reading his face rather than asking him straight out.

"So, uh, you're getting married?"

She blinked. *What?*

Oh. It hit her like water on a hot skillet. "I'm the chef partner at Weddings by Design, and we have a big outdoor wedding in late October, and I like to have things planned out ahead of time, but with my gas shut off, I'm out of commission, and. . ."

She was rambling.

"Did you happen to do the Lander wedding last February?" He was watching her, clearly not excited about trying the fried cheese.

She pushed her hair behind her ear. "Yes, as a matter of fact we did." *Had he been there?*

"Those barbecued beans were great. And the cake." He shook his head in a way she knew meant *yes* rather than *no*.

"Thank you. Felicity, our cake specialist, is a genius. And the beans, well, my Gramma 'Cine should get credit for those."

"Seen?" His forehead wrinkled.

"C-i-n-e. Short for Francine—also my mother's name."

"Did she cook 'em? Your grandmother, I mean."

"Oh no. She's been gone for twenty years. But she taught me how to make them when I was a little girl."

Not exactly the time to get all puddly, but Gramma 'Cine had laid the foundation for nearly everything Ronnie did, from cooking to trusting God, both of which often went hand in hand.

Polite won out over petrified, and Cowboy reached for a tortilla wedge while she poured him a glass of the juice. "Sounds Japanese, not Greek." His mouth hitched up on one side with a little chuckle deep in his chest. But when he bit into one of the cheese-topped triangles, his eyes slid closed in pleasure.

Bingo.

Tortillas were not part of the traditional saganaki recipe, but in a pinch, they served as a handy scoop and worked better than a fork and knife in an informal setting. Not much was more informal than her incapacitated kitchen.

He took another.

Her heart smiled. Apparently his taste buds worked as well as his nose. She made a mental note to offer this informal appetizer for the Gardner-Mitchell tasting.

"You're right. It does sound Japanese. But if you saw those little wedges at a party, maybe a Western-themed party, what would you call them?"

Picking up a third one, he shoved the whole thing in his mouth, glancing at her off and on. He swallowed, then tasted the juice before downing half of it. "Cheese wedges?"

Wonderful. Just wonderful. She'd hired Mr. Original Thought himself.

⁓

The cheese wedges hadn't looked bad—they just smelled like the inside of Ty's boots after a long day gathering cattle.

And by the look on Ronnie Fare's pretty face, that's what she thought of his answer to her question.

How was he supposed to know what to call these things? He tried out another idea. "Fried-cheese chip?"

She rolled her eyes.

Guess not.

But he did know she hoped he'd like them. Her anticipation was a dead giveaway, and for a split second he weighed the cost of a bald-faced lie to keep from hurting her feelings. A scary proposition no matter how he viewed it, and a whole lot like his aunt Gert's friend insisting he try gefilte fish when he was ten years old.

But this time the taste overrode the smell. No lie necessary.

The fancy cheese was good enough that he had three and chased them with the pink juice. "Not what I was expecting, I admit, but it's good."

He felt a little guilty for asking her what he already knew about her job, but he wanted to compare her version to Casey's, though her sigh seemed heavy for a gal who cooked for a living. She ought to know if her wares were any good, but she'd looked worried for a second. Watched him like a hawk watches a gopher hole.

He reset his cap. "I'm gonna get started on the leak. But for safety's sake, make sure all your pilot lights are off. And all the burners."

Her side-eye said even more than her mouth. "Everything's been off for a couple of days."

Fine and dandy. But he couldn't take anything for granted. He was a professional, after all.

Well before noon, he had the leak repaired and the gas back on, but he took his time filling the hole in the front yard and packing up his tools. Took time to walk around the outside of the house and inspect the storm windows that looked like they hadn't been removed in a decade. Found chunks missing in the gingerbread trim—that's what he'd heard it called. And a couple busted rain gutters to boot.

For a gal with a commercial-class kitchen, she hadn't done much else around the place. Maybe she was as cash-strapped as Casey had said.

But it wouldn't take much in the way of manpower. Ty could patch up a few things, do some repairs that would prevent major problems come winter if left to worsen, and maybe sample a little more of her cooking. He had the time. It would take a week at most. What'd he have to lose?

Other than your heart?

He yanked off his hat and scrubbed his hair, already sweaty, and it was only ten o'clock. It was going to be another warm day.

The front screen door screeched and slapped shut. Sounded like a chicken caught in a hay baler.

He strode around the east end of the house and caught her holding a tray of lemonade, leaning out over the porch railing, looking the other way. When she turned in his direction, her face took on relief, like she might have been worried that he'd left.

A guy could hope, right?

"Thirsty?"

Long sun-browned legs belied her indoor occupation, and he forced his gaze elsewhere as he climbed the porch steps. "As a duck in the desert."

She laughed, and the tray jerked, spilling a little over the rim of two frosty glasses.

"Here, let me help you with that." He reached for the tray, but she turned before he could grab it and set it on the wicker table with the red flowers.

"Please, have a seat." Handing him a glass, she sat on an old swing suspended from the porch roof that looked like it might let go in a stiff wind.

He took the white rocker on the other side of the table and a long swig of cold lemonade better than any he'd ever had. A mint leaf floated on top and smelled like spring and summer all rolled into one.

The woman was a genius. And she was watching him again.

A small white plate with dusted cookies waited on the tray.

"Help yourself," she said, catching his glance. "They're my lemon cooler cookies."

He bit into one, and powdered sugar melted on his tongue. Good thing his mouth was full, or he might make a fool of himself and ask her to marry him.

Ronnie pulled a folded check from the back pocket of her cutoffs and held it out to him. "Thanks for your help with the gas leak."

He stared for a second as if he didn't know what she was talking about, then took the check.

"My pleasure, ma'am."

Sheesh. He was born in the wrong century.

Without looking at the check, he slid it into his shirt pocket, then made quick work of the lemonade and cookies.

How could she keep him around until she went shopping, restocked her freezer and refrigerator, and started in on her appetizers and entrée samples? She sipped the ice-cold but bland lemonade already condensing moisture on the clear glass.

He pushed his ball cap up off sweaty hair. "That hits the spot." A quick glance her way. "I take it this isn't from a mix."

She didn't need taste buds to identify true appreciation. Not that her partners didn't appreciate her, or the brides and mothers she worked with. But to have the approval of someone not connected to her business somehow made things a little sweeter. In a metaphorical sort of way.

With his cap up a smidgen, she had a clear view of his eyes as they scanned the porch railing, worn floorboards, and chipped paint on her toenails.

She tucked her feet back under the swing, an idea simmering. "Do you work on other things besides plumbing?"

His gaze locked with hers and held for that eternal moment

that catches one's breath in a romance novel or during a rom-com movie.

Blink. Look away. Do something. But she couldn't break the connection. She didn't *want* to break the connection.

"I do."

Bad choice of words.

She felt her mouth open and her pulse make a mad dash for escape. How many times had she heard those words in her profession? They meant nothing to her. Nothing. Ever.

Oh boy.

Without looking away, he lifted his chin to the right, as if pointing with it. "That screen door's got a killer screech. How 'bout I work on that?"

She swallowed and reached for whatever dignity remained. "I've WD-40'd the hinges, but there seems to be more to it than that."

His eyes smiled, and then his mouth.

Hers went dry. "This house is a work in progress. When my career makes progress, so will renovations."

Looking away, he tipped the bill of his Ellicott Ropes cap toward the railing. "You've got a few balusters that need to be repaired."

Didn't she know it.

"I've got a little extra time Monday. I could take care of that for you."

His expression sobered, and he shot her a quick glance, as if testing the proverbial waters. "No charge of course. Just a hobby of mine. I have a lathe and enjoy working with my hands every chance I get."

Hobby. Right. And working with his hands? Where was a cooling breeze when she needed one? The backs of her legs were sticking to the swing. "That's very generous of you, but I don't mind paying you for your time." With what, she wasn't sure.

He adjusted his cap, set his empty glass on the tray by the geraniums, then went to the railing, where he dislodged a decrepit spindle with little effort. "I'll see how many of these have split and should be replaced. The top railing might need replacing as well."

She shot to her feet. The porch railing was all cedar, and she wanted to renovate as close to the original as possible, which wasn't cheap.

"That's very generous of you, but seriously, all that can wait. My budget is set aside for food for the next several weeks, so maybe just the screen door—"

His smile dislodged her argument. "It's no trouble, really. That lemonade of yours is pretty good on a hot day, and Monday is supposed to be a scorcher."

After she agreed and he left, Ronnie peeled paint chips from the backs of her legs and took the tray inside. Ideas. She needed ideas for this wedding, at least three of everything to offer the clients who were meeting today with Felicity to taste cake samples. Monday the bride was discussing her wedding dress with Kiki, and the groom was meeting with Cassie to sign on the dotted line and make transportation arrangements.

And also on Monday, Ronnie was meeting the couple at the shop, so she had a lot to do. This gas-leak delay and the loss of so much food had set her way behind.

She had no time to waste on Mr. Fix-it with coffee-colored eyes.

Chapter Four

I sn't he dreamy?"

Ronnie rolled her eyes, hidden by the luxury of a phone conversation with her friend and former client. "You did not just say dreamy, Cindy. Nobody says dreamy. And you're married now, remember?"

Anticipatory silence preceded a huff. "Well?"

"Okay, he's dreamy."

"I *knew* you'd think so. That's why I insisted Casey call him for you. Besides, he saved our bacon when the old hot water heater downstairs burst in the middle of the night. My idea of a true hero."

Ronnie's image of hero didn't quite match the ball-cap wearing cowboy, but he might win a medal for tenacity and stunningly gorgeous eyes.

"He's been here every day doing something. After fixing the gas leak on Saturday, he came back Monday and worked on my screen door. *Screeching*, he called it, which was a bit insulting but completely true. Then he reset a half dozen balusters he'd sanded, repaired, or remade, and it certainly spruced up the porch railing and the front steps."

"You don't say."

Cindy's smirk was audible, but Ronnie ignored it.

"Yesterday I met with the Gardner-Mitchell couple for sample tasting, and when I returned, I noticed the old furnace filter was in the dumpster next to the garage."

"He changed the furnace filter? Seriously?" Cindy's voice popped up an octave on the last word.

"Yes. And this morning when I went outside to investigate a scraping sound, I found him doing just that to the porch deck."

Cindy giggled.

"What are you, twelve?"

"Don't you see? He's sweet on you."

Grateful that she wasn't face-to-face, another eye roll hit the front-porch ceiling. "You read too many historical romances. He's not *sweet* on me. But he does come in handy as a taste tester."

"Why would you need a taste tester?"

Ronnie clapped her hand over her mouth and set her feet on the porch floor. The swing creaked. If she let it slip that she couldn't taste the difference between a sweet potato and a pineapple, her career could be down the disposal. Who would trust a chef who couldn't taste what she made? Or smell it either.

"I repeat," Cindy said. "Why do you need—"

"This ranch wedding I'm working on is scheduled for October—a real last-minute affair—so I'm trying out a couple different things on him. He is a *cowboy*, you know."

Not that she'd heard or seen him do anything even remotely Western, but he was definitely a willing participant when it came to sampling what she served. And now that she thought about it, he always managed to be there during breakfast or lunch.

Apparently satisfied with the diversion, Cindy eased off.

"What's he charging you for all this work?"

"I expect I'll get a bill any day now. The guy's gotta make a living, right?"

"Oh, he makes a living."

"What—doing odd jobs and driving that old beat-up Chevy truck?"

"I take it you haven't heard of Ellicott Ropes. Or driven out past his place off Highway 34?"

"No. Should I have?" Though she'd seen plenty of *Ellicott Ropes* stitched on the front of his ball caps—a different one every day.

"Come over for lunch Sunday, and I'll drive you out there. And don't say no. Do you realize how much chutzpah it takes to ask a chef over for a meal?"

Ronnie laughed, conceding that Cindy did have a point. That gave her the rest of the week to get ready for the weekend's wedding that had been booked a year ago and also organize for the Gardner-Mitchell event now that they'd made their selections. But she wouldn't have a job if she didn't get this taste-and-smell issue settled.

As soon as she hung up, she called her doctor's office and asked for the first opening they had. One month out. She could be unemployed by then.

"But this really is an emergency. Isn't there anything earlier, like say, tomorrow?"

The receptionist maintained her professionally neutral tone. "If you have blood or burns, go to the ER. Other than that, try the walk-in health clinic."

"But I need to see a specialist, and I can't get into one without a referral."

"I'm sorry, but late October is the best I can do. Or you can go to the clinic."

Ronnie mumbled a polite goodbye and went upstairs to change into publicly presentable clothes.

Clinic it was. Right after she dropped off her mother's swimsuit that somehow ended up in Ronnie's suitcase.

⌒

"I wondered where this was." Francine Fare stood in her living room, holding the turquoise, black, and lime-green suit against her still shapely body. "Do you think it made me look fat?"

"*Mo–om*. Honestly, you looked great. Stop already."

At a knock on the door, her mother jumped.

A man's voice called from the other side. "Francine, you home?"

"Coming!" She tossed the suit at Ronnie. "Will you put that in my bedroom please? How do I look?"

"What?"

Her mother went to the entryway mirror, fluffed her shoulder-length hair, tugged on her navy cowl-neck shirt, and whispered, "Tom's here. How do I look? Do I need lipstick? Do you have any in your purse I can borrow? I don't want to run upstairs."

"Francine?"

"Be right there!" She bit her lip and pinched her cheeks.

Ronnie rolled her eyes. "You look beautiful, Mom. But who's Tom?"

When her mother opened the front door, a sun-bronzed man walked in, his white hair a veritable crown of glory. "I'm sorry. I didn't know you had company."

Her mother blushed and tugged Ronnie close to her side as

they faced the casually dressed man holding a bouquet of mixed flowers.

Ronnie hid the swimsuit behind her back.

"Ronnie, I'd like you to meet my friend Tom. Tom, this is my daughter, Ronnie."

Aside from being shell-shocked, dumbfounded, and speechless, she managed to accept the handshake he offered.

"I'm happy to meet you. Your mother talks about you all the time and tells me what a wonderful chef you are. You cater special events, I hear." His eyes actually twinkled when he said it.

"Weddings. We do weddings. Weddings by Design. That's the name of the business."

Her mother reached for the flowers. "I'll just put these in a vase while you two chat."

Ronnie snapped out of her stupor, scrunching the swimsuit in a wad at her back. "Oh, I really must go. I have quite a bit to do to get ready for this weekend."

"A wedding?" Tom asked.

"Yes."

She made her getaway when he walked into the kitchen. At the car, she tossed her mother's swimsuit onto the passenger seat. She'd have to try delivering it again another day.

On her way home, reality wrapped around her as snug as her seat belt. Her mother had a boyfriend. Ronnie found it hard to believe, in spite of the fact that she had prayed for something like this to happen.

No, not something like. *Exactly* like. Her mother was lonely for companionship with someone her own age. Male companionship.

God had been listening.

At the corner of Fifth and Colorado Avenue, Ronnie turned west and followed the tree-lined street to her own little shady spot of struggling lawn and narrow driveway.

Of course God had been listening. He always listened. She didn't always get what she wanted, but He always listened. Yet the way Tom latched onto Ronnie's business information left her trembling. Was he thinking of proposing to her mother? Her *mother*! Could she plan a wedding for her *mother*?

Completely befuddled, she pulled into her driveway then immediately backed out and headed for the clinic across town.

⁓

The biggest roping clinic of the year was this weekend at Brace Ryder's arena, and Ty was behind on loading his stock trailer with product and practice dummies.

Though he didn't have a plastic head and rebar body like the roping dummies he sold, he might be the biggest dummy of them all, the way he'd been hanging out at Ronnie Fare's place every day for more than a week.

Boy, could she cook. Not to mention listen to everything he said and watch him with those gray-green eyes that saw all the way through him. But hang it all anyway—he hadn't seen a gal like her in years. Not with his head buried in work and his heart put on hold.

He shoved the bent-pipe body of a "steer" into the stock trailer, complete with fake back legs that allowed a heeler to rope them during a practice session. And if there was one thing ropers did consistently, it was practice. That's why he carried molded steer and calf heads mounted on two rebar rods that could be stuck into a bale of hay, and fancier pipe stands bent to imitate a calf or steer's body. He even carried a wooden contraption with four movable legs that emulated calf legs and allowed calf ropers, young and old, to practice their tie-down roping skills—with a selection of Ellicott piggin' strings, of course.

Ronnie had listened wide-eyed to his explanation of what a piggin' string was after teasing him that it must have something to do with bacon.

"It's a short rope used to tie three of the calf's legs together. In competition the calf has to stay tied for six seconds or the run doesn't count."

"Competition? Why compete over tying up three calf legs, and why tie them up to begin with, poor little guys."

"Back in the day when cattlemen needed to doctor a calf, they roped it and tied it down to hold it still, keep it safe. A lot of ranchers still do. Not everyone has a squeeze chute. Over the years, cowboys took pride in the speed with which they could rope an animal and tie its legs. Same with team roping, only that's a two-man event. One ropes a steer's head and the other ropes the hind feet."

"And that's timed too, I imagine."

"Yes, ma'am. And I make the ropes that help those ropers get their best time."

At that point, he'd popped the rest of her bacon-wrapped date appetizer into his mouth and watched her watch him. That fast, she went from asking him about rodeo to searching his face. Every day she offered him something different and said, "Taste this—I want to see what you think."

Couldn't she just taste it herself? Or did she want a man's opinion? Either way, he wouldn't look a gift horse in the mouth.

Serving as taste tester was about the best part-time job he'd ever had, whether he got paid for it in real money or not.

A longtime bachelor did not turn down real food.

Five more practice dummies in the trailer and several boxes of new ropes and piggin' strings, and he had just enough time to mow the grass before dinner.

Every time he climbed on the little tractor, he appreciated his father's foresight to get a riding mower. There was no other way to sufficiently take care of three acres of grass around the house, garage, and outbuildings. He kept cow/calf pairs on his hayfield late winter and early spring, then moved them off and let it grow to the first cutting in either May or June. But the "yard" simply had to be mowed to keep the place looking well-kept. Like everything else, that fell to him.

Life hadn't seemed as hard when he was growing up. Labor was divided among four people. And even in the early days before he and his brother came along, his mom and dad had done all right. How many times had he listened to them reminisce at the dinner table?

"Two are better than one," his mother would say, stirring a twinkle in his dad's eye and a blush in her cheek.

"The good Lord knew what He was talkin' about," Dad always said. Then he'd lean over and kiss her soundly on the cheek. On the lips if he could get away with it.

A lot of Ty's school buddies had parents that had divorced, so he knew his growing-up years had been a real blessing. Now, after five years alone, he longed even more for what his folks had.

The image of a lanky blond-haired gal circled his brain as he looped the mower behind the barn and back toward the house.

He had searched online for saffron, remembering it as a reddish spice. It came from a purple crocus that bloomed in the fall. Danged if he could figure that out, but it sure enough meant yellow flower, just like she said. Maybe something got lost in translation from one language to another.

Ronnie's hair wasn't exactly yellow, more honey-colored. And her gray-green eyes—maybe they were hazel. He wasn't an expert on eye color, but he knew they cut through him like a laser at her bidding.

It was hard to tell her age, and he sure wasn't going to ask her outright. She might think him an old man with the stray white hairs showing over his ears. But it didn't take much to imagine her here at the ranch, working as a partner beside him. He'd teach her to ride—if she wanted to learn. Make whatever improvements she wanted in the house, especially the kitchen. He hadn't done much in that department himself, but working at her place and seeing the pleasure in her eyes over something he repaired or replaced was worth every minute of toil.

His mother had been right about that "two are better than one" theory. For whoever those two were, they did have a reward for their labor, like the scripture said. Even Dally and Short-Go proved the point. They had each other, whether they got along all the time or not.

At least they weren't doing everything on their own.

That night's dinner was a frozen bean burrito that he'd be embarrassed to let Ronnie see. He knew how to cook. His mom had seen to it that he and his brother could fend for themselves in the kitchen. But he just didn't have the heart to make the effort lately. *Alone* was getting old, and so was he. Maybe it was time to look for the other half of his two.

And maybe he'd already found her.

With that thought wiggling through his brain, he tore the plastic wrapper off his insta-meal, laid it on a plate, and set the microwave for two minutes. A quick hunt through his refrigerator netted a jar of month-old salsa and a cold soda, and he set it all on a tray his mother had used for eating outside on the deck.

She'd been on his mind a lot lately, ever since he saw the barnwood sign in Ronnie Fare's kitchen.

He set the tray on the family picnic table beneath the sprawling overhang and sat on the side facing the cut grass that sloped down toward the arena. Crickets took up a chorus from the pond south of the barn while the sun slid toward the mountains. He unscrewed the lid from the salsa jar and dumped a pile of it on one end of his burrito.

"Thanks, Lord."

Lifelong habit forced a cursory nod to God, but the fullmouth prayer wasn't the kind of blessing he'd grown up with. Prayers like his father prayed had faded after the three-in-one funeral. It'd been hard to thank God for anything when Ty felt like everything had been ripped from him.

He took another bite of burrito and chased it with cold cola. Not exactly Ronnie Fare's sweet lemonade and fried cheese.

The memory of her golden hair and tanned legs swamped his good sense as an arrow of Canada geese sailed past on their way to the pond. He wondered what she was making for dinner.

And he wondered what his mom would think of a girl with a boy's name and a smile that made him want to be a better man.

Chapter Five

Ronnie agreed to leave her car at Cindy's house after Sunday lunch and ride along with her out Highway 34. A fan of the Front Range, Ronnie enjoyed drinking in the view without having to watch traffic on the busy two-lane road that drew motorists into the heart of the Rocky Mountains.

She would have enjoyed it more without the mind-numbing pain relievers she'd been taking. The long line at the medical clinic last week had turned her right around, and she'd been trying to tough it out ever since. The narrow, winding road wasn't helping.

Following a queasy left turn, they took another left at Trail West Road into ranch country—irrigated pastures, neat barns, grazing cattle, and horses.

Just past a tree-lined pond, Cindy slowed at a set-back entrance where a sign on the right said ELLICOTT RANCH & ROPES. The *E* and the *R*s were made with actual rope.

"No-o-o-o." Ronnie powered down her window and laid her arm on the door. The ball-cap-wearing, old-truck guy in jeans and a T-shirt lived here?

"Yes." Cindy pulled onto the shoulder to let a couple of other cars go by. "Gorgeous, isn't it?"

Green pasturelike grass sloped away from a sprawling ranch

house, barn, and narrow steel building longer than the barn. Trim fence line separated sections of land, and a long oval of board-fenced dirt with gates at one end looked like something from a rodeo.

"He must have a crew of groundskeepers working for him."

"Nope."

Ronnie's hair swished against her neck and her head and sinuses throbbed as she turned to face her friend. "You're serious."

"As mozzarella on lasagna."

Massive cottonwoods hugged the ranch house. Ronnie imagined the setting pristine and golden come fall.

"He's single and alone since a plane crash took his parents and brother about five years ago. And he's the most eligible bachelor among the ranch and rodeo set, now that Casey is out of circulation." Cindy smiled possessively.

"How do you know all this?"

"Casey and Ty have been friends since middle school."

Ronnie craned her neck and scoped the countryside. "My next venue isn't far from here. The Sweetheart Ranch."

"Wanna drive by?"

"No—I'm familiar with it, but thanks."

She leaned back in her seat and looked again at Ty Ellicott's home, curious about what else he was hiding behind his warm smile and quiet laugh. She never dreamed that his carob-colored eyes masked such loss, pain, and. . .peaceful repose.

"Like I said, he's the most eligible bachelor—"

"I'm not looking."

"Well, he is."

"For what—bachelors?"

"No, silly. At you."

Ronnie's pulse hiccupped and she avoided her friend's gaze. "And you know this how?"

Cindy checked her mirror and made a U-turn back onto Trail West Road. "Let's just say I have inside connections."

Ronnie snorted, a poor decoy for the unfamiliar flutter beneath her ribs. Heartburn—emotional or otherwise. Exactly what she didn't need right now.

With one last look as they sailed past the pond, she found it even harder to believe the cowboy lived on that place all alone.

On the way home from Cindy's, Ronnie stopped by her mother's townhouse, where laughter from beyond the door paused her raised hand. Francine Fare hadn't laughed like that in years—not even on their cruise.

"Oh, it's you." Her mother drew her into the entryway and a hug. "I'm so glad you stopped by."

Ronnie followed dutifully around the corner and into the kitchen where Tom sat at the counter with a cup of coffee in hand.

"Care for a cup?" her mother asked as she poured.

"Sure, Mom."

Tom chuckled. "Persuasive, isn't she?"

Ronnie took a seat at the counter, leaving the middle one of three empty between herself and Tom. Her mother slid a white ceramic cup to her, then leaned on her elbows, looking across the sink at her guests. A little more at Tom than Ronnie, blushing like a seventeen-year-old at the prom.

Tom's happiness was palpable. So was her mother's, for that matter.

A corner of Ronnie's heart warmed at the attention her mother responded to so instinctively. But from another corner stepped a coldhearted drill sergeant with clipboard in hand. Who was this Tom guy, and why was he at her mother's townhouse all the time? What did he want?

One question popped out of its own accord. "How did you two meet?"

Her mother's back straightened defensively—a response Ronnie knew well. "At church," she said, answering the question directed at Tom. "We met last week at church."

Tom nodded in agreement. "I've been attending there for more than a year, but I always went to the evening service." He sent her mother a tender glance.

Ronnie shoved aside an envious tug in the pit of her stomach.

She had stopped by to commiserate single-woman to single-woman, but clearly that ship had sailed right along with their cruise liner. She had fully expected her mother to meet men on her birthday cruise and, therefore, had all of her weaponry trained hard on any man who gave Francine Fare a second glance. Ronnie had heard stories about vultures who trolled for lonely, financially stable women. Not on her watch.

She'd missed church the last two Sundays in a row. So much for watching.

⁓

Monday morning Ronnie was up early icing a pan of warm cinnamon rolls with cream cheese frosting. Amazed at how easy it was to say no to her favorite diet buster, she took some consolation in knowing she wouldn't pig out on what she couldn't taste.

With the pan cooling on a trivet, she washed a batch of brussels sprouts and pulled off the leaves. Her Gardner-Mitchells wanted chips for one of their appetizers, but not the corn and potato variety.

Ronnie was thrilled that they'd gone with her suggestion of brussels sprout chips, lightly roasted with olive oil and sea salt.

Was anything better—other than fresh cinnamon rolls?

Well, she wasn't sure anymore. The crunch was still there—that wonderfully fun texture. But the taste was gone.

The familiar slam of an old truck door popped her pulse up a couple of degrees as she slid a sheet of leaves into the oven and set the timer for eight minutes. Then, using her reflection in the top oven-door glass, she pulled out her messy bun and fluffed her hair. Rolled her lips. She'd already applied an extra coat of lip gloss—

What was she doing?

The door buzzer trilled. She wiped her mouth on a paper towel and tossed it in the trash. Too late to put her hair up.

Smoothing her crocus-purple T-shirt over the top of her jeans, she pulled her shoulders back and walked down the central hallway to the front door as sedately as she knew how.

He stood with his back to the door, just like he had that first day. Same broad shoulders and well-fitting jeans. White T-shirt and dark hair. Ball cap in place.

Nothing about him said Loveland's most eligible bachelor, bereft of family and companionship. Which was fine. She wasn't looking for either.

Lord, have mercy. She wasn't interested in a man. She was interested in what her cooking tasted like.

"Hey there." *Shoot.* Had she lost her vocabulary as well as her sense of smell?

He turned and gave her that slow-burn smile through the screen door that didn't moan anymore. "Morning, sunshine."

Whoa. Hold your horses, Cowboy. No nicknames, thank you very much. She fingered her hair behind one ear, then flicked it back out.

She pushed the screen door open. "Would you like a cup of coffee before you get started?"

"You've got yourself a deal." He came in, smelling-distance close, and her nose reached for the scent of hay or horse or motor oil.

Nada.

"Smells like you've been up and at 'em already this morning," he said.

She blinked, distracted by his use of the word *smell.* Had she heard right? "Adam?"

The slow smile slipped around her shoulders, knees, and toes.

"*At 'em.* You know—at work. Busy." He indicated the hallway, closed his eyes, and sniffed. "Cinnamon?"

"Oh. Sure. Yeah." He had long, brown lashes. So unfair. "Cinnamon rolls. Want one?"

His eyes opened and poured hot coffee all over her brain. "Don't mind if I do."

She was in way over her head. *Way* over.

He followed her and stopped at the booted sunflowers.

She looked over her shoulder in time to catch him fingering the petals of a giant yellow face.

"Looks almost real."

"Yeah, they do."

The timer went off, and she hurried to the oven, removed the sheet of perfectly browned brussels sprout chips, and set it on a brass flower-shaped trivet.

⌒

Her hair was down today.

Ty had to stop at the old boot with the sunflowers to give

his hands something to do other than what they wanted. Ronnie Fare was quickly transforming from needy homeowner into a seriously attractive woman. Single woman, according to Casey and his wife. No husband or boyfriend in the shadows.

He followed his nose to a pan of frosted cinnamon rolls, but instead of offering him one, Ronnie slid miniature toasted basketball skins onto a fancy plate.

He folded his arms and tried not to growl.

"Give me a sec here, and I'll plate a roll for you."

Plate a roll?

She held out a napkin filled with toasted leaves "Wanna try one?"

No.

She looked at him. Tipped her head. Her hair fell away from her ear and a white pearl earring winked at him.

"Sure." The leaf crunched in his mouth like a real salted chip. *Not bad.* He took another one. "What are these?"

"Brussels sprout chips."

He would have eaten more vegetables if his mother had thought of this. He took the napkin and finished off the scoop-shaped leaves, hoping to free Ronnie's hands for dishing up a roll.

She obliged, set the plate and fork on the counter in front of a stool, and poured him a cup of coffee.

She was the first client who'd ever fed him on the job, and he decided right on the spot that he could find plenty to do around her place to keep him busy until snow fell. With time off for his last hay cutting.

She poured her own cup and took the stool at the end of the counter, watching him eat. Last time he'd been watched like that, his mother was doing surveillance on his table manners.

"Aren't you gonna have one of these? They're great." He made sure to wipe his mouth on the napkin tucked next to his plate.

She glanced at the pan of icing-covered heaven like she hadn't thought of it as food. "Sure. Yeah."

Turnaround was fair play, so he watched her closely as she used a spatula to lift a cinnamon circle from the pan and set it on another plate.

"Would you mind if I had another one?"

She flicked him a look and smiled, then served him a center roll. He used to fight with his brother over who got the center rolls their mother baked rather than those around the edge of the pan. He hadn't thought of his family this much all summer, but something about Ronnie Fare made him feel at home. And home was about family.

"What do you really think?" She slid a forked-off bite in her mouth.

"I think they're great."

She waved her fork in a circle while she chewed, then asked. "I mean specifically. How would you describe the taste, the smell? Too much cinnamon? Too much cream cheese in the frosting?"

Was she kidding?

"They taste like home. Like what my mom used to make when I was a kid and I'd sneak a taste of frosting from the bowl if she wasn't looking."

Ronnie stared at him—deep into his past as if she could see his gangly self shouldering past his beefier brother.

Uncomfortable, he attacked the breakfast treat. He didn't talk to other people about his folks and was frankly surprised that he was doing so now. In spite of the home-and-family triggers.

Her sigh drew his glance, and she tilted her head a little to one side. "That's the nicest description I've ever heard."

She cut off another bite and looked at him with a sudden threat. "But dip your finger in my bowl of icing and you're liable to pull back a bloody stump."

Unable to help himself, he choked on her words and clapped the napkin over his mouth rather than spray the counter with half-chewed cinnamon roll.

Defensively, she perked up. "I'm serious. This is a commercial kitchen, and I can't have people sticking their fingers in bowls and pans."

"If you don't swipe a taste now and then, how do you know if it's any good?"

She tensed—not much, but a little—like his horse when they backed into the roping box before chasing a steer down the arena. Her nostrils even flared.

A push at her hair and a tug on her T-shirt confirmed his suspicion.

"That's why I have taste testers. To get other opinions as well as my own."

Made sense. She cooked for other people more than she did herself. Yet his gut said she was hedging the truth—and he was getting too close to it.

When he finished, she took his plate and cup to the sink, and he ambled over to the corkboard and perused her Hopeful Renovations list.

Nothing like having a helpful road map.

Chapter Six

Desperate.

By Wednesday morning, Ronnie was desperate for help in the truest sense of the word. That desperation—and the increasing sinus pain—propelled her to the clinic as soon as it opened.

"Have you traveled outside the country in the last thirty days?"

The receptionist trained her eyes on her clipboard, recording Ronnie's affirmative answer, and immediately followed up with "Where?" and "For how long?"

After the obligatory temperature check, she was ushered into an examination room where a nurse practitioner looked in her ears and down her throat, then pressed on her sinuses with silicone-gloved thumbs.

"Does this hurt?"

Rather than scream, Ronnie gripped the middle-aged woman's wrists, pulled down on them, and managed a controlled *yes*.

Compassion filled the nurse's blue eyes. "I'm sorry, but it's part of the drill."

Ronnie understood. She really did. But that didn't make her face hurt any less.

"You have contracted a serious sinus infection that has affected your sense of smell. It could be simply from the swelling of your sinuses, or it could be what is clinically known as anosmia. The everyday name is smell blindness."

Smell blindness? How could her nose be blind when it didn't see to begin with? "Is it rare?"

The nurse sat down at a wall-mounted computer. "It's not necessarily common, but I've seen a few other cases this year. I'll call in a week's worth of antibiotics, and that should knock out the infection. Where do you get your prescriptions?"

Ronnie's hopes ballooned as she gave the name of her pharmacy. "I can't taste anything either. Will my taste and smell return by the end of the week?"

The woman remained silent as she signed off from the computer. No smiling eyes. No affirmative nod.

Ronnie deflated.

"There are two types of anosmia: partial and total. And it can be temporary or permanent. Sometimes the sense of smell returns slowly, sometimes not at all. We just have to wait and see."

"Does it affect taste as well?"

The practitioner faced her, looking anything but encouraging. "Have you noticed that food seems to have lost its taste? If so, it's more likely a *sense* of flavor you're missing. We actually smell more than we taste, and the two senses are tied together. Taste is highly dependent on smell."

"I'm a chef." Ronnie's voice caught on the last word. "I make my living cooking, and I have to be able to taste and smell what I'm cooking."

"I'm sorry." A motherly pat on Ronnie's hand. "There are no guarantees. Wait and see is the best we can do. But make sure you have a working smoke detector and carbon monoxide sensor. The sense of smell is often a first line of defense, so make sure you're prepared for emergencies."

Ronnie cried all the way to the drive-through pharmacy, increasing the pain in her sinuses to nuclear levels. Hiding behind her vacation sunglasses, she handed over her credit card and then cried all the way home. By the time she parked in front of her run-down garage, she had to breathe through her mouth.

And her head was killing her. "Wait and see" was not what she wanted to hear and not what she needed in her line of work. *Lord, what happened to "taste and see"?*

Wagner's "Bridal Chorus" chimed from her purse as she entered her kitchen, and nearly sent her into orbit. She silenced the ringer on her phone and put it on vibrate before answering.

"Ronnie. Glad I caught you."

Kiki's cheerful voice struck fear and envy in a single blow. Fear that the sharp-eared seamstress would hear Ronnie's thick throat and thicker sinuses. Envy because her friend had recently found Mr. Right where she didn't expect him to be. In fact, the future was looking pretty good for Felicity and Cassie too, and in the romance department, Ronnie was the odd man out.

"I haven't talked to you since you got back from your mom's birthday cruise. How was it?"

"Pretty good." Until she got sick.

Kiki skipped a beat and her voice came back different. "Only *pretty* good? All that sun and high-seas sailing. You all right? You sound a little plugged up."

"Oh, I'm fine. Probably just fall allergens floating around." *Forgive me, Lord.*

"Well, I just wanted to remind you of our meeting next week.

Are you going to be able to make it? We need to compare notes and track progress on the Gardner-Mitchell wedding."

"Absolutely. I'll be there with my menu and a couple of appetizers to get us in the mood."

"Oh good. Felicity is bringing the unchosen cake samples she's had in the freezer, and I have photos from the dress fitting last week. Cassie will have our timeline."

Ronnie signed off and peered through teary eyes at the barn-wood sign her mother had given her when she graduated from her culinary training. The black script letters were only half of the verse in Psalm 34—the challenge part.

The encouragement part wasn't there, but it had been tattooed on her heart by two loving women over the years and even now ran through her mind in her Gramma 'Cine's voice: *"Blessed is the woman who trusts in Him."*

For as long as Ronnie could remember, Gramma had added *wo* to the verse, insisting that it didn't alter the promise but directed it to a more specific audience.

Years of hearing that affirmation had laid a foundation of trust.

Trust sounded a whole lot like *taste*. And right now it was just about the only thing she could do in the face of this potentially life-altering challenge.

That night she propped herself up in bed with extra pillows and a warm compress on her forehead while she watched cooking shows on her laptop. How would she manage if she couldn't taste or smell what she was doing?

What would her business partners do if they learned the truth?

Felicity, Kiki, and Cassie depended on her to be a fully functioning chef. The fourth corner of their business, holding up her share of Weddings by Design.

"Oh Lord," she whispered. "Help me, please."

Much more than her health was involved, and the stakes crystalized in her mind like Waterford stemware. She had two weeks to prepare for one of the bigger weddings they had booked. The business's success could hinge on how well her food and beverages were received.

Could she put together a menu based on what she *thought* would work?

Contrary to an old cliché, seeing was not believing. She needed to *taste* and see.

On Friday morning, Ty set his toolbox on Ronnie Fare's porch and knelt by the screen door. The heavy oak stood open behind it as usual, and the heady scent of maple-cured bacon told him she was cooking up a storm for breakfast. He couldn't wait to be hit with the full force of it, and his mouth watered just thinking about it.

The gal could definitely cook, but for some reason, she seemed insecure. It didn't add up. She had killer talent and worked as a wedding planner. Everything she offered him was amazing. Yet she always had a question in her eyes and her fingers folded into the bottom of her shirt, twisting and turning it into a knot.

Instinct told him the knot was on her insides, but he couldn't figure out why.

The week before, he'd bumped against her antique mailbox attached to the front of the house and knocked it off the wall.

Red, no less, and looking like it had been knocked off the wall on a regular basis. Another contradiction in Ronnie Fare's combination state-of-the-art kitchen and crumbling-house setup.

If she wasn't careful, the place would fall apart around her, yet a growing connection made him determined to see that didn't happen.

A warm spot behind his ribs spread across his chest and shot into his head. Hot enough to short-circuit every working brain cell he had left. What was the matter with him? And what did it matter that some fanatic woman's house needed serious repair and upkeep? Or that he'd neglected things at the ranch so he could hang around every day for a sweet view of long tanned legs and eat whatever their owner had concocted in her kitchen.

He held a level against the wall and marked off a line, then shoved his cap up and slid the carpenter's pencil behind his ear.

The screen door opened, and his stomach wrapped around his backbone.

"Good morning."

No kidding.

With her hair twisted up, sunshine in her eyes, and a plate of fresh something-or-other in her hands, he was toast.

His hands itched. One tug of the chopsticks holding her hair would tumble it down around her shoulders.

And he would tumble right off the front steps.

"Hello?" Her head cocked to the side like the corgis' when they waited for his signal to bring in the calves.

"Hello. I mean, good morning." He swallowed and fastened his eyes on the white platter she held with toothpick-skewered bacon rolls.

"Care for a bacon roll? You have a choice today: water chestnuts or the pitted dates."

Wanna run away together? He rubbed the back of his neck. "Sure." He was losing his mind.

"Good. I want to see what you think."

No—no, you don't. You do not want to see what I'm thinking.

She set the platter on the wicker table by the swing and rocker and went inside, voice trailing behind her. "I'll be right back with coffee."

He pushed to his feet, pulled off his cap, and scrubbed his hair. The pencil dropped to the floor. She'd said it again—"see what you think."

Thank God she couldn't really do that, though she sure enough tried to read his face like a good tracker read sign.

He planted himself on the chair, leaving the swing clear for her, and picked up a roll of bacon that looked like it had been dipped in syrup and smelled like it came straight from heaven.

"Well?" The screen whispered shut behind her.

He held the plate out. "Wow. Here—try one."

She exchanged the plate for a heavy white mug with a sunflower on one side. "Two sugars in your coffee, if I remember correctly."

He swallowed. "You do."

A smile tilted her lips as she planted herself on the swing, set the plate on the table, and toed the swing into slow motion.

"Why don't you ever eat anything you make?"

"Because I can't—" The swing stopped. Her face blanched and she clapped her hand over her mouth, eyes bigger than the skewered rolls.

He'd broken a barrier—just like the barrier on a roping chute that added time to his score if he didn't give the calf enough of a head start.

He backpedaled, picked up another roll. "These are great."

She said nothing, clearly holding her breath as if she was about to cut and run.

Think, Ty. Think.

"You know, I've been thinking. You've fed me every time I've come over here. How about you come out to my place this evening and I'll barbecue. Burgers, ribs, chicken. Whatever you'd like."

She blinked, hand still over her mouth.

"Maybe you could bring some of those beans you served at Casey and Cindy's wedding."

At that, her shoulders relaxed and her hand lowered, options flying through her eyes. He had to convince her before she said no.

"I haven't fired up the grill since July, and this would be a good excuse to clean it and enjoy some late barbecue before fall really sets in."

Her head tilted and she looked over his shoulder. Probably at the unfaded paint on the wall marking where the red mailbox belonged.

"All right," she said, eyes sliding back to his. "It's a deal. What time?"

Chapter Seven

Guilt shook a finger in Ronnie's face for not admitting that she knew where Ty lived. He'd volunteered directions, and she'd let him, because the last thing she wanted to do was appear too interested. Or eager. Or look like a stalker.

At five thirty that evening, she turned off Highway 34 at Trail West Road and wound toward the cross-bar gate standing open at Ellicott Ranch & Ropes.

Her insides twisted like the two rope *R*s, and she prayed her grandmother's sweet chili recipe had turned out as good this time as it usually did. But she couldn't smell its baked-bean aroma filling the car, though she'd checked beneath the Dutch oven lid to make sure it hadn't cooked too long and dried out.

Two short-legged dogs greeted her as she parked near the ranch-style home, barking a warning and dashing in and out as if the Subaru would tuck tail and run any minute. Ty came from around the corner with a long-handled meat fork that made up for the short dogs.

"Dally! Short-Go!"

Both dogs responded to his hand signal with flattened ears and trotted to the barn, where they plopped in its lengthening shade, heads on paws, back legs out like frogs.

Wow. If only he could make her tastelessness disappear as easily.

She reached for her basket of hard rolls and a napkin-wrapped ladle, and before she could open the car door, Ty did it for her. A backward ball cap, big grin, and a gallant bow had her giggling without effort.

Kiss the Kook lettered the bib of a faded red apron that had clearly earned its favored status, based on the frayed edges and missing front pocket.

"What?" Mock offense rimmed his expression as he glanced down at the apron.

"Nothing." She swallowed a laugh but could feel the twinkle in her eyes. "Nice apron."

"You're just jealous because you don't have one like it." He closed her door and opened the one behind it, retrieving the pot of beans.

"You don't know that."

Under his breath, he mumbled something that sounded a lot like, *I'd bet on it.*

He struck off toward the corner of the barn but not so fast that he was leading her. More like *herding* her, walking beside her and hinting at direction while letting her make her own choice. Her eye caught a breath of smoke puffing from an old Weber kettle grill, drawing her toward a covered patio that ran the length of the ranch house not far away. She couldn't smell it, but she imagined it was a heavenly aroma.

"Smells great," she said.

He eyed her with suspicion.

What was that about? Surely he didn't know her secret. And surely it smelled wonderful. She just couldn't prove it.

"Thanks." He lifted the Dutch oven toward his nose. "So does this."

A picnic table waited invitingly, complete with a blue-checked cloth laid at an angle. Tableware, plates, and napkins indicated place settings for two.

Her heart did a funny little skip, and she shushed it like an impatient puppy while setting the breadbasket on the table and the ladle in the kettle Ty had placed front and center.

"Thanks for bringing rolls. I forgot to mention it this morning."

"No problem. Bread is easy to forget—and easy to freeze if there's too much."

He gave her that hot coffee smile, and she turned away to drink in the view instead.

A breeze danced through the giant cottonwoods skirting the house, and in the distance Canada geese drifted on a shimmering pond. Low-angled sunlight scattered diamonds across the water's surface, and Ronnie wondered if the night sky glittered like that after dark.

Idealistic drivel, she scolded silently, and wrapped her arms around her middle to hold herself together. For too long she'd been watching his facial reaction for a hint at what he really thought. Trouble was, the habit was giving her romantic heartburn. Dangerously distracting.

"Dinner is served."

Ty set a platter of ribs, chicken, and tri-tip on the table, and snuggled it up next to the Dutch oven. Ronnie forced herself to come up with a less romantic word than *snuggled.* Her emotional balance was skittering after her wayward senses of taste and smell.

She slid onto the bench on her side of the table, and Ty did the same across from her. Then he held his hand out palm up with a purely innocent look on his face.

She took it.

He bowed his head and offered a brief but heartfelt prayer of thanks.

"Amen," she whispered afterward, struggling against a catch in her throat. Mr. Fix-it Cowboy was a multifaceted piece of work.

"So why'd you become a chef?"

And he knew how to cut to the chase.

She scooped a helping of beans, images of her grandmother's kitchen rising to the surface. "My Gramma 'Cine was an incredible cook. She grew up in what she called 'the Great Depression.' As a little girl, I thought she was talking about the dip in a pile of mashed potatoes where you pour the gravy."

Ty laughed out loud and snatched up his napkin as a barrier.

She glared at him. It wasn't *that* funny.

"I'm sorry." He dropped the napkin and scrubbed a hand down his face, failing miserably at erasing the humor. Spreading two fingers around one eye, he looked at her. "Did you ever see the movie *Close Encounters of the Third Kind*?"

Was he serious? Of course she'd seen it. With Gramma 'Cine, who recorded it on her VCR player. Fork trails down the side of the "mountain" and all.

He forked his own finger-trail through his hair, a gesture she'd seen him make at her house when he was working out a problem. Not that she spent an inordinate amount of time watching him work.

Exchanging a coconspirator glance with him, she wiped her mouth and cut into the dark crispy skin of a chicken breast. Juice ran onto her plate, and she prayed that God would let her taste it. Just one little taste—*please*.

Nada.

She wasn't easily offended, thank goodness. But Ty was still an idiot.

Close Encounters? Really?

Ronnie Fare put on a good act, but she showed no reaction to his barbecuing skills, which he knew for a fact were second to none. His dad had taught him well.

"That board in your kitchen." He glanced up from chomping on a rib. "Clever sign for a chef."

Her brows bounced together then back, quick enough to miss if he hadn't been watching. He'd touched a nerve.

Her head cocked to the side, and she cut into her chicken. "It's a good reminder."

Odd comment. "How so?"

"Gramma 'Cine used to say it all the time. Usually before she filled her wooden spoon with a sample of what she was stirring and offered it to me."

The back of his neck crawled. Coincidence? He hunched his shoulders. "No sticking your fingers in the bowl?"

She raised her steak knife and pointed its shiny tip in warning, but the softness around her eyes belied the threat.

"Try that at your own risk."

"I was talking about you. With your grandmother. Didn't she ever let you lick the beaters or clean out the frosting bowl?"

Ronnie cut off a chunk of chicken. "That's entirely different than polluting the recipe with a grimy finger."

"Oh. Polluting, is it?"

Her eyes smiled as she chewed closed-mouthed, and he sensed an intimate exchange. A companionable comfort he hadn't felt in a long time. The last woman he'd brought home for dinner seemed more interested in his business plan and property holdings than the meal.

The sun dipped behind the mountain while they shared childhood tales of what they'd wanted to be when they grew up. Memories of first loves—good times and some not so good. Close calls and "Thank You, God," prayers for not always getting what they asked for.

But when her eyes glistened at mention of her father's death, he took her hand and held it lightly, warmed it between both of his, connecting with her through the pain.

They sat in the stillness, and he wanted nothing more than to lean in and kiss her. A pond frog bellowed a bass note, crickets joined in, and Ronnie's hair swayed against her neck as she turned her head. The evening cloaked her expression.

"I didn't realize it was so late." Regret weighted her words. "I should be going."

She stood and gathered the plates and silverware, stacking them at the end of the table. "If you'd like, I'd be happy to leave the remaining rolls with you."

Her voice was as hushed as the night and drew soft fingers over his skin.

"Does that offer go for the beans too?" A guy could hope.

Warm laughter gave answer. And suddenly he didn't want her to leave. She'd brought something with her that hadn't been around his place in a long time, and it had nothing to do with food.

"I'll be right back with a bowl. Wait for me?"

Her eyes flicked his way with promise.

Finally, he'd met a woman who made him wonder if God had a plan after all, and what was he doing?

He was on his way to the house, hoping to find a plastic bowl with a lid that fit.

Chapter Eight

Three days later, Ronnie made yet another trip from her kitchen to her car for that afternoon's wedding delivery, still reliving her dinner with Ty at the ranch.

It was a fairy tale.

Okay, she wasn't twelve.

It was delightful.

Sheesh. That sounded like something her mother would say.

And speak of the dear woman, there she was, pulling up in front of the house, dressed in her I'm-here-to-help outfit.

"I'm here to help." Her mother tugged on the sleeves of a black shirt tucked neatly into black jeans.

Ronnie had forgotten she'd asked for help toting chafing dishes, warming pans, and a dozen other items critical to an evening buffet line.

"Thanks, Mom. Can you grab the table linens and serving utensils I stacked on the kitchen counter?"

After securing the overloaded car and locking up the house, Ronnie backed into the street and headed for the newest venue. Felicity would be there staging the cake. Kiki would be taking last-minute tucks in the bride's wedding dress, and Cassie would be wrangling everyone through her well-planned steps for seamless sentimentality and picture-perfect nuptials.

Picture perfect. That was it. That was Monday's dinner with Ty as she drank in the peacefulness of the Ellicott ranch. She'd felt so at home that the evening slipped away before she realized it, embarrassing her for overstaying her welcome. Or so she'd thought. Leaving hadn't felt like an option after he'd taken her hand in his, cradling it like a wounded bird when she spoke about her dad.

And her sweet beans must have tasted like they were supposed to, because Ty had scraped every last bean into an old plastic container that looked like something his mother had used.

His mother. Oh Lord, what a heartbreak. Family barbecues when he and his brother were growing up, how they vied for the last chicken leg or piece of pie or anything that remained. How his mother had taught her boys to cook so they could survive.

Even now, her heart squeezed at the image of Ty standing by the graves of every other family member. Alone.

He'd given no details, but the tightness on his face was enough to say the pain was still very present.

He'd also mentioned how his mother had often quoted the "Taste and see" verse. Eerie, in a way, that both of them had family members who had appreciated the same biblical admonition.

Eerie—or a God thing.

"Are you sure you got enough?" he'd asked her, a knot in his brow. "You didn't eat much."

Instinctively, she'd held her hand to her stomach. "Absolutely. And it was delicious." More of a declaration of faith than out-and-out deceit, she hoped. . .

"Ronnie? You there?"

Her mother's voice came from a distance, filtering through

her thoughts of Ty until she jumped at the touch on her arm.

"Are you all right? You're a hundred miles away."

Actually, just about ten. "Sorry." She smiled at her mother's worried expression. "I'm back now."

"Mind telling me where you were?"

Yes.

She redirected. "So tell me about Tom."

Her mother's right eyebrow cocked over the frame of her black-rimmed glasses, still as capable as ever of saying a mouthful.

Clearly an obvious decoy, but Francine Fare's dimples made an appearance, and she tucked a perfectly placed lock of white hair behind her ear. No tucking necessary—a dead giveaway.

"We drove up to see the aspens after church on Sunday, and then he took me to dinner at that new steak place downtown."

Ronnie gave her mother a side glance, confirming the blush of happiness she heard in her voice.

An internal parent stepped forward in Ronnie's brain. "How much do you know about this guy?"

"Enough."

That made her twitchy. Her mother sounded like a high schooler dodging questions about a date. "Seriously, Mom. You've known him how long—two weeks?"

Her mother's laughter fell like spring rapids in the Big Thompson River. Clear and fresh and full of promise.

Ronnie wanted to cry but didn't know the reason.

"Don't worry, honey. I've checked him out. He's a close friend of the pastor. We talk about the Lord and His faithfulness a lot. He's a widower, lonely like me, and has been waiting to meet someone with similar faith and interests."

Her mother reached across the gearshift and squeezed her hand. "He's a retired teacher too, and he likes to travel."

They would continue the conversation on the drive home, because the immediate wedding venue was just around the corner, in the expansive backyard of one of Loveland's wealthier entrepreneurs. And Ronnie couldn't be in watchdog mode while setting up an appetizer table and buffet.

True to form, Felicity's wedding cake graced a separate table, complete with elegant lilies and ribbon twisting around an arch matching the arch beneath which the bride and groom would be married.

Cassie had the buffet table ready to go, and Ronnie's mother took over spreading the cloths and spacing the warming dishes. A smaller round table awaited an assortment of appetizers, one of which was the bacon-wrapped water chestnuts and dates Ty had devoured, three and four at a time.

The man could put away the food.

The evening went off without a hitch, aside from the bride lighting her veil during the candle ceremony.

The MOB nearly fell out of her garland-draped folding chair, but the pastor clapped the flames into smoke, sending relief rippling through the wedding guests in waves of gentle laughter.

Kiki, who was standing at the back of the crowd with Ronnie and her mother, covered her face with both hands.

"Well, it wasn't the dress," Ronnie assured her friend with a hug. "It could have been worse."

Ronnie wasn't sure if Kiki was sobbing or laughing. With weddings, one never knew where tears were involved.

Kiki finally swiped beneath her eyes and snorted. "That was close."

On Sunday morning, Ty had trouble concentrating on the pastor's message. He'd been attending Loveland Community Church off and on since he was a kid, and the familiar setting was a comfort. But images of Saffron Fare in the moonlight kept drifting through his thoughts.

Did she attend church? It hadn't come up in conversation that night at the ranch, or any other time when he was working at her place, which was most days. In fact, it was entirely possible that she attended *this* church during the second, later service. Her Saturdays were probably booked with weddings followed by late-evening cleanups, which led to late Sunday mornings.

Maybe he'd hang around after church and find out.

Or he could just invite her to come with him next Sunday. A casual, no-pressure *non*date. She'd accepted his invitation to the barbecue at the ranch. And she'd held his hand as he asked a blessing over their meal without rolling her eyes first.

An hour later, he waited near a clump of decorative juniper trees in the churchyard to see if his first hunch panned out. Sure enough, just before eleven, Ronnie parked her gray Subaru at the back of the lot and headed toward the church.

He cowboyed up and walked her way. Decisive. Manly.

A nervous wreck.

As he neared, she smiled, surprise lifting her fine brows. "Well, hi there, Cowboy."

Hope and his pulse galloped in side by side.

She carried a Bible and a small bag that hung over her

shoulder, but the sunny skirt that swished against her slender legs locked in his attention like a heat-seeking missile.

"Good morning," he managed. "I didn't know you attended here."

Holding one hand above her eyes, she tipped her head. "Do you come to the early service?"

"Yes, ma'am." *Dang. So much for stealth.* "Mind if I sit with you this morning?" He had nothing—and everything—to lose.

Her mouth quirked on one side, sure sign of a debate going on in her pretty head.

"I'd like that." Sincerity edged her tone.

Risking a hand against the back of her waist, he urged her on ahead at the door. She responded quickly and gave him a smile that twisted his insides tighter than a new rope.

She passed the back row where he usually sat. Then the next to the last. And two in front of that.

He was about to jerk her slack when she stepped into the next row and took a seat, leaving room for him on her left.

Joining her, he drew a long, deep breath through his nose, making eye contact with Pastor King, who did a double take, shifting his gaze from Ty to Ronnie and back again. The man could play a mean hand of poker if he had a mind to.

Now what?

Chapter Nine

Ty Ellicott went to church twice last Sunday. Because of her.
Ronnie still had a warm spot at the back of her waist where he had touched her briefly as they entered the building. And again when they went for a sandwich at a sidewalk café downtown. And when he later opened her car door in the church parking lot and helped her in.

Of course he didn't actually help her. She didn't need help. But it was a thoughtful gesture that she could get used to. Somehow gallant and supportive. Something she'd never experienced in any other man's company, which probably played into her lack of interest where other men had been concerned. They simply hadn't drawn her from her calling long enough for her to take much notice.

So was she a prude?

She worked her neck from side to side, massaging her shoulders and staring out the kitchen window at yellow leaves fluttering to the ground. If prude meant attentive to a man's conduct and behavior that unwittingly announced his intentions, then yes, she was a prude. Just like her mother, from whom she'd learned how a man should treat a woman. And if that was still the case with Francine Fare, then this Tom fellow must be gallant as well.

But Ronnie wanted to see for herself. Perhaps dinner at her place for Mom and Tom was in order.

She snickered at the rhyme. But no dinner until after the Gardner-Mitchell wedding, which was less than two weeks out.

The timer dinged, and Ronnie grabbed a pot holder on her way to the oven for fresh apple-cinnamon rolls. Thanks to her current malady, she'd lost five pounds since returning from the cruise. Amazing how much weight a taste or two here and there could add, though she'd rather be happier than thinner. Life included enjoyment of what the Lord had given, and taste and smell were critical elements of that enjoyment.

Ty said he would be back to work this morning. He'd taken two days "off" to stack hay and catch up on chores at the ranch. Memories of the ranch setting rose in her mind's eye, and she imagined what it must smell like—pine from mountain forests wafting down in the evenings, freshly cut hay, the doggy smell of Dally and Short-Go, Ty's two low-rider corgis.

If she was honest with herself, she missed him being around. Missed the sounds of him working outside, the clomp of his boots when he came indoors to use the "facilities," as he called the bathroom, and the timbre of his voice when he raved about her cooking.

He always raved about her cooking, even over things she knew he didn't want to try at first, like brussels sprout chips.

Today she was sure he'd rave over her latest recipe. She had a thing about cinnamon rolls. They were never part of her wedding menus, but she was driven to bake them and eat them—until she couldn't taste their gooey goodness.

She depended on Ty to let her know.

The thought stopped her in her tracks, and she stared at the pan of pinwheels. She did not depend on men for anything. Never had, until now, and she wasn't sure how she felt about that. She was an independent woman who did most things herself, even if it involved power tools. But God had seen fit to let her experience tastelessness. Why? She *needed* that ability.

Tasting was even a biblical admonition, based on what her barnwood sign said.

She looked at the painted script, words that had drawn her and encouraged her since she was a little girl. Why, *now*, did she lack a most critical ingredient for her life's work?

Heavy footfalls on the front porch drew her from her shadowy thoughts, and she set the pan on the counter, where she drizzled cream cheese frosting over the rolls. Still warm, they melted the icing, and it filled every crease and crevice until it banked against the edges of the pan.

In an act of desperation, she spooned out a bit of the sugary goodness and licked the spoon. *Please. . .*

Nothing. Just warm, smooth, tasteless icing.

⁓

Apples and cinnamon.

Lord, have mercy. Ty had never considered good home cooking a torment until he had to smell it long before he could eat it.

The red mailbox held its place against the faded gray porch paint, and he was pleased when it didn't give way to his nudge. He pushed the door buzzer.

"Coming." Ronnie's voice wafted through the screen door, buoyed on the promise of hot, sweet bread. If he wasn't careful, he'd be letting a notch out of his belt sooner than later.

He stepped back, and the screen door opened. Her sunny smile floated above a plate of giant rolls swamped with icing. Those chopsticks held her hair up off the back of her neck again. God help him.

"Good morning. Would you care for an apple-cinnamon roll?"

"Absolutely." *Would you care for a kiss?*

"Coffee's perking, and I'll have it right out."

"Need any help with that?"

She gave him a quick laugh. "No, but thank you. I'm sure you have enough on your to-do list for today."

Setting the plate on the wicker table, she stepped back and rubbed her hands down the apron tied at her waist. "I'll be right back. Help yourself."

She pulled a napkin from her apron pocket and pressed it against his chest as she walked by. He nearly followed her.

Instead, he took a center roll, licked the frosting around the edges, then laid it in the napkin he held in his other hand. A guy could get used to this.

⁓

Two sugars in the first cup, a spoon of honey in hers. Ronnie stirred each and took them out to the porch, where she set one on the wicker table next to Ty and cradled the other as she settled on the swing.

It wouldn't be long until autumn pulled on its thick white coat and scurried away with winter. Would Ty keep coming? Fixing things indoors? Could she afford to pay his ridiculously small invoices? Could she afford not to? Was there enough for him to do?

"Aren't you going to try one of these?" He squinted at her, his dark brows bunching like a storm off the mountains.

She sipped her coffee from the heavy white mug, then looked over the brim and shook her head.

And the clouds parted. The sky cleared. A smile pulled his mouth up on one side, and cream cheese icing peeked from one corner.

He swallowed, licked the frosting from his lips, and leaned toward her. "You can't taste it, can you?"

Fear ripped through her veins. She shot off the swing, snatched the plate of cinnamon rolls, and turned for the door. "You're fired."

He rose to his feet right behind her and touched her arm. "Now hold on a minute."

She pulled away. "Let go of me."

The screen door slapped behind her. "Send me a bill, I'll send you a check."

She hooked a foot around the oak door and kicked it closed. It slammed hard, jarring up her spine and into her teeth.

Or was that the door to her heart?

Ty stared at the wooden scrollwork on the screen door that Ronnie called gingerbread. He felt like a gingerbread man that had been dropped and stepped on.

What just happened?

The red mailbox stared at him, its slot mouth open. He flicked the flap down, gathered his toolbox, and threw it in the back of the truck.

All the way to the ranch he replayed scenarios from the last four weeks, from everything she'd wanted him to taste to their lunch Sunday after church. The evening at the ranch when he'd barbecued everything that could be barbecued, and she'd given no visible sign of enjoying any of it.

By the time he made his entrance off Trail West Road, he was convinced he'd hit her nerve-nail squarely on the head.

She couldn't taste a blasted thing, and she was trying to keep it a secret.

Every time she'd ask him to try something, she added, "so I can *see* what you think." That white barnwood sign in her kitchen must rub it in every time she looked at it—*taste and see.*

Anger fizzled into pity until pride punched it square in the eye. He jerked the truck to a stop at the barn, sending up a spray of gravel, and slammed out of it.

Dally and Short-Go tucked what tails they had and skedaddled for the arena.

Tears dripped from Ronnie's chin like the icing on her cinnamon rolls. She set the platter on the work counter, right beneath the scripture shouting from the wall—*"O taste and see that the Lord is good."*

What had the psalmist meant when he wrote that? She knew it was from David's bid for survival when he pretended madness before an enemy king. But what had David been thinking? What had prompted him to say, "taste and see"?

Squeezing her eyes shut, she covered her face with her hands and let the sobs roll up and out until she slid down the face of the cabinets and hunched against them on the floor. It wouldn't take much to provoke madness for her at the moment.

If Ty Ellicott figured out that she couldn't taste what she was cooking, how long before her business partners and clients figured it out?

She pulled the chopsticks from her messy bun. Her hair fell around her face like a curtain, and she laid her forehead on her drawn-up knees. It didn't matter if she cried her sinuses shut. She couldn't smell anyway. And she had no guarantee that she ever would again.

Fear and panic had pushed the wrong buttons, and now she was in a real fix. But worst of all, she missed him, and it had been only ten minutes. He was that unique ingredient she'd been lacking in her life, and she had begun to believe he felt the same way about her.

She'd thought he could possibly, maybe, might share not only her love of food but her faith as well. Might even love—

A Caribbean rumba ringtone interrupted from her back pocket with morbid hilarity, signaling her mother's call. Loving but persistent.

She took a deep breath. "Hi."

Momentary silence hung in the air—parental intuition kicking in.

"Ronnie, are you all right?"

It wasn't the words but the *tone* of the words that broke the dam.

"I'll be right there."

Chapter Ten

"Why didn't you tell me sooner?"

Ronnie blew her nose into a tissue, pushing the pressure in her sinuses even deeper. "I was afraid if I told you, I might let it slip to the others. I could lose my job over this, Mom. My *job*."

Her mother brought another box of tissues from the pantry and set it on the floor next to Ronnie. "I'm making you a cup of ginger tea."

Ever the pragmatist, Francine Fare always knew what to do in a crisis. And tea usually figured into the equation.

"These rolls look delicious. We can have these too."

Fresh tears welled in Ronnie's eyes. Those rolls were what brought her charade crumbling down around her.

Her mother plated two, popped them in the microwave for a few seconds, then joined Ronnie on the floor—so typical of the woman who never belittled pain but simply shared it. Ronnie still had a lot to learn from her.

"I'm not trying to change the subject, but I couldn't help but notice all the improvements outside. Things are really shaping up. How do you have time to do all that and fulfill your chef duties as well?"

The sob caught Ronnie in the chest as she tried to swallow a tasteless bite, and she nearly choked.

"Honey, what is it? There's more to this situation than not tasting."

Leave it to her mother to read between the fork tines.

"Remember when I told you I hired a plumber to fix my gas line? Well, he's been fixing other things too."

Her mother didn't flinch, but the bulge in her jaw said plenty.

"His name is Ty Ellicott, and he owns a ranch off Highway 34, and he barbecues and twists poly-nylon ropes to sell, and he has two dogs named Dally and Short-Go, and he's been tasting everything I cook and telling me what he thinks."

Ronnie tipped her head back against the cupboard and took a deep breath.

A motherly sigh, a sip of tea. "And you're in love with him."

She closed her eyes and let her mother's quiet statement seep through her skin and into her bones.

Until her meltdown, she'd felt completely comfortable with Ty. Safe, yet tingly about life and its possibilities. How could she be in love with someone she'd known only a few short weeks?

And how did her mother know?

"Could this Ty fellow be the reason you've been giving me the third degree about Tom?"

Ronnie looked into her mother's eyes and saw herself mirrored there. "I didn't know I was lonely, Mom. I didn't know that deep down I wanted someone to laugh with. Touch and talk to."

Her mother reached for her hand. "Oh honey. I know so well what you mean, and I had hoped you would understand when I said similar things to you about Tom. He will never replace your father, whom I still dearly love. But I'm lonely for companionship too. Someone who makes me feel safe even though I know I can take care of myself."

Ronnie leaned her head on her mother's shoulder, sensing a profound kinship with this woman who had given her life.

"I know it sounds cliché, but God is going to see you through this. He's been faithful to me my whole life, and I raised you to believe in His fidelity."

"I know, Mom. It's just so hard. . ."

"Why? What exactly is so hard?"

She swiped at her tears. "I fired him."

In two short weeks, all but the evergreen trees had draped themselves in gold and yellow and russet, and leaves were flying on the crisp morning breeze. The Gardner-Mitchell wedding was the next evening, and Ronnie had prepped as much as she could in advance. Tomorrow's last-minute cooking was all that remained, as well as transporting the food, chafing dishes, holding pans, serving platters, and bowls.

Experience, training, and long-standing habit had her checking every appliance in her kitchen, every burner, switch, and knob, because everything had to be a "go" tomorrow. No last-minute glitches.

She reached for the switch on the hood above her stovetop. Pushed it to *on*, awaiting the gentle whir of the fan.

No whir.

She pushed the switch again, then again, but got the same results. Einstein was right about insanity. Doing the same thing over and over while hoping for different results was crazy.

She dug her flashlight out of a drawer, popped the filter out of the hood, and inspected the fan. Though she understood how the intricate exhaust system worked, she was powerless to trouble-shoot it.

Health department regulations required a fully functional hood for safety reasons. Grill and stovetop surface temperatures climbed incredibly high, and fire became a serious threat. Heat could be a dangerous thing. Without that hood, her entire kitchen was shut down.

She swallowed her heart and phoned Felicity to ask about the commercial kitchen at Weddings by Design.

"I'm good to go," Felicity assured her, "so if you need to cook there, it's all yours. And if I can help prep, let me know."

Of course Felicity would offer to help. All four of the partners had one another's backs. But this time it didn't work for Ronnie. She couldn't let them discover her career-crushing secret.

"Thanks, Felicity, but I'll be fine. My mom's with me on this event—I just didn't want to crowd you in the kitchen there at the last minute."

By the time Ronnie disconnected the call, she was strategizing the next twenty-four hours at breakneck speed.

A thought crossed her radar. *Call Ty and ask if he'll repair the hood.*

"No."

The force of her answer shocked her, mainly because she could *taste* it—pride. Fear. Regret. A bitter combination if ever there was one, and difficult to swallow.

She glanced over her shoulder at the barnwood sign and mentally skipped to the remainder of the verse that wasn't printed there. *"Blessed is the woman who trusts in Him."*

Gramma 'Cine's voice rose from her heart. *"The good Lord was talking to all of his children, dear, not just the boys."*

Tears pricked Ronnie's eyes again. She was tired of crying. Tired of fighting. Tired of being afraid.

She had Ty's number in her phone. It had been there since the first invoice he'd given her when she added him to her contacts, just in case.

With a deep breath and a quick prayer, she pulled up his name.

Ty's phone buzzed from his belt. He coiled his rope, gathered his reins, and turned his horse for the roping box.

On the second buzz, he checked the caller ID.

Ronnie.

He hadn't listed her as Saffron Fare, because that wasn't how he knew her.

He returned the phone to its case, backed into the box, tripped the release, and chased the calf all the way down the arena without trying to catch it.

Blasted woman.

She hadn't even told him why she'd fired him, but he knew. He'd guessed her secret, and she'd run faster than any calf he had.

The phone buzzed again. Was she calling to apologize? Probably not. Well, maybe. If he remembered right, she had a big wedding at Sweetheart Ranch this weekend.

Well, he was busy.

Buzz.

He trotted back to the roping box, opened the slide to the chute, and let the next calf in. The little critter was in no hurry, unlike its former buddy. It sauntered in, head down, as if moping about its predicament, reminding Ty of himself and all the lonely meals he'd eaten in the last two weeks.

He could have called up a friend. Casey and Cindy. A woman even. He knew plenty of gals from ropings and jackpots, but most of them had eyes for his assets, not him.

He nudged his horse out of the box, formed a loop in his rope, and took a couple of swings over his head to get the feel of it. Brand-new, lightweight, but stiff. Like his life lately.

It hadn't just been lonely meals, but lonely nights as well. Ever since Ronnie came out for barbecue—sharing the table with him, the meal, the evening—nothing had been the same.

The place felt empty with no one to say, "Hey, Cowboy," in the morning, have coffee with, or offer the latest thing she'd concocted in her high-dollar kitchen.

He'd wondered what she looked like with bed head and no makeup. And he knew it'd take a ring on her finger before he'd get that view. The idea wasn't disagreeable, and he'd thought of a half dozen ways he could ask her.

His phone rang again—a different kind of ring than the one he was thinking of. He hung his rope over the saddle horn and pulled out the phone.

"Hello?"

She'd hung up.

He checked his voice mail. Empty.

Would it make him look desperate if he called her back?

How lonely did he want to be? Pride, he'd learned, was a lousy companion and an even worse cook.

Chapter Eleven

The phone rang in Ronnie's hand, and she jumped.

Ty. Returning her call. Her *third* call.

She breathed deeply through her nose, pushed her hair back from her face.

"Hello?" As if she didn't know it was him on the other end.

"Hey."

That little word had power to curl her toes when he said it.

"Hi. Um, you busy?" Shoot. "I mean—I'm sorry. For firing you without explanation."

No comment.

"You never sent an invoice."

"Is that what you called for?"

"No. I called to apologize and to ask a favor. A paying favor of course."

He scoffed. Scoffed!

She deserved it.

"Like I said, I'm sorry. You scared me, that's all, and I didn't handle it well."

"No, you didn't."

Her eyes started to sting. She couldn't afford tears right now. She cleared her throat, but he interrupted.

"Why were you scared? Because I figured out your secret?"

Cutting to the chase was his strong suit. "I was afraid that if you figured it out, so would my business partners, and I'd lose my job."

His settling sigh came through the phone and nuzzled up against her neck. "Do you ask them to taste everything you cook so you can *see* what they think?"

"Well. . .no."

He chuckled deep in his chest, and it rippled from the phone into her ear and through every cell in her body.

He waited a beat.

She opened her mouth, but he spoke again, tenderly, as if he really meant it.

"What do you need?"

Surprisingly, she had several answers to that simple question, but she forced the most pressing to the forefront. "I need you to look at the hood over my stovetop and see if you can get it running before tomorrow."

A horse whinnied in the background, and a dog barked.

She closed her eyes, imagining those short-legged cow dogs, Ty's Weber grill under a star-flung night, and his arms around her.

"I'll be right there."

⌒

Ty had to give her credit. There wasn't a spot of grease anywhere inside or out on her massive canopy hood. It covered her entire cooking area—from the six-burner stove-top range with two fourteen-inch grates for stockpots to a twenty-four-inch griddle and double ovens.

No wonder she didn't have money for outside repairs.

He started with the easier parts first: air filters and ducts, fan switch, motor, and blades, then checked the control board. The switch was the culprit, and while he worked, she leaned against the counter and talked more to him than she had at any time since he'd known her. The pretense was over, the shield down, and she spilled her heart.

"I didn't think I was afraid of anything until this happened. I mean, a chef who can't taste or smell? Who wants that?"

He replaced the fan cover. "But everything I've tried has been great. You've got this."

She shook her head, worry pulling at her eyes. "But how do I tell the others—Kiki, Felicity, and Cassie? How do I tell them and still keep my job? It doesn't seem right that the Weddings by Design chef is completely tasteless."

In thirty minutes, he had her commercial kitchen up and running again. He double-checked the switch, replaced the cover pieces, and ran through everything else for good measure. Then her took her in his arms and kissed her.

She melted against him like the frosting on her warm cinnamon rolls. It didn't matter how or where she talked to him, just so she did. It didn't matter where or how he kissed her, just so he could. And it didn't matter how long he had to wait for her to say yes, because he knew deep down that she would.

⌒

By late Saturday afternoon, Cassie had done it again, and the Sweetheart Ranch was "dressed to the nines" as Gramma 'Cine would say. With Western elegance, sunflower garlands draped the arched entryway to the ceremony seating area as well as the food tables and dining area. Ronnie and her mother headed that way.

They set up three small-plate food stations, one with appetizers, including bacon-wrapped dates and water chestnuts, as well as individual servings of colorful fruits and nuts. Flavored lemonades and sweet tea topped a second table, and the third boasted braised short ribs with roasted red potatoes, and brussels sprout chips.

The food selections did not mirror the wedding's Western flavor, which was the bride's nod to her groom and his ranching background, but Ronnie's presentation made up for it. Thanks to Ty and her mother's taste testing, no one would complain about the more elegant menu, nor would they miss chips, burgers, and beans.

Small sunflower cupcakes were scattered across the larger wedding cake table with Felicity's exquisite creation front and center.

With everything set up and ready to go as soon as the "I dos" were spoken, Ronnie left her mother to keep an eagle eye on the three small-plate tables and went to the barn in search of Kiki.

The bride's dressing room was an elegantly draped horse stall, complete with cheval mirrors, sunflower garlands, lounges, and overstuffed chairs arranged strategically on plush carpet. No straw or oats anywhere to be seen.

In front of one of the mirrors, Kiki was setting the headpiece on the teary-eyed bride. She had worked wonders with the mother's bridal veil, shaping and edging it to fit the updated style of wedding dress she had made. Mrs. Gardner watched with a tissue to her eyes as Kiki connected the past, present, and future in a bouffant bow attached to the daughter's braided updo.

Soon after, the music began, and Ronnie didn't need to taste or smell to feel her heart overflowing. This time she saw more than the Gardner-Mitchell bride and groom and their families. She heard more than a song about someone finding what they always wanted. And she brushed tears from her eyes at camera flashes that paled against the smiles of the young woman and her new husband.

When Ronnie closed her eyes, all she sensed was Ty Ellicott holding her in his arms and kissing her until her knees went weak. Right in front of the white barnwood sign in her kitchen.

Cheering broke through her reverie as booted bridesmaids in sassy gowns and groomsmen wearing starched jeans and sunflower boutonnieres lined up for dancing. Guests made their way to the food, and Ronnie worked relay between the braised ribs table and the sweet tea and lemonade. Her mother held down the appetizer fort, and Felicity stood guard at the three-tiered waterfall of sunflowers on the wedding cake.

Perfection reigned. And Ronnie had never felt more alone in her life.

⁓

Crashing a wedding was one thing. Crashing a wedding where you know the groom and are in love with the chef is another.

Dressed in his best jeans, starched shirt, and El Presidente silver-belly Stetson, Ty slipped in at the edge of the crowd just as one of his clients, Wade Mitchell, planted a home-run kiss on his new bride, Jenny Gardner.

Cheers and hats filled the air, and Wade and Jenny led the wedding party to the dance floor. Ty had never seen so many sunflowers in one place other than a field of them on his way across Kansas a couple years before.

Braised ribs tickled his nose, and he scoped out the food

section where sweet Saffron Fare manned a glorified lemonade stand. Just what he needed.

He waited out of her view for several guests to be served, then slipped in front of the table when her back was turned.

"Is this your recipe?"

She whirled around with what he hoped was hope on her face, and he broke out in a laugh at her surprise.

"What are you doing here?"

"I know the groom."

She blushed to match an embroidered WBD on her high collared chef coat and pushed at the back of her hair. Chopsticks peeked over the top of her head, and his fingers started itching.

She crossed and uncrossed her arms.

He lowered his voice. "And the chef."

"Stop," she whispered.

He leaned over the table and returned her whisper. "I'm her official taste tester."

"Shush! Someone will hear you!"

It was hard not to laugh at her expense, but she was so pretty when she was flustered that he wanted to kiss her right there in front of everyone. Show Wade Mitchell how it was *really* done.

With no hopes of getting to dance with—or kiss—the cook, Ty meandered through the crowd, congratulated the bride and groom, and fended off a few questions from potential clients. He refused to talk shop. This was a celebration. He hoped to repeat it at his own place, so he was paying close attention.

When guests started leaving, he stowed his hat in the truck and returned to Ronnie, rolling up his sleeves. "Tell me what I can do."

She looked at him for a second before a smile tugged her lips. "Okay, if you insist."

"I do." He liked that phrase. Rolled right off the tongue with no effort at all.

"But first, I want you to meet someone." She waved over a white-haired woman in black with the same gray-green eyes, contagious smile, and WBD on her shirt. Ronnie Fare thirty years in the future.

"Mom, I'd like you to meet Ty Ellicott, the man I told you about who fixed my gas leak and has helped me so much around my place."

She touched his arm. "Ty, this is my mother, Francine Fare."

From the look on the woman's face, she knew more about him than he'd ever know about her. His collar got a little tight, and he offered his hand. "Nice to meet you, ma'am. Ronnie speaks highly of you."

She leaned in and spoke in a hushed voice. "I hear you're her taste tester."

Her eyes sparkled at Ronnie's playful nudge and full blush, and Ty hoped he'd someday get to know this woman who had done so much to secure her fatherless daughter's growing-up years.

Two hours later, he loaded the last of Ronnie's silver pans into the back of her car, then helped her partners fold up chairs and tables, take down flower garlands, and pack up what needed to be packed up.

A couple he guessed were the bride's parents came up to Ronnie and her three friends as they finalized the cleanup, and the woman offered both hands. "It was perfect. All of you—thank you so much."

"You're most welcome, Mrs. Gardner," the brunette said. Also bearing a pink WBD on her shirt, she seemed to be in charge. "It was our pleasure."

Ronnie's tension was growing. She fidgeted with her hair, her white jacket, and the dirty tablecloths she held in one arm.

"Thanks for your help," another partner said as Ty folded up the last table. "I take it you're a friend of Ronnie's?"

"Yes, ma'am."

Ronnie came over and linked her arm through his. "Cassie, Kiki, Felicity—this is Ty Ellicott. He's been helping me."

"Oh, you must be the plumber who repaired her gas leak. I'm Kiki, the seamstress on the team."

"Yes." Ronnie's arm tightened in his. "Felicity here does all our cakes, and Cassie runs the show and keeps everything organized."

"Nice to meet you all. You've got a great operation going."

"Well, it wouldn't be as great without Ronnie and her culinary skills." Cassie turned to Ronnie. "I heard rave reviews tonight over those braised ribs and brussels sprout chips."

"About that." Ronnie's cheeks pinked, and she dipped her chin.

He knew where she was headed and tugged on her arm, attempting to distract her. She didn't have to do this. Not tonight.

"Ty here has helped me with more than the gas leak—"

"I made some minor repairs around the house too. You know, screen doors, mailboxes, banisters."

The three women had worked themselves into a straight line, firing-squad style, watching him ramble and Ronnie squirm. This wasn't right. He couldn't let her do this tonight.

She dropped his arm and straightened. Her chin came up, her shoulders squared, and he wouldn't have been surprised if she'd nodded her head, calling for the next roping calf to be let out of the chute.

"Ty has been my taste tester."

All three monogrammed women blinked in unison.

"He's tasted everything I've made since I returned from the cruise with my mom. I. . .I can't taste or smell anything because of an infection I got on the ship."

The three glanced at each other and then back at Ronnie.

"Why didn't you tell us?" the baker asked.

Ronnie took a shaky breath. "Because who wants a chef who can't smell or taste?"

"From what I heard tonight," Cassie said, "it didn't make a bit of difference."

"And it doesn't make any difference to us," the baker added. "You know what you're doing, and you do it well. I certainly hope you're not thinking of quitting."

"But I may never get my taste and smell back. There are no guarantees."

"You nailed it tonight, Ronnie. Just like always," Cassie said. "We're not worried."

The other two agreed, and by the time they'd all hugged and parted ways, Ronnie's eyes were shining with tears.

Ty pulled her close. "Come on," he offered. "I'll follow you home and help you get everything inside."

Chapter Twelve

Ronnie curled up in the middle of her brass bed, every quilt she owned piled on top. As was so often the case along Colorado's Front Range, one blustery fall blast had dropped the temperature by thirty degrees overnight, but the coming day was supposed to return to the low eighties. She certainly hoped so, because Ty was coming by to take her to dinner at the ranch.

She had pointed out several times that she was perfectly capable of driving there herself, but he wanted it to be an official date, which meant he would come to "collect" her.

Where he came up with such vocabulary was beyond her. Very un-cowboy.

So she insisted he drive his old truck, not the newer one she'd seen parked near his barn.

Burrowing deeper, she watched the brightening sky fill her eastern window with promise of a glorious display. Her grown-up self said she should get up, get dressed, and get outside for a walk to witness the glory firsthand.

The teenage side of her said fluff the pillows, pull the quilts tighter, and watch from bed.

If she hurried, she could run downstairs, brew a cup of tea, and be back under the covers before dawn. She threw back the quilts and made a dash for it.

Caribbean rumba rang from her phone.

Returning to her room, she grabbed her phone from the charger and ran down again, feet stinging against the cold hardwood at the bottom.

"Hello, Mom."

"Good morning. I just wanted you to know I'm going to Denver today with Tom. He has business there, and we probably won't be back until this evening."

"Have a good time."

Silence, and then the Mom quiz. "Are you all right?"

"Yes, I'm just in a hurry to make tea and get back upstairs before the sunrise."

Her mother chuckled. "You always did like that first wink of the sun. I'll let you go then. But first I wanted to tell you what a lovely meal you presented last night and what a gallant young man Ty seems to be. I expect him to ride up on a white horse someday."

So did Ronnie, but she refused to admit it out loud. "Have fun today and be safe." Somewhere in the back of her mind, those words echoed in her mother's voice from days gone by, as if their roles had switched.

"I will. Love you."

Against every culinary nerve in her body, Ronnie stuck a mug of water in the microwave to heat while she grabbed a tea bag and the honey jar. The five minutes it took to boil water could make the difference between seeing dawn split the sky and watching clouds fade from pale pink to white. She wanted the whole show this morning.

Running upstairs was trickier while covering her mug with a pot holder, but very little spilled on the way, and she slipped beneath her covers just in time. Warmed by the hot tea, she snuggled against her pillows and curled around the mug as the sun broke through a low cloud bank.

"More than those who watch for the morning. . ."

The partial verse ribboned through her mind as she sipped her tea. What was the rest of it? Something about waiting—not exactly her favorite thing to do.

She'd waited for everything in her life, from schooling, to business loans, to home ownership. Now she was waiting for the return of her senses and waiting to see if Ty Ellicott was the man she'd been, well, *waiting* for.

"Waiting is so hard, Lord." Yet if she was honest with herself, nothing important was easy. Everything that mattered to her required determination and effort. And what was wrong with that? Was life supposed to be easy?

Microwaves were easy. Did she want a microwave life—something that never really held the heat over time?

It took time to prepare a good meal. It took time to establish a career. And it often took time to see God working. In retrospect, she begrudged none of it.

"Lord, help me wait graciously—on Your healing and on Your direction for my life."

Ty pulled up in front of Ronnie's two-story house just after five, turned off the truck, but didn't hop out. Instead, he sat behind the wheel waiting, for what he wasn't sure. But he sensed the need not to hurry. To listen and watch. He'd worked all day getting everything just right for this evening. He wanted it all to be perfect. Perfect food, perfect weather, perfect timing when he asked her to marry him.

A chill rippled over his skin as he merely thought the words. How was he going to get them past his teeth and through his lips?

Her porch light flicked on. Busted.

He picked up the sunflower bouquet he'd bought at the market and climbed out his groaning driver's side door. He should fix that. He'd fixed her screen but not his own truck door. He'd be in his good pickup if he'd done what he wanted, but she wanted to ride in the "old truck."

He smiled to himself. She was a keeper.

He half expected her to come to the door before he rang the buzzer. His other half proved right, and she didn't.

But it wasn't long before she opened the ornate oak masterpiece, eyes flicking from the sunflowers in his hand to his face. "Are those for me?"

No, they're for my horse. He squelched the remark before it fell out of his mouth, pulled the screen door open, and handed them to her. "I thought you might like these flowers since they're all over your doormat and coffee mugs and in the boot on the table behind you."

Scrunching her shoulders, she giggled like a little girl. He hoped he'd make it to the ranch and through dinner before he popped the question.

In the kitchen, she took a large Mason jar from a cupboard, filled it with water, and set the flowers in it, turning their faces outward at just the right angles. Then she set it on her work counter right under the white barnwood sign, faced him, and smiled.

"Thank you. They're perfect."

She pushed up on her toes and brushed her lips across his cheek. He caught her around the waist and captured her lips in a real kiss before his brain engaged.

Wrapping her arms around him, she laid her head against his chest.

"We'd better go," he managed against every other desire. "I don't want dinner to burn. I am feeding a chef, you know."

Following a quick squeeze and a laugh, she flicked off the kitchen light and picked up her purse and sweater from the hall table. "Ready if you are."

In the falling light of day, Canada geese arrowed down to the pond like feathered pontoons, squawking and splashing their arrival.

After dinner, Ty led Ronnie to the rise where he'd set up the hammock not far from the pond, and pulled her into it after him. She curled up against him like one of her bacon-wrapped appetizers, and he marveled at how well she fit next to him.

In that moment, life was perfect.

And in that moment, he understood that it might not stay that way. That sorrow would visit again. Suffering or pain. But he also understood that God would be with him through it all. That He'd be with *them*.

He tightened his arms around her, and with her head beneath his chin, he pulled back and kissed her hair.

She sighed into him—a sound he wanted to hear the rest of his life.

"Do you realize how many things you've fixed at my house?"

He ran his fingers through her loose hair, recalling the first time he saw her. "And to think, you initially doubted my qualifications."

She huffed out a laugh. "A girl can't be too careful these days."

"You know what my favorite job was?" He could just make out her profile in the fading light, the way she tilted her head and wrinkled her brows in thought.

"The screen door. You made it not sound like a dying chicken anymore."

He chuckled and gave her a light squeeze. "Nope. Guess again."

She tipped her head up and looked at him. A clear invitation to graze her lips with his.

"Three guesses," he said and kissed her once.

"The red mailbox."

Another kiss. "Nope."

"The leak in the gas line."

"Nope. One more guess." Another kiss, longer.

"But that *was* three things."

"One more." He brushed her cheek.

She shook her head no. "I surrender."

Leaning back in mock surprise, he looked at her straight on. "Really?"

A little shove. "You know what I mean. No more guesses. Just tell me."

He pulled her closer, buried his fingers in her hair, and breathed in the scent of her. "I liked being your taste tester. And if you'll have me, I'd like to sign on permanently."

She straightened and pressed both hands against his chest. "What?"

He couldn't help but laugh at her surprise. "Will you marry me so I can taste everything you ever cook and grow old with you?"

Squirming out of his embrace, she sat up, rocking the hammock until he thought it would flip.

"Do you love me or my cooking?"

Unable to resist the temptation, he palmed his jaw and looked up at the sky as if thinking the matter over.

She slugged him and tried to climb out. "Ty Ellicott!"

Wrapping his arms around her, he pulled her back down, laughing and kissing her, and laughing some more. "I love *you*, Saffron Fare—which you're not being."

"What are you talking about?"

He stole a kiss from her perplexed mouth. "You're not being fair."

"Different word, different meaning."

He tugged his earlobe. "Sounds like. . ."

"That is so not funny." But her not-funny laughter spilled over him like the icing on her apple-cinnamon rolls.

"Well?"

"Well what?"

"Will you."

"Will I what?"

"Will you—"

"Oh!" She pushed until the hammock twisted, and she slid out of his arms to the grass.

"What? What's wrong?" He jumped down beside her. "Did you hurt yourself? Are you all right?"

Straightening, she brushed grass off her jeans, then stared at the patio where they'd shared grilled steaks and baked potatoes. Both hands covered her cheeks, and tears caught the moonlight in her lashes.

"I smell what you cooked for dinner. The steak. I smell it."

She bent and tore off a handful of grass then held it against her nose as if it were a rich perfume.

With both hands, she reached for him and nuzzled his neck. "I smell your aftershave—spice and pine, like a forest. Have you always worn that, or is it new? Something you just bought."

He couldn't help but laugh, and he picked her up and whirled her around. "Since I was twelve and sneaked into my parents' bathroom to *borrow* my dad's aftershave."

"You've worn it all this time and I never noticed?"

"You didn't notice how I smelled when I was all sweaty either, now did you?"

Instead of answering, she tore off for the picnic table, where she picked up the leftover peeling of her baked potato and bit off a chunk. As he approached, she clapped her hands over her mouth and bent in half.

He kicked into a trot. Was she choking?

She was crying.

"I can taste it. Oh God, thank You, I can *taste* it. Salty butter and bitter potato peel. Pepper. It's beautiful, so beautiful!"

———

Ronnie swiped her eyes with a greasy hand and didn't care at all if she had butter on her face. She could taste!

Was there anything better?

"Does this mean I'm out of a job?"

Ty stood off to the side of the patio, hands hanging limp beside him, not shoved in his pockets or cocked proudly at his belt. He looked like the twelve-year-old caught poking through his dad's things, wanting desperately to be a man like the one he admired.

Yes, *yes*, there was something abundantly better than tasting.

She wiped her hands on a napkin and went to him. Wrapped her arms around his neck and kissed him like her life depended on it.

"No," she whispered. "You're not out of a job. In fact, you're hired."

His responding kiss set her knees to wondering if they'd ever be strong enough to hold her up again.

"You taste like baked potato," he said with a slow-burn smile.

"I can see that you like it. I've learned to read your face pretty well, you know."

"Taste and see." He tipped his forehead to hers.

"That the Lord is good." She closed her eyes in anticipation.

"Taste and see—Ty and Saffron. Has a nice ring to it, wouldn't you say?"

"Yes, it does," she whispered. "We could be onto something here."

Davalynn Spencer is a *Publishers Weekly* and ECPA bestselling author with novellas in three Barbour collections, *The 12 Brides of Christmas, The 12 Brides of Summer,* and *The Cowboy's Bride.* She won the Will Rogers Gold Medallion for Inspirational Western Fiction and is the author of ten additional titles, both contemporary and historical. She blogs monthly for Christian Authors Network, contributes to the *American Christian Fiction Writers* blog, and writes her own weekly inspirational blog. She appears on the radio broadcast *Write Time Radio* and teaches writing workshops when not wrangling Keeper the Cowdog and mouse detectors Annie and Oakley. Connect with her at https://www.davalynnspencer.com. *May all that you read be uplifting.*